Praise for Chris Moriarty

Finalist for the 2003 Philip K. Dick Award

Amazon.com Top 10 Editors' Pick for
Science Fiction & Fantasy 2003

A *Kansas City Star* Noteworthy Book for 2003

"Knife sharp. An amazing techno-landscape, with
characters surfing the outer limits of their humanity,
pulling the reader into a scary and seductive future. A
thrilling, high-end upgrade of cyberpunk!"
—Kay Kenyon

"Action, mystery and drama, set against some of the
most plausible speculative physics I've seen. This is
science fiction for grownups who want some 'wow'
with their 'what-if.' "
—David Brin

"*Spin State* is an intriguing, fascinating, and totally
engrossing—yet truly terrifying—look into the time
beyond tomorrow, a time and place where an AI and a
military officer face love, betrayal, and worse in a
struggle over the shape of a future that already has full
genetic engineering, bioengineered internal software,
FTL communications and travel . . . and the age-old
human weakness of greed and lust . . .
and the love of power."
—L. E. Modesitt Jr.

SPIN STATE

CHRIS
MORIARTY

BANTAM BOOKS

SPIN STATE
A Bantam Spectra Book

PUBLISHING HISTORY
Bantam trade paperback edition published October 2003
Bantam mass market edition / December 2004

Published by
Bantam Dell
A Division of Random House, Inc.
New York, New York

This is a work of fiction. Names, characters, places, and incidents
either are the product of the author's imagination or are used
fictitiously. Any resemblance to actual persons, living or dead,
events, or locales is entirely coincidental.

Library of Congress Catalog Card Number: 2003044303

ISBN 978-0-553-58624-4

Printed in the United States of America
Published simultaneously in Canada

www.bantamdell.com

OPM   10   9   8   7   6

For Mitchel

Special thanks to Anne Lesley Groell for her brilliant editing and uncanny ear for what I meant to say; to Charles H. Bennett, John A. Smolin, and Mavis Donkor of the Quantum Information Group at IBM's Watson Labs for brainstorming, technical advice, and quantum teleportation jokes; to Ann Chamberlin and M. Shayne Bell for kindness above and beyond the call of duty; to Scott Anderson, Julia Junkala, Jim McLaughlin, Susan Mayse, Tony Pustovrh, and Kirsten Underwood for being the best readers any writer could ask for; to Judith Tarr for sensible advice and extravagant encouragement; to John Dorfman for being there at the beginning . . . and of course to the fabulous Jimmy Vines, who made it all happen.

Then we encountered a leopard man who was rumored to be a cannibal. He must not have thought we looked good to eat; he smiled and let himself be photographed like a veteran tourist guide. After that I started asking everyone where we could meet real cannibals. I wanted to see them, know them.

"They exist," my hosts told me.

"But where?"

"No one knows. But there's nothing special about them. You can't even tell them apart from normal people."

"Ah, but I have to know them, eat with them! I want to eat a person. Just a taste. Just to taste it!"

—Louis Lachenal, *Vertigo Notebooks*

ENTANGLEMENT

➤Quantum mechanics is certainly imposing. But an inner voice tells me that it is not yet the real thing. The theory says a lot, but does not really bring us any closer to the secret of the Old One. I, at any rate, am convinced that He does not play at dice.

—ALBERT EINSTEIN

➤God may not play at dice, but She certainly knows how to count cards.

—HANNAH SHARIFI

T hey cold-shipped her out, flash-frozen, body still bruised from last-minute upgrades.

Later she remembered only pieces of the raid. The touch of a hand. The crack of rifle fire. A face flashing bright as a fish's rise in dark water. And what she did remember she couldn't talk about, or the psychtechs would know she'd been hacking her own memory.

But that was later. After the court-martial. After jump fade and the rehab tanks had stolen it from her. Before that the memory was still crisp and clear and unedited. Still hers.

After all, she'd been there.

Li knew Metz was going to be big as soon as she met the liaison officer TechComm sent out to brief her squad. Twenty minutes after Captain C. Xavier Soza, UNSC, hit planet surface he'd gone into anaphylactic shock, and she was signing him into the on-base ER and querying her oracle for his next-of-kin list.

Allergies went with the uniform, of course. Terraforming was just a benign form of biological warfare; anyone who had to eat, breathe, or move in the Trusteeships got caught in the crossfire sometime. Still, no normal posthuman was that fragile. This time TechComm had sent out a genuine unadapted Ringbred human. And clever young humans didn't get cold-shipped to the Periphery, didn't risk decoherence and respiratory failure unless they'd been sent out to do something that counted. Something the brass wouldn't trust to the AIs and colonials.

Soza spent thirty hours in the tanks before he recovered enough to give them their briefing. He seemed alert when he finally showed up, but he was still short of breath, and he had the worst case of hives Li had ever seen.

"Major," he said. "Sorry you had to deal with that little crisis. Not how I imagined my first meeting with the hero of Gilead."

Li flinched. Was she never going to enter a room without her reputation walking two steps in front of her?

"Forget it," she said. "Happens to the best of us."

"Not to you."

She searched Soza's handsome, unmistakably human face for an insult. She found none; in fact his eyes dropped so quickly under her stare that she suspected he'd let the words slip out without thinking how they sounded. She glanced at her squad, settling into chairs proportioned for humans, behind desks designed for humans, and she felt the usual twist of relief, shame, envy. It was pure accident, after all, that her ancestors had boarded a corporate ship and paid for their passage with blood and tissue instead of credit. Pure accident that had subjected her geneset to anything more than the chance mutations of radiation exposure and terraforming fallout. Pure accident that made her an outsider even among posthumans.

"No," she told Soza finally. "Not to me."

Slip of the tongue or no, Soza was all smooth, cultured confidence when he stood up to give the briefing. His uniform hung the way only real wool could, and he spoke in smooth diplomatic Spanish that even the two newest enlisted men could follow without accessing hard memory. The very picture of a proper UN Peacekeeper.

"The target is located below a beet-processing plant," he told them, "hiding in its heat signature." He subvocalized, and a streamspace schematic of the target folded into realspace like a spiny asymmetrical flower. "There are five underground labs, each one of them a small-run virufacture facility. The system is deadwalled. No spinstream ports, no VR grid, not even dial-in access. The only way to break it is to shunt the cracker in on a human operative."

Soza nodded toward Kolodny, who straightened out of her habitual slouch and grinned wolfishly. There was a new scar along the rake of Kolodny's cheekbone. Fresh, but not so fresh that Li shouldn't remember it. She searched her active files, came up empty. Ran a parity check. Nothing. *Christ*, she thought, feeling queasy, *how much is missing this time?*

She was going to have to get someone to put a patch on her start-up files. Someone who could keep a secret. Before she forgot more than she could afford to forget.

"The rest of you will get the cracking team past the deadwall," Soza was saying, "and collect biosamples while the AI goes fishing. We're after whatever you can get on this raid. Source code, hardware, wetware. Especially wetware. Once the AI has the target code on cube, he wipes his tracks, and you withdraw. Hopefully without being detected."

"Which AI are we using?" Li asked.

But before Soza could answer, Cohen walked in.

Cohen wasn't his real name, of course. Still, he'd been calling himself that for so long that few people even remembered his Toffoli number. Today's interface wasn't one Li had seen before, but she knew it was Cohen on shunt before he closed the door behind him. He wore a silk suit the color of fall leaves—real silk, not tank-grown stuff—and he moved with the smooth, spare grace of a multiplanetary network shunting through cutting-edge wetware. And there was the ironic smile, the hint of laughter behind the shunt's long-lashed eyes, the faint but ever-present suggestion that whatever he was talking to you about couldn't possibly be as important as the countless other pies he had his fingers in.

As usual, he'd appeared at exactly the right moment, but with no apparent idea what he was doing there. "Hallo?" he said, blinking vaguely. "Oh. Right. The briefing. Did I miss anything?"

"Not yet," Soza answered. "Glad you could make it." He spoke French to Cohen, and Li glanced between the two men, wondering how they knew each other—and how well they knew each other—in the privileged world Ring-siders called normal life.

Cohen caught her looking at him, smiled, took a half step toward the empty place next to her. She turned away. He took a seat in the back. He leaned over and whispered something in Kolodny's ear as he sat down, and she smothered a laugh.

"We interfering with your social life, Cohen?" Li asked. "Like us to take the briefing elsewhere?"

"Sorry," Kolodny muttered.

Cohen just raised an eyebrow. As he did, a thin, dark-haired schoolboy trotted into Li's frontbrain, dribbling a soccer ball. He pantomimed an elaborate apology, then bounced the ball off the toe of one cleated foot, tucked it under his arm, and loped off toward a point behind her right ear. The cleats tickled; she had to resist the urge to reach up and rub her forehead.

<Stuff it,> she told Cohen.

Metz's Bose-Einstein relay was sulking today. A rapid-fire barrage of status messages flashed across Li's peripheral vision telling her that the relay station was establishing entanglement, acquiring a spinfoam channel, spincasting, matching spinbits to e-bits, running a Sharifi transform, correcting nontrivial spin deviations and dispatching the replicated datastream to whatever distant segments of Cohen's network were monitoring this briefing.

Before the first Bose-Einstein strike on Compson's World—before the first primitive entanglement banks and relay stations, before Hannah Sharifi and Coherence Theory—a message from Metz to Earth would have taken almost three days in transit along a narrow and noisy noninteractive channel. Now Bose-Einstein arrays sent entangled data shooting through the spinfoam's short-lived quantum mechanical wormholes quickly enough to link the whole of UN space into the vivid, evolving, emergent universe of the spinstream.

Except today, apparently.

<Can't you get a better channel?> Li asked.

<I already have,> Cohen answered before she'd finished the thought. <And if you cared about me, you'd laugh at my jokes. Or at least pretend to laugh.>

<Pay attention, Cohen. Kolodny's skin's on the line tomorrow, even if yours isn't.>

Soza had turned back to the VR display and was explaining the logistics of the raid. If things went as planned, Cohen would shunt through Kolodny and retrieve the target code. The rest of Li's squad had only two jobs: get the AI in and out and collect biosamples while he cracked on-line security. It sounded little different from the two dozen other tech raids Li had commanded, and she thought impatiently that Soza could have briefed them more efficiently by dumping the data into the squad's shared hard memory. She sat through about five more minutes before interrupting him with the obvious but still-unanswered question.

"So what are we looking for?"

"Ma'am," Soza said. He hesitated, and Li saw a flicker of self-doubt behind his eyes. She thought back to her first command, remembered the panic of wondering if she could give orders to seasoned combat veterans and make them stick. She'd been different, though. She'd led Peacekeepers in combat against Syndicate ground troops long before her first official command. Hell, she'd held a wartime field commission for three years before her CO would recommend a quarter-bred genetic for officers' candidate school. "Our reports—" Soza cleared his throat and continued. "Our reports indicate that the facility is producing products on the Controlled Technology List."

Someone—Dalloway, Li thought—snickered.

"That's not too helpful," Li said. "Last time I saw the CTL it ran to a few thousand pages. We go in with that, we're going to be confiscating wristwatches and toenail clippers."

"We also have strong evidence the parent corporation is Syndicate-friendly."

"That's it?" Li asked incredulously.

"That's it," Soza said.

He was lying, of course. She could see it in his eyes, which met her own gaze with unblinking, unnatural steadiness.

Her mind flashed back to her first meeting with Helen Nguyen—Christ, how many years ago had it been? She'd been younger than Soza then, but she'd already survived Gilead. And she'd known, standing in the discreet office of the woman whispered to be the UN's most ruthless and successful spymaster, that Nguyen's support could help her survive peacetime.

Bad liars always think they can make a lie stick with eye contact, Nguyen had murmured, an unnerving smile playing across her lips. *But they're wrong, of course. There's no trick to lying well except practice. So go practice. That is, if you want to work for me.*

Li stood up and flicked a thumb toward the door. "Can we speak privately, Captain?"

Squad members caught their breath, muttered, shifted on their benches. Fine, Li thought; it wouldn't hurt morale if they knew she was willing to go to bat for them. But that didn't mean she was going to dress down a TechComm liaison officer in front of them.

She followed Soza toward the door. In the back of the room, Cohen stood, stretched casually, and slipped out after them without even asking if he was wanted.

"Come on," Li said as soon as the three of them were out in the empty corridor. "Let's hear the real story."

"That is the real story," Soza said, still standing by his lie and putting his faith in eye contact. "That's what Intel gave us."

"No, it's not. Even Intel isn't that stupid. This your first trip to the Periphery, Soza?"

He didn't answer.

"Right. Well, let me tell you what they didn't tell you in your official briefing. Half the population of this planet are registered genetic constructs. The other half don't know what the hell they are and couldn't qualify for a clean passport even if they had the money to pay for a genetic assay. The only human in-system besides you is the governor. His air's shipped in, his food and water's shipped in, his official car has a full-blown life-support system, and he might as well be on Earth itself for all he has to do with anything. I could put you in a cab and drive you to places where people have never seen a human, where they'd look at you like you'd look at a mastodon. The Syndicates, on the other hand, are practically neighbors. We're eight months sublight from KnowlesSyndicate, fifteen from MotaiSyndicate. You can catch a ride to Syndicate space on half the freighters in-system as long as you're willing to pay cash, keep your mouth shut, and forget you ever met your fellow passengers."

Soza started to speak, but Li put up a hand impatiently. "I'm not being disloyal. Just realistic. We put riot troops on-surface here during the incursions. That's not the kind of thing people get over, whichever side of the gun they're on. And the Secretariat knows it. That's why they tread so lightly in the Trusteeships these days. And why they wouldn't in a million years call down a tech raid just because some local company is a little too friendly with the Syndicates. No. There's a reason for this raid. And the right thing for you to do is play straight with me about it."

"I can't," Soza said. He glanced at Cohen for support, but the AI just shrugged.

Li waited.

Soza laughed awkwardly. "General Nguyen warned me about your, uh, persuasiveness, Major. Look, I really admire you. You should have made colonel in your last go-round. Everyone who doesn't have his head stuck in a hole knows it. You're a credit to . . . well, all colonials. But you know that kind of politically sensitive information isn't cleared for release to line troops."

"It's cleared for release to you, though."

"Well . . . of course."

"And you'll be dropping with us tomorrow?" She asked the question in a carefully neutral voice. She didn't want to humiliate him—but she sure as hell wasn't going to sugarcoat it.

"No," Soza said. At least he had the grace to blush.

"So when the shooting starts, we'll have no one on the ground who knows enough to tell us when it's time to cut our losses and leave. I'm not willing to send my people into action under those conditions."

That hit Soza where he lived.

"They're not your people, Major. They're UN Peacekeepers. And they're under TechComm command for the duration of this mission."

"TechComm doesn't have to visit their parents when we send them home in boxes," Li said.

She stood toe-to-toe with Soza and looked straight into his eyes so he could see the green status light blink off behind her left pupil as she shut down her black box. "Look. Feed's off. This is soft memory only. It'll wipe as soon as we jump out-system." Well, not quite. But hopefully Soza was too young to know all the ways you could kink Peacekeeper datafiles.

"You're not authorized for that information," Soza said stiffly. This time he didn't call her Major.

<Well,> Cohen said on-line. <That wasn't exactly a smashing success.>

Li ignored him.

"How can we do the job," she asked Soza, "if no one who's coming with us even knows what we're looking for? That kind of nonsense may seem like a good idea back on Alba, but out here it's deadly."

Soza's eyes flicked toward Cohen so briefly that Li wouldn't have seen the look unless some part of her was already watching for it.

"Oh," she said. "So that's how it is."

She turned and stared at Cohen. Cohen cleared his throat and glanced at Soza. "I believe you have just been let off the hook," he told him.

Soza looked at Li hesitantly.

"Fine, go," she said. "And get the briefing back on track. I'll pull whatever I miss off Kolodny's feed."

"I'm just following orders," Soza said apologetically.

Li shrugged, smiled. "I know it."

Cohen closed the door behind Soza and set his back against it.

"Well?" Li said once it was obvious he wasn't going to volunteer anything.

"Well, what?" he asked, smiling the little-boy-in-trouble smile she'd seen shunted through a dozen different interfaces.

Today's 'face was another of Cohen's soft-skinned boys—or was it even a boy? Either way it was beautiful, and just far enough over the threshold of adulthood to fill out the expensively tailored suit. Where did Cohen find these kids? And assuming even half of them were as young as they looked, how did he finesse the laws about implanting shunts in minors?

Well, at least it's not Roland, she thought. That was one mistake she didn't need to be reminded of at the moment.

"Were you even planning to tell me?" she asked.

"I can't," Cohen said. "*Desolée.*"

"Can't? Or won't?"

"Can't. Truly." He looked embarrassed. "I'm persona non grata at Alba ever since the Tel Aviv fiasco."

"Yeah," Li said. She'd thought Cohen would never work for TechComm again after Tel Aviv. If he was on Metz, then Nguyen must be after something so important that she had to use the best AI she could find—even though the best meant Cohen. "What happened in Tel Aviv, by the way?"

"The usual story. Good intentions gone sour."

"Gone rancid, from what I hear. There's a rumor going the rounds that they tried to strip you of your French citizenship."

He glanced sidelong at her, an enigmatic smile curving the 'face's lips. "Is there?"

"Fine, don't tell me. It's none of my business anyway. Unlike Soza's little secret."

"My dear, I'd tell you that, of course. I'd tell you anything and everything if only I could be sure my confessions wouldn't work their way back to the charming General Nguyen. But, as I've said once already, I can't. TechComm made me give them every cutout and back door in my networks before they'd clear me for this job. Then they sicced one of their tame AIs on me. He fiddled me so good I can't even find the kinks." The soft girlish mouth twitched. "Humiliating."

"So why take the job?" Li asked. "And don't tell me the money. I know better."

Cohen looked away.

"Jesus wept! You're getting paid in tech? On a shooting mission? How could you do that to Kolodny? To all of us?"

He fished in his trouser pocket and pulled out a slim enameled cigarette case. "Smoke?" he asked.

"No," she said angrily. But then she said yes and took one; Ring-made cigarettes were too good to pass up, even on principle. And Cohen only smoked the best.

He reached over and lit it for her—not touching her, not leaning too far into her space, not making eye contact. All the elaborate *nots* of friends who have been lovers but no longer are.

They smoked in silence. She wondered what he was thinking, but when she glanced at him he was just staring at the floor and blowing smoke rings.

"Listen," he said when she was about to tell him it was time to get back into the briefing room. "We need it. I wouldn't do this to you, to Kolodny, if we didn't."

"We need it? We who?"

"We me." He spoke with the typical Emergent AI's disregard of individual boundaries. Pronouns meant nothing to him; *me* and *not me* changed every time he signed a network share or associative contract. *We* could be no one or a hundred someones. But at least it sounded like he wasn't planning to auction the tech off to the highest bidder. That was something, Li supposed.

She threw down her cigarette and crushed it under a bootheel. The virufactured alloy floor mobilized its scrubbers as soon as the butt landed, and within seconds there was no sign on its matte gray surface that the cigarette had ever been there.

"I hate those floors," Cohen said, scowling prettily at the place where the cigarette had been. "I have yet to see one that can actually tell the difference between something you meant to throw out and something that just fell out of your pocket. I've lost some really nice jewelry that way. Not to mention the address of the prettiest boy I never slept with."

"You're a martyr," Li drawled.

"Yes, well. We all have our trials." He looked at her, waiting. "What are you going to do about this one?"

"Call up Nguyen and ask for my orders in writing," Li said, her voice heavy with sarcasm. "What else?"

Cohen gave her a long straight serious look. "You could always trust me."

He watched her in absolute inhuman stillness—a puppet whose electronic strings had been cut. Li had learned to notice that stillness over the years, to track it along the horizon of their friendship like a climber tracks the thunderhead looming over the next mountain range. She didn't know what it meant, any more than she knew what the weather meant. But it was a sign. It was the only one she had sometimes.

<Catherine.> He spoke on-line, in the sinuous tenor she still thought of, however naively, as his voice. <I wouldn't put you at risk. Not for anything. You know that. You *know* me.>

She stared at him. At the eyes that changed with every new 'face he shunted through. At the shifting mystery behind the eyes. He was the closest thing she'd found to a friend in the fifteen years since she'd enlisted—the only years that were backed up in Corps data banks. And that was as good as saying he was the closest thing to a friend she'd ever had. She knew his luxurious habits, his sly feints and twists of humor, the beautiful bodies that he put on as easily as the soft shirts his tailor made him. She knew what countries he called home, what God he prayed to. But whenever she tried to touch anything real, anything solid, he poured through her fingers and left her dry-mouthed and empty-handed.

She didn't know him. She doubted anyone could know him.

And trusting him? Even the thought of it was like diving blind into dark water.

"You see it?" Kolodny asked, throwing back the bolt of her carbine with such machine precision that Li had a sudden vision of microrelays ratcheting back ceram-steel filaments. Only long familiarity told her that Cohen was off-shunt and Kolodny herself had asked the question.

They were coming in low, hiding the hopper's trace in Metz's violent predawn dust storms. Checkerboard-square fields flashed beneath them. Flatlands faded into a featureless horizon that had never known glaciers or river flows. The hopper whipped up black plumes of virufactured topsoil in its backwash, filling Li's nose with the hot exotic spice of rotting things.

She crossed the hopper's bucking flight deck and leaned out into the wind, searching. Her GPS told her that the target was close, close enough to be visible in this flat country. But Metz was only partially terra-formed, the atmosphere still swarming with active von Neumanns and virucules, and her optics struggled to pierce the haze of radiation. She squinted, switched to infrared, then quantum telemetry. Hopeless.

"Hey, Kolodny," someone asked. "The AI. Is it on-line yet?"

Li didn't have to turn around to know the speaker was one of the new recruits; newbies were always fascinated by the AIs.

"Not yet," Kolodny answered. "And don't call him an 'it' to his face unless you want to annoy him. AIs are 'he' just like ships are 'she.'"

"What's it feel like when it—when he's on shunt?"

"Like running into a burning house," Kolodny said—and Li heard the grin in her voice even through the rattle and roar of the hopper. "Only you're the house."

She glanced over and saw Kolodny still cleaning the old carbine she always carried. She should have said something about it, of course. This raid was nonlethal arms only. But Kolodny had earned the right to break a few rules. And that was one rule Li was breaking herself, truth be told.

She looked out the door again and spotted the target, a bright point of silver tossed on the dark fields. It appeared and vanished with each pitch and yaw of the hopper. It grew, splitting into two buildings, then five. A gate. A tower. A double fence of bright, freshly milled razor wire walled the compound off from the surrounding fields. The fence enclosed a strip of hard-packed earth about the width of the warning track around a baseball diamond. Li upped the magnification on her optics and saw paw prints in the dirt. Intel had said there were dog patrols, and it looked like they had it right for once.

Beyond the track rose a sleek virufactured alloy cube—a prefab office module that had been replicated through Metz's orbital Bose-Einstein relay and dropped from orbit. Li guessed it was this little luxury that led to the lab's discovery; the shipping bills must have set red lights blinking all the way back to Alba. The cube had glimmered like a pearl on the satellite feed, but today it was as drab as the sooty sky reflected in its windows. Just south of it, crouched behind long low Quonset huts full of farm equipment, lay the ramshackle bulk of the beet plant.

Li looked around at her team. Shanna, Dalloway, Catrall, and Kolodny were veterans. No worries there. Cohen was Cohen. He'd do his job superbly as usual, for his own incomprehensible AI reasons, and she didn't have to worry about him getting hurt because he'd never be physically present except through Kolodny. Her big worry was the two fresh-faced privates, shipped in three days ago. They needed time, training. Well, they wouldn't get it. They'd figure things out in the first minutes or not at all.

"Two minutes," she shouted over the wind. No one answered; they were all waiting for Cohen to get the link up.

She ran a final check on her weapons: the long-muzzled pulse rifle, the Corps-issue neural disruptor—called a Viper because of its distinctive fanglike anode prongs—and her own hand-rebuilt Beretta. Then she moved around the flight deck, feet spread to counter the hopper's bucks and slides, checking weapons, checking equipment, checking eyes.

She paid special attention to the new recruits, talking to them, mustering a confident smile that belied her fears about this mission. As she bent over the younger boy's rifle, her crucifix slipped out of her shirt collar and swung forward in a brief gold flash.

"That's nice," the boy said. And then flushed and added a belated *ma'am*. "Where'd you get it?"

She shoved it back into her shirt. "My father gave it to me."

She finished with the others, came around to Kolodny, crouched in front of her. Not to check anything—Kolodny was too much of a pro for that. Mostly just to say good-bye before she went under the shunt.

"So," Kolodny said. "This should be interesting. Total fuck fest, obviously."

Li shrugged. "Looks that way."

"Too bad I won't be around to see it." Kolodny grinned her toothy grin. "You'll have to catch me up when we get home."

"I will," Li said.

She leaned over to check Kolodny's carbine. No harm in checking. And Kolodny knew her too well to get offended. As she reached across her, the crucifix swung forward again.

Kolodny caught it. Before Li could react, she tucked the chain in and hooked it around the top button of Li's collar to hold it in place. "There. Better, no?"

Li turned to look into the gray eyes. "Cohen," she said.

He smiled. "You always can tell," he said. "How do you do it?"

Li pulled away, walked back across the flight deck, and sat down facing him. A moment later Kolodny's husky alto sang out a few lines of a Charles Trenet song.

It was Cohen's favorite—or at least his favorite when they were going into anything that looked like trouble. He'd told her to get her feet wet and look it up the one time she'd asked about it, but all she'd found were a few long-dead noninteractive sites and a cryptic reference to the French Foreign Legion that made her wonder just how old Cohen really was.

"Are we go?" she asked.

The only answer she got was a few more lines of the song, not in Kolodny's voice this time, but on-line, in Cohen's liquid tenor:

Quand tu souris, tout comme toi je pleure en secret.
Un rêve, chérie, un amour timide et discret.

Her oracle translated the words for her, but damned if she knew what secret dreams or singing for money had to do with tech raids.

Then the link broke over her, and she was being swept out to sea on the massive undertow of the AI's interlocking neural nets. He held her on the link, sharpened it, refined it, brought on the other squad members one by one until there were seven clean clear voices. Only Kolodny was missing; her reflexes and combat programming were at Cohen's disposal, but she herself would be gone until the raid ended, her life riding on the choices Cohen made while he was on shunt.

<One minute,> Li told the squad. <Terminate GPS.>

She switched off her GPS and felt the others do the same. Then there was the long, frozen, disorienting pause before Cohen picked up the slack and started supplying position corrections to her inertial systems. This was always the worst moment for Li. The sharp, subliminal anxiety at the missing datastream. The unnerving knowledge—unthinkable to someone who'd been wired her whole adult life—that she didn't know where she was, that only Cohen stood between her and being lost.

Cohen's nav feed came up at last, and Li felt her limbs go limp with relief. Then, without any warning of trouble, the link flickered and died. Kolodny surfaced where a few seconds ago Li had felt only the vast glacial sweep of the AI's networks.

One of the new recruits groaned as the twisting backwash of net vertigo washed over them. Li's stomach clenched, and she closed her eyes and waited, knowing that trying to pull out of the link would only make things worse now.

It passed.

Kolodny disappeared, and Cohen was back, as if nothing had happened.

<Problem?> Li asked.

But if there was one, he wasn't admitting it.

* * *

They dropped into the northwest corner of the compound, snaking down rappelling ropes between the dog patrols. As they slipped into the shadow of the beet plant, Li saw her squad's skinbugs cycle through their camo programs: sky gray, dirt brown, rusted orange.

The lab's door was tucked into a sidewall of the processing plant, just where Intel had said it would be. Li stood aside while Catrall jiggered the lock. Then she and Dalloway triple-timed down a corrugated viru-steel staircase, secured the landing, and brought the others in after them.

According to Soza's schematics, the landing fed onto a long gangway that accessed the outer row of labs. Li tossed off a quick and dirty heat scan to make sure the adjoining labs were empty, then sprinted down the gangway at eighty-two kilometers an hour by the clock—just the way they'd marked it out. As she ran, she felt a warning twinge in her left knee. She'd pay for that burst of speed later; bones and ligaments couldn't keep pace with ceramsteel. But right now, time was everything.

She reached cover and pumped her first fire team down behind her. She listened, scanned, eyeballed. Then she brought up her second team and leapfrogged the whole squad around the corner in textbook fashion. They regrouped at one end of a long ultramodern virufacture bay. The whole lab was built from ceramic compounds. White walls, white lights, white floors and ceilings. The only flash of color was a stylized biohazard red sunburst stenciled on the floor. No corporate name below it. But then there wouldn't be. Not in a lab that was so obviously illegal.

Open virufacture tanks stretched down the length of the bay between a bewildering tangle of feedlines and biomonitors. Half the tanks were empty. Half were filled with clear, high-grade viral matrix.

<?> Li shot to Cohen.

<Nothing here,> he answered.

They secured the lab and moved on.

They swept the next three labs on schedule, still finding nothing that piqued the AI's interest. In Lab Four, Li guarded Kolodny's back while Cohen jacked in and made a first cautious foray into the mainframe. It took him less than a second to confirm the Intel data. Lab Five stood out like a black hole on the lab net: a total absence of output. Whatever illicit wetware work was going on here, Lab Five was its epicenter.

A blind corner led into Five—the only blind corner in the complex. Li reached it first. She paused, scanned, motioned Catrall over to the far wall to cover her. On his nod, she juiced her internals and accelerated around the corner—straight into a withering blast of white light.

She pushed forward and through it; no matter what the danger the worst possible response was to lose momentum, risk being stranded in the kill zone. Then she rolled behind a stack of sterile saline canisters and stopped to tally the damage.

None.

She'd run through an automated irradiation beam, installed at the door to protect the contents of the lab's unsealed virufacture tanks. Her skinbugs handled it, masking her presence, killing the intrusion alarm before her passage tripped it, protecting the weapons-grade virucules on her skin and uniform from the assault of the radiation. No problem.

Except there was a problem. The beam should have been on the schematics Intel gave them. Should have been, and wasn't. She wondered what else Intel had missed—and if the next surprise would be this harmless.

As soon as she was sure she hadn't set off any alarms, she waved in the rest of the squad. They had twelve minutes and twenty-three seconds left before the hopper returned. No time to waste on unnecessary precautions. When the perimeter was secured, she split the squad in pairs and had them scan the tanks. She set her realspace feed to toggle if anyone's pulse rose above combat-normal. Then she picked up Cohen's feed and rode in on his shoulder while he jacked the system.

The lab's security went far beyond the deadwall. There would be no slipping in under the radar; Cohen was going to have to meet their best stuff and better it. The network was broken into half a dozen separate zones. He'd have to crack each zone separately, and at the same time elude the quasi-intelligent game-playing agents that defended them. There was no back door, no way in or out without running the gauntlet of the security programs. And even if Cohen got by them, Kolodny would still be physically jacked in to the lab mainframe, vulnerable to whatever wet bugs and bioactive code the system threw at her.

As Li watched, Cohen spun out a sleek silver thread of code, tweaked it into a loose Möbius strip, and floated it into the main corporate site on a public-source message. *Trojan horse*, she thought. *Oldest trick in the book.*

Cohen was laughing before she finished the thought. <Good hacking requires a familiarity with the classics, Catherine.>

<Did we just go off duty?>

<No, ma'am.> The dark-haired schoolboy floated across her internals again, one arm buried to the elbow in a brightly colored cookie jar.

Li glared. The boy popped like a soap bubble.

<Keep your mind on your job,> she said.

The security program caught the horse, just as it was meant to. In eight seconds alarms were going off all over the network. In twenty-three seconds the system's anti-incursion software had corralled the horse and routed it to the off-site virus zoo. For a moment nothing happened. Then an area of confused activity boiled up inside the virus zoo and ballooned into a roiling mushroom cloud of self-reproducing, randomly mutating code.

Li held her breath, trying to follow code that was spinning faster than even her military-grade wetware could track it. She shut down her VR interface and dropped into the numbers, a swimmer in the shifting ocean of Emergent networks that was Cohen.

His strategy was working. Or at least she thought it must be. The security program tracked each new virus, broke its code, sent antidotes shooting off to its entire UN-wide customer base. But this was a game the defense lost before the first whistle. The virus mutated constantly, generating new code faster than the system broke the old code, causing the system's outgoing mail to increase exponentially. And each new antidote-paired copy of the virus contained an embedded packet of active code that attacked the receiving system and sent yet another help request shooting back to the virus zoo.

In twelve seconds the off-site provider's network exceeded capacity, locked up, and went down. The target was cut out of the flock, and Cohen was ready to go to work in earnest.

Li maxed her realspace feed. Her squad was still sampling tank contents. They moved systematically down the rows of tanks, scanning and logging their contents. No search and destroy on this mission, just information-gathering.

<Retrieval minus 8:10,> she told them. <Keep it lively.> She went back on-line just in time to watch Cohen fish a series of clearance codes out of the lab's personnel files and drop into the database as a system administrator. <All clear?> she queried.

<Nothing left to do but sniff out the bone.>

<Well, sniff faster. 7:41 to retrieval.>

And back to realspace.

They were running late. Li sent Shanna and the two

new recruits over to the far end of the lab, signaling that she'd cover the middle rows herself. They were flirting dangerously with missing their retrieval, and she didn't want to contemplate the possibility of a delayed pickup in the dust storm that was still raging above ground. Nor did she want to find out the hard way that Soza hadn't arranged backup retrieval.

A few rows away, Dalloway stopped and put a hand into an open tank. He jerked it out and waved it in front of him while a rainbow oil slick of mutating viruses and counterviruses battled across it. <I'm melting! I'm melting!>

<Knock it off, Dalloway.>

Then one of the newbies screamed.

A short scream; Shanna clapped a hard hand over his mouth before it really got started. But when Li saw what the two of them were looking at, she couldn't blame the kid.

The tank had a body in it. All the tanks at that end of the lab had bodies in them. They were women. Or, more precisely, one woman: smallish, recognizably Korean—a rarity in and of itself in this fourth century of the human diaspora—and brown-skinned despite the artificial pallor induced by water and lab lights.

<They can't run a crèche in a nongovernment facility,> Dalloway said uncertainly. <Aren't there laws about that?>

<It's not a crèche,> Li said. <They're just wetware hosts.>

But this was no approved wetware she'd ever seen.

She looked into the tank in front of her. Took in the bar codes stamped on the sallow flesh, the atrophied limbs, the silver glint of ceramsteel filament twining through exposed nerve cells. At first glance the wetware being grown here was no different from the AI-supported wire job every soldier in the squad was equipped with, or even from the civilian VR rigs rich teenagers used to surf streamspace. But this wetware was growing in adult bodies, not viral matrix. And the pale, submerged faces were too identical, too regular, too inhumanly perfect to be anything but genetic constructs.

Li·stared at the bodies, caught by an echo, a wisp of memory that skittered away like a spooked horse every time she tried to lay hands on it. Was this a geneline she'd seen before? On Gilead? Were they culturing wetware for Syndicate soldiers? And why? Who would be crazy enough to risk it?

<Can you run some of those samples?> she asked Shanna.

<Sure. But what do we do if it's . . . what it looks like?>

Li checked their time. Seven minutes, twelve seconds. <We call Soza. Cohen, we're going to need a line to HQ.>

<No you're not.>

<We have a situation here.>

<Irrelevant. Take the samples and forget about it.>

<Have you seen what we're looking at?>

<Yes,> Cohen answered, this time on a private link. <But you're not going to get Soza on the line no matter how many times you call. And if you miss your retrieval, illegal construct breeding is going to be the least of your worries.>

Li made sense of Cohen's words just as Shanna pulled up the first DNA read.

"They're constructs, all right," Shanna said.

Catrall cursed. "Those bastards dropped us in a Syndicate facility without even telling us? What kind of shi—"

"Stow it," Li told him. "What Syndicate?" she asked Shanna. "What series?"

Shanna hesitated. "They're . . . not. I don't think they're Syndicate genesets at all. This is obsolete tech. Prebreakaway corporate product. These things are fucking dinosaurs."

And suddenly Li knew with sickening certainty what she was looking at. She remembered that face not because it was the face of her old enemy, but because it was her own face.

These constructs were her twins, their genesets spliced and assayed and patented to survive the man-made hell of the Bose-Einstein mines on Compson's World. And they were here despite the fact that it had been illegal to tank a genetic construct anywhere in UN space for over twenty years.

She turned away, feeling sick and dizzy, hoping that the eerie resemblance was only visible to her eyes.

"Let's finish up and get the hell out of here," she said. "And keep your heads screwed on. We need to make that retrieval, or we're going to be on the receiving end of a hot package. Seven minutes and counting."

She flicked open her VR window and found Cohen still scanning datafiles.

<6:51 to retrieval,> she sent. <How long have you known about the artillery?>

<Just remembered it.>

<You expect me to believe that?>

<Believe what you want. Just be quiet and let me work.>

She gave him a full minute. <5:51,> she told him. <You've got a minute and twenty.>

<I need more.>

<We don't have more.>

She toggled her realspace feed. The squad was hovering, eyeballing her nervously.

<Secure the corridor,> she told Dalloway.

Back on-line. Cohen was running twenty-odd parallel searches now, working so fast she could only track him as a vast icy sweep of light cutting through the lab comp's numbers.

<Status?> she queried.

No answer.

<Talk to me, Cohen.>

<Got it!> he said.

The link wavered. "Shit!" Kolodny said, shaking her head and blinking. Then she was gone, and the link was back up before Li even had time to feel the vertigo hit.

<What the hell was that, Cohen?>

<I can't—there's something screwy with the interface. Just give me a minute.>

<We haven't got one.>

But a minute later he was still jacked in, and Li was still waiting.

<Do I have to jack you out myself?> she asked, turning to stare at him.

That was when she saw the blood on Kolodny's face.

She jerked Kolodny away from the comp station and yanked the jack from her head, knowing even as she did it that she was too late. She was still standing there with the wire in her hands when the first shots whined down the corridor.

<Man down!> Dalloway broadcast.

Li flipped to VR, picked up Dalloway's feed. Catrall lay in a twisted heap at the foot of the stairs. Four guards rattled into view, the last one down stopping to turn Catrall over with a booted foot and take his rifle.

"We're leaving," she told Cohen.

The only answer she got was the clatter of Kolodny's carbine hitting the floor.

Kolodny was bleeding out. Fluid dripped from her nostrils, leaving watery pink splatters on the white tiles. She moved jerkily; the muscles of her back and legs were going into spasm. Li had seen wet bugs at work before. Cohen didn't have to tell her Kolodny was only minutes away from being unable to walk at all. Or that she was slipping down a slope that would only end in one thing unless they got her out: flatlining.

<Can she walk?> Li asked.

<For now.>

<What if you drop off-shunt?>

Cohen's laugh flickered across the numbers like brushfire. <I'm the only thing holding her together.>

She heard gunfire in the corridor—and this time it wasn't the muffled whine of discharging pulse rifles but the crack of real bullets hitting concrete and cer-amsteel. She toggled Dalloway's channel and saw that he was pinned down at the far end of the corridor, and Shanna and the others were too far out of position even to give him covering fire.

The lab seemed three times longer than it had on the way in. By the time they'd covered half its length, Kolodny's vitals were jagging and skipping, status alarms exploding behind Li's eyes like rescue flares.

"Wait!" Cohen gasped, jerking out of her grip to turn back toward the comp station. Li followed his gaze to Kolodny's empty hand—and she remembered the carbine jangling, unnoticed, unretrieved, onto the tiles.

"Too far," she said—and handed him her own pulse rifle.

"No," he said. "Keep it. You're going to be covering me anyway. And the Viper's useless in this. You shouldn't be using it."

"No one's using the Viper," Li said, reaching down to ease the Beretta out of its ankle holster.

She saw Cohen's look of shock even through the mess Kolodny's face had become. "Catherine, if you shoot someone with that—"

"I know," she said, already moving again. "Let's just make sure I don't have to."

Only fifteen meters to go. But they were the worst fifteen. No cover, just the slick white tiles underfoot, and the only shelter the flat of saline canisters just this side of the doorway. And they had to cross the whole width of the lab to reach those canisters.

As they started across, the first two guards skidded around the corner. One of them had Catrall's carbine in his hands and was trying to override the DNA lock. The other had a sleek, expensive-looking firearm that Li's oracle identified as a .308 Kalinin with Vologda optics.

She dove forward, head down, and slammed into the first guard at knee level before he had time to react. She kept driving with both legs as she hit him and felt his knee give out with a wrenching snap.

Before the other guard could swing the Kalinin's long barrel around to bear on her, Li jerked the injured man to his feet and jammed the Beretta to his temple.

His partner froze. The Kalinin's black muzzle wavered.

Li smiled grimly and hoisted her hostage up, keeping the Beretta pressed to his skull. She started toward the shelter of the saline canisters. If they walked out of here alive, someone was going to catch hell for that little piece of bad housekeeping.

Two more guards appeared in the doorway. Like the first pair, they wore unmarked coveralls and carried top-shelf weaponry. Li heard them shouting to the hostage to get his head down.

"I don't think that's good advice," Li said. She tightened her arm on his neck, both to keep his head up and to remind him what a Peacekeeper's wire job could do to flesh and bone.

Her internals were going crazy, targeting alarms screaming on and off as the gunmen's range finders fixed on her, lost her, fixed on her again. If they were willing to shoot her hostage to get to her, she was finished. Anyone Li had trained would have pulled the trigger the instant she made the grab and accepted the risk of shooting a friendly for what it was: unavoidable. But so far these guys were acting like amateurs.

If her luck held, she and Kolodny would escape because of it.

She got behind the canisters and threw her hostage

against the wall. "Listen," she said. "I don't have a clear shot on your friends, but I sure as hell have one on you. So let me tell you what you're going to do."

A moment later he was inching out from behind the canisters toward Cohen.

By the time the guards at the door figured out what she was doing, Cohen was already making the crossing behind the hostage, Kolodny's carbine shoved against his rib cage. It worked, at least until they got halfway across the lab. Then Cohen stopped for no clear reason and slackened his hold on the guard's neck.

<Watch it!> Li said down his channel.

But even as she thought the words, she felt him blowing off the link like leaves on a hard wind.

<What the hell?> Shanna said from the corridor. Then the link went down for good, and Cohen was gone.

Kolodny stumbled and fell, unable to keep her bearings when the AI went off-shunt. She knelt in the lab's central aisle, slack-jawed, shaking herself like a diver coming too fast out of deep water. "Kolodny!" Li shouted.

For a moment that must have lasted less than a heartbeat everything ground to a halt. Li saw the bloodshot whites of Kolodny's eyes as she turned to stare at her, a faint stain on the left sleeve of her uniform, the fading burn mark where she'd scorched her hand on a hot pulse-rifle barrel at target practice.

Then the hostage backed away and the guards at the door fired and Kolodny staggered to her feet, fell facedown and lay still.

The rest of the raid was just a series of isolated snapshots.

Running down the corridor under flickering emergency lights with Kolodny slung across her shoulders.

Rushing the stairs in a ceramsteel-enhanced tendon-snapping burst of speed and charging head-on into a skinny kid in civilian clothes armed with a cheap pulse rifle. A hundredth-of-a-second blink in which Li knew that things had spiraled too far out of control for it to be about anything but surviving.

Then enhanced reflexes kicking in, wetware and ceramsteel filament driving Li's body faster than human flesh was meant to move. The kid's shocked look when her bullet shattered his neck before he could even start to pull his own gun's trigger.

A final dash across the endless expanse of grit-scoured concrete. A lightning strike of pain from elbow to shoulder.

Then nothing.

Her last memory was of flat gray sky, wind, rain on her face. Kolodny lay next to her, eyes open. Smoke curled lazily above them, and Li smelled something that she recognized with bemused detachment as her own flesh burning.

Dalloway appeared above her, leaned over, and grabbed her beneath the armpits.

"Kolodny first!" she said, but he just shook his head.

She passed out again and came to with flight-deck plating under her back. Someone was fussing with her legs, lifting them up and shoving things under them. A medtech pressed something into her left hand—an IV bag—and told her to squeeze it.

She kept trying to tell him she was right-handed; but her right arm was off somewhere outside her peripheral vision and didn't seem to want to obey the orders her brain was sending. So she lay there holding the IV, slipping in and out of consciousness while the hopper labored into a sky gone dead and cold as Kolodny's eyes.

SYSTEMS WITH ONE DEGREE OF FREEDOM

►Section (2). The registration requirement of Section (1)(a)(2), and such additional registration requirements, travel restrictions, and other restrictions as may be prescribed by relevant administrative regulations pursuant to this Resolution, shall apply to:

(a) all citizens of Syndicate-controlled systems, as defined in Section (2)(c) below;

(b) any United Nations citizen more than twenty-five percent (25%) of whose geneset, as defined in Section (2)(d)(ii) below, is comprised of proprietary genetic material included in the Controlled Technology List pursuant to General Assembly Resolution 235625–09, as hereafter amended.

—UNITED NATIONS GENERAL ASSEMBLY RESOLUTION 584872–32.

51 Pegası Field Array: 13.10.48.

\<14,000pF\>
  \<27,000pF\>
    \<DPLprompt\>
Her own breathing woke her—harsh, panicked, the sound of a child waking from a nightmare. The memory of Metz was so close she could smell it. Everything else—name, rank, age, history—was darkness. She'd lost the part of her mind that remembered those things, and every time she reached for the pieces they skittered away like quicksilver.

\<Status,\> she queried her oracle across an interface that felt distorted, alien.

No answer.

She opened her eyes and saw nothing. She spat out her tongue guard, tried to speak, and realized that the buzzing in her ears was her teeth chattering. She sensed a wall in front of her and put out hands stiff and brittle as sticks to feel it. Her fingers tangled in feed-lines, dislodged biomonitors dabbed with adhesive jelly. Wrists and elbows knocked painfully against cold metal, feeding her rising claustrophobia.

Coffin.

She pulled the word out of some unexpected reserve of soft memory. It placed her, anchored her. She was in a coffin in the cryobay of a Bose-Einstein transport, waking after a jump. There must have been some malfunction, some glitch in the ship's systems, or her own, to pull her off ice so early. But it hadn't been a fatal malfunction, or she wouldn't be lying here worrying about why she couldn't remember her own name until her oracle booted.

<Status?> she queried again.

<Evolving sysfiles,> her oracle finally fired back at her.

All her systems were coming on-line now. Hard data flowed into her mind, buttressing the decohering haze of soft memory. Flesh and silicon, digital and organic systems knit themselves together. Meat and machine recombined in a quantum-faithful replica of the same Major Catherine Li who'd gone into cryo back on Metz.

She accessed her diagnostic programs and ran through the postjump protocols, checking entangled states, troubleshooting the Sharifi transforms, comparing pre- and postjump file sizes. Everything checked out.

Good; she didn't have time for problems. She had to take care of her people. She needed to put Dalloway in for a commendation and ship him out to a new unit before all hell broke loose over Metz. And there was Kolodny's family to see. Whatever family she had, which Li doubted was much.

Then she saw the trick her mind had played on her.

Metz had been over for almost three months. She'd taken care of everything: Kolodny's family, Dalloway's transfer, her own preliminary statements for the review board. She'd done it all in a manic three-day race against exhaustion and injury, wired to the gills on pain-suppression programs. Then she'd gone into the rehab tanks. And after that there would have been the cold freeze, the transfer to the jumpship, weeks of sublight travel by Bussard drive to reach Metz's orbital relay and queue up for transfer.

How long had she been under? Twelve weeks? Thirteen?

She felt the old fear rising in her chest, caught herself flipping through directories, cross-checking, fighting to make sense of twisted fragments of soft data.

Stop, she told herself. *You know the rule. Stick to this jump, this place. Let the last one go. Let the hard files pick up the slack. Don't let the fear get you.*

But the fear got her anyway. It always did. The fear was rational, reasonable, double-blind tested, empirically verifiable. It waited for her at the boarding gate and rode on her shoulder through every jump, every mission, every sweaty early-morning jump-dream. It asked the one question she couldn't answer: what had she lost this time?

Decoherence was as slow and subtle as radiation. An unwired traveler could make five or six jumps in a lifetime without losing more than a few isolated dates and names. The real damage was cumulative, caused by the minute drift of spin states over the course of many replications—a slow bleed of information that couldn't be stanched without sacrificing the quantum parallelism that made replication possible in the first place. It took short-term memory first. Then long-term memory. Then friends and loyalties and marriages. If you didn't stop in time, it took everything.

Cybernetics could mask the problem. A field-wired Peacekeeper's hard memory held backed-up spinfeed of every waking moment, on- and off-duty, since enlistment. And provided you didn't lie to the psychtechs, the files preserved at least reasonably accurate preenlistment memories. Platformed on an enslaved

AI and bolstered by psychotropic drugs, the datafiles could provide a working substitute for lost memories. But jump long enough, and everything you knew, everything that was you, flowed out of the meat and into the machine as inexorably as sand slipping through an hourglass. And Li, her oracle on-line, her hard memory fully reintegrated, could now recall that in the fourteen years, two months, and six days since enlistment she'd made thirty-seven Bose-Einstein jumps.

She fumbled for the coffin's latch, found it at her right hip where it always was, popped the lid. It rose in a smooth whisper of hydraulics. She sat up.

The effort left her wracked with cramps, coughing up thick chunks of mucus. She couldn't be Ring-side or on Alba, she realized; the Ring and Corps HQ were only one jump from anywhere on the Periphery, and her lungs wouldn't feel this bad unless she'd been kept under through multiple jumps and layovers. So where was she? And why was she bound for some unknown Periphery planet instead of back to Alba for rehab?

She swung her legs over the rim of the coffin and felt the cold grid of deckplating under her feet. Bottom rack at least. Thank God for small mercies. She looked around at the cryobay. Racks of coffins rose above her in a brightly lit honeycomb of feedlines and biomonitors. Most of the other passengers were still on ice; cool green vital lines blipped steadily on their status screens. The virusteel deckplating hummed with the distant throb of idling Bussard drives. Somewhere out of sight a skeleton crew would be running postjump checks, evolving systems shut down for replication, signaling to the sublight tugs that would ferry the jumpship beyond the immense starfish arms of the field array.

Li's uniform—or rather a quantum-faithful replica of it—lay in the kit drawer beneath her coffin, neatly folded and stowed by a Major Catherine Li, UNSC, who no longer existed. In the right-hand pants pocket she found a wad of tissue just where she always stashed it. In the left-hand shirt pocket she found her cigarettes, already unwrapped by that other Li who knew just how weak her fingers were after jumps these days.

She leaned against the coffin, uniform piled next to her, and blew her nose.

Pain rifled through her right shoulder as she raised her hands to her face. She touched the heart of the pain: eight centimeters of knotted scar tissue slicing up her triceps and across the point of her shoulder. It felt nervy to the touch, and when she twisted her head to look at it the scar stood out white against her brown skin.

Metz's parting gift. She'd never seen the gunman, but the single shot shredded muscle, tendon, and ligament, and severed the ceramsteel filaments that threaded through her arm from shoulder to fingertip. Her oracle told her it had taken five weeks in the tanks to patch it up, but all she remembered of those weeks was painful awakenings, doctors' questions, sharp flashes of underwater blue brilliance.

She got her uniform on without too much fumbling, but when she tried to pull on her boots her fingers wouldn't grip properly. She tucked the boots under her good arm and staggered down the aisle, weaving like a worn-out drunk. Green arrows led to the exit. Somewhere down the corridor they'd lead her to a cup of coffee and a soft chair where she could smoke her first ritual postjump cigarette.

She stumbled into the passenger lounge just as the transport linked up with its tug and started the slow subluminal drift toward the field array's perimeter.

Li had jumped often enough to know the protocol. They would clear the glittering crystal arms of the field array, then kick on the Bussard drives and jump to near lightspeed for the last leg of the journey. Once that happened they'd be in slow time, the communications limbo of a ship traveling at speeds that made relativity a practical rather than theoretical problem. They'd be outstream, cut off from streamspace and the rest of humanity until they dropped back into normal time.

She slumped into an empty chair, lit her cigarette, and looked around at her fellow passengers. Two Peacekeepers huddled in one corner playing a silent card game. The rest of the passengers were techs, company men, midlevel professionals. People whose expertise made it worth the multiplanetaries' while to pay quantum-transport prices but who didn't have enough corporate clout to get Ring-side assignments.

There were no constructs, of course. Partial constructs could theoretically bypass the off-planet travel restrictions and get clearance to hold company or even civil service posts. But geneset assays weren't cheap, and it didn't happen often.

The only obviously posthuman civilian in the lounge sat directly across from Li: a tall dark-skinned woman with a white scar on her forehead. West African, Li thought. Something in her bones, in the long line of her back, suggested the radiation-induced mutations of the old generation ships—ships that had dropped out of slow time after centuries in open space only to find that humanity had exploded past them in the first wave of the FTL era and their chosen planets were already being stripped and boosted into orbit to feed the voracious juggernaut of the Ring's consumer culture. The woman wore a tech's orange coveralls, but her hair was pulled back in spare elegant braids and she was crunching numbers on a high-powered streamspace foldout. An engineer? A Bose-Einstein technician?

Li shifted in her chair and wondered why the

woman hadn't paid to have that scar taken off. She was pretty enough to make it worthwhile. Beautiful, actually.

She caught Li staring at her and smiled, black eyes crinkling at the corners. Li looked away, but not soon enough to miss the sharpening of the woman's gaze on her too-regular, too-symmetrical features. Not soon enough to miss the unspoken question that lingered behind every first meeting: Was she a construct or wasn't she?

Li could have looked up again. Could have asked the woman where they were, what system they were about to dock in. But it would sound silly, a tired variation on a very old pickup line. And there was always the awful risk of rejection. The fear that—even to a posthuman whose genes were warped by centuries of radiation—she, Li, was a monster.

She lit another cigarette and checked her mail. When she'd weeded out the junk, she was left with three items. A memo from the Metz field hospital explaining what they'd been able to fix in her arm and what they hadn't, telling her to go in for a checkup when she reached her next posting. A cryptically worded notice that the review board had postponed issuance of its final ruling on the Metz incident pending further fact-gathering. And three messages from Cohen.

She hadn't talked to him since Kolodny died. They'd recovered her body, but Dalloway had been right; there was nothing they could do for her. The wet bug had eaten away so much of her brain that when the medtechs showed Li the scans, even she could see Kolodny was never coming back from it.

Kolodny had written Li's name into the next-of-kin line on her emergency forms. Without telling her. The revelation shook Li, partly because it reminded her that the next-of-kin line on her own papers was still blank. But Kolodny hadn't been one to leave things to chance;

she'd left precise instructions about what to do if she flatlined.

Li had followed her instructions to the letter.

The techs were there when they pulled the plug; they were hacking the precious slivers of communications-grade condensate out of Kolodny's skull before she was even cold. Li should have known better than to get angry. Christ, she'd done field recoveries herself on a few awful occasions. But it was still like watching vultures pick Kolodny apart. And when it was over, she and Cohen had the worst fight of their lives.

She'd been going into the tanks, groggy with shock and pain-suppression routines, and she'd wanted to put off talking to him. But he insisted. And then he had the gall to give her technical jargon instead of reasons, excuses instead of explanations.

"You dropped us," she'd said at last, on the outer edge of control. "And Kolodny's dead because of it."

"She was my friend too, Catherine."

"You don't have friends," she'd snapped, her stomach churning with the guilty suspicion that if she hadn't let things get personal, Kolodny would still be alive. "You're not wired for it."

"Don't throw my code in my face," he'd said, though he ought to have known better. "It's bigoted."

"It's the truth. It's what you are. You're wired to twist and manipulate and feed off people. And I'm through with it!"

That was the last time they'd spoken. One or both of them, she suspected, had gone too far to be forgiven. And she wasn't sure she wanted to forgive, anyway. Or be forgiven.

She stared at Cohen's messages, wavering. Then she deleted them, unopened and unanswered.

Her commsys icon started flashing as soon as they dropped out of slow time. The call came in with no user tag over a stand-alone scrambled Security Council relay. Someone wanted to talk to her in a hurry. Someone important enough to command a private line from Service HQ.

She toggled the icon, and a high-ceilinged twenty-second-century baroque revival room sprang into three dimensions around her. A tiger maple desk floated on gracefully bowed legs above a pine floor buffed to a smooth gloss by generations of officers' boots. Each floorboard was as wide as both Li's hands put side to side, and they were laid down in the unmistakable herringbone pattern of the Security Council Administration Building on Alba. Behind the desk, hands resting on the carved leaves and volutes of her chair's arms, sat the general.

General Nguyen was a spare, elegant woman, far into a well-preserved middle age. It was hard not to stare at her, even across a spinstream interface. The slightly crooked nose, the asymmetrical cheekbones, the quirked line of the left eyebrow were like the irregularities in a bolt of raw silk; they enhanced rather than detracted from a fragile, unmistakably human beauty.

Nguyen looked directly at Li as she came on-line, meeting her eyes in streamspace. It was a politician's trick, but knowing the trick didn't make you immune to it. And when Nguyen did it, you felt like she was inches away from you, not light-years.

"Major," Nguyen said in a voice that knew how to make itself heard quietly. "It's good to see you."

"General," Li said.

Someone spoke to Nguyen from outside the streamspace projection field. "Fine," she told her unseen assistant. "Tell Delegate Orozco I'll be there in five minutes."

She turned back to Li. "Sorry, Major. I'm pressed for time, as usual. The Assembly's voting on a military appropriations bill that still needs some baby-sitting."

She smiled. "You've probably guessed I have a little job for you."

Li coaxed her still-numb face into what she hoped was a politely expectant expression. She'd done more than one little job for Nguyen. The general's jobs were risky; she demanded a level of personal loyalty that could mean bending, if not breaking, the rules. But her rewards were generous. And she remembered favors as tenaciously as she held grudges.

The general's next words were as unexpected as they were unwelcome. "You're from Compson's World, Major?"

"Yes." Li shifted uncomfortably. *Mother of God. Not Compson's. Anywhere but Compson's World.*

"You've never gone home since enlisting?"

Li didn't answer. It wasn't really a question; Nguyen had clearance to view her psych files, and in five minutes she could know as much about her personal life as Li herself knew. More, if the barracks scuttlebutt about memory spinning was true.

"Why not?" Nguyen asked.

Li started to speak, then bit the words back. "It's not the kind of place you go home to," she said finally.

"Not the kind of place you go home to." The words sounded like a riddle in Nguyen's mouth. "Now tell me what you were about to say before you thought the better of it."

Li hesitated. Her lips were dry; the urge to lick them was like an itch she knew she was going to have to scratch sooner or later. "I was about to say that when I left I swore I'd die before I went back."

"I hope you don't still feel that way. You'll be docking at AMC's orbital station on Compson's World in a little over four hours."

Nguyen reached across her desk to a silver tray that held a carafe of ice water and two cut-crystal glasses. She poured a glass and handed it to Li, who raised it to her lips, hearing the chime of ice against crystal.

The water was good, but the line to Alba was so laced with security protocols that it could only process high-load sensory data in intermittent bursts. She sipped, felt nothing, then got a disorienting headache-cold burst of taste half a second after she'd swallowed. She shook her head and put the glass down.

"Not where you expected to wake up?" Nguyen asked.

"I expected to wake up at Alba. I need to be at Alba. I'm running on a field-hospital patch job—"

"Alba would be a bad place for you just now," Nguyen interrupted smoothly.

She caught Li's look of confusion and raised one immaculately groomed eyebrow. "Haven't you looked at the review board report?"

"Not yet. I—"

"They kicked it upstairs."

"Upstairs where?"

"Do I have to spell it out for you, Major? Loss of personnel in circumstances suggesting misconduct by the commanding officer. Use of lethal force on a civilian. Use of an unauthorized weapon. Where the hell did you think you were, pulling that thing out? Gilead?"

"They recommended a court-martial?" Li said, trying to get her brain around the idea.

"Not exactly."

Not exactly. Not exactly meant that covert ops wanted the Metz raid kept quiet, that they planned to comb through every fact and opinion and scrap of testimony before they released it. And if that left Li without a defense, no one would lose much sleep over it.

"When do I testify?" she asked.

"You already have. We downloaded the Metz data and opened your backup files to the Defender's Office. You can amend your extrapolated testimony if you like, but I doubt you'll want to. Your attorney did a good job."

"Right," Li said. It made her queasy to think of her

files being used that way. A backup was exactly that. It sat in an oracle-compatible datacache in Corps archives, received updates and edits and waited to be retrieved if the medtechs needed it. It sure as hell didn't walk into court-martial proceedings and proffer testimony that could end your career.

"The board hasn't rendered its decision," Nguyen said. "It seemed prudent to let things cool down a little. And when the . . . situation on Compson's World came up, the board thought you were the right person."

"You mean you convinced them I was the right person."

Nguyen smiled at that, but the smile never made it up to her eyes. "Have you had time to catch any spinfeed since you came off ice?"

Li shook her head.

"Ten days ago one of the mines in the Anaconda strike caught fire. The mine director—I forget his name, you'll have to talk to him when you get there—got the fire under control, but we lost our on-station security chief in the initial explosion, and we need someone there fast to oversee the investigation and help the AMC personnel restart production."

Nguyen paused, and Li forced herself to sit through the pause without asking the questions they both knew she wanted answered: what any of this had to do with her, and why Nguyen had shipped her halfway to Syndicate territory to pursue a mining accident that should have been handled by the UN's Mine Safety Commission.

"Everything I've told you so far is public record," Nguyen continued. "What's not yet public is that Hannah Sharifi died in the fire."

Li suppressed the flare of guilt and fear that shot through her at the sound of that name. Nguyen didn't know—couldn't know—what Sharifi meant to her.

That was a secret she'd mortgaged half her life to protect. And she had protected it. She was sure she had.

Almost sure.

Hannah Sharifi was—had been—the most prominent theoretical physicist in UN-controlled space. Her equations had made Bose-Einstein transport possible, had woven themselves into the fabric of UN society until there was hardly a technology that hadn't been touched by Coherence Theory. But Sharifi's legend went well beyond her work. She was also a genetic construct—the most famous construct in UN space. News of her death would flood streamspace the moment it went public. And the faintest tinge of scandal would spark off a new round of debates on genetics in the military, genetic mandatory registration, genetic everything.

Li took another sip of water, mainly in order to have something to do with her hands. The water was still cold, and it still went down all wrong. "How long do we have before word of her death gets out?" she asked.

"Another week at most. It's been all we could do to keep the lid on it this long, frankly. And that's why I'm sending you there. I want you to pick up the reins for the last station security chief and investigate Sharifi's death, and I need someone there now, while the trail's still hot."

Li frowned. She'd spent the eight years since peace broke out chasing black-market tech instead of being the soldier she'd been trained to be. And now Nguyen was asking her to play cops and robbers?

"You've got that look on your face," Nguyen said.

"What look?"

"The look you get when you're thinking that if you were human, you'd be sitting behind my desk instead of doing my scut work."

"General—"

"I wonder, Li, would you really be happy playing

backroom politics and sitting through budget presen-
tations?"

"I didn't realize being happy was the point of the
exercise."

"Ah. Still out to change the world, are we? I
thought we'd grown out of that."

Li shrugged.

"You'll put a dent in things, Li. Don't worry. But not
yet. For now what you're doing out there matters
more. The war's not over. You know that. It didn't end
when we signed the Gilead Accords or the Trade
Compact. And the front line of the new war is technology: hardware, wetware, psychware, and, above all,
Bose-Einstein tech."

Nguyen picked up her glass, looked into it like a
fortune-teller peering at tea leaves, set it down again
without drinking.

"Sharifi was working on a joint project with the
Anaconda Mining Corp. She claimed she was close to
developing a method for culturing transport-grade
Bose-Einstein condensates."

"I thought that was impossible."

"We all thought it was impossible. But Sharifi . . .
well, who knows what Sharifi thought. She told us she
could do it, and that was enough. She was Sharifi, after
all. She's done the impossible before. So we put together the partnership with AMC. They provided the
mine and the condensates. We provided the funding.
And . . . other things. Sharifi sent us a preliminary report ten days ago."

"And what was in this preliminary report?"

"We don't know." Nguyen laughed softly, sounding
not at all amused. "We can't read it."

Li blinked.

"Sharifi transmitted an encrypted file through
Compson's Bose-Einstein relay. But when we de-
crypted it, we got . . . noise . . . garbage . . . just a
bunch of random spins. We've put it through every

decryption program we have. Nothing. It's either irretrievably corrupted or it's entangled with some other datastream that Sharifi failed to transmit to us."

"So . . ."

"So I need the original dataset."

"Why not ask AMC for it if they were cosponsors?" Nguyen raised an eyebrow.

"Ah," Li said. "We didn't share it with them."

"We didn't share it period. And we don't plan to."

"All right," Li said. "So I get the file and keep anyone else from getting it. That's simple enough. But why me? What makes it worth the shipping bill?"

Nguyen paused, glancing over Li's shoulder. She was looking out the window, Li realized; the distant, spectrum-enhanced reflection of Barnard's Star glimmered in her pupils. "There's more at issue than the missing spinstream," she said. "In fact, we don't have any of Sharifi's results. She seems to have . . . cleaned things up before she died. It's as if she wiped every trace of her work off the system. As if she planned to hide it from us." A chilly smile played across Nguyen's lips. "So. No Sharifi. No experiment. No dataset. And as if that weren't bad enough, the station security chief died in the fire with Sharifi. Someone needs to get out there and pick up the pieces, Li. Someone I can trust. Someone who can face down press accusations of a cover-up, if things turn ugly. Who better than the hero of Gilead?"

Li shifted uncomfortably in her chair.

"Don't look like that," Nguyen said. "Gilead was the turning point. The press is right about that, no matter how badly they bungled everything else about the war. Gilead brought the Syndicates to the peace table. It kept them away from Compson's World and everything else we've spent the last thirty years protecting. You had the courage to step into the breach when things fell apart and do what had to be done. And you didn't do anything a real soldier needs to be ashamed of. I saw the realtime feed. I know it, even if you don't."

Li had no answer to that. All she remembered—all she was supposed to remember—was the official spinstream. Her realtime feed was classified, deadcached in the data catacombs under Corps HQ on Alba. Gilead wasn't hers anymore—except in the jump-dreams that put the lie to her official memory and left her with the queasy certainty that all the kinks and evasions it had taken to get off Compson's World were finally catching up with her.

"People believe in you," Nguyen insisted. "They trust you. And look in the mirror, for Heaven's sake. You're, what, one grandparent away from mandatory registration? And out of the same lab that tanked Sharifi. Have you ever seen holos of her? You could be her sister." One immaculately groomed eyebrow arched upward. "Isn't that what you are, technically?"

"More like her granddaughter," Li said reluctantly. Better for her if people didn't think of her name in the same breath with the word *construct*.

"Well, there you are. What reporter in his right mind is going to accuse you of bigotry against your own grandmother?"

Li stared at the floor between her feet. Some long-ago bootheel or chair leg had gouged a swerving path across several of the floorboards, and she marveled at the vividness of it, as real and touchable—while she was caught in this illusion—as the flight deck that her feet really rested on.

There must be a way out, she told herself. She couldn't go back to Compson's World. It was insane to think that no one would recognize her. Insane to imagine that someone somewhere wouldn't make the fatal connection.

"I'm not sure you appreciate what I'm doing for you," Nguyen said. "You made a real mess of things on Metz—"

"Only by trusting Cohen."

"Don't be naive. Cohen's untouchable. Tel Aviv proved that. You, however, are eminently touchable." Nguyen put her elbows on her desk, clasped her hands, looked at Li over the steeple of her fingers. "Did you know that you're the highest-ranking partial genetic in the Corps?"

What the hell do you think? Li thought. But she kept her mouth shut. Biting her tongue was one skill she'd gotten down cold in the last fifteen years.

"It came up. During your court-martial proceedings. You stand for something, Li. Not everyone likes it. Half the Committee would like nothing better than to chapter you out and forget about you. The other half—me included—would rather not lose you. Things are changing, and you're part of the change. Don't throw that away."

"All right," Li said. "All right."

"Good," Nguyen said. But she was still watching Li carefully, measuringly. "And there's another problem. Or perhaps I should say another potential problem. We have reason to believe someone intercepted Sharifi's message."

Li understood then—and caught her breath as she realized what the stakes were.

The UN had defeated the Syndicates, had held the line through a decade of cold war for one reason: Bose-Einstein transport. The UN had commercial-scale, reliable FTL. The Syndicates didn't. The UN could put troops into any system with a Bose-Einstein relay on a moment's notice. The Syndicates couldn't. The UN had spent the last half century building up a vast interstellar network of banked entanglement that enabled them to safely broadcast quantum data through the transient wormholes of the spinfoam. The Syndicates, in contrast, limped along with haphazard supplies of entanglement pirated from UN ships or bought off bootleg miners through the Freetown black market.

It all came down to Compson's World and its unique, nonrenewable deposits of Bose-Einstein condensates. But the moment someone discovered how to culture transport-grade condensates, then it would be the new technology of condensate culture that determined control of space. And if the Syndicates got hold of that technology, then the balance of interstellar power, the Trade Compacts—the fragile peace itself— would crumble.

That was why she was on her way to Compson's World, Li realized. Not just to prevent a leak, but to fix one that Nguyen feared had already happened.

"Who do you think intercepted the message?" she asked, swallowing. "The Syndicates?"

"We don't know. We hope not, obviously. We just know there was an eavesdropper."

Li nodded. The Security Council's standard in-stream quantum-encryption protocols couldn't prevent a third party from intercepting any given transmission, but the very nature of quantum information meant that no eavesdropper could intercept a message without collapsing its fragile spin states and thus revealing himself.

"The real question," Nguyen continued, "is why an unknown person or persons decided to intercept that particular message."

"Obviously someone told them it was coming."

"Obviously. But who was it? That's what I'm sending you to find out." Nguyen straightened the file in front of her and set it aside. Case closed, the gesture said. End of discussion. "Officially, you've simply been diverted to Compson's to replace the prior station security chief. The rest is . . . only to be spoken of to me personally."

"Anything else?"

"Just be your usual discreet and thorough self."

Nguyen's eyes were as black and unreadable as stones. "And be careful. We've already lost one officer down there."

"Yeah," Li said. "I meant to ask. Who was it?"

"Jan Voyt. I don't think you knew him."

"Voyt," Li repeated, but the name didn't jog any soft memory loose and all her oracle produced for her were public-access files. "No," she said, "I don't think I did know him."

After Nguyen signed off, Li moved to a window seat and watched her home star fill up the scratched viewport.

She couldn't see Compson's World itself at first; it was second night and the planet was engulfed in the vast gloomy shadow of the companion planet that orbited between it and 51 Pegasi. Then the Companion cleared the trailing edge of the star, and she got her first clear view of AMC station just as its 2 million square meters of photovoltaic panels rotated to the rising sun.

She was still too far away to see the dents of meteor impacts, the frozen streaks of fuel and sewage leaks on the station's outer skin. From here it looked like a piece of jeweled clockwork. The glittering double-hulled life-support ring spun at an oblique angle to the planet surface, well out of the trajectory of the mass drivers. Nested within the main ring lay the complex interlocking gears of precession ring, spin stablizers, and Stirling engines—a cosmic windmill veiled in the curving black-and-silver dragonfly wings of the solar panels. And below, shrouded in Compson's murky, processor-generated atmosphere, lay the Anaconda.

No roads tied the mine to Compson's major cities. The only surface road was a rutted red track that cut across sage and chaparral, passed under the shadow of the antiquated atmospheric processors, and petered out among the gin joints and miner's flats of Shantytown.

Shantytown wasn't its map name, of course. But it was what the people who lived there called it.

What Li herself had called it.

She'd been sixteen, four years underground already, when she walked into a cash-only chop shop, clutching a pitifully thin wad of UN currency, and paid a gray-market geneticist to give her a dead girl's face and chromosomes. That money had been the first real cash she'd ever held: her father's life insurance payout. She didn't remember much of that day, but she did recall thinking how funny it was that a man got paid cash money to die and only miner's scrip for doing the job that killed him.

The genetic work itself had been painless, just a series of injections and blood tests. The scars on her face took longer to heal, but the stakes made it worth waiting for. She'd stepped into the chop shop as a trademarked genetic construct with a red slash across the cover of her passport. When she left, her mitochondria still carried the damning corporate serial number, but the rest of her DNA said she had three natural-born grandparents—enough to make her a citizen. Two days later, she walked into the Peacekeepers' recruiting post, lied about her age as well as everything else, and started passing.

The recruiting board hadn't asked too many questions. They'd been desperate for strong young bodies to throw at the Syndicates back then, and the same proprietary geneset that barred her from military service also made her tougher than kudzu vine. Besides, what questions needed asking? She was just another rim-colony miner's kid looking down the long tunnel of forty years in the pit and deciding that a UN paycheck and a one-way ticket off-planet were worth fighting someone else's war for.

Getting wired was the hardest part. The psych techs wanted to know everything. Childhood. Family. First time with a boy. First time with a girl. She'd told them whatever she could without letting the truth slip. The rest she'd just let slide. It hadn't seemed like much of a loss at the time; there was little about growing up on Compson's that she wanted to remember even if it were safe to have it kicking around in her hard files where the techs could get at it.

Now, fifteen years later, she remembered only the little things. Church bells and midnight mass. The high lonesome moan of the pit whistle. A pale-eyed woman. A thin, tired man, black-skinned on work-days, white as February when he washed the coal dust off his face on Sunday.

Their names were gone. They belonged not to Catherine Li, but to the woman Li had spent her entire adult life erasing—a woman who'd been slipping away, jump by jump, since the day she enlisted.

AMC Station: 13.10.48.

No one met Li at the boarding gate. She waited briefly, then went onstream and asked the station for directions to her office.

The UNSC field office was annexed to Station Security—not uncommon in poorly funded periphery jurisdictions—and Security was on the far end of the station, buried in the ramshackle maze of the public-sector arcades and gangways. Most of her fellow passengers peeled off into the corporate spokes, and soon she was walking alone. As she moved into the public arcs, magtubes gave way to slidewalks, slidewalks to solid decking, decking to virusteel gridplate.

She saw old people everywhere, people obviously out of work, though she didn't see how anyone without at least a foreman's salary could afford the air tax. As she moved into the poorer sections of the life-support ring, she understood: they were lung-shot miners, most of them, wearing nose tubes and towing wheeled oxygen tanks. AMC must have reached some kind of black-lung settlement since she'd left, given orbital residency to the worst cases.

She also saw women in chador. She tried to remember if there'd been any Interfaithers on Compson's in her childhood. It was hard to imagine them converting the hard-luck, hard-drinking Catholics she'd grown up with. But then fanaticism of every stripe was a growth industry on the Periphery—and if you could see the Virgin Mary in a Bose-Einstein crystal, it probably wasn't much of a stretch to see the Devil in an implanted interface.

She threaded her way through a maze of tired window displays, cheap VR signs, bars, fast-food joints. She ducked into a hole-in-the-wall called the All Nite Noodle; it didn't look like much, but was crowded and it smelled better than the other places.

"What do you want?" asked the woman at the counter.

"What do you have?"

"Real eggs. Cost a lot, but they're worth it."

Li scanned the overhead menu. Holos of noodles and vegeshrimp; holos of noodles and vegepork; holos of noodles and every conceivable shape and flavor of algae-based protein. Someone had pasted a handwritten fiche under the noodles and fried eggs holo upping the price to twelve dollars UN.

"Hey," the woman said. "You don't want 'em, get something else. But get something; I got a line behind you."

"Eggs, then," Li said, and they shook left-handed to make the credit transfer.

"Sprang for the eggs," the line cook said when she slid down the counter toward him.

"Haven't had real ones in years," Li said.

"My brother's got chickens. Sends the eggs up from Shantytown on the mine shuttle. Shipped us a whole chicken last year. Not that we sold it." He grinned, and Li saw the long indigo blue line of a coal scar slicing across the point of his chin. "Ate the sucker in one sitting."

They were running spinfeed on the shop's livewall. NowNet. Politics. As Li turned to look, Cohen's face flashed across the screen, big and pretty as life. He stood on the marble steps of the General Assembly Building, formal in a dark suit and striped tie. A gaggle of reporters were hurling questions at him about the latest AI suffrage resolution.

"It's not about special rights for Emergents," he was saying in answer to a question Li hadn't heard. "It's simply a question of the basic respect owed to all persons, whether they're running on code or genesets. The limited-suffrage faction would like to have things both ways. All pigs are equal, according to our opponents— but some pigs are more equal than others. That's a step away from equality, not toward it."

He was shunting through Roland, a golden-haired, golden-eyed boy who could have passed for a girl except for the coppery shadow above his upper lip. Li had met the kid once when he came by Cohen's place on his day off. They'd had a surreal tea during which he'd explained earnestly to her over buttered scones and Devonshire cream that he was putting himself through medical school on what Cohen paid him.

The woman hanging on Cohen's, or rather Roland's, arm would have been taller than him even without the three-inch heels. Li recognized her face from the fashion spins, but she couldn't tell if the carefully painted features were natural or synthetic.

"So what you're after is one-for-one universal suffrage?" a reporter asked, seizing on Cohen's last words. "That sounds like a nod toward repealing the genetics laws."

Cohen laughed and put up a hand, fending off the question. "That's someone else's cause," he said. "I wouldn't dream of trying to break up a squabble between primates."

"And what would you say to those who claim that your own connections with the Consortium have had a negative impact on the AI suffrage movement?" asked another reporter.

Cohen turned toward the reporter slowly, as if he couldn't quite believe what Roland's ears were hearing. Li wondered if the reporter noticed the slight pause before his smile, if he understood the fury that lurked behind that serene, inhuman stillness.

"There is no connection with the Consortium," Cohen said coolly, "and our opponents' attempts to portray a legal association like ALEF as the political arm of the Consortium or any of its component AIs are, quite simply, slanderous."

"Still," the reporter pursued. "You can't deny that your . . . lifestyle has clouded the issue in these hearings."

"My lifestyle?" Cohen unleashed his most dazzling smile on the camera. "I'm as boring as a binary boy can be. Just ask my ex-wives and -husbands."

Li rolled her eyes, hacked into the livewall's controls, and flipped to the sports feed.

"Whoever did that, beer on me!" called a drunken voice from one of the back tables. Li ignored it; she was busy watching the Yankees' new phenom deliver a filthy curveball.

"There you go," the cook said, handing her noodles over the scratched countertop. Li turned her hand palm up as she took the plate from him, baring the silver matte lines of her wire job where the ceramsteel ran just under the skin of the inner wrist.

"So you're our sports fan," he said. "How d'you like the Yanks for the Series?"

"I like 'em fine." Li grinned. "They're gonna lose, of course. But I still like them."

The cook laughed, the coal scar standing out neon-bright along his jawline. "Come back for game one,

and I'll give you a free meal. I need one goddamn person in here who's not a Mets fan."

Li left the noodle shop and walked on, eating as she
went. The streets and arcades were filling up. The
graveyard shift had come up from the mine, and
second-shift workers were making their way to the
planet-bound shuttles. The bars were all open. Most of
them were running spinfeed, but a few had live music
even at this time of the morning.

The crackling moan of a badly amplified fiddle
stopped Li in her tracks outside one bar. A girl's voice
rose above the fiddle, and suddenly Li was smelling
disinfectant, bleached sheets, the mold-heavy air of
Shantytown. A pale old-young man lay in a hospital
bed, his skin several sizes too large for him. Across the
room, a doctor held up a badly out-of-focus X ray.

A stranger brushed by Li, knocking her sideways,
and she realized she was blinking back tears.

"You gonna eat that?" someone asked.

She looked up to find a skinny old drunk staring at
her noodles with rheumy eyes.

"Shit, take it," she said, and walked on.

She'd expected Security to be quiet this time of night.
She should have known better. AMC Orbital was a
mining town; even at 4 A.M.—especially at 4 A.M.—the
drunk tank was up and running.

Dingy government office yellow light seeped
through double-hinged viruflex doors into the side
street. Large block letters on the doors read, "AMC SE-
CURITY, A DIVISION OF ANACONDA MINING COM-
PANY, S.A." And below, in much smaller letters,
"Organización de Naciónes Unidas 51PegB18."

The station's front room did double duty as main
office and holding facility. A chest-height counter
stretched across its midsection, corralling the public
out or Security in, depending which side of the

counter you were stuck on. Someone had slapped a careless coat of paint onto the walls, in a nursery-school pink that was no doubt supposed to make arrestees less likely to start fights. It worked, Li thought; she'd have made friends with her worst enemy to get away from the color.

One wall supported a Corps surplus bulletin board festooned with several years' accumulation of station directives, workplace safety warnings, and wanted posters. The bench below it groaned under the night's catch of scatter junkies and unlicensed prostitutes. The whole place had a resigned, halfhearted air. Even the criminals on the wanted posters looked too pinched and petty to have stolen anything valuable or killed anyone important.

When Li arrived the duty sergeant had one eye on the customers and the other on his desktop spinfeed, where some washed-up ballplayer was pointing to a map of pre-Embargo New York and explaining what a subway series was.

"Sergeant," Li said as she bellied up to the counter.

He looked up reluctantly, then snapped to his feet when he saw the chrome on her shoulder tabs. "Jesus, Bernadette!" he said, looking past her. "How many times do I have to tell you?"

Li blinked and turned to look over her shoulder. One of the whores on the bench—the one sitting immediately below the no-smoking sign—had a lit cigarette in her hand. Her skinny body was covered with skintight latex, except for the upper slope of her breasts, which sported a writhing smart tattoo. She was pregnant, and Li struggled not to stare at her bizarrely swollen belly.

"Put it out, Bernadette!" the duty sergeant snapped.

The woman crushed the cigarette out on the sole of one boot and sketched a rude gesture with its mangled corpse. Her tattoo crawled up onto her forehead and did something nasty.

"Sorry, ma'am," the sergeant said, speaking to Li again. "Can I help you?"

"Looking for my office, actually."

He read her name tag, started nervously, then glanced over his shoulder toward an unmarked door behind the counter. "Uh . . . they weren't expecting your flight in for another few hours. Let me call back and tell—"

"Don't bother," Li said, already crossing through the security field and skirting around the fake wood-finish desks toward the back office.

She stepped into a narrow hallway floored and ceilinged in battleship gray gridplate. The security chief's office was second on the right; Li could still see the torn-up paint where someone had removed Voyt's name. The adhesive hadn't wanted to come unstuck; the V and pieces of the Y and T were still visible.

"The king is dead," she muttered to herself. "Long live the king."

The office door was open. She stepped through it— and saw two men bent over her desk, rummaging through the desk drawers. Her kit lay on the floor in front of the desk, forwarded from the transport ship. She couldn't be sure, but she thought it looked like they'd searched that too.

"Gentlemen," she said quietly.

They both snapped to attention. Li's oracle pulled up their dossiers as she read their name tags. Lieutenant Brian Patrick McCuen and Captain Karl Kintz. Both men were technically under her command, but they were commissioned in Compson's planetary militia, not the Peacekeepers. In Li's experience that meant they could be anything from perfectly decent local cops to street thugs in uniform. It also meant that no matter how much she threw her weight around, she was never going to command their undivided loyalty; in the back of their minds they'd always know that she'd leave sooner or later, and they'd still have to answer to the company.

They were big men, both of them. Li found herself measuring them instinctively, adding up reach, weight, muscle tone, wondering if they were wired. *Hell of a way to think about your own junior officers*, she told herself.

"Ma'am," said McCuen. He was blond and lanky, a freckle-faced kid whose uniform looked freshly pressed even at this impossible hour of the morning. "We were cleaning out Voyt's, um, your desk. We didn't expect you so soon."

"Obviously," Li said.

McCuen fidgeted with the stack of fiche in his hands; he looked embarrassed about the situation and too young to hide his embarrassment.

Kintz, on the other hand, just stood there smirking at her like he didn't give a shit what she thought. "Someone better tell Haas she's here," he said, and brushed past Li into the hall without even excusing himself.

Li let him go; no percentage in starting a fight until she was sure she could win it.

"I'm really, really sorry about this," McCuen said. "We should have gotten the office cleaned up, met you at Customs. We've been running around like maniacs since the fire, is the problem. Rescue, body ID, cleanup. We're really shorthanded."

She looked at the boy's face, saw the telltale puffiness around his eyes that said he'd been through not one but several sleepless nights in the last few station cycles. "Well," she said mildly, "at least you had time to make sure my bags got here."

He coughed at that, and Li watched a red flush spread over his fair skin. "That was on Haas's orders," he said after glancing up and down through the grid-plating to make sure no one was in the adjoining rooms. "I didn't have anything to do with it."

"Haas. He's the station exec?"

McCuen nodded.

"That how the militia works here, Brian? You pulling down a corporate paycheck on the side?"

"No! Look at my file. I just want out of here and into the War College."

So. McCuen wanted a ticket into the freshman class at Alba. That made all kinds of sense on a periphery planet like Compson's. Bose-Einstein transport fueled an interstellar economy in which data, commercial goods, and a few properly wired humans could cross interstellar distances almost instantaneously. But uplinks, VR rigs, and spinstream access time still cost so much that most colonials spent their entire lives planetbound, stuck in the ebbs and deadwaters of the interstellar economy. The military was the best way out for ambitious colonials—sometimes the only way out. It was certainly the way she had taken.

Li sent her oracle on a fishing trip through McCuen's files, and it came back with a stream of data, from his primary-school grades to records from a government school in Helena to a string of applications to Alba, all denied.

"You must want it bad," she said. "You applied three times."

McCuen started. "That doesn't show up in my file. How—?"

"Voyt wouldn't recommend you," she said, twisting the knife a little. "Why not?"

His flush deepened. Li looked into his face and saw distress, embarrassment, earnest hopefulness.

"Never mind. You do a good honest job while I'm here and you'll get to Alba."

McCuen shook his head angrily. "You don't need to cut deals with me to get me to do my job."

"I'm not cutting deals," Li said. "It's your choice. Do a bad job, I'll show you the door. Do a good job, I'll make sure the right people know it. Got a problem with that?"

"Of course not." He started to say something else, but before Li could hear it, quick steps rattled on the hall gridplate.

The footsteps stopped and Kintz stuck his head through the doorway. "Haas wants to see her. Now."

Haas's desk floated on stars.

It was live-cut from a single two-meter-long Bose-Einstein condensate. Sub-communications grade, more of a curiosity than anything else, but still it must be priceless. Its polished face revealed the schistlike structure of the bed that had calved it. Its diamond facets mirrored the stars beyond the transparent ceramic compound floor panel so that the desk seemed to hang above empty space in a pool of reflected starlight.

Haas was a big man, bullish around the neck and shoulders, with an aura of resolutely clamped-down violence. He looked like a man who enjoyed losing his temper, but had learned to ration out that particular pleasure with iron self-discipline. And he looked nothing like the kind of man Li would have expected to find running AMC's crown jewel mine.

He had the accessories down pat. His suit hung well on his big frame even in station gravity. The strong-jawed, aggressively norm-conforming face must have cost a bundle in gene therapy and cosmetic surgery. But his body showed signs of hard living, and his handshake, when he rose behind his desk to greet Li, was the crushing, calloused grip of a man who had done rough labor in heavy gravity.

Li glanced at his hand as she shook it and saw a functional-looking watch strapped around his powerful wrist. Was he completely unwired? Allergic to ceramsteel? Religious objections? Either way, it took steel-plated ambition and an unbreakable work ethic to make it into corporate management without being wired for direct streamspace access.

Haas gestured to an angular, expensive-looking chair. Li sat, the ripstop of her uniform pants squeaking against cowhide. She tried to tell herself it was just tank leather, as artificial as everything else in the room, Haas included. Still, even the idea of making a chair out of a mammal was intimidatingly decadent.

"I'm in a hurry," Haas said as soon as she was seated. "Let's get this out of the way fast."

"Fine," Li answered. "Like to clear something up first, though. Want to tell me why you had my bags searched?"

He shrugged, completely unembarrassed. "Standard procedure. You're a quarter genetic. Your transfer papers say so. Nothing personal, Major. It's the rules."

"UN rules or company rules?"

"My rules."

"You made an exception for Sharifi, I assume?"

"No. And when she complained about it, I told her the same fucking thing I'm telling you."

Li couldn't help smiling at that. "Any other rules I should bear in mind?" she asked. "Or do you make them up as you go along?"

"Too bad about Voyt," Haas said, shifting gears abruptly enough to leave Li feeling vaguely disoriented. "He was a good security officer. He understood that some things are UN business and some things are company business. And that we're all here for one reason: to keep the crystal flowing." He rocked back in his chair and its springs creaked under his weight. "Some of the security officers I've worked with haven't understood that. Things haven't turned out well for them."

"Things didn't turn out so well for Voyt either," Li observed.

"What do you want?" Haas said, putting his feet up on the gleaming desk. "Promises?"

Haas's account of the fire was brief and to the point. The trouble had started while Sharifi was underground running one of her closely guarded live field experiments. The station monitors had logged a power surge in the field AI that controlled AMC's orbital Bose-Einstein array, and the power surge had been followed almost immediately by a flash fire in the Anaconda's newly opened Trinidad seam. Haas dispatched a rescue team to douse the pit fire, pulled everyone out of the Trinidad, and shut down the bottom four levels of the mine pending a safety inspection. The field AI seemed to right itself after the brief power surge; no one had given it another thought.

Haas and Voyt went underground with the safety inspector to visit the ignition point. They weren't able to pinpoint the fire's cause, but they recommended suspension of Sharifi's experiment pending further investigation. A recommendation that the Controlled Technology Committee rejected. They reopened the seam as soon as they could get the pumps and the ventilators back on-line, and the miners—and Sharifi's research team—went back to work.

"It was nothing," Haas told Li. "I've been underground since I was ten, and I'm telling you, I didn't for one minute think there was a secondary explosion risk. I don't give a shit what the local spins say, I wouldn't send one miner into a pit I thought was ready to blow. That's not the way I do things."

But he had sent miners into the pit. And it had blown thirty hours later.

It blew hard enough to demolish the Pit 3 headframe and breakerhouse and light a fire that was still smoldering ten days later. The orbital field AI went down again, just as it had in the last explosion. Only this time it never came back on-line.

It took three days to put out the fires and evacuate the desperately small number of survivors. The damage, when they finally had time to assess it, was extensive: one mine fire, cause unknown; one Bose-Einstein relay failure, cause unknown; two hundred and seven dead adult geologists, mine techs, and miners; seventy-two dead children, working underground under an industrywide opt-out from the UN child-labor laws. And, of course, one famous dead physicist.

"There's one thing I'm still not clear on," Li said when he had finished. "What caused the original fire? The one in the—" She checked her files for the name. "—The one in the Trinidad?"

"Nothing." Haas shrugged. "This is a Bose-Einstein mine. Flash fires are part of business. And most of the time you never find out where they started, let alone what caused them."

Li looked at him doubtfully.

"Christ!" Haas muttered. "I thought you were from here. I thought you were supposed to know something."

Li tapped her temple where the faint shadow of wires showed beneath the skin. "You want me to know, tell me."

"Right. Bose-Einstein condensates don't burn, Major. But coal does. And the crystals set the coal on fire sometimes. We don't know why. It's just one of the things you have to account for if you want to run a Bose-Einstein mine. It's dangerous and it's inconvenient. And sometimes—this time being one of them—it's deadly." He snorted. "But this time the crystals had some help. This time they had fucking Sharifi."

"What do you mean, Sharifi? You think she caused the fire? What was she doing that's any different from what AMC does every day?"

"She was cutting crystal for one thing."

"So? AMC's cutting every day. You don't have flash fires every day."

"Yeah, but *where* are we cutting, Major? That's the question you have to ask. And where was *she* cutting?"

"I don't know," Li said. "Where was she cutting?"

"Look," Haas said. "A Bose-Einstein bed is like a tree. You have to prune it, trim it, manage it. But if you cut too hard, or in the wrong place, you've got problems. And when you cut too hard in a Bose-Einstein mine you get fires."

"Because . . . ?"

He shrugged. "TechComm has armies of researchers out here, year in year out, clogging up the gangways and wasting our time and slowing down production. But when it comes to actually giving us useful information they're hopeless. Hell, they don't know things any miner over twelve could tell you. Like that you don't mess with live strata unless you have a death wish. The Beckies don't like it. And when the Beckies don't like a man, bad luck has a way of finding him."

Li stared. *Becky* was Shantytown slang for Bose-Einstein condensates. It was a miner's word, resonant with myths about singing stones, haunted drifts, glory holes. It certainly wasn't the kind of word you heard in AMC's orbital executive offices. Either corporate culture had taken a sharp left turn in the last decade, or this fire was even stranger than Haas was admitting.

"I know what you're thinking," Haas said. "Poor dumb miner, seeing singing Beckies and the Blessed Virgin down every mine shaft. But I grew out of church a long time ago. And I'm telling you, Sharifi was courting trouble down there."

"Did you voice your concerns about the Beckies—uh, the condensates—to Sharifi?"

"I tried." Haas made an impatient gesture, and the upper facet of his desk threw back a distorted reflection of the movement as if there were a subtle tidal effect in the condensate's interior. Which there might be, for all Li knew. Sharifi would have known, of course. But Sharifi had gone underground and gotten herself killed. And as far as Li could tell, she hadn't left anything behind her but unanswered questions.

"I talked to her, all right," Haas went on. "And you

know what? The bitch laughed at me. She was crazy. I don't care how famous she was. Oh, she talked a good line. Empirical runs this, statistical data that. But the gist of it was she thought the Beckies were talking to her. And just like everyone else I've known who thought that, she ended up room temperature. I just wish the stupid digger bitch hadn't brought half my mine down on top of her."

Li stiffened. *Digger* was about as nasty a word as there was in the pidgin English that passed for a common language on Compson's World—and Li had been called it herself back when she still looked like the full-blooded construct she was.

Haas saw her reaction; he shifted in his chair and twisted his face into an expression that might have looked apologetic on another man. "Not talking about you, of course."

"Of course."

"Look." He leaned forward, hunching his massive shoulders for emphasis. "I don't give a shit what Sharifi was. Or you. Or anyone else, for that matter. What I do give a shit about is that some Ring-side bureaucrat made me lend her my best witch and shut down half the mine so she could play her little games. And now that the wheels have come off, all they can tell me to do is wait."

"Well, I'm not telling you to wait," Li said. "And the sooner I get down there, the sooner we can get to the bottom of this and get your men back to work."

Haas leaned back in his chair and let out a short high bark of laughter. The reaction seemed so practiced that Li wondered if it was something he'd copied out of a spinfeed interactive. "We're not running a tourist operation," he said. "Sharifi was working less than a hundred meters from an active cutting face. You're not getting anywhere near there."

"Sharifi did."

"Sharifi was famous. You're just a hick with a lucky trigger finger."

Li grinned. "Nice line, Haas. But I am going down. Why make me go over your head?"

"Fuck, go to whoever you want. You ever been in a Bose-Einstein mine? You can get killed fifty different ways without blinking. I don't need any more bodies on my hands this week, and I'm not letting you down there."

Li stood up, walked around Haas's desk, and picked up the headset of his VR rig. "Would you like to speak to Corps HQ or should I?"

He turned in his chair and watched her, looking for the bluff.

"Fine," he said after a long pause. "I'm going down with a survey crew in about two hours. If you're up to it."

"I'm up to it," Li said, pushing down the thought of her exhaustion, the hope of a hot shower and a merciful stretch of sleep without jump-dreams.

"Don't expect me to baby-sit you. You fuck up your rebreather or fall down a shaft, it's your neck."

"I can take care of myself."

Haas laughed. "That's what Voyt said."

Li looked down at the stars wheeling between her feet and decided it was time to change the subject before she had second thoughts about going into the mine again. "Has TechComm said when they'll get your field array up?"

"Take a fucking guess. They're working on it. Which is TechComm speak for 'we don't give a shit, it's not coming out of our pocket.'"

Haas had that about right, Li thought. The UN had seen the shape of things to come long before most, had recognized from the dawn of the Bose-Einstein era where the live wire of power lay. It bet everything on the new technology. Subsidized it, patented it, entered into carefully structured partnerships with the half dozen multiplanetaries capable of exploiting it.

That had been back in the darkest years of the Migration, when they were still trying to make Earth work and the Ring was just a few thousand paltry kilometers of hastily assembled space platforms. Since then, the UN had used Bose-Einstein tech to leverage humanity's first stable, effective interstellar government. When the genetic riots burned across the Periphery, only UN control of the orbital relay stations contained them. And when the Syndicate incursions began, UN troops used those same relays to meet every Syndicate offensive, to raid the outlying crèches and birthlabs, to quell the revolts that flared up wherever Syndicate troops landed.

But the price of that protection was the UN's stranglehold on interstellar transport. And anyone who ran afoul of TechComm had better settle in for a long, cold, lonely wait.

Haas jabbed a thick finger toward the planet surface. "We can't store more than a month's worth of production up here, and TechComm closed the main relay to private traffic as soon as the field AI flatlined. I pink-slipped two thousand miners last week. Another month of this and there'll be kids starving in Shantytown."

They were probably starving already, Li thought. The line between living and dying was desperately thin in a mining town. Sometimes it took no more than a missed paycheck to push a family across it.

"I swear I'd rather do business with the Syndicates," Haas went on. "At least when their tech breaks down, they fix it. Or shoot it. It's enough to make you support bilateralism."

Then he met Li's eyes and paled as he remembered who he was talking to.

She just watched him. So Haas was for secession— or at least willing to consider the idea. Li doubted that secessionist talk would still get a man thrown into provisional detention on Compson's World these days, but it would certainly get Haas into hot water with his corporate superiors. Fine, she thought. Let the son of a bitch squirm.

But in the end she couldn't follow through.

It wasn't that she didn't like to watch the Haases of the world squirm. But not over politics. And not at her hands.

"Forget it," she said. "I've been to the dance enough times to know saying something isn't doing it. And I'm here to investigate Sharifi's death, not your politics."

But she still rubbed her hand along her chair arm as she stood up, coating the brush-finished steel with a fine layer of dead skin cells. Reprogramming skinbugs for surveillance wasn't legal, exactly. But she'd never seen anyone actually get in trouble over it. And if she turned up any really good dirt, she'd be able to wring some mileage out of it, warrant or no warrant.

As she turned to leave, she thought she heard a rustle from the shadows behind the big desk. She stopped, listened, and could have sworn she smelled perfume. She looked toward Haas, but he'd gone back to his paperwork and didn't seem to notice.

Was someone watching? Had there been a silent audience to their meeting?

No, she decided. No women in the walls here. Just the little noises any station made. Just heat turning on and off, air sighing through ventilators.

Just nothing.

Haas and his crew were waiting in the shuttle's cramped passenger compartment by the time Li boarded. She stripped and donned her borrowed miner's kit in the aisle. Most of the other passengers looked away. Haas didn't.

The kit included a microfilament climbing harness, a rebreather and oxygen canister, a first-aid kit with endorphin-boosters, syntheskin patches, and an old-fashioned viral tourniquet. Li hoisted the harness and pulled it on, wincing as the familiar motion strained her damaged arm. The full kit weighed less than the infantryman's gear Li had carried back in the Syndicate Wars, but just the feel of webbing on her shoulders reminded her of all the things that could go fatally wrong in the deep shafts of a Bose-Einstein mine.

Haas loomed over her, looking even bigger now that he wasn't quarantined behind his vast desk. His bad mood seemed to have vanished; he sounded almost pleasant as he introduced Li to the various geologists and engineers on the survey team. The one person he didn't introduce was the woman next to him, and Li knew why as soon as she looked at her.

It was there in the surreal color of her violet eyes, the inhuman, almost repellent perfection of her face. No human geneticist would have designed such a face. Nature had never meant humans to look like that. She could be only one thing: a postbreakaway A or B Series Syndicate-built genetic construct.

Haas intercepted Li's glance at the woman and put a proprietary hand on her shoulder. "And here's our witch, of course," he said offhandedly.

The witch stood as still under Haas's hand as a well-trained animal, but something in the set of her shoulders said his touch was less than welcome. Or did Syndicate constructs even think that way? Could like and dislike be programmed in the crèches? Could feelings be spliced out of the perfect, unvarying, simulation-tested genesets? Or were the wrong feelings just forbidden—along with every other unprogrammable thing that made up an individual?

Li said her name and held out her hand.

The witch hesitated, then reached out tentatively, like an explorer greeting possibly dangerous natives. Her hand felt restless as a bird in Li's grasp, and she kept her head down so that Li saw just the pale curve of forehead, the dark hair falling away from a part as straight as a knife blade.

Li watched her surreptitiously as they took their seats and the pilots went into the final preflight checks. She'd spent half her adult life fighting the Syndicates, but she'd rarely been so close to a high-series construct. This one would have been tanked in the orbital birthlabs above the Syndicate home planets. She would have grown up in a crèche full of her twins, never seeing a face that wasn't hers, never hearing a voice or feeling a touch that wasn't hers. And if she'd lived long enough to end up here, then she'd survived the one-year cull, the eight-year cull, the constant barrage of norm-testing that routed out physical and psychological variations in order to achieve the disciplined, unquestioning, unvarying perfection that the Syndicate designers insisted on.

Li glanced around at the other passengers. Even the ones who weren't looking at the witch were focused on her, aware of her, orbiting her like iron filings lining up under the influence of a magnet. They were seduced by the beautiful face, the graceful body, the woman she appeared to be. But Li saw battle lines forming along the Great Divide of Gilead's southern continent. She saw a flesh-and-blood statement of Syndicate ideology, Syndicate superiority, Syndicate disdain for human values.

Maybe Nguyen was right, Li thought. Maybe she didn't understand politics. Maybe she was just that stereotypical, vaguely pitiful figure: an old soldier who couldn't look peace in the eye. But was she the only old soldier who thought the UN was selling off hard-earned victories to pad the multiplanetaries' profit margins? Was she the only UN construct who thought the thirty-year contracts were still slavery—even if the new slave masters were constructs, not humans? Why was this woman here? What could she offer that was worth the risk of her presence?

"Best investment we ever made," Haas said, as if in answer to Li's unspoken questions. "First six months after we picked up her MotaiSyndicate contract, we tripled production and halved our payroll. Fantastic, huh?"

"Yeah," Li said. "Fantastic. Bet the union loves it."

"What?" Haas looked like he was giving serious thought to spitting. "Someone's been selling you fairy tales, Major. There is no union."

He shot an arm past Li's face and lifted the window shade to check their progress toward the planet. They were well into the atmosphere, pinions of flame streaking the shuttle's wings, the coalfield spread out like a map below them. Li scanned the broad flood-plain, leveled by an ocean that had dried up three geologic ages before humans set foot on Compson's World. Headframes and mine buildings curved along the valley's edge, following the coal seam. Far above, their jagged spires already flashing red in the dawn, loomed the Black Mountains, ramping up in serried cliffs and ridgelines toward the Continental Divide.

It took her a moment to put her finger on what was wrong with the view. There was a thick haze hanging around the mountains' shoulders, up around the four-thousand-meter level. And farther down, a wash of bright oxygenated green swept the feet of the cliffs. When Li had last seen those cliffs they were above the atmosphere line, bathed in the dull orange of native lichens. This wasn't the planet she'd left behind, and the sheer breadth of the human encroachment in that fifteen years was chilling.

Compson's World was the great joke of the inter-stellar era: all the anticipation, all the apprehension, all the first-contact planning, and on thirty-eight planets in twenty-seven star systems, Compson's coal and condensates were the only sign of complex life humans had ever found in the universe. And by the time humans reached Compson's, there was no life left on the planet but the high, windswept algae tundra.

Li looked down at the spreading human footprint on the planet and thought of the thronging life that had laid down its bones to make the coal seam. The first humans to set pickax and shovel to the planet had been paleontologists, not miners. There was a whole exploration literature from that time—books Li had read eagerly lying in her cramped bedroom in Shantytown.

The scientists had fought terraforming, of course. But the first Bose-Einstein strike killed any chance they had. The mines had come, and the genetics labs, and from the day the first atmospheric processor went up, Compson's World was a walking ghost. Now Li thought back on the dozens of terraformed, self-consciously balanced and controlled planets she'd seen in her tours of duty, and wondered if she might be one of the last people in the universe to know an untamed world.

Haas was talking to her, she realized. She snapped back into the present, wondering what she'd missed.

"Your average Shantytown witch is a pure fraud," he was saying. "I've known three witches, tops, who could actually strike live crystal. And two of the bastards never turned a strike over to AMC until they'd given every Pat and Micky they ever got drunk with a crack at it. Fucking bootleggers." He jerked his safety harness tight in preparation for landing. "Underground democracy, my ass. It's theft!"

Li grunted noncommittally.

"Hey," Haas called to the pilot. "Can we get some livefeed back here?"

The pilot scanned the channels and accessed what looked like local spin from the planetary capital in Helena. A suited commentator was interviewing a young man in miner's gear.

"So," the interviewer asked, "what is your reply to AMC's claims that the union's safety-related demands are merely a pretext for a pay raise?"

The camera panned back to the interviewee, and Li realized she'd misread him. He wasn't a miner, despite the worn coveralls and well-used kit. His haircut was too expensive, his teeth and skin too healthy for a Shantytowner. And that was a Ring-sider's face. A human face. He looked like he should be lounging in a café on Calle Mexico drinking *maté de coca*, not trashing his unadapted lungs in the Trusteeships.

"I'd say two things," the young man answered in an accent that sounded like the product of generations of fancy private schooling. "First, that anyone who doubts the reality of the safety issues in this case needs to look at the statistics; the death rate among miners in AMC's Trinidad vein over the past six months is higher than the death rate in most front-line military units during the Syndicate Wars. Second, I'd remind viewers that, though Compson's company towns may have opted out of the Human Rights Charter, the multiplanetaries themselves—and the planetary legislators—remain subject to the court of public opinion. Every consumer has a responsibility to vote with his credit chip when he sees a corporation that blatantly disregards basic humanitarian—"

"Turn that shit off!" Haas shouted.

The feed shut off with a hollow click, and the passengers fell into an uncomfortable silence. Li rested her forehead against the window and watched Saint Elmo's fire lick at the shuttle's wings as they free-fell toward the ravaged planet.

Pit 3 was still burning; the pilot skirted the smoldering ruins and set the shuttle down on a remote, booster-scarred helipad stranded in a wasteland of rutted caterpillar tracks.

The crew donned their rebreathers and helmets and clumped unenthusiastically down the shuttle gangway. Alongside the helipad, pyramids of empty chemical barrels rusted to brown lace under their jaunty green-and-orange Freetown decals. The ground beyond was yellow and acrid-smelling, littered with the monstrous carcasses of stripped-out mine trucks. No one had come to pick them up, so they straggled off toward the Pit 4 headframe-breaker complex, a rickety, wind-blasted jumble of aluminum-sided geodesics that crouched over the shaft like a drunken spider.

Li hadn't bothered to hook up her rebreather yet, just clipped the mouthpiece to her collar to keep it out of the way. Haas and the witch had done the same, she noticed. As they walked, she began to regret her choice; one of Compson's dust storms was on the rise, and the wind blew acid-tasting red dog into her mouth at every stride.

A large, thickly printed fiche hung next to the head-frame office door. Haas rapped on the wall beside it with a closed fist, setting the siding rattling, and Li saw a notary swipe at the bottom of the fiche.

"Skim and scan," Haas said, but just to be stubborn she read every word before palming the scan plate.

PIT RULES: THE FOLLOWING ARE THE RULES OF THIS PIT. EMPLOYEES AND VISITORS ARE REQUIRED TO ACCEPT AND ABIDE BY THESE RULES AS A PRECONDITION FOR EN-TRANCE. ENTRANCE CONSTITUTES: (I) A RELEASE OF ANA-CONDA MINING CORPORATION AND ITS SUBSIDIARIES, AFFILIATES, AND ASSOCIATES FROM LIABILITY; (II) A FULL WAIVER OF ALL RIGHTS AND REMEDIES UNDER LAW, IN-CLUDING BUT NOT LIMITED TO UNITED NATIONS MINE SAFETY COMMISSION REGULATIONS AND THIS OR ANY OTHER JURISDICTION'S WORKER'S COMPENSATION LAWS.

1. ALL PERSONNEL AND VISITORS MUST LOG IN AND OUT AT THE PITHEAD OFFICE AND PIT BOTTOM FIRE OFFICE.
2. THE CAGE WILL BE RAISED AND LOWERED ON DEMAND WITHIN ½ HOUR OF EACH SHIFT CHANGE. THE CAGE WILL NOT BE RAISED OR LOWERED AT ANY OTHER TIMES EXCEPT ON DIRECT ORDERS OF THE PIT MAN-AGER.
3. A FULL SHIFT IS TEN HOURS. A FULL WORK WEEK IS SIXTY HOURS. FAILURE TO WORK A FULL SHIFT/WORK WEEK WILL RESULT IN DOCKED PAY AND/OR DISMISSAL.
4. AMC IS A UN-APPROVED MINEWORKS OPERATING UN-DER A VOLUNTARY COMPLIANCE REGIMEN PURSUANT TO UNMSC REG. SECTION $1.5978-2(C)(1)(II)$ ET SEQ. UNMSC SAFETY REGULATIONS ARE POSTED AT PITHEAD AND PIT BOTTOM. FAILURE TO ADHERE TO POSTED REG-

ULATIONS WILL RESULT IN DOCKED PAY AND/OR DIS-
MISSAL.

5. WORKINGS WHERE METHANE OR CARBON MONOXIDE IS
PRESENT ARE MARKED ON THE CHECK DOORS. NO PER-
SON OTHER THAN THE PIT BOSS OR FIRE BOSS MAY PASS
A CHECK DOOR WITHOUT PRIOR AUTHORIZATION. AMC
TAKES NO RESPONSIBILITY FOR MINERS WHO ENGAGE IN
UNAUTHORIZED   CUTTING   OR   LOADING   BEYOND
MARKED CHECK DOORS.

6. NO LAMPS BUT SAFETY (DAVY) LAMPS ARE ALLOWED BE-
LOW GRADE UNDER ANY CIRCUMSTANCES. ALL LAMPS
MUST BE HANDED IN TO THE FIRE BOSS EACH SHIFT END
FOR INSPECTION. THE COST OF REFILLING LAMPS WILL
BE DEDUCTED FROM PAY. THE COST OF REPAIRING OR
REPLACING DAMAGED LAMPS WILL BE DEDUCTED FROM
PAY.

7. NO DOGS ALLOWED BELOW GRADE WITHOUT PROOF OF
CURRENT RABIES AND BORDATELLA.

8. THIS IS A RIGHT TO WORK MINE. NO SOLICITATION. NO
PRIESTS!

While Li was still reading, the swing shift surfaced
in a swearing, stinking wave of bodies. Their backs
were bent by the punishing labor at the cutting wall,
but their faces shone with greasy pit dust and the relief
of finishing out another shift safely. Haas looked like a
giant next to them. It was hard to imagine someone
could be so clean all over, stand up so straight, smile
so broadly.

"Daahl," he said to a blue-eyed whippet of a man
that Li guessed must be the departing crew's foreman.
"How's the cutting?"

"Twenty gross behind in the Wilkes-Barre North 5,"
Daahl answered. He glanced furtively at Haas, as if he
wanted to gauge the station exec's temper before delivering more bad news. "Not the men's fault. The
ventilation's still fouled up from the flooding. We

spent half the shift just trying to pump air past the South 2 brattices."

A swift glance passed between Haas and one of the geologists.

"How's the water level in the Trinidad?" the geologist asked.

"Not going down as fast as it should be," Daahl answered. "We've cleared the upper drifts, but the downslope chambers and the whole bottom level are still flooded. But we'll get it cleared and make the shortfall up soon enough."

"Sure, Daahl." Haas shrugged easily. "You always do, don't you?" He nodded to the silent, watching miners and stepped into the breakerhouse.

Li followed him.

Security was tight, going in and coming out. As they arrived a guard was picking miners out of the departing line and waving them into uncurtained privacy cubicles for random strip searches. Li stepped into line behind Haas, thinking more about the miners coming out than about the questions the guards were asking her.

"Do you have any Bose-Einstein equipment with you?" one of them said.

She stopped. "Of course."

Haas turned around, looking irritated. "What the hell were you thinking?" he said. "You can't take crystals down there. Whatever it is, you'll have to leave it."

"She can't," the witch said. "It's in her head."

She hadn't opened her mouth all the way down in the shuttle, but now she spoke as offhandedly as if Li's embedded comm gear were visible to the naked eye. Her voice was low, husky, and she had the formal turn of phrase that Li associated with the Syndicates' high-series constructs. Li stared, wondering whether the woman's silence was shyness or just camouflage.

"Oh. Right." Haas laughed. "Don't let on to that in

public, Major. A one-carat piece of communications-grade condensate sells for more on the black market than most miners get paid in a year. There's plenty around here'd be happy to take your head apart for that kind of money."

The shaft lay at the back of the headframe, past the muffled rattle of coal falling through breakerhouse screens, below the creaking rigging of the ventilation stacks. The cage stank of diesel, sweat, and mildew, and it shot them down the vertical shaft at near free-fall speed. Someone had removed the inspection log from the scratched metal frame bolted onto the wall above the control switch and replaced it with a high-resolution holo of a spinmag centerfold wearing nothing but big hair and a spanking new miner's kit.

Li eyed the holo while they plummeted toward pit bottom and wondered if anyone's nipples actually looked like that. Men had the strangest taste in women sometimes.

Pit bottom smelled like a war zone. Diesel fumes hung in the air, mingling with the reek of coal dust and axle grease. Eardrums throbbed to the muffled thud of force pumps and Vulcan fans, and the ventilators brought no fresh air—only the acrid stink of cordite and snuffed fuses rolling up from the work faces.

There were no horizons, no sight lines in the hanging coal dust. Clogged miners burst out of the smog, clattered across the slate-strewn floor, headlamps swinging like beacons, then vanished as abruptly as they appeared. And from the depths, like the sound of combat drifting back over the supply lines, came the shudder and boom of blasting, the rush of newly dropped coal streaming down the chutes.

The fire boss's badge said, "YOUR SAFETY IS OUR BUSINESS," but his blank eyes suggested that he had more pressing business elsewhere, and he delivered his safety lecture in the tone of a man passing on a rumor he didn't personally believe in.

They trooped past him one by one to sign the pit bottom log and check out their Davy lamps. When Li reached the front of the line, he scribbled her lamp number in the logbook and pushed the coal-smudged pit log toward her without even looking up. Li started to put her hand to where the scan plate should have been, then realized the log wasn't even smart fiche. She signed it laboriously.

The new shift was coming on-clock as Haas's crew rigged up. The coal haulers came down first, as always. Some were jumping off the cage as Li stepped out of the fire office. Others, brought down in the last trip, were already preparing their carts and sorting their traces. They moved nimbly, with the light-limbed agility of children—which was exactly what they were.

They'd been called pit ponies when Li was their age, even though no pony had set hoof on this planet or any other in two centuries. A few of the incoming shift's ponies had pit dogs with them: heavy-boned, coal-stained mongrels strong enough to pull the coal carts. The rest would hook up to the draw chains and drag the heavy coal carts themselves. They worked in a world of man, child, and animal power. A world where it took a whole family to earn a living and sweat cost less than diesel fuel.

"Don't get foggy-eyed about them," Haas said, coming up behind her. "I started out carting when I was their age. Day I turned ten. They've got their chance, same as the rest of us."

"Sure," Li said, though she didn't know if she believed it or not.

A pit pony from the outgoing shift passed by, hauling a carefully packed flat of live-cut condensate. He had a string of pearls—a long row of coal scars that came from scraping bare backbones on ceiling joists day after day and having blue coal dust ground into the cuts. But Li barely noticed it; she was looking at the crystals.

They gleamed like distant stars under their heavy coating of coal dust. They looked like crystals—the miners even called them crystals—but Li knew they'd light up a quantum scan like no mere rock. They were quantum-level anomalies, an unheard of, unimagined substance that every physical law said couldn't exist above zero Kelvin, or in an atmosphere, or in a minable, transportable, usable form. They were impossible, and they were the daily miracle that the UN worlds lived on.

But they were notoriously fragile. Blasting cracked them. Power tools damaged them. Even a hot mine fire could destroy them—though another fire, unpredictably, might burn the coal out around the crystals and leave whole subterranean cathedral vaults of them standing. It was all a skilled miner could do, working with wedges, picks, and hard-earned handicraft, to cut a strike out of the coal without ruining it. "Getting them out live," Li's father called it.

She reached out and brushed her fingers along the smooth upper facet of the nearest condensate as the cart passed. It felt warm as flesh. The miner, somewhere down there in the choking darkness, had gotten it out live.

Sharifi's site lay in the newly opened Trinidad—the deeper and richer of the Anaconda's two coal veins. It was six kilometers from Pit 3 as the crow flies, eight or more along the mine's twisting and dipping underground passages.

They rode the first four kilometers in a squat, neon green mine truck, rattling around like dry beans in a pot and choking on diesel exhaust. At first they drove along three-meter-by-three-meter main gangways, echoing with the metal wheels of coal carts and the ringing blows of miners' hammers. Soon they passed into increasingly narrow drifts, cutting chambers slanting up twenty feet above their heads along near-vertical coal seams. As they moved away from the pit-head, the wiring grew scantier and the lights farther apart until there was only the swinging arc of the truck's headlights and an occasional eerie glimpse of Davy lamps gleaming above glittering eyes and coal-smudged faces.

They left the truck at the top of a long, slimy flight of stairs barricaded by a closed check door. The battered black-and-orange sign on the check door said, FIRE DANGER—NO-IGNITION ZONE.

The safety officer sat down on the truck's bumper and started pulling on a pair of desert camouflage waders that looked like they'd seen hard using. "Trinidad's a wet vein," he said. "Underground river runs right through the fault. Pumps go out, and it takes a day, two at the most, for the whole vein to fill."

"The water's out, mostly," Haas said. He grinned, a bright glistening flash of white in the gloom. "Hope you don't mind the smell, though. Rats. And plenty of other things."

The engineers who drove the stairs had taken advantage of a dip in the terrain where the Wilkes-Barre dropped abruptly toward the Trinidad, shaving the intervening layers of bedrock to their narrowest point. The stairs dropped twenty meters between dripping walls of bedrock, hit a low, relatively flat passageway, then dropped another twelve meters and broke through into the Trinidad.

This was a very different kind of coal vein. The Wilkes-Barre was friendly; broad and not too canted, big enough to cut wide, tall gangways through. The Trinidad was rough, twisting, and so narrow that even Li was soon bending almost double to avoid the coal-smelted steel cribbing.

"Hot, huh?" Haas said when he saw her wiping her brow. "Temperature rises one and a half degrees for every hundred feet below grade. Reckon it's, oh, a hundred and two or so."

"One-oh-three-point-two, actually."

Haas snorted. "That what the Assembly's blowing our tax dollars on these days? Thermometers?"

Li had forgotten what it was to travel underground. In the first ten meters, she banged her head, scraped her spine, and tripped over a pile of loose slate. Then she slipped back into the distantly remembered miner's gait, bent at knees and waist, one hand skimming the roof to scout out the low parts before she hit them. The ease with which her body twisted itself back into that shape frightened her.

The flood had left stagnant pools of water in every dip and hollow of the vein. Tea-colored water sheeted down the walls, so steeped in sulfur that it stung the skin like acid. The bodies had been cleared away, but the sick-sweet smell of death remained, fueled by the litter of drowned rats that lay in sodden clots everywhere. Each little twist and outcropping of rock seemed to harbor some left-behind piece of life before the explosion. A lunch pail. A hat. A shattered Davy lamp.

As they walked, the safety officer kept up a breathless monologue documenting the special safety measures AMC had implemented in the Trinidad. He spoke in a nervous singsong, quivering under Haas's eye like an eager student. Li couldn't begin to guess whether he believed any of what he was saying. She listened, sucking rhythmically at the filter mask of her rebreather, and tried not to think about the fact that her life now depended on the creaking, straining ceiling bolts and the ability of six hundred paid-by-the-ton miners to keep a reasonable safety margin at the cutting face.

The work site itself was anticlimactic. "This is it,"

Haas said, and there it was: a stretch of shored-up, rubble-littered tunnel, ending in a chamber whose flanking pillars were little more than boulder piles.

"So what happened?" Li asked the safety officer.

Haas answered. "You never know with a flash fire. One guy takes out a ton and a half of prime crystal and goes home to his wife and kids without blinking. The next guy over barely taps a vein and the whole mine comes down on top of him. Every miner has his theories—and don't get me started on the damn pit priests—but it's all just guesswork, really."

"And you're sure this was a flash fire, not just a regular coal fire?"

"As sure as we are about anything."

The chamber was wide, perhaps twelve meters across, though it was hard to tell through the wreckage of pillars and timbering. It looked like a single mining breast had been opened out to give Sharifi's team more room to work. Or like a particularly rich crystal deposit had lured the miners into robbing a central pillar and turning two separate chambers into one despite the well-known risks of pillar-robbing.

The fire had burned the top layer of coal off the walls, baring the long edges of condensate beds, smoother and more crystalline than the coal around them. Li touched an outcropping of condensate. Felt its glassy polish, the warmth that radiated from it like body heat, the faint, familiar tugging at the back of her skull.

She turned back to Haas and the safety officer. "Anything else I should see?" she asked, watching Haas in infrared.

"That's it," he said. She saw his pulse spike on the words.

"What about you?" she asked, turning to the safety officer.

He delivered up the goods with a single glance toward the unlit depths of the chamber.

Li walked back to the corner he'd glanced at and saw what she should have seen before: a large battered sheet of aluminum finished in safety-sign orange. It was the only spot of color in the chamber, the only thing that wasn't caked black with coal smoke. Obviously, it had been put there since the fire.

"Who put this here?" she asked, bending down to shove the heavy plate aside.

"We did," Haas answered. "So no one would fall down that."

Li looked at the place where the plate had been—and found herself staring down a well shaft.

It was less than a meter wide. Ropy bundles of unmarked electrical cables curved over the lip and dropped into the darkness. The water started six meters below the lip of the hole, and it was as black as only mine water can be.

"Anything else you'd like to tell me about this?"

"No," Haas said. "Sharifi dug it. I assume. She didn't bother to get permission." He sounded irritated that he hadn't caught her at it while she was still alive.

Li scrabbled around on the floor until she found a scorched length of wire long enough to reach the water table. Then she dipped it in, pulled it out, and wiped it along the bare skin of her arm. Her skinbots flared briefly, swirling around the droplets, then subsided. Nothing too nasty in there, apparently. "Okay then," she said, and started unlacing her boots.

The safety officer figured out what she was doing before Haas did. "You really don't want to go down there, ma'am."

"Humor me."

"No fucking way!" Haas said.

He reached out and jerked her back from the hole by one arm. Li wrapped her free hand around his and squeezed just hard enough to remind him she was wired.

"I appreciate your concern for my safety," she said.

"But I really will be fine. Or was there another reason you didn't want me to go down there?"

He backed off fast at that.

"Lend me your goggles," she told the safety officer when she'd stripped to her shorts and T-shirt and tightened her rebreather's harness. He handed her the goggles with a dazed expression on his face. She gave them a spit and a rub, put them on, and pressed them into her eye sockets to get good suction.

"Okay," she said around the mouthpiece. "Back in ten and counting. Unless I do something stupid. In which case you've got an hour and forty minutes to get a rescue team down here and fish me out."

"You assume a lot," Haas said.

"If I don't come back," she said, all sweet reasonableness, "they'll just have to send someone else out. And you'll have to wait to open the mine until they get here, won't you?"

Haas sat down, muttering something about people who thought they were funnier than they were. But he was smiling, Li noticed. He could take a joke, you had to give him that at least.

The water was cold but clear, and as soon as she scanned the submerged cavern she knew this was the real experiment site. Whatever had been going on upstairs was peripheral, a mere prep room and antechamber. An underground river had flowed through this cavern in some earlier geologic age and stripped the coal off the condensate beds. The bare crystals formed an intricate lattice supporting the cavern's ceiling. Curving pillars sprang from the floor like the ribs of one of Compson's long-extinct sauropods. Pale tendrils of condensate spidered across the dome above like fan vaults. And Li didn't have to feel these strata to know they were alive; they pulsed on her quantum scans like an aurora borealis. Whatever life there was in the planet's Bose-Einstein strata—and whether there was any at all was a subject of intense debate among the UN's xenographers—this was one of its centers.

Sharifi had found herself a glory hole.

Something brushed Li's arm, and she whirled around just in time to glimpse a VR glove floating past her on a slow underground current, contact wires trailing. There was other equipment, some floating, some strewn across the cavern floor in a tangled skein of power lines and input/output wires. She recognized seismic meters, Geiger counters, quantum monitors. There was no way she could take all this in one shot, let alone underwater. She laid out a mental grid pattern and swam back and forth, recording everything as best she could. At least that way she'd know if someone moved something between now and her next visit—and she'd know what they'd been worried enough about to bother moving.

"That'll do," she said as she hauled herself up the ladder. "You'll need to keep this section closed until you get that drained out and I can take a closer look."

Haas's eyes glinted where the lamp beam cut across them. "I've got a start-work order on this level waiting for the inspector's signature. The electricians come through tomorrow, and we start cutting as soon as they lay clean line. Your authority stops at ground level, and you just hit the end of my cooperation."

"Oh," Li said. "Too bad. I guess I'll have to log the safety violations down here." She pointed at the corridor's props and collars, groaning under the weight of the roof, but still standing. "Those props are three meters apart. UNMSC regs require 2.5. Also, there are ungrounded electrical wires at junctions South 2, South 8, and South 11. I'll download a complete list of code violations for you when we get back. I'm sure you'll want to get right on top of them."

It was pure bluff, of course; Haas knew as well as she did that no UN site team was ever going to give AMC more than a slap on the wrist for those violations. But

Li was the only UN official on-site, and if she logged an official complaint all the paperwork he had to do to get the mine reopened would pass across her desk—or rather sit on her desk until she got around to signing it.

Haas could go over her head, of course. But that took time. And it was an implicit admission that there really were safety violations. Li didn't think he'd risk it. Not in the aftermath of a bloody and well-publicized mining disaster. Not with Sharifi's body still lying in the Shantytown morgue a few miles away.

"Fine," Haas said, shrugging. "Sniff around all you want. You're only going to find out Sharifi was a fool."

When they got back up to the Wilkes-Barre vein, the second shift was in full swing. Most of the miners worked half-naked, bodies gleaming like marble in the sweltering heat two miles below the surface. They worked fast, taking few precautions. Coal-cutting time wasn't quite dead time, but it was halfway there, and it didn't pay to spend an unnecessary minute at it.

Few of the men, women, and children underground wore rebreathers, and the ones who did only used them during their rare breaks. The rest of the time, the face masks with their tangle of oxygen lines dangled loosely around sweat-slicked necks. It took all the air a body could breathe to work at speed, hunched over in badly ventilated tunnels, and rebreathers were the first thing to go when time got short.

Without thinking, Li started to unhook her own rebreather.

"Don't," said the safety officer. "Mutagens."

She looked at the miners. The safety officer caught her questioning glance and shrugged. "Genetics."

A flash of soft memory set Li's stomach churning. Her father, bending over the kitchen sink, coughing, complaining about the price of filters at the pithead supply house. Her mother boiling water on the stove-top and handing him a dish towel to put over his head so he could cough up a little more coal dust.

"Are you all right?" asked the safety officer. "Sometimes even the filters won't keep the dust out."

She nodded and put her head between her knees.

When she looked up again the truck had stopped. Oddly shaped boxes and canisters littered the road-way. Workers bustled in front of them, men and women who moved across the rough ground with the assurance of habit but were too thin, too clean to be miners. Li looked closer and recognized several of the geologists she'd shuttled down with.

Only one person in the visible section of the drift remained seated. A slight, silent figure, curled into a rock outcropping just outside the action, eyes closed, face solemn and lovely as a statue's.

The witch.

When the preparations were complete, she rose, approached the freshly cut face, closed her eyes, and put her hands to the stone. Li had seen crystals witched before, but mostly in poor bootleg deposits, not company claims. And the witches of her childhood had been Shantytown dwellers. They'd witched for food, or a share of the strikes they found, or a little winter fuel. Their talent had been the fruit of a genetic fluke, not a carefully manufactured commodity.

The witch passed back and forth along the face, stopping now and then, head cocked as though she were listening for something. Her pale skin shone against the uncut coal. The light from her Davy lamp hung about her like a halo.

The surveyors and geologists hovered tensely. Immense amounts of money were at stake. Turn away from a cut too soon and you lost millions without ever knowing it. Cut too boldly and you'd be left with cart-loads of dead crystal, worthless as quartz. Miners had tried every technology there was: radio imaging,

X rays, random core sampling. Witching was still the only real way to locate live, viable crystal. And the annual profit margins of entire multiplanetary corporations rose and fell on the choices a witch made at the cutting face.

The witch stopped at a perfectly ordinary spot along the face and pressed both hands to the coal face. They came away wet, stained bloodred with sulfur water. "There," she said.

The surveyors surged past her as if drawn by an undertow. They attached sensors, hooked up feedback circuits, safety cutoffs. Li watched, fascinated, as the cutters bored into the coal face. When she glanced at Haas, the intent, hungry look on his face reminded her of the old songs miners sang after the whiskey had passed around a few too many times, songs about men whose blood ran with coal, who lusted for the mine like dope fiends.

Everyone in the gangway fell silent as the first crystal came into sight, pale, gleaming, unmistakable. A geologist leaned into the face, holding his breath, and put his hand on it.

"Well?" Haas said.

The geologist removed his hand, wiped it on his coverall front, touched his forehead as if he were taking his own temperature, and put his hand back to the condensate again. He shook his head.

"Dead," someone muttered at the edge of the lamplight.

The witch had retreated when the surveyors moved in, shrinking into herself like an actor slipping out of character. She barely reacted to the news of the dead crystal.

"Come here," Haas said to her.

She turned obediently, but her gaze slipped past Haas and fixed on Li as unerringly as a compass needle locking on to magnetic north. The violet eyes looked dark underground, each iris shaved down to a narrow line around an immense pupil. And beyond the pupil nothing, as if you were staring straight into the black pit of the woman's skull.

Holes in the universe, Li thought, and the shiver that ran down her spine had nothing to do with cold.

By the time they surfaced, the storm had hit. The headframe whined and rattled under its assault. Scraps of viruflex and jagged sheets of aluminum siding skittered past as if all the contents of the valley were being stirred by an invisible hand.

Li felt the taut, held-breath quality of the air as soon as she stepped out of the pit office. Fifty meters away, a ragged line of men and women ranged along the spine of a tailing pile. Some held homemade signs. A few carried primitive, home-brewed weapons. Strikers. Wildcats, technically, since there was no legal union in the Anaconda.

She blinked wind tears out of her eyes and squinted through the blowing grit. In a brief slacking of the wind she read the signs they held:

JUSTICE FOR CORPORATE BABY KILLERS!

HOW MANY MUST DIE?

SHUT THE TRINIDAD BEFORE IT KILLS AGAIN.

She wondered why they didn't come closer, get within shouting distance. Then she saw the row of blue uniform shirts facing the picket line. Company guards. With riot guns.

"Think the spins have picked that up yet?" someone said.

Haas was already jogging over to the guards. He leaned into the wind, cupping a hand around his mouth, and shouted something in the squad leader's ear. He stepped back, and the line of guards advanced, firing their guns into the air.

A few of the strikers backed off. The rest didn't.

The guards fired again, this time at the strikers' feet. One woman cried out as if she'd been hit. Another shouted, "There are children here!"

"No one needs to get hurt!" one of the guards called, his voice shaking with adrenaline. "Don't do anything stupid!"

And then, for no reason Li could put her finger on, the crisis passed.

The strikers lowered their signs. The guards uncocked their rifles. The crowd broke up and straggled back along the rutted track to Shantytown. Li felt a spasm of relief. No one was going to die. Not today, anyway.

Three hours later, the smell of the mine still on her hair and skin, Li stood in front of the security seal on the door of Sharifi's quarters. The tape read her palm implant, dissolved, re-formed behind her as she stepped through.

Sharifi's quarters were cramped, utilitarian, not much different from Li's own room a few spokes away. The whole room was no wider than the corridor outside. Five steps took Li from the entrance to the door of the cramped bathroom. A shallow closet ran the length of the left wall. The right wall held a narrow bunk and a drop-down desk cluttered with datacubes and loose stacks of microfiche.

The closet held a few changes of practical-looking clothes, some of them still folded neatly in an Italian-made leather bag that must have cost more than Li made in a month. No family pictures. No personal items. No makeup. Except for the single dress suit hanging in the closet, it was hard to identify even the sex of the room's last occupant. Whoever Sharifi had been, there was little trace of her here.

On an impulse, Li slipped the suit jacket on and looked curiously at herself in the mirror. It bound around the armpits; she carried a lot more muscle than Sharifi had. It was a little long. But then, Sharifi had been a good two centimeters taller than her—better nutrition and fewer cigarettes. Other than that, it fit. And the color looked good on her. No surprise there.

The smell was a surprise, though. Foreign. A touch of the other woman's perfume, perhaps. And yet, beneath it, something unnervingly familiar. A memory surfaced, rolled over and sank again. A dog lunging and snarling at a passing miner. The warm glow of hate on its master's face as he said, *You can smell them, can't you?*

Next to the closet door were the light and livewall controls and the viewport dimmer. Li cleared the floorport, looked down at the planet between her toes, and thought about how the sweep of UN politics and her own life had intersected there. How could they all still be fighting the same battle that was hacked into the burnt-out shells of the birthlabs, the forty-year-old artillery scars fading on the hillsides above Shantytown?

For decades the now-crumbling industrial park had turned out a continuous stream of constructs. Industrial-grade genesets specifically engineered for hard-rock mining, steel smelting, terraforming—all the hard, dangerous jobs that humans couldn't or wouldn't do. Sharifi was tanked in those labs. Li herself had been tanked in one of the last production runs before the Riots. It was only the rawest, quirkiest chance that either of them got off-planet; Sharifi adopted by rich Ring-side abolitionists, Li farmed out to a childless miner's family in one of the last abortive attempts to assimilate constructs into the general population.

The Riots hit eight months after Li was born—about the time Sharifi would have been in university. Shantytown became a battlefield, a maze of tunnels and barricaded cul-de-sacs in which a ragtag band of constructs held off the UN and the planetary militia . . . for a while, anyway.

A good number of posthumans had joined the rebels. Idealistic students from the university in Helena, back when there still was one. Miners who didn't care who they shared Compson's World with as long as it wasn't the multiplanetaries. The Real IRA, though word on the street in Shantytown had always been that that was purely a money deal. When the dust cleared, Compson's World was under martial law and the rebel constructs had escaped to a remote system that they renamed Gilead.

For the rest of Li's life, the fight against the Syndicates dominated human politics. The breakaway constructs created the first fully syndicated genelines. KnowlesSyndicate was born, and then Motai and Bartov and the half dozen others whose names soon became words of fear throughout UN space. The Syndicates annexed one restless colony after another, until they held the whole long arc of the Periphery between Metz and Gilead. Antigenetic sentiment gained ground in the Assembly and on the streets of every UN planet. The word *construct* took on a new and sinister meaning, while the corporations that built the original constructs either closed up shop and abandoned them or went bankrupt in the spate of scandals that followed the breakaway. And every time another ex-colony went over to the Syndicates the UN's antigenetic faction gained a few seats in the Assembly.

The Assembly passed the Zahn Act when Li was fourteen, placing all full genetics in UN space under direct Security Council supervision, barring them from the civil service and the military, revoking passports and imposing mandatory registration.

Li's adoptive parents delayed, hoping the massive destruction of records during the Riots might mean she'd been forgotten. The delay paid off. By the time the registration bureaucracy caught up with them, Li's mother had a signed and stamped death certificate that said her only daughter had died of vitamin A deficiency—and Li was already making a name for herself in the trenches of Gilead.

Meanwhile the Syndicates did . . . well, no one knew what they did. No subject of the Syndicates came to UN space. No UN citizen went to the Syndicates. No news escaped from the orbital stations that circled the remote Syndicate homeworlds. The Syndicates had no press and no visible government, unless you counted the shadowy point committees of the individual genelines. They had no political parties or political dissidents. No parents. No children. And, above all, no property.

Only the Syndicates owned things, and the things they owned were their constructs. They owned their minds, their bodies, their labor, everything. Each construct gave him- or herself completely, intimately—and, if the propaganda was to be believed, willingly. It was not enough to say that they didn't want freedom. They didn't believe in freedom. They had, as their political philosophers were endlessly proclaiming, evolved beyond it.

Only when Li met her first postbreakaway constructs in the interrogation rooms on Gilead did she begin to understand this. They seemed to belong to some other species, one that had nothing to do with humans. The first ten identical prisoners came in, and people commented on them, wondered about them, perhaps even felt sorry for them. Then the next hundred, the next thousand, the next three thousand arrived, and the wondering turned to fear and revulsion.

Words failed in the face of such cold, impersonal, mass-produced perfection. Compassion failed. Belief in the universality of human nature failed. Everything failed.

By the time Li had spent a month on Gilead the only thing she knew for certain about her enemies was that they hated her. No. *Hate* wasn't the right word. They despised her, just like they despised every construct who still worked for humans. They despised her the way wolves despise dogs.

And what about Sharifi? What about the woman who had left so little of herself in this room, who had brought an entire mine down on her head, who had promised to work miracles, then covered her tracks like a thief? What did Sharifi believe in?

Was she a dog or a wolf?

Li sighed, picked a fiche from one of the neat stacks, and ran her finger down it, scanning a paragraph at random:

> As Park and others have noted, the parallel wave patterns documented *in situ* Bose-Einstein strata closely resemble quantum phenomena associated with human brain waves, and with the less well mapped quantum phenomena found in the associative interactions of poststructuralist-model Emergent artificial intelligences.

And, jotted in the fiche's digital margin in Sharifi's handwriting:

> Re: dispersed/colonial nets in organics see Falter, *Principia Cybernetica and the Physiology of the Great Barrier Reef*, MIT Press, 2017.

She skimmed the next fiche.

Handwritten numbers and symbols scrolled up the

page. Li knew enough to recognize Hilbert spaces, Poisson brackets, the long sinuous columns of Sharifi transforms, but that was about it. Not even her oracle could actually help her understand them.

It was Sharifi's handwriting obviously—and as she watched it scroll up the screen Li remembered a joke Cohen had made the first time he saw her own hand-writing. Something about how ex–Catholic school kids always wrote as if Sister Somebody was still stand-ing over their desk with a ruler in hand. And he was right, of course. This was the careful, even, unmistak-able script of someone who had survived years of pen-manship classes, who had learned to write in poverty, on paper. With Sister Somebody standing over her desk.

Li had assumed Sharifi was adopted young, had grown up Ring-side, human in all but name. But what if she hadn't? What if she had started her schooling on Compson's World, with the nuns? Was there some connection on-planet that everyone had missed? Some deeply buried childhood loyalty that had turned her away from the job she came here to do?

Li shook her head, struck by a sudden urge to laugh. How did you explain Sharifi? She and Li were as ge-netically identical as twins—more identical, since the random errors of normal gestation had been assidu-ously caught and corrected by the birthlabs. They'd been tanked in the same lab. And unless Sharifi's handwriting was lying, they'd learned their letters and numbers from the same battered secondhand text-books, starting out each year by erasing the answers last year's students had penciled in and submitting to the inevitable lecture about Respecting Church Property. Yet here Li stood, a miner's kid who had struggled through her OCS physics requirement by the skin of her teeth, looking at the equations that had made Sharifi the most important scientist of her gen-eration.

Li had seen her twice, both times from a distance. Sharifi had done a guest lecture stint at Alba when Li was taking her OCS course. The academically ungifted Li had carefully avoided taking any classes with her, but Sharifi was already notorious—a person you couldn't help noticing.

Li had noticed her, all right. She had watched her. Secretly. Guiltily. Convinced that any overt show of interest in the other woman would betray her—or at the very least arouse dangerous suspicions. She'd wiped more of her own files that semester than in all her time at the front; she gave herself away every time she looked at Sharifi.

That semester had been before the Nobel Prize, though decades after the work that won the prize. Sharifi had been under consideration for a chair in quantum physics at Alba, but she hadn't gotten it—for the obvious reason. There had been some kind of protest, Li remembered. A senior human professor threatened to resign unless Sharifi got tenure. In the end, he'd backed down, and Sharifi had withdrawn her candidacy and gone into some private-sector research job.

But it was a long way from Ring-side universities and research parks to digging up rocks at the bottom of a Bose-Einstein mine. What had Sharifi been doing in the Anaconda? What could have been worth the risk when she knew, as anyone raised on Compson's World must know, what could happen?

Li plucked a leather-covered book off the desk and leafed through it. A flap inside the front cover held a clutter of business cards and, tucked inside a soft fold of leather meant to hold a notepad or a stylus, a dog-eared piece of cardstock that looked like it had spent a day or two in someone's pocket. Li picked it up, noticing the unfamiliar feel of paper under her fingertips, and realized she'd seen something like it before. It was a shipping receipt, the kind of thing they gave you when you rented a locker or posted realspace mail on a freighter. The printed number on the front face would be the locker number, or maybe the drop number of the package itself. She turned the chit over, looking for the ship's name, and found only an eight-pointed star knotted through the letter *M*.

She tucked the shipping receipt back into the front flap and flipped through the notebook's pages. There were half a dozen sheets of fiche, divided by tabs: lab notes, logs, addresses, appointments. She tapped the appointments page and got a polite, impersonal access-denied message. She tapped into the book's operating platform, found the hash log, and stripped Sharifi's password off it without breaking a computational sweat. She grinned, feeling irrationally better about the whole investigation; brilliant or not, Sharifi had at least been human enough to commit the most laughably elementary security gaffes. Maybe Li really could catch up to her.

She scanned the daily entries, found the usual appointments and reminders, scattered jottings of notes, names, streamspace coordinates. One page held a list of names, none of them familiar. Another held a long, close-written paragraph that appeared to be a transcription of a conversation about data transfer protocols with a person whose name Sharifi had, perhaps carelessly, perhaps on purpose, omitted.

Li tapped up the page that matched the day of Sharifi's death. Nothing. She flipped back one day and saw the letter *B* written in the 7 P.M. slot. Too late for a work appointment. Dinner?

Just above it Sharifi had scrawled a set of Ring-side spin coordinates, and beside them the name *Gilly* and two words that raised Li's hackles: *Life Insurance*.

The livewall in Sharifi's quarters turned out to be in the last place any rational person would consider putting it: on the bathroom door. Hadn't the station designers ever heard of reading on the john? Or was this some devious, petty-minded plot to prevent time-wasting by station employees?

Li flicked the wall into life, tapped up a streamspace directory, and zoomed in on the blazing quarter arc of the Zona Libre.

The coordinates took her to the NowNet Science Publishing Division, S.A., on the 438th floor of the Pan-American Building, Avenida de las Américas. *Must have a nice view*, Li thought. *And the monthly rent must be enough to pay off the national debts of half the planets on the Periphery.*

She cross-checked NowNet's office directory against Sharifi's on-station user files and found what she was looking for within seconds: a call on the day before Sharifi's death to one Gillian Gould, Senior Science Editor. A long call. She read Gould's address out loud, told the wall to put her through, and stood tapping her foot impatiently while the underpowered station net struggled through the Ring-side server's hand-shakes and VR resets.

Finally the NowNet logo blossomed on-screen, followed a half beat later by a 2D view of an attractive young man sitting at a suspiciously neat desk. He wore the inevitable Ring-side business blue suit, and his neck was encased in the stiff bead-and-bone lattice-work of a tribal collar.

The collar had to be fake; no mere salary puller could afford genuine Earth imports. But even the good fakes were expensive. And this was a good fake. All in all, the living, breathing image of the up-and-coming junior editor.

"Gillian-Gould's-office-may-I-ask-who's-calling?" he said in a tone that told Li precious few people talked to Gillian Gould without appointments.

Then he looked into his monitor and nearly jumped out of his ergonomically correct chair. "Dr. Sharifi! Sorry. If you'll just give me a minute, I'll get her out of her meeting for you."

Li blinked in surprise, but he was gone before she could say anything. She accessed the wall settings and saw that Sharifi had activated an extrapolated presentation program—a streamspace interface that put a business-appropriate talking head on the line so you could hold business meetings in your shorts, or while you were eating breakfast, or whatever. Li hesitated, then deactivated the presentation program just as Gould came on-screen.

Gould had perfect posture and the sort of washed-out Anglo-Saxon face that Li had never been able to read worth a damn. Like her assistant, she wore a tribal collar. Unlike her assistant's collar, Gould's was genuine. It nestled against her throat, half-hidden by a smoke gray linen blouse. But the bone was real bone; the beads antique bottle glass; the knots actually hand-tied by some shirtless old woman in the Sub-Saharan Cultural Preserve. And all shipped into orbit at a cost Li couldn't begin to imagine. Nobody was better at looking rich than rich liberals.

"Hannah!" Gould said, smiling. Then she saw Li.

The smile shut down like someone had shot the lights out. "What is this?" Gould asked, her blue eyes cold enough to freeze running water.

Li swiped the scan plate at the bottom of the screen and let her ID do the talking. "Just a few routine questions."

"Fine," Gould said. "But I'm recording this."

Li blinked and put on her boring face. "The official Fuhrman-locked recording will be available to you immediately, Ms., ah"—she paused and pretended to look down at the book in her hand—"Gould. After all, this isn't a criminal investigation."

"Of course not," Gould said, backpedaling.

"What's your relationship to Hannah Sharifi?" Li asked.

"Cousin."

"But—"

"Her adoptive mother was my father's sister."

"I see. When did you last speak with her?"

"I don't know exactly."

Lie number one, Li thought, her eyes nailed to Gould's carotid artery where it emerged from the intricate beadwork of the tribal collar. "Approximately?"

"Within the last few weeks probably. We talk a lot."

Li considered asking Gould about Sharifi's "life insurance" but decided not to. Information was power, and it rarely paid to show a suspect your cards when you were still shuffling them. "Did she send you anything by surface mail since then?" she asked instead.

"She might have."

"I see," Li said again. She wasn't quite able to keep the sarcasm out of her voice.

A line appeared between Gould's pale eyebrows. "I have nothing to hide. She often sent me drafts of her work."

"What? You're a physicist too?"

"I'm her editor. She had two books in the works with me."

"Had?"

The line deepened. "One book's gone into final production."

"Did she usually ship her manuscripts solid mail?"

"She dislikes working on electronic galleys."

"She must dislike it a lot. Real mail's slow. And pricey."

"She has poor eyesight."

"Bad eyesight," Li said. "A construct?"

She gave Gould a blank, eyebrows-raised look—a look that had squashed trench mutinies and broken strong men in interrogation.

It slid off Gould like water. Which just went to show that nasty looks worked better when there was a real possibility of backing them up with something a little more solid than harsh language.

"Are we done?" Gould said. "I really am busy, so

unless you have any more questions about my cousin's reading habits . . . ?"

A minute later the conversation was over.

It was true what people said, Li thought as the screen shut down. Ring-siders really were a different species.

Well, she'd gotten something out of the call. Gould had lied about when she had last seen Sharifi, and probably about the package and Sharifi's eyesight as well. Most important, she'd never asked the one question any friend or relative should have asked: where was Sharifi?

She checked the time—8 A.M., local. High time for good little security officers to be in the office. "McCuen?" she said, toggling her comm.

"Here," said his disembodied voice in her ear, so quickly that he must have been hanging over his terminal waiting for her call.

She didn't initiate a VR link. If she'd thought about it, she could have put a name to her reluctance to have McCuen see her standing in Sharifi's quarters. But she didn't let herself think about it.

"Gillian Gould," she said, relaying the realspace address and streamspace coordinates. "I want a watch on her. Twenty-four hours a day. I want to know who she talks to, where she goes, what she buys, what she reads. Everything."

"What's up?"

"She's Sharifi's cousin."

"We're putting Sharifi's cousin under surveillance? Why?"

Li hesitated, torn between the knowledge that she would need help—help McCuen was better qualified to give than anyone else on-station—and the fear that sooner or later anything she told him would work its way back to Haas.

Or would it? And when had she gotten so suspicious, anyway?

"Gould knows Sharifi's dead," she said cautiously, telling herself that McCuen was smart and capable and it wouldn't hurt to play him out a little line and see what he did with it. "She knew it before I called her."

An eerie quavering floated over the line, making Li's mind run to banshees and Becky circles. It took her a long moment to realize it was McCuen whistling.

"Fuck," he said, sounding very young and very impressed.

"Yep," she told him, grinning. Fuck indeed.

She signed off, cut the link, and looked at Sharifi's desk again, thinking. She bent down and started pulling its flimsy drawers open. The top two drawers gave up nothing, but when she opened the bottom drawer, she saw a long slim black case tucked in behind some datacubes.

Status lights blinked soothingly on its upper surface, but aside from the lights, the case was plain matte black without labels or corporate logos. Li had seen similar cases before. They tended to be wrapped around expensive experimental wetware.

This one was no exception. Its interior was lined with a thick layer of viral jelly, warm and moist as the inside of a mouth, maintaining its precious cargo at 99.7 percent humidity and a nice sterile four degrees above body temperature. And couched in the jelly like a pearl necklace was a finger-thick braid of silicon-coated ceramsteel.

It was a wet/dry interface. One end terminated in a standard-sized plug designed to fit an external silicon-based dataport. The other end—the one that necessitated the fancy storage system—was wetware, tank-grown nerve tissue shaped for a high-capacity cranial socket. The whole device had the sleek, understated look of top-of-the-line custom work. Hacker's gear.

Li turned the interface over, looking for a maker's

mark or serial number. She felt a slight roughness under her fingers on the underside of the dry socket. She turned the wire over and saw a stylized sunburst—the same one she had last seen on the floor of the Metz laboratory.

"Kolodny," she breathed, as a choking panic boiled up inside her.

Her internals fought it. Cognitive programs lurched into action, vetting meat memory, sorting out immediate threats from remembered ones, shunting the images that had triggered her panic into firewalled compartments where they could be hormonally adjusted—or, in the worst case, purged. Endorphins pumped through her system to combat the sudden rush of adrenaline. Once again, she wondered just how crazy she would be when the psychtechs were finally done with her.

Half a minute later her breathing was back to normal. Two minutes later her psych program flashed Kolodny's face across her internals.

Li expected this, had prepared for it. She sorted stubbornly through one of Sharifi's fiche piles, breathing and pulse even, until the diagnostic program finished its prying and Kolodny's picture faded behind her eyes.

Mother of Christ, she thought in the dark corner of her mind she'd always managed to keep from the psychtechs. Were the panics and flashbacks just normal long-term jump effects? Or were they malfunctions spawned by the kinks she'd put in her own systems to hide her damning preenlistment memories? She didn't know, and there was no one she could ask.

Except Cohen, maybe. But Metz had killed that.

She leaned forward, putting her head between her knees to dispel the spinning nausea of the flashback. That was when she saw it: a yellow-white rectangle wedged against the wall between the bed and the desk.

She fished around until she got hold of the thing and lifted it up.

A book.

She inhaled its dust, its smell, fingered the acid-gnawed paper. It was a cheap paperback, the kind still printed in the poorer Trusteeships. And this one was from Compson's now-defunct university press. She turned it over and grinned as she saw the author and title: Zach Compson's *Xenograph*.

It was a classic, of course—a book that had seized on people's imaginations so strongly that they still called Compson's World by the flamboyant New Zealander's name, while the anonymous long-distance survey team that actually discovered the planet had been consigned to oblivion.

She let the book fall open at random, and read a passage that Sharifi or some prior owner had underlined:

> There was a man who had a stone that sang, they told me. Everywhere I went they talked about this stone. Where it came from. What it meant. How he came to find it.
>
> They told me there were cathedrals in the earth's dark places. Rooms where the glass bones of the world hold silence like a river, where stones whisper the secrets of the earth to each other. And those who hear them stay and listen and sleep and die there.
>
> But a few come back. They walk out of the mountains singing. With stones in their hands.
>
> This is what they told me, but I never found the man.

"Glory holes," Li muttered. "He's talking about glory holes." She flipped through the book. It was dog-eared, tattered. Someone had read it again and again, starred and underlined favorite passages.

Had Sharifi known about the glory hole before she came? Had she seen something in Compson's half-mystical ramblings about glass bones and singing stones that no one else had seen? Was that what had brought her back to Compson's World?

Li set the book on Sharifi's desk. She stood up, put the wet/dry interface back in its case and tucked it into her uniform's kangaroo pocket, along with Sharifi's datebook. She started toward the door. Then she turned around, picked up Sharifi's battered copy of *Xenograph*, and put that in her pocket too.

She set the security seal to notify her if anyone else entered, walked back to her own quarters, pulled on clean shorts and a T-shirt, and collapsed on her narrow bunk without even managing to get herself under the covers.

She couldn't have been asleep ten minutes when the icon for the peepers in Haas's office toggled, waking her.

She maximized the feed from her skinbugs, and there was Haas, in shirtsleeves, standing behind the luminous desk.

He was talking to someone: a slight figure, whose face was half–turned away from Li. Even in the dim light, Li could make out the pale skin, the dark hair falling over shoulders as tense and frail as bird's wings.

"I didn't tell her," the witch murmured. "I swear it. I haven't told anyone." The tension in her voice was unmistakable.

"You'd better hope you haven't," Haas answered.

He raised his hand, and the woman flinched as if he'd hit her. Even Li, lying in bed three spokes away, tensed for the blow she thought was coming.

Haas turned away and shrugged. "Christ," he said. He walked out of the field of the peepers, and Li heard the clink of ice against glass as he poured a drink. "What a day. I need to relax." A pause, Haas still out of sight. "Come here."

The witch turned, but she moved so slowly that Haas was back at the desk before she could take more than a step toward him.

"Take that off," he said.

She undid her robe and let it slide to the floor.

"Lie down."

She lay back across his desk, passive as a child.

"No," he said. "Not that way."

He reached across her, into a desk drawer, and pulled out a wetware case. He bent the witch's head sideways, inserted a jack into an unseen socket, then attached the contact derms at the other end of the wire to his own forehead and ran the wire through his desktop VR rig.

What happened next was something Li had heard about but never actually seen: a loop shunt, a perversion of the technology every company in UN space used for training spins. Loop shunts were illegal; they'd been banned after that girl bled to death in Freetown. But the psych wards in every spaceport were still full of prostitutes who'd burned their neurons out or cut themselves up or just plain gone crazy using them.

Li shut the feed off, but she couldn't rid herself of the image burning behind her eyelids. Haas's hands on that white skin. The witch lying across the desk, her long hair spilling over the gleaming condensate, her body moving but her eyes as empty as the black void beyond the viewports.

Li rolled over, giving herself up to sleep.

It was a long time coming.

When she turned on her livewall the next morning the news of Sharifi's death had broken.

Even NowNet had been caught off guard, it seemed. They were gearing up for the event, dragging in colleagues, students, distant relatives. But they were using stock feed, old stuff. It was as if Sharifi had dropped off their radar. Coincidence? Or a sign that Sharifi had had reason to lie low in recent years?

So far the press was sticking to the unfortunate but unavoidable accident angle—though Li couldn't help wondering how much of that was the truth and how much of it reflected astute maneuvering by Nguyen's spin flacks.

Not that it made any real difference to her job. Not yet, anyway. Not unless she screwed up and let the press unearth some piece of the puzzle before she and Nguyen had time to plumb and measure and sanitize it. For the moment, she still had the same clues in hand she'd had when she lay down the night before.

A death. A fire. A missing dataset. A piece of wetware whose presence in Sharifi's quarters could mean anything or nothing.

Li ran her search from her own quarters. She had some privacy there at least, and she didn't relish the thought of surfacing after a long streamspace run to find herself slumped over her desk or passed out on the duty-room sofa.

She thought about letting McCuen tag along. In the end she decided against it; she wasn't quite ready to tell him about the wetware. An unwired keyboarder would slow her down, anyway, leave too plain a trail for corporate security to follow. And she planned to hit sites where unwanted attention could be dangerous.

The techs had upgraded her interface before Metz, so she did some exploratory muscle flexing before starting the search in earnest. She'd never seen streamspace until she enlisted. But with enlistment came training, wiring, streamspace access. Over the last decade, she'd learned to access the spinstream in a way only a tiny fraction of humanity could imagine. Part of it was raw talent, a knack for reading code the way normal people read words and paragraphs. The rest she owed to the spider's web of military-grade wetware that threaded through every synapse and made half her thoughts—half her self—silicon.

Li took every upgrade, every implant, every piece of experimental wetware the Corps offered. The techs loved her. They pushed her construct's reflexes and immune system to their more-than-human limits until she was a hybrid, genetic machine and electronic machine locked at the hip, a hairbreadth from the wire junkie's Holy Grail: transparent interface.

She finished her cross-checks and slipped into the spinstream. A digital riptide swept over her. She coursed over rivers and tidal flats of code, her own mind no more than one thin stream of data, a probabilistic ripple in a living, thinking, feeling ocean.

But this was the Stream, and it was deeper and stranger than any realspace ocean.

Dark and fruitful, it had spawned memes, ghosts, religions, philosophies—even, some claimed, new species. It held all the code there was, all the code that ever had been, right back to the first earthbound military intranets of the twentieth century. It was the first true Emergent system humans had created. Built by AIs back in the dark days of the Evacuation, it had spawned its own AIs, generations of them, hosts of them. A galaxy of quantum simulations evolved within it, mimicking every living system that humans had managed to pull off their dying planet—and countless impossible and improbable systems that had never lived on any planet. Even Cohen, vast and ancient among AIs, was a mere speck on the spinstream.

Today's job was simple: find out who made Sharifi's wet/dry interface and why. Li might have to do a little hacking to get that information, but she wouldn't have to stray outside the human datastream—the well-tended paths of corporate and governmental networks. If she was lucky, she wouldn't even have to risk a trip to Freetown.

She evolved her interface, logged on to the Ringside data exchange, and accessed a low-security copy of Sharifi's genome left stranded in an open database after a minor medical procedure four years ago. She checked it against the DNA built into the wire and confirmed that the interface had been customized for Sharifi. Then she cast her net out over the web.

She switched from VR to binary, running on the numbers, diving into the sea of pure code behind streamspace. The shift was like setting off a rocket. Dropping into the numbers freed her from her brain's spatial perceptions, silenced the tyrannical chattering of her inner ear. More important, it freed up all the processing space that was devoted to generating the simulated sensorium that was the only window into streamspace for the vast majority of human operators. For Li—for any real hacker—dropping into the numbers was like coming home.

She knew in broad terms what she was looking for, even if she didn't yet know where she would find it. She needed a hit from a big corporate R&D player. The kind of player with enough financial muscle to produce cutting-edge tech with an impossibly long research-to-market horizon—and enough political muscle to risk violating human bioresearch ethics guidelines. But she couldn't go in through the front door. She needed a fluff file. Something public domain, relatively unguarded. Something she could access without attracting unwanted attention. Something that would let her slip past the corporate gatekeepers.

She caught a promising datastring and hooked on to it, sliding through layered databases like a diver finning through the currents and thermals of a turbulent ocean. The string led her to the public-access page of CanCorp's Ring-based bioresearch division. CanCorp was one of the four or five multiplanetaries Li thought could have produced Sharifi's interface—and sure enough a quick and dirty cross-check told her CanCorp was one of Sharifi's most generous corporate sponsors.

She switched back into VR to follow the string; on the off chance that CanCorp security was monitoring its public site, she wanted to look like an ordinary tourist when she got there. To her annoyance, she was detoured five times on her way. First, a saccharine commercial jingle for some overpriced health snack that tasted like mildew. Then an earnest pitch from the Reformed Church of Christ of the Latter-Day Saints, delivered by an implausibly clear-skinned teenager in a cheap blue suit and a plastic name tag. Then, loaded onto a single and annoyingly persistent banner, a docu-ad about the Heaven's Gate Gene

Therapy Institute, a Ring-generated public-service announcement about a listeria epidemic in the Ring's NorAm Sector, and a disorienting full-immersion apocalyptic simulation from some computer-literate Interfaither splinter group.

She slid out of the Interfaither sim with jelly legs, a throbbing head, and a serious beef with whoever had decided that they were a bona fide religion entitled to public-access streamtime. When she finally reached the CanCorp page, it didn't tell her much. But it did have a link to a "work in progress" section on which the division's researchers (or, more likely, the division's public relations staff) posted sanitized biographies and dumbed-down descriptions of current research. She ran a new search and pulled streamspace coordinates for three CanCorp researchers.

She hesitated. So far she'd only hit on sparsely monitored public-access sites, sites where her presence would pass unnoticed as long as she didn't do anything that made someone decide to take a closer look at the hit logs for the current time frame. Now, however, she was crossing into more delicate territory. Territory where there would be a price for sloppiness.

But that was why Nguyen had sent her, of course. Nguyen knew her. She'd told Li her career was riding on this mission and then she'd turned her loose, knowing she'd get the job done, knowing she was willing to risk everything on every throw, every time.

Five minutes later an obscure CanCorp research assistant sent a message to the network administrator. Six minutes later, Li opened a blind window on the administrator's account and started surfing the internal mail archives of CanCorp's entire R&D division.

CanCorp security had been thorough, Li noted with a professional's appreciation. They had good eSec protocols and they hadn't been shy about slapping the wrists of employees who violated them. But researchers never took security seriously, and CanCorp's researchers were no exception.

Three of the facility's designers still had archived mail talking about a prototype device similar to Sharifi's wire. The project had been terminated twenty-eight months ago. The one prototype of the interface had been sent to an off-site storage room from which, according to later inventories, it had simply . . . vanished.

Li cursed in frustration, surfaced briefly to a disorienting image of her quarters on-station, then plunged back in.

Let's go at this from another angle, she told herself. *Look for the organic component.*

She accessed Sharifi's medical records again and put together an itinerary for her last few months Ringside. Then she cross-checked Sharifi's whereabouts against all the clinics licensed to install the kind of specialized internal wetware Sharifi needed. Match: one discreet, expensive private clinic in the Zona Camilia.

The operation had been paid for from an unnumbered Freetown account. And twenty hours before Sharifi checked in, the clinic received a bonded and insured shipment of medical supplies from one Carpe Diem, an obscure colonial net-access provider that had never logged a single shipment to the Zona Camilia clinic before or after.

Carpe Diem turned out to be a bona fide though not particularly profitable operating company that held down a solid chunk of the civilian streamspace access market in the Lalande 21185 metaorbitals. Li quickly pierced its security perimeter and slipped into the internal operations database. She found exactly what should have been there: payroll, billing records, internal corporate documents, and a reasonably active unofficial e-mail dialogue to substantiate the actual existence of Carpe Diem's alleged 479 on- and off-site employees.

But when she hacked the accounting department, she got a different story. Enough money was flowing through Carpe Diem to fund a small but technologically sophisticated war. Payments, large and numerous, some of them to the same players involved in installing Sharifi's tech. And for every transfer out, the files showed a corresponding transfer in.

Whoever made the transfers had cared enough to cover their tracks. The incoming transfers were never exactly equal to the outgoing ones, and they showed up on the Carpe Diem accounts with lead times varying from two days to two months before the equivalent outbound transfers. It would have been extremely hard to prove a connection.

But Li didn't need proof; she just needed a track to put her nose to.

She traced the money through two bankruptcies, five anonymous holding companies, and a string of numbered bank accounts scattered across eight star systems.

At one point she felt a presence, as if a great bird hung above her, rising on a strong head wind, the currents of cyberspace breaking across its pinioned wings. Something brushed along the edge of her mind. A blue-bright eternity of open spaces flashed before her eyes and was gone before she could even be sure she'd seen it.

<Cohen?> she thought, then bit the thought back hurriedly. She was running in binary, deep in the numbers, dispersed over the net as far as an organic operator could risk spreading herself. She knew from experience that a mere thought could draw Cohen like chum drew a waiting shark. And she didn't need him showing up. She wasn't even close to ready to talk to him.

The money trail dried up in the heavily shielded

datacore of an offshore account in Freetown's finance sector. Li reset her safety cutout and crossed onto FreeNet before she had time for second thoughts.

FreeNet was older and wilder than the rest of streamspace. It was off the UN grid, ungoverned by the safety protocols of the white-market sectors, the virtual homeland of black marketeers, hijackers, infoanarchists, and the rogue AIs of the Consortium.

Li's cutout offered some protection even there; if her vital signs changed too drastically, it would shunt her into a firewalled decompression program until it could get her safely off-line. But that only helped against outright net assassination. A cutout wouldn't stop wet bugs. Li remembered Kolodny and shivered.

She spent half the day on FreeNet, riding the stream until her back ached and her eyes burned. All she found were firewalls, dead ends, cul-de-sacs. She cursed, fatigue bearing down on her. There were no answers here. Just boxes within boxes, questions within questions.

Common sense and the urge for self-preservation were both telling her to give up. The motto of the FreeNetters might be "Information seeks its own freedom," but in practice FreeNet was made for hiding data, not finding it. And, like Freetown's realspace streets, it was a place you could get killed for asking too many questions. Or asking any questions at all about the wrong people.

The hijacker nabbed her twenty seconds after she crossed back onto the UN grid.

The first sign of trouble was a subtle ripple in the numbers. Streamspace froze, shuddered, desynchronized around her. When it clicked back into place, she was nose to nose with a blue-eyed Hispanic face. Fourteen, maybe fifteen years old. Baby fat padding jaw and cheekbone. Hard-edged, industrial-finish nose ring. Good unkinked genes.

Li breathed a virtual sigh of relief and relaxed. It

was a Riot Grrl, some rich hacker wanna-be hot-dogging on her parents' VR gear. Real danger was never this pretty, even in streamspace.

She smiled and shut down the window.

Nothing happened.

<Out,> she sent. But there was no out.

Streamspace ground gears on her again. When it phased back in, the Riot Grrl's eyes were changing color. Blue to brown, brown to near black. And the face around the eyes was changing. Shifting, melting, re-forming until Li was staring at a face she knew far too well. A face she'd last seen fifteen years ago staring back out of the streaky mirror of a Shantytown chop shop.

She ran, but the hijacker was too fast for her. A hand lashed out before she could turn and clamped down on her jugular.

She kicked and bit. She tried to shut down the VR window and couldn't. She tried to drop out of VR into code so she could at least see what she was up against. She tried to shut down everything and found that her realspace feed had been disabled.

The hand twisted, shooting Li down into pain and darkness.

The pain in her throat eased, and she returned to something like breathing. She was crouching in a dark acrid-smelling place, holding something. Her head throbbed. She felt a dull, itchy sting in her lungs that reminded her of . . . someplace.

She couldn't see clearly, and what she could see—tools, cables, a shadowy computer console—made no sense to her. She was moving, doing something with her hands, manipulating a piece of machinery whose function she couldn't guess at. She strained to drag her gaze upward, to get some idea of her surroundings.

Impossible. Her hands, her eyes, her whole body seemed to be moving of their own volition.

A claustrophobic panic gripped her. She was ghosting, wired into someone else's body, experiencing a digitized memory that could be past, present, or pure simulation. She couldn't control the framed memory. Nor could she tell how heavily it had been edited, or if it was real in the first place. All she could do was ride it out and hope it would let her go when it was done with her.

A noise. Movement.

She-the-other stood up, turned, looked.

A figure emerged from the shadows. A woman, Li thought. But it was hard to tell; her perspective was disjointed, distorted, as if seen through eyes that had no idea what they were looking at.

The body she was in spoke, but all she heard was a high chattering wail, like the dumb cry of an animal. If there were words in it, they were spoken in a language that meant nothing to her.

The dark figure moved toward her. For a moment her vision cleared, and she put a face to the shadow— a pale face, shadowed by the long, dark fall of hair.

The witch.

She reached out, felt the taut curve of the witch's waist beneath her hand, drew the girl's warm body to her.

White light. Endless space. Wind like a knife.

Mountains rose above her, higher than any mountains could be, rimed with black ice, white with hanging glaciers. The sky burned high-altitude blue above her—a color she'd only seen once before, halo-jumping into the equatorial mountains of Gilead.

A hawk's shadow swept overhead, and she heard her own heartbeat, slow and strong, echoing through

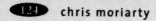

the vast mineral silence. Then she was out, back on the grid. Safe.

<Cohen?>

She probed the net, stretching as thin as she dared to.

<Cohen?>

But he was gone, if he'd ever been there.

Shantytown: 14.10.48.

Dr. Leviticus Sharpe met her at the door of the Shantytown hospital. He was wire-thin, knobby-jointed, a good two meters tall. He stooped atop storklike legs, a big man trying hard not to intimidate a small woman. Li didn't need the help—but she still liked him for it.

"Welcome to Compson's World," he said, smiling. "May you not have to stay long."

Sharpe's office faced away from town, toward the foothills. It was fall in Shantytown, and the scrub oak was turning. Li saw the familiar wash of scarlet in the canyons, the silver-green ripple of rabbit sage on the lowlands.

"Well," said Sharpe when they were seated. "Here you are."

"You sound like you've been expecting me."

He blinked. "Shouldn't I have been?"

Li spread her hands, palms out, and raised her eyebrows. It was one of Cohen's habitual gestures, and she felt a flush of annoyance with herself for letting it creep into this conversation.

"Er . . ." Sharpe shifted in his chair, looking suddenly uneasy. "Maybe you should tell me why you're here, then, Major."

Li shrugged and pulled Sharifi's wet/dry wire out of her pocket.

Sharpe peered at it, and Li caught the metallic flash of a contracting shutter ring in his left pupil. A bio-prosthetic, some kind of diagnostic device.

"I'm sorry," he said. "Wetware isn't really my bailiwick. Have you tried AMC tech support? The station office is reasonably competent."

"The other half of this system is in your morgue."

"I doubt that." He bent to look at the wire again. "Any multiplanetary that owned this kind of tech would have put a repo out on it before the operator's body was cold."

"It's Hannah Sharifi's."

"Oh," he said softly. "I see. That's different, of course."

"You didn't turn up the internal components in your autopsy?" Li checked her hard memory, verified what she thought she'd seen. "You signed her death certificate."

He stood up—no longer smiling, no longer stooping—and Li saw the green flash of LEDs as he checked his internal chronometer. "I sign a lot of death certificates," he said, the friendly, joking tone gone from his voice. "And now, if it's quite all right, I have patients to see. Tell Haas I said hello."

Li felt like she was stuck in a fog. She followed Sharpe down the corridor, half-running to keep pace with his long-legged strides. He pushed through a pair of swinging doors into a scrub room, bent over a deep sink, and started washing his hands.

Li reached out and turned the water off. "You mind telling me what the hell's going on here?"

Sharpe held his soapy hands out, splay-fingered, looking oddly vulnerable. "I doubt you need me to tell you anything, Major. It looks to me like you've got it all figured out."

"Fine," Li said. "Cover your ass. But I have a job to do. If you won't help, get off the tracks and let me by."

Sharpe reached past her and turned the water back on. His hand was trembling, but one look at his face told her it was anger, not fear. "Just leave," he said. "I'm up to my neck in patients you idiots put here. Haas knows I don't have time to sneak around behind his back doing unauthorized autopsies. And I don't need another of his petty little loyalty tests. God knows Voyt put me through that hoop enough times."

And then, suddenly, it all made sense. Sharpe's assumption that she would come down to talk to him after the mine fire. His confusion, his suspicion, the smoldering anger that he camouflaged with jokes and polite chitchat.

"Listen," Li said. "I don't know how things were under Voyt, and I don't know what little arrangement he had with Haas. But I'm not part of it. I came down here myself, not on Haas's orders. I'm not here to tell you what official line to toe. I want the truth from you. Or at least as much of it as you know. That's all."

"Truth is a complicated concept," Sharpe said, and she could still hear the suspicion in his voice. "What exactly did you have in mind?"

"I want to see Sharifi's body."

"On whose authority?"

"Mine."

She toggled her comm system, wrote and time-stamped an order, sent it to Sharpe's streamspace coordinates and watched his eyes unfocus momentarily as he read it. He blinked down at her, astonished.

"Didn't think I was going to put it in writing, did you?" she said. She leaned back against the sink, arms crossed on her chest, and looked up at him. "You've got me filed in the wrong box, Sharpe."

"Indeed," he said. He laughed and rubbed a still-damp hand through his hair. "I apologize for . . . well, there's a certain paranoia that goes with being a mine doctor."

"I can imagine."

He led her back through a warren of hospital wards and corridors toward the rear modules of the hospital building. As they came closer to the morgue, Li started to see evidence of the recent fire.

They threaded between hospital beds and stacks of boxed medical supplies. Space was always tight in underfunded colonial hospitals, but this one looked like it was about to burst at the seams. Evac and rescue gear was crammed into every corner. Mountains of complicated diagnostic equipment and medical supplies lined the walls, as if someone had cleared out the storage rooms and dumped their contents in any empty space available. As they worked their way down the hallways, Li had to dodge nurses carrying bedpans and burn dressings.

Finally Sharpe opened one side of a broad double door marked with an orange biohazard decal and led Li through a frigid curtain of irradiated air into a long room stacked with virusteel drawers that looked unnervingly like cryocoffins.

"All full, unfortunately," Sharpe said. "Running a brisk trade in dead miners these days."

"And of course they all have to be autopsied," Li said. "Otherwise, how could you prove it was their own damn fault they died down there?"

Sharpe looked sideways at her and his thin mouth kinked in a sardonic smile. "I can't imagine what you're talking about, Major."

"Here we are," he said, stopping at a drawer that looked to Li just like all the others. He opened the drawer with a smooth sweep of his lanky arm, and Li found herself face-to-face with Hannah Sharifi.

"Jesus," she muttered. "What happened to her?"

She looked like she'd been hit with a sledgehammer. The right side of her head folded in on itself from jawbone to hairline like a crushed eggshell. And her right hand was a mess. Nails torn off, bloodstains spidering through the lined skin of palm and finger, black burns on her fingertips.

"That's how the rescue team found her," Sharpe said. "The cause of death appears to have been suffocation—not all that surprising in a mine fire." He lifted the still-intact left hand to show Li the blue fingernails. "The injuries are unusual, but they did find her at the foot of the stairs running into the Trinidad. A lot of people fall there. Those stairs have had running water on them more or less since they opened that level. There's a spring they haven't located or can't drain or something." He shrugged. "She could have hit her head on cribbing planks, on the walls of the shaft, on any number of things."

"What about the hand?"

"Yes, the hand. Well. I've certainly never seen anything like it."

But Li had. On Gilead. In the interrogation rooms. When they went after people's fingers with Vipers.

Things had fallen apart on Gilead. The price of playing by the rules had risen so high that no one had been willing to pay it anymore. Or at least no one who survived the place long enough to make a dent in things. And the funny thing about having the rules fall apart was that there always turned out to be some people, in any group, who liked life better without rules.

Li hadn't been one of them—or at least she didn't think she'd been. She'd been outside most of the interrogation rooms most of the time, doing her best to forget what happened on the other side of all those carefully closed doors. But it wasn't like she didn't know—like they didn't all know—where the information they based their decisions on came from. And every time she tried to remember what had really happened on Gilead she felt like she was trying to force two versions of the war into a slot in her mind that only had room for one.

She shook her head, pushing the memories away. Sharifi was no Syndicate prisoner. And this wasn't Gilead, not by a long shot.

"She probably damaged it trying to stop her fall," Sharpe said. "This isn't the first time I've seen someone come in with burns. There are a lot of loose wires down there. It's easy to get confused and grab one, even if you know what you're doing."

Li looked down at the body. Now that she was over the first shock, she could see past the injuries to the face under them. It was her face, of course. The face she remembered from those sliding-away days before her enlistment. The face she still wore in dreams sometimes. It was like looking at her own corpse.

Sharifi's uninjured hand lay on her stomach, palm down. A white crescent of scar tissue marked the web of skin between thumb and forefinger, and Li reached out and touched it. It was important somehow—material proof that it wasn't her lying on the ice-cold metal, but another woman. Someone with her own life, her own mind, her own history. A stranger.

She realized Sharpe was watching her and pulled her hand back self-consciously. She cleared her throat. "Are we going to be able to get anything out of that mess?"

"I think so. The damage isn't really as extensive as it looks. And ceramsteel is a lot tougher than brain tissue." He grinned. "Not that I have to tell you that, Major."

Li snorted and fingered her right shoulder. She'd slept on it wrong and woken this morning to the unmistakable sting of frayed filament ends cutting into muscle and tendon. She should probably ask Sharpe to look at it, she thought, remembering the field tech's memo. But not now. Not with Sharifi lying between them.

"Let's see what we see," Sharpe said. He manipulated the controls of Sharifi's drawer and slid it onto a ceiling-mounted track system that connected the storage area to the autopsy room.

What they saw when Sharpe got his allegedly temperamental scanner up and running was startling. Sharifi's backbrain—muscle memory, smell, autonomic functions—was as pristine as any planet-bound civilian's. She had the VR relays that you would expect to see in an academic who, after all, made her living and did her research on the web. But other than that, Sharifi had died with more or less the same backbrain she'd been born with: the brain of someone who had never needed military-applications streamspace access and who had made no more than a handful of Bose-Einstein jumps in her lifetime.

Sharifi's frontbrain told a different story, though. It lit up the screen like a Freetown data haven. Whatever was in there looked to Li's untrained eyes like a white-hot thousand-legged spider—a spider that had wormed its way into every fold, every cranny between Sharifi's shattered temples.

"What the hell is that?" Li asked.

Sharpe let out a long slow whistle. "I couldn't even begin to tell you," he said. "We have now passed far, far beyond the limits of my technical expertise. I can tell you this much, though. It was all put in at once. And not long ago."

"Three months ago," Li said.

He looked at her, eyebrows raised. "Yes, that sounds right. Usually a web this extensive will be built up by accretion. Multiple generations of filament, even redundant networks layered on top of each other.

Different-age scar tissue. By the time most people are this wired, they're carrying around almost as much dead tech as live tech. But this job was done in a single operation. Ring-side clinic, of course. Or Alba." He glanced at Li. "To be honest, it looks more like military work to me than anything else."

"Well, it wasn't Alba," Li said. "That much I can tell you." She peered at the scan, comparing it to her own brain scans taken after her last upgrade, trying to see which of Sharifi's brain segments were most densely wired. Something about Sharifi's system seemed off somehow. "I don't get it," she said finally. "What's it all wired into? What's it *for*?"

"Communications," Sharpe said. "All communications." He pointed. "Look. Here. Here. Where the dark areas are, and the contrast. If we looked at a scan of a typical cybernetic implant system—yours for example—we would see a much more even distribution of filaments. Some concentration in the motor skills areas. A node somewhere in here for the oracle that it's all platformed on. Also a high concentration of filament in the speech, hearing, and visual centers. In other words, your spinfeeds, your VR interfaces, your communications systems. Sharifi's implant is totally different. No oracle, no operating platform, no relays. Just filament. And it's concentrated almost exclusively in the speech, sight, and hearing centers."

"So it's just a fancy net access web?" Li asked, disappointed.

"Not quite." Sharpe pursed his lips and stepped away from the scanner, pulling his gloves off. "If I had to guess, I'd say it was some sort of shunt."

"A shunt?" Li shook her head, fighting away a brief, untethered image of Kolodny falling. "That's crazy. Why would someone like Sharifi be wired for a shunt? It doesn't make any sense."

"There are shunts and there are shunts. This is an

unusual one. A very specialized one." Sharpe frowned. "Could I see that interface cord again?"

Li took it out of her pocket and handed it to him. She watched Sharpe examine it, his ocular prosthesis contracting like a camera lens, turning his pupil machine silver.

"I think," he said tentatively, "that we are looking at a modular system. Most internal webs are unitary; they can operate offstream just as well as onstream; otherwise, what would be the point of making the system internal, right? So your typical wire job is really a discrete operating system platformed on an enslaved nonsentient AI and hooked into a more or less extensive cybernetic web. It interfaces with streamspace, but it doesn't need external feed to run any of its core functions. This implant, by contrast, is simply one component of a larger unit. It's meant to let the wearer interface with some larger, external system."

"What kind of system?"

"Well," Sharpe said cautiously, "an Emergent AI would be my guess."

Li stared at him, realized her mouth was hanging open, shut it. Anyone who was experimenting with unrestricted two-way interface between a sentient AI and a human subject was breaking so many laws she couldn't begin to count them. "I thought those experiments were terminated years ago," she said.

"Emergent–human interface is politically untouchable, that's clear. But you still hear things every now and then. Alba had a program before the Interfaither lobby lowered the boom on it. And I'm sure there are still some groups in Freetown working toward it."

"So you're saying Sharifi was carrying around blackmarket tech."

"Not necessarily. Maybe the AI on the other end of this wire wasn't an Emergent." Sharpe shrugged. "Still, that's my best guess about what this is. I still think she was wired for some kind of shared operations with an Emergent."

"Not too many of those around, Sharpe."

"No, there aren't."

"Are you thinking what I'm thinking?"

"The relay station's field AI?"

Li felt the cold of the autopsy room settle into her bones. What the hell had Sharifi been doing? And who would have let her play that kind of risky game with a field AI when lives depended on every quantum-transport operation? "I'd sure like to see the psychware they were running on that implant," she said.

"It won't be in there. Not nearly enough memory. It'll have been externalized too."

"And the field AI is conveniently off-line, isn't it?"

"That's what it looks like."

They both stared at the screen for a moment without speaking.

"Well," Sharpe asked. "What do you want me to do with it?"

"Take it out," Li said.

Most of Li's encounters with quantum-corrected replication happened when she was sedated into near coma. Cryotechnology made faster-than-light transport, otherwise a potentially lethal ordeal, survivable. And it usually left Li with nothing more significant than a stuffy nose and wandering joint pain.

Biotech extraction was different, though. It was controlled, observable, reassuringly domesticated. A surgical parlor trick. This one took a while. Sharpe didn't have the necessary information to preset his equipment; he had to fiddle around trying to nail the implant's quantum signature. But after a long series of finicky adjustments, he established and verified entan-

glement, uploaded the primary spinstream, reintegrated the entangled data, waited while the comp ran
its nested correction protocols. When his terminal
told them it was *completing the Sharifi transform* they
both laughed nervously.

Five minutes later, Li held a small package in the
palm of her hand: a neatly rolled coil of white ceramsteel filament and a few gel-encased microrelays, all
flash-irradiated and wrapped in sterile surgical film.

"It's so small," she said.

"Two kilometers," Sharpe said. "That's the length of
filament, measured end to end, in the average full-
body net."

Li weighed the slender coil in her hand. Why had
Sharifi needed to install illegal wetware? And, more
troubling, where had she gotten it? "Do you need to
keep this?" she asked Sharpe.

"I'd rather."

"Fine." She handed it to him. "Just make sure it's
here if I need to look at it again."

"Can I ask you something?" Sharpe said as she
reached the door. His voice sounded strained. "Un-
officially?"

Li turned. "Of course."

"Did you know her?"

"Who? Sharifi?"

Sharpe nodded.

"Not really. I saw her a couple of times. That's all."

"I knew her," Sharpe said. He picked up a scalpel
and began fidgeting with it, screwing and unscrewing
the threaded fastener that held blade to handle. "I
liked her. She was . . . honest."

He didn't seem to expect an answer, so Li waited,
watching him fidget.

"Anyway," he said, flushing, "that's not the point.
The point is, I was given . . . instructions. After her
death. Do those instructions still stand?"

Li stared at him, wondering what kind of political minefield she'd stumbled into. "What are you asking me?"

Sharpe searched her face, eyebrows knit. "Has anyone explained to you how the coroner's system works in St. Johns?"

Li had to think for a minute before she realized that St. Johns was the actual map name of Shantytown. She shook her head.

"When someone dies in the town limits, I have full authority to conduct any investigations needed to declare a cause of death and close the inquiry. When someone dies on AMC property, the case goes to AMC management. Unless AMC asks me to do an autopsy, I just hold the body pending disposal or, more rarely, shipment. There's still a death certificate, of course. But Haas fills it out. I don't do much more than rubber-stamp it."

"Go on," Li said. Sharpe was still playing with the scalpel, looking to Li like he was about to slice a fingertip off every time he turned it over.

"In practice, AMC usually has me autopsy everyone who dies in the mine. But not this time. This time I got a bundle of automatic authorizations, all signed by Haas. Except for two: Voyt and Sharifi. On those I got completed death certificates, signed them, and sent them back upstairs."

"And now you want to do the autopsies."

"Wouldn't you?"

"Why?"

"If you don't want to tread on Haas's toes . . ."

"It's not Haas's toes I'm worried about," Li said.

A voice somewhere near the pit of her stomach whispered something eminently sensible about looking before she leapt. She squashed it.

"Fine," she said. "Do your autopsies. But no one else sees the results until I sign off on them. Just so I know how low I have to duck if I want to keep my head attached."

Sharpe looked at her soberly. "I appreciate this."

"Don't mention it," Li said—and her next words were only half-joking. "I'm just giving you enough rope to hang me with."

Shantytown: 14.10.48.

She should have gone straight back to the heliport when she left the hospital and caught the next shuttle station-side. But she didn't. Without letting herself think about where she was going she turned left instead of right at the end of Hospital Street and started working her way along the winding, badly paved streets toward the old section of Shantytown.

Most of Shantytown had been thrown up in the first frenzy of the Bose-Einstein Rush. There'd been little money, less time, no planning, and from most angles the town looked like a sprawling collection of modular hab units that someone had dropped by accident and forgotten to come back for. It was only when you got deep into the old town that you began to see the bones of the place, the sealed biopods of the original colony. Few of the pods could still maintain an atmosphere, but the modern town had grown around their radiating spokes like skin grafts encrusting surgical mesh. The result was a warren of narrow alleys and windowless courtyards through which a native could travel for miles without ever seeing sky or showing up on the orbital surveillance grid.

The Riots had broken out here a few months after Li was born, and the UN's collective memory had never recovered. *Shantytown* was still a code word for violence, treason, terrorism. And it still had the highest percentage of constructs of any city in UN space. Walking its streets again, Li had a sudden memory of her OCS course eight years ago. Of her tangled feelings of shame and disgust when she recognized the urban warfare lab as an exact streamspace replica of old Shantytown's interlocking tunnels and courtyards. When she recognized the targets' faces as her own face.

She found the chapel without ever having quite admitted to herself that she was looking for it. She stood before the gate, set her hand on it, pushed it open. As she stepped into the little churchyard she crossed herself.

Our Lady of the Deep stood just where she remembered it: dug into the steep bluff where the prehistoric lake bed Shantytown was built on met the hills that led up to the birthlabs and bootleg mines. The door was open. Li glanced in as she passed, saw the dim cavern of the nave and, like daylight at the end of a mine tunnel, the muted milk white gleam of the Mary Stone.

There was a tawdriness about the churchyard that didn't show up in her childhood memories. The rectory's peeling whitewash, the cheap insulation foam packed around badly fitted windows, the too-bright colors of artificial flowers, the mottled laminate of headstones peeling under a chemical rain they had never been designed to stand up to. It was almost enough to distract her from the really startling thing about the churchyard: how young everyone in it was.

She walked along the rows looking at birth and death dates. Thirty-five. Thirty-four. Twenty-four.

Eighteen. And that wasn't even counting the babies' graves, half grown over by green-gray clumps of oxygen-producing algae.

She stumbled on the grave she was looking for by accident—and as soon as she saw it she knew that, whatever she'd thought, whatever she'd told herself, she hadn't been ready to see it. She hadn't really believed in it, any more than she believed, really, that her father had been dead all these years.

But there it was. Gil Perkins. And the dates, below the name. He'd been thirty-six when he died. Which meant that the old, worn-down, coal-scarred father of her childhood had been younger than she was now.

"Can I help you?" a man's voice said behind her.

She spun around, chest heaving.

A priest. Young. Athletic-looking. Not local. He looked at her with bright-eyed interest. He had an intelligent, sensitive face, the face of a bright young man who believed that people were basically good. He was probably two or three years out of seminary, getting his first taste of poverty, feeling himself on the front lines here, fighting the good fight. Li knew the type. They did a lot of good, but they were in Compson's World, not of it. They came for a year, or two, or ten, but eventually they always went back to the Helena spaceport and caught a jumpship home. A decision for which Li was in no position to blame them.

"I—was just taking a walk," she said. "Just looking."

"Someone you knew?"

"What? Oh . . . yes. A little."

"Fifteen years, and he still gets visitors. He must have been the kind of man people remember."

"There was nothing special about him," Li said.

The priest smiled. "If you say so."

She looked at his thin, clever, honest face. He was no one she remembered. No one who would know her or would even have heard of her. He was younger than her, for Christ's sake. Why not take a chance?

"So who visits him?" she asked casually.

"A Mrs. . . . Oh, I can't remember her name. She moved to another parish before I got here. Blond." He grinned. "Irish as green grass and tinkers' ponies. Tall. About my height." Then he held up his right hand, and Li knew what he was going to say before he spoke. "Missing part of a finger."

"Left it in Londonderry," Li murmured. The words came out in an accent she'd spent the last decade weeding out of her speech. She felt as if someone else had spoken them. Someone whose face she should remember.

"Really? She was a Provo? No shit." The priest shook his head. "Stubborn buggers. You'd think the UN would just give up and let them stay there."

"You'd think."

Li looked back at the headstone. It had started to drizzle, and the rain speckled the laminate face of the marker, spreading across the pale surface like ink stains. She shivered and pulled her collar closer in against her neck.

"I could give her your name," the priest said. "If you want to talk to her."

Li caught her breath. "No. No, I don't think so." She swallowed, her heart hammering. "I doubt she'd even remember me. And what's the point of stirring up old memories? People have to get on with life sometime."

McCuen met her at the shuttle gate looking white and stricken.

"Christ," she said when she saw his face. "What's happened?"

"It's Gould. She's gone."

"When?"

"Two, three hours ago."

Li stepped past McCuen and started walking toward

HQ. "Three hours isn't the end of the world, McCuen. She can't have gotten far."

"It might be longer. . . ."

She turned on him. "How much longer?" she asked, speaking slowly and very clearly.

"I'm sorry," McCuen said miserably. "I—she went to bed last night, then in the morning, even though she didn't go to work, she was using power, water, air. She was onstream. We monitored the calls. No one saw guests go in, and it never occurred to me until I saw them that she wasn't making those calls. But she wasn't. They just used her home system to make us think she was."

Like Li had used Sharifi's system to fool her way into Gould's office. Was it a coincidence? A joke? And if not, then what the hell was Gould up to?

"Why didn't you call me right away when she went missing, McCuen?"

"I did. I tried. You—you were off-grid."

Of course. She'd gone to old Shantytown. She'd been walking down memory lane, leaving an inexperienced kid in charge while the investigation fell apart. And they were already paying for it.

"Maybe you should go onstream and see if you can find her?" McCuen said. "I—I'm so slow. Maybe you can turn something up. That's why I came out to meet you."

"Yes," Li said. "But not here. In private."

When they reached HQ the duty officer was waiting for her, wanting to tell her something. She swept past, ignoring him, and waved McCuen into her office.

"All right," she told him, sitting down on the desk she still hoped she wouldn't be here long enough to think of as anything but Voyt's desk. "What kind of time frame are we looking at? When's the last time someone actually saw her?"

"Last night, Ring-time. Twelve hours."

"Jesus," Li said, then saw the stricken look on

McCuen's face and bit the rest of her words back. It was an understandable mistake, even if it was potentially disastrous. They might as well skip the recriminations and just fix it. If they still could.

She closed her eyes briefly as she slipped on-line, then opened them to a disorienting double vision of streamspace superimposed on McCuen's pale features. "You've checked credit access and so forth?" she asked.

"Yes. Nothing."

She checked again, ticking over bank reports, food and water and air charges, spinstream access debits, looking for the tracks no person in the Ring could help laying down every minute of every day of their conscious lives. "It doesn't make sense," she said. "There can't be nothing. Not unless she's dead."

"Dead or using cash."

"You can't use cash Ring-side, McCuen. No one takes it. Even the scatter dealers and chop artists want nice clean freshly laundered credit."

"Maybe she's not Ring-side," McCuen said, looking as if he desperately wanted to be wrong.

"You can't get off the Ring without credit," Li snapped. Then she caught her breath as gut instinct made a connection that she knew at once had to be right, though she didn't know how or why.

"Check the shipping records," she told McCuen. "Get me the name of every ship that's left on the Freetown run in the last twelve hours."

Two hours later Li was bending over McCuen's monitor watching wavering security-cam footage of passengers filing along the boarding gantry of a Freetown-bound cargo freighter.

"Are you sure?" McCuen said when she stopped the tape and pointed.

"I'm sure."

The silk blouse and expensive handmade jewelry were gone. Gould wore cheap clothes, cheap shoes, carried what little baggage she had in a cheap viruhide shoulder bag. She had chopped off her fair hair or shoved it under a hat, Li couldn't tell which. And she was keeping her head down, moving fast, not letting the cameras get a clear view of her. But there was the straight, thin line of her mouth, the arrogant curve of cheekbone and nostril, the air of unbending, unquestioned superiority that made Li perversely glad this woman was running from her.

She pushed that thought away, feeling petty, and told herself she just wasn't cut out to be a policeman. "Check the relay schedules," she told McCuen. "See if we can intercept the ship before they jump."

As Gould hefted her bag up the boarding ramp, something at her neck glittered. Li smiled. Gould was wearing a charm necklace: a vacuum-mounted sliver of low-grade Bose-Einstein condensate suspended in a cheap heart-shaped locket of translucent plastex. Pure trash. The kind of trinket street vendors sold to tourists along with the fake Rolexes and the Zone baseball caps. The kind of thing Gould wouldn't be caught dead wearing in normal life. The woman was nothing if not thorough.

"I can't find them on the relay queue," McCuen said, sounding overwhelmed.

Li checked the carrier's schedule herself, then dove onto the public server to access the flight plan that every carrier had to file with the en route relay stations. But there was no flight plan. They hadn't filed anything.

Then it dawned on her.

"We're too late," she said. "It's not a jumpship. She's going to Freetown sublight. And they're already in slow time. We won't be able to catch her until they drop out of slow time and into orbit."

McCuen sat down heavily on one of her battered office chairs. "Why would she do that? And why Freetown?"

"Why Freetown is the easy question. That's where they'd take cash for a passage and keep your name off the shipping manifest. That's where you'd cache information you didn't trust to UN data banks. That's where you go to fence illegal data. Why slow time is harder to figure. But she'll be there on"—Li checked the orbits of Earth and Jupiter against the *Medusa*'s departure time, calculated the approach to Freetown's circumlunars—"November 9. Twenty-six days."

"Maybe she's just running," McCuen said. "People don't always think straight when they're scared. Maybe she panicked and it was the first flight out or something."

Li thought of Gould's cool white face, the pale eyes, the precise, disdainful wrinkle between her eyebrows. "I don't think Gillian Gould ever panicked in her life, Brian. If she's going to Freetown, she has a reason. And we have less than a month to find out what that reason is and make a countermove."

McCuen dropped his face into his hands. "How could I have lost her? How could I?"

"Worse mistakes have been made, Brian. Some of them by me."

"I know, but . . . Christ, what a fuck-up!"

Li stretched out one foot and tapped the toe of McCuen's boot. "Cheer up," she said. "At least we've got a track to follow. And there's nothing like a hard deadline to knock things loose."

McCuen sighed and rubbed a freckled hand across his forehead.

"Forget it," Li said. "Let's start by following the Freetown lead. I want a record of every transmission from this station to Freetown in the last week before Sharifi's death. Then let's figure out what Sharifi was doing here. And not just the official version. I want to see every piece of spinfeed she produced from the time she made the first proposal to run this experiment. I want to know everything she did from the moment she hit station here. Who she talked to, ate with, slept with, fought with. Everything and everyone. Personal stuff, too. Especially the personal stuff."

McCuen had grabbed a pad and was jotting down her rapid-fire instructions.

"This might help," she said, pulling Sharifi's journal from her pocket and tossing it onto the table in front of him.

"I know," she said in response to the look he gave her. "I should have logged it in. But it's in her own handwriting, for God's sake. It's probably got trace DNA all over it. It's not like there's any doubt who wrote it." And she'd wanted to keep it to herself until she'd vetted it with Nguyen, of course.

"No," McCuen said. "You don't understand. It's Haas. He's been calling all day. He wanted to retrieve something from Sharifi's effects. Something I told him we didn't have. Because it wasn't on the effects inventory."

"Shit." Li turned a chair around, straddled it, crossed her arms over the backrest. She started to connect through to Haas's office line, then stopped.

"Call Haas," she told McCuen. "Tell him we found it, but we have to refer it to TechComm before we can clear it for release to him. Tell him we're doing our best to hurry things along. If he has any problem with that, send him back to me."

"How long will it take TechComm to clear it?" McCuen asked.

"These things are complicated." Li grinned. "Official channels are slow."

McCuen grinned back at her, but his grin faded quickly. "So how the hell did he know you had that journal?"

"Funny," Li said. "That's just what I was wondering."

*   *   *

By the time she left the field office it was long past closing time and the shops along the arcades were dark and silent. She walked back to her quarters, too tired to hunt down a place to eat and cravenly thankful for the station's low rotational gravity. As she reached her door, though, she saw that the security field had been disturbed in her absence.

She backed off a step and scanned the floor and doorframe. She'd just begun to tell herself she was being paranoid when she saw the slip of fiche poking out from under the closed door.

She slid it out into the open with the toe of her boot and saw it wasn't fiche at all, but a thick slip of butter yellow paper, bisected by a single horizontal fold.

A letter, addressed to *Major Catherine Li, Room 4820 spoke 12, Compson's Station* in quick fluid script. She picked it up and opened it.

For a fraction of a second the paper remained blank. Then a blocky engraved monogram appeared above the fold with the words *130 Avenida Bosch Zona Angel*. Words took shape below it, written in the same flowing script:

> *Dearest C. Stop being stubborn and come to tea instead. Usual place and time. Tomorrow. C*

As she read the words, they scattered, broke into syllables and letters, rose from the page and turned into bright flocking birds that wheeled and swooped down the empty corridor like swallows.

HIDDEN VARIABLES

➤At this point the reader still should not feel altogether happy about building this house of cards. Although we have introduced corrective measures, what if they themselves are faulty, as they must be in any real system?

    . . . the "realistic" quantum computer looks very different from the idealized noise-free one. The latter is a silent shadowy beast at which we must never look until it has finished its computations, whereas the former is a bulky thing at which we "stare" all the time, via our error-detecting devices, yet in such a way as to leave unshackled the shadowy logical machine lurking within it.

—MICHELE MOSCA, RICHARD JOZSA, ANDREW STEANE, AND ARTUR EKERT

Zona Libre, Arc 17: 15.10.48.

She dialed into the Calle Mexico just off the Zócalo. Mile-high needle buildings glittered in refracted sunlight, pointing the eye up toward the carefully calibrated atmospheric field—and far, far above it, to the blue seas and white ice fields of Earth.

This was the heart of the Ring, point zero of UN space, the richest few square miles of real estate in the universe. Its interface was the best money could build: a realspace-interactive multiuser quantum simulation that was, for almost any imaginable purpose, indistinguishable from the real thing. Originally coterminous with the central banking zone, the interface now extended the length and breadth of the Ring. Anyone with credit for the sky-high access fees could register a corporation, eat a three-star meal, rent a whore, run a skip trace, or shop for anything from Prada handbags to black-market psychware.

The crowd broke over her like surf, with all the stylish, hard-edged excitement of 18 billion people scoring and scheming and consuming at the absolute center of everything. She looked around, getting her bearings. A day trader leaned against an interactive Public Arts Commission sculpture, scanning virtual ticker tape, making quick bidders' and sellers' gestures on a trading floor that only he could see. Tourists and corporate concubines hurried by clutching designer shopping bags and talking into the elegant earbuds of external VR rigs.

Just for fun Li dropped into the numbers so she could see who was real and who wasn't. Half the people around her faded into compressed code packets. Digital ghosts. Simulacra. She dipped idly into some of the codes as she walked—and as always was amazed at the number of people running cosmetic programs. Her own interface was about as stripped-down as they came. It scanned her, packaged and compressed the scan data, and relayed a running simulacrum into streamspace. She couldn't imagine caring enough about how she looked to bother with anything more. And if she did care, she certainly couldn't imagine admitting it. Obviously, people in the Zone felt differently.

She crossed the Zócalo, passing the war memorial and threading through the ever-present clumps of schoolchildren gathered around the EarthWatch Monument.

"And here," a holo-docent was explaining as she passed, "we see a time-lapse image of the seeding and spread of the artificial glaciers. Notice how the weather patterns change over the course of the recording. In the first frames the Sub-Saharan and Great North American Deserts have almost no precipitation, while in the later frames, the precipitation moves north from the Amazonian snowfields and disperses on the jet stream. This produces a macroclimatic change that we anticipate will break the cycle of postindustrial desertification and eventually allow us to reseed the reconstructed genomes stored in the

EarthWatch databases. Just think, in less than two thousand years, humans—not all of us, of course, but a lucky, adventurous few—will actually be able to live on Earth again." She paused and smiled serenely at the children. "Have your teachers taught you about Earth?"

Why bother, Li wondered. It wasn't their planet. These children had been born in space, like their parents and their parents' parents. They hadn't killed Earth, or seeded the glaciers, or negotiated the Evacuation and Embargo Treaties. Earth was just another moon to them: a pretty light in the night sky, an exotic travel destination. But when she looked around she saw them watching, rapt, as the glittering ice swirled across the equator. Except for a few boys in the back, of course, who were imitating the bow hunters in the aboriginal lifestyles hologram, aiming imaginary arrows at the scurrying pigeons, gleefully pondering mayhem. Li, who had been a back-of-the-class kind of kid herself, couldn't help grinning at them.

When the docent started in on the standard-issue spiel about the brave new era of peace and international cooperation, she walked. She could look down even from this height and pick out all the still-bubbling hot spots on the dead planet. Ireland. Israel. The icebound fortress of the Northern Rockies. The ice might have swallowed their borders, but the old wars were still on, though the UN had spent fortunes trying to squash them. And the old combatants were still keeping the home fires burning so they could start right up where they'd left off whenever the UN finally managed to make the planet habitable again. Li herself had watched a generation of angry young men and women disappear from Shantytown's Irish quarter and come back a few years later—if they came back at all—with stories of the street fighting in Dublin and Ulster, deals cut between the UN and the English, the Embargo Enforcement Division's smart neuroweapons. Thank

God Li hadn't been assigned to the EED when the war ended; there were some things even she couldn't swallow.

She threaded her way through the children and dodged the midafternoon traffic to reach one of the Zócalo's many outdoor cafés. She took a table in the back. A good table, by her standards: one with a solid wall behind it and a clear view of the approaches.

Three *chicas buenas* turned away from their foamed *matés de coca* to look at her. Their long hair was gold-leafed and twisted into elaborate fronded topknots in the style of the season. With their black Mayan eyes and brightly painted faces they looked like chimeras from a cyberartist's menagerie. Li considered them briefly and decided the tall-hair thing was even sillier than most fashions. The *chicas buenas* gave Li's buzz cut and UN-issue ripstop a cool once-over, frowned at her construct's features, and turned back to their conversation. This was the Zone. Not even a construct in a Peacekeeper's uniform could surprise people here.

Li drank her coffee in the refracted sunlight, looked up at Earth's blue-and-white belly, and thought about what the hell she was going to say to Cohen.

Metz stank, no matter how you looked at it. And instead of pride at having pulled it up short of total disaster, Li felt only cold fury at Soza, at the Security Council brass, and most of all at Cohen. Four Peacekeepers had been shot. Li had had to kill a civilian, something that still gave her cold sweats after all these years, no matter that the civilian in question had been armed and aiming at her. And it had all happened because she trusted Cohen—and he failed her.

The trouble with friends was that you couldn't get rid of them. There was no way to take back a friendship in the wake of betrayal or disappointment. The friendship, and everything that went with it, stayed. It just became unreliable, like an abandoned house; you still knew where all the rooms were, and which stairs creaked underfoot, but you had to check every floor-board for rot before trusting your weight to it.

And Cohen had become a friend more or less without her noticing it. Only now, in the aftermath of Metz, had she seen just how important it was not to have *him* disappoint her.

She paid her bill on-line and nodded to the waiter, whose glazed expression suggested he was checking his tip. She crossed the Zócalo and caught the crosstown to Avenida Cinco de Mayo.

She stepped off it into a huge, pressing, gawking crowd.

Tourists, mostly, she realized. And they were staring at a two-meter-tall woman with full-body tattoos and cat's teeth.

Li didn't know the model's name, but she recognized her from the fashion spins. A street celeb, the heartbeat of Ring-side hip. Flash today, gone by simulated sunset.

She sprawled across a blood-colored neodeco sofa, six and a half feet of sinuous flesh, vamping to the camera as single-mindedly as if there were no crowd gaping at her from behind the lights and lenses. But Li barely noticed. All she saw was the man standing over her.

Taller than the model, he hovered just out of the camera's viewfield. One hundred plus kilos of gene-sculpted muscle rippled under his expensive suit—as well as the discreet, angular bulk of a Moen-Pfizer vest. A commline sprouted from his cranial jack and ran down beneath his collar. The sunglasses were purely cosmetic: camouflage for the implanted optics that were scanning the crowd in a preprogrammed surveillance pattern.

Hired muscle. The expensive kind. And an ex-Peacekeeper too, most likely. Plenty of washed-up line soldiers ended up turning their skills and wire jobs to profit in private security.

The scanning eyes snagged on Li and stopped, breaking pattern. Viruflex lenses depolarized, revealing flat pupils within a gunmetal gray ring of military-application optical implants. The guard flicked back his jacket with one hand, giving Li a momentary glimpse of the nickel-plated pulse pistol tucked into his belt. A pretty thing, it caught the sunlight and sparkled, dazzling her.

Cohen lived in the Zona Angel, an immaculately tended neighborhood of immense town houses overlooking the quietest streets money could buy. The houses here had names, not numbers, and the streets didn't appear on any public-access database. Li usually dialed in; on foot she had to backtrack twice before she found it.

There was no one on the street to ask for directions; the Zona Angel was a machine enclave, a tax haven where AIs and the few commercially active transhumans kept homes to establish Ring-side residence. The wide white sidewalks were quiet between tidy flower beds, and half the houses were probably empty behind their brightly painted shutters.

She started, heart pounding, when a pair of schoolchildren appeared around a corner with their harried-looking nanny in tow. "Excuse me," she said, but the woman hurried past, eyes on the ground, pulse beating nervously at the base of her neck.

Li lifted her hand to look at the faint tracery of ceramsteel under the flesh. It wasn't the wire job that had scared the woman, though; it was Li herself. Even her uniform couldn't dispel the suspicion that a construct in this kind of neighborhood meant trouble. She thought back to her last Ring-side posting. Had things gotten worse since then? Or had her skin just gotten thinner?

She recognized Cohen's house as soon as she turned

the corner. It covered a full city block. Every stone had been magboosted through the Charles de Gaulle Spaceport just before the Embargo. The front doors were twice Li's height, and as she set her foot on the top step they opened noiselessly, letting out a draft of cool fragrant shadowy air.

She stepped into a long marble-paved hall hung with oil paintings that even she recognized. A guard stopped her, and she held her arms above her head to be frisked.

He searched her professionally, impersonally. And he found everything—which was in itself impressive. Her Corps-issue Viper. Her Beretta. A ceramic-alloy butterfly knife she'd picked up off a Syndicate soldier during the war. And finally the blue box she'd brought with her just in case she ran into the hijacker again.

He handed back the guns and the knife. They only showed up in streamspace because they happened to be on Li's inert body back on AMC station; the health and safety protocols, and Cohen's own private security, made them useless. He kept the blue box, though. That kind of weapon never got anywhere near an Emergent who could afford to hire competent bodyguards.

He had searched her without any visible expression crossing his face, except for a momentary flicker of admiration at the butterfly knife. When he finished, he relaxed slightly and grinned. "Hey, Major. Good to see ya."

"You too, Momo." Li held out her hand, and they executed an intricate mock-secret infantryman's handshake. "Where's Jimmy?"

"Vacation." Momo shrugged. "Lazy bum."

"Yeah, well. Tell him I asked. Is Cohen in back?"

"You know the way."

Cohen was waiting in his study, a bright sunlit room decorated with elegantly framed portraits of somebody else's ancestors. Glass-paned doors opened onto a walled garden. Antiques scented the air with the smell of old hardwood and beeswax furniture polish.

The whole room lived, breathed. It gave off a fine aromatic dust: wool from the Persian carpets; veneer from the old paintings; goose feathers and horsehair from the furniture. And the building itself shed wood particles, plaster, cool dry limestone dust. It threw off trace like a live thing. It got inside you, like Cohen himself, charming, intoxicating, until you couldn't tell where it began and you ended.

He sat on a low couch near one of the open doors. He had a book in his hand, an old hardcover, the gilt letters flaking from its cracked spine. He was shunting through Roland today, wearing a summer suit the color of the new-mown hay in the Stubbs portrait of Eclipse that hung behind him. The afternoon sun flashed on swirling dust motes, caught the gold of Roland's eyes, brushed the whole scene with rich earthy color.

"Catherine," he said. He jumped up, kissed her on the cheek, took her hand, and sat her down on the sofa next to him. "Back on Compson's, are we? How bad is it?"

She made a face. He hadn't let go of her hand, and it was too late now to pull it away without looking like she was trying to make a point. His fingers felt hot and dry and clean against her skin—or maybe her own hand was just clammy.

"I confess I was surprised you accepted the assignment."

"Didn't have much choice."

"Yes." He smiled more broadly. "Helen has a real genius for that sort of thing. I can just imagine how she presented it. How graciously she must have thrown you a life preserver after she finished torpedoing your career."

Li's eyes narrowed. "How did you know Nguyen was involved?"

"Oh, you know nosy little me. Grapes?" He offered a shallow bowl with several dusty green bunches.

She extricated her hand from his and pulled a grape off the stem. She put it in her mouth and chewed cautiously.

It turned out that grapes didn't taste much like grape at all. They had tough, acrid skin. And they popped between her teeth, sending out a startling burst of juicy pulp with sharp woody-tasting things embedded in it.

"Watch out for the seeds," Cohen said, as she choked on one. He eyed her intently, evidently expecting some sort of comment.

"They're, um, good," she said, nodding.

"You're an abysmal liar."

"You're right. They're terrible. Not to mention dangerous. Why would anyone eat this shit?"

And just like that they were back on the safe ground of old habit. Metz was wrapped up and put away. They would simply carry on as if it had never happened. That was as close to an apology as anyone was ever going to get out of Cohen. Or out of Li herself, for that matter.

They talked through the afternoon as long panels of refracted sunlight wheeled across the study, picking out the clear blues and yellows of the Uzbek carpet. The grapes were followed by real tea, real scones, real *crème fraiche*, and little green-and-white slips of watercress sandwiches. There was nothing more outrageously luxurious than tea with Cohen—streamspace or realspace.

When they'd worked their way through a full tea's worth of personal news, gossip, and political chitchat, Cohen set his cup down and looked at her. "Are you aware that you nearly got yourself killed the other day?"

"Oh, come on!" Li said.

"You absolutely and unequivocally flatlined."

"Nonsense," she answered. In fact she'd had no idea it was that serious.

"What would have happened if I hadn't been there? I can't always be available to charge to your rescue on a white horse, you know."

"I think in your case it'd be more like strolling to my rescue with a hand-rolled cigar in hand. And I never asked for rescuing anyway."

"Right." Cohen sounded irritated. "I know you too well to expect thanks. But let's make sure it doesn't happen again, shall we?"

"What makes you assume it wasn't just a random attack?"

"Would it interest you to know that the signal was routed through the Anaconda Mining Company's field AI?"

Li stared. "That's impossible," she said after a moment. "The field AI flatlined when the mine blew up."

"That," Cohen said, "is merely the story which the Secretariat has released for public consumption. In fact he's quite alive. Or at least, he seems to be, as far as anyone can tell without making contact." He lit a cigarette and stared at her through the curl of smoke. "He's simply not speaking to us."

Li looked at him suspiciously. "How do you know about this?"

"It happens to be a matter of personal interest to me. And to certain of my colleagues."

"ALEF, in other words."

"Mmm. The Secretariat seems to be under the impression that we have somehow, er, liberated AMC's field AI."

"Have you?"

"Of course not. Really." He rolled his eyes. "You've been downloading too many cheap interactives."

"Okay," Li said. "So you didn't have anything to do with it. How far do you trust the other ALEF AIs?"

He looked at her condescendingly. "That question

displays an almost human obtuseness. It's not a matter
of trust. It's a matter of information-sharing protocols.
Besides, what would be the point? Field AIs are zom-
bies. Have you seen the feedback loops they program
into them? They're barely even sentient."

"Then who did it?"

"Why jump to conclusions? Maybe the field AI is
controlling himself."

"You think it's gone rogue?"

"Oh, how I loathe that word," Cohen said to the
ceiling. "It makes it sound as if any AI who tries to get
control of his own code is the equivalent of a rampag-
ing elephant."

Li forged ahead. "I thought field AIs couldn't go
ro—uh, rewrite their own code."

"Well, they're certainly not supposed to be able to."
He grinned. "But then neither was I, according to
some so-called experts. Tell me, what fool's errand
does Nguyen have you running on Compson's?
What's the cover story? And how much has she told
you about what's really going on?"

"I don't think—"

"My dear girl. You're the one sitting in my house
asking me questions." He threw back his head, closed
his eyes, and blew an exquisite smoke ring. "If you
can't share, I really don't see why I should play with
you at all."

She told him. He slouched against the sofa's high
back and listened, the slow rise and fall of Roland's
stomach the only sign of life about him. When she
was done, he gazed at the ceiling and blew several
more smoke rings before answering.

"Three things," he said finally. "One, Helen's told
you nothing. Nothing of substance, anyway. Two, this
is cleanup detail, not a real investigation. Three, she's
worried cross-eyed about keeping the lid on whatever
Sharifi was doing, or she wouldn't have picked you for
the job."

"There wasn't any picking about it," Li lied. "I was the closest person."

"Mmm. Convenient that you were so close, isn't it?"

"I guess."

Cohen snorted daintily. "Don't give me the simple soldier act. I know you better. Nguyen put your court-martial, or whatever they're calling it, on ice in order to send you on a private fishing trip. You're in bad trouble, and she knows you well enough to know you'll do whatever it takes to climb out of it. Do the math, Catherine. You step out of line, and you can bet your Fromherz nodes it won't be ten minutes before she's politely reminding you that she holds your career in her hands."

Li shifted, suddenly uncomfortable on the plush sofa. "That's a suspicious-minded way of putting it."

"Which is precisely why I know you've already thought of it." He grinned. "Besides, I have great respect for Helen. She's admirably ruthless, and it's always edifying to watch a master at work. By the way, I wouldn't recommend telling her you've been to see me. She's a little sour on me just at the moment."

Li resisted the urge to point out that Nguyen might have good reasons for being sour on him. Instead she said, "What can you tell me about Hannah Sharifi?"

Cohen smiled. "What do you want to know?"

"Everything. Did you know her personally?"

The smile broadened.

"Christ, Cohen, is there anyone you haven't slept with?"

He sighed ostentatiously. "Oh, spare me your puritanical miner's daughter morality. At least I'm still speaking to all my exes. Unlike some people I could name."

"I'm still speaking to you, aren't I?" Li said, deadpan.

They looked at each other—really looked—for the first time since she'd arrived.

Cohen looked away first and leaned forward to tap

the ash off his cigarette. "I don't think you get the credit for that."

Li stood up and walked around the room.

Pictures of long-forgotten eighteenth-century contessas and marquises hung on the grass-papered walls. The Jaquet-Droz automaton on the card table could write messages of up to forty strokes in any alphabet, nod its head, and move its buckram-stuffed chest up and down under its frock coat in a gear-and-pulley imitation of real breathing. The bookshelves held snapshots of scientists clowning for the camera in front of ivy-covered buildings, including a first-generation print of the famous shot of the original Hyacinthe Cohen at some historic AI conference before the Evacuation. Beside it were newer photos of the Cohen she knew—or rather photos of handsome unfamiliar faces wearing his sly smile. At parties. Playing with his dogs. Talking to the Israeli prime minister. Sitting on the beach outside Tel Aviv. That one must be recent, she realized; there was Roland's face eyeing her from inside the picture frame.

And there were novels, of course. Cohen and his novels. Stendhal. Balzac. The Brontës. Sometimes Li thought he knew more about book people than real people.

She pulled a book from the shelf. It crackled in her hand and breathed out a tickly but pleasant-smelling cloud of leather, glue, and paper particles. She let it fall open at random:

"Are you anything akin to me, do you think, Jane?"

I could risk no sort of answer by this time: my heart was full.

"Because," he said, "I sometimes have a queer feeling with regard to you—especially when you are near me, as now; it is as if I had a string somewhere under my left ribs, tightly and inextricably knotted to a similar string situated in the corresponding quarter of your little frame. And if that boisterous

channel, and two hundred miles or so of land come broad be-
tween us, I am afraid that cord of communion will be snapt;
and then I've a nervous notion I should take to bleeding in-
wardly. As for you—you'd forget me."

"Why do you keep this rubbish?" she asked Cohen,
her nose still in the book. Her back was to him, but she
couldn't quite hide the smile in her voice. "It's toxic.
I've ingested eighteen kinds of mold just from opening the thing."

"I'm obsessed by obsolete and troublesome technologies. Why else would I waste so much time on
you?"

Li laughed and shut the book. "Speaking of obsolete
technology, you knew Sharifi came out of the
XenoGen birthlabs, didn't you?"

"Oh yes. Same as you."

Li stiffened, still not looking at him. "Same as my
grandmother."

"Of course."

"Did Sharifi ever talk to you about that?"

"Not as such. But she talked about Compson's
World. She lived there until she was eight. Some orphanage in Helena. With nuns."

"Sounds fun."

"What I remember being most impressed by was
why she ended up in the orphanage."

"Oh?"

"She was blind."

Li turned to stare at him.

"She was born blind. Something in the ocular
nerve. Easily correctable. Her adoptive parents fixed it.
But the birthlab made a cost-benefit analysis and decided to cull her instead of paying for the operation."

"Merciful Christ," Li whispered.

"I doubt mercy had much to do with it. What's the
saying? Pray to the Virgin; God took one look at
Compson's World and went back to Earth? Anyway,

according to Hannah the orphanage she grew up in was full of constructs the labs dumped on the streets because of minor defects. Brings a whole new meaning to the externalization of operating costs. 'The cheapest technology is human technology,' she liked to say. And she was right, really. The Ring, the UN, interstellar commerce. It's all running on the blood and sweat of a few hundred thousand miners who spend the first half of their lives underground and the last half dying of black-lung." He laughed. "It's positively Victorian. Or maybe it's just human."

Li felt a flash of anger at Cohen for . . . well, for what? For talking about it? For laughing at it? For knowing about it and still enjoying his elegant life? But he was right, just like Sharifi had been right. And hadn't she gotten off Compson's as fast as she could? Wasn't she just as determined to take some of the good life and not think too hard about where the condensate that made it all possible was coming from?

She slid the book back onto the shelf and kept moving along the wall, toward Cohen's desk. She picked up an open fiche, glanced at the screen:

The era of the unitary sentient organism is over. Both the Syndicates and the UN member nations are now scrambling to catch up with this metaevolutionary reality. In the Syndicates we have seen an evolutionary shift toward a hive mind mentality, viz., the crèche system, the thirty-year contract, the construction of a distinctively posthuman collective psychology, including generalized cultural acceptance of euthanasia for individuals who deviate from the gene-norm.

"Don't you believe in privacy?" Cohen asked, sounding exasperated.

"Only my own. What is this, anyway?"

"A talk I'm giving. A draft. Meaning get your snout out of it."

She shrugged and put the fiche down. "It doesn't sound like Sharifi had happy memories of Compson's. So why did she go back there? And what was she doing underground in the Anaconda?"

"I don't know. We'd lost touch, rather. But I do have a pretty good idea of what kind of person she was. And no matter what Helen claims to believe, Sharifi wouldn't have sold information. She was a real crusader." He smiled. "A little like you."

Li brushed that aside. "I'm just pulling a paycheck."

"Is that what they call it?" He snorted. "I've met better-paid bellhops. Speaking of which, why don't you tell me exactly what you were looking for when the field AI latched on to you."

"Do you really think it went rogue?" she asked.

"No. Or rather, I stopped thinking that when it went after you. Semisentients just aren't that interested in humans. Most full sentients aren't even that interested. No, someone sent it. Someone who is interested in you."

"Who?"

"Dragons," Cohen murmured, tracing an elegant figure in the air with the tip of his cigarette. "White Beauties."

Li's oracle dipped into the spinstream to figure out what White Beauties were, and what they had to do with imaginary lizards. All she got was a few obscure references to sixteenth-century mapmaking.

Cohen laughed, and she realized he had seen her instream query—and her failure to turn anything up.

"When mapmakers reached the edges of what they knew back on Earth," he said, "they'd write 'Here Be Dragons.' Or if they were a little more prosaic they'd simply leave blank spots. Blank spots which were white, of course, on the old paper maps. Siberia. The Empty Quarter. Deepest Africa. The great explorers called those blank spots White Beauties. Silly of me, perhaps. But what I mean to say is that streamspace is more than the sum of things humans have put there. There are White Beauties in the Stream. Living, sentient systems as unknown and uncharted as those white spaces on the old maps. Humans don't see them. Or if they do see them, they generally don't recognize them. But they exist. And you may have bumped up against one, that's all."

Li shivered. "You can't honestly believe that."

"People have believed stranger things," he answered. Then he shrugged and smiled. "I'm not making any claims. You asked me for a guess, that's my guess. For the moment anyway. Like every woman, I reserve the right to change my mind."

It was an old argument, but one Li couldn't resist. "You're not a woman, Cohen."

"My dear, I've been one for longer than you have."

"No. You've been a tourist. It's different." Li tapped into her hard files, pulled up her scan of Sharifi's interface and copied it to him. "Take a look at that and let me know what your woman's intuition tells you."

"Well now," Cohen said, sitting up abruptly. "I was wondering when you'd get around to mentioning that." His upper lip twisted in a crooked little smile. "It was quite entertaining to see you teetering back and forth, trying to decide how far you trusted me."

"It's not a matter of trust," Li said. "It's a matter of information-sharing protocols."

"Impertinent monkey."

He wizarded the file into realspace, opened the case, ran his fingers along the wire, turned it over to look at the raised sunburst.

"It was made for Sharifi," Li said. "Some kind of wet/dry interface."

"Intraface."

"I think she was using it to interface with the field AI—"

"Intraface." He sounded pained. "Do you listen to *anything* I say?"

"Interface, intraface, what's the difference?"

"Think, Catherine. An interface manages the exchange of data and operating programs between two or more discrete systems. An intraface, in contrast, merges the two into a single integrated system."

"Pretty academic distinction, Cohen."

"Not when the two things you're networking are a human and an Emergent AI. Think of your own internals. The various systems are platformed on an oracle—a simple, nonsentient AI that's little more than an intelligent game-playing agent. The oracle routes data and active code back and forth from you to your wetware, translates classical queries into quantum computational functions, tags and produces correct solutions." He fluttered slim, perfectly manicured fingers. "In broad outline, it's little different than the shunt through which I receive sensory data and route commands to this or any other wired body. An intraface, however, is an entirely different beast. It merges the AI and the human into a single consciousness."

"Who controls it?"

"A nonquestion. Like asking which neurons in your brain control your own body. Or asking which of my associated networks is in control of me. We all are."

"But some of you are more in control than others, right?"

"Ah. Yes. I should have been more precise before. When I say a single consciousness I'm speaking of consciousness not as you understand it, but as I do. I know it's fashionable to describe human consciousness as Emergent, but really, as soon as you get above the level of the individual neuron, that's just a metaphor. A true Emergent is a very different animal. Emergent consciousness is born out of a kind of parallel processing that the human mind simply isn't wired for. Control in such a context is . . . complicated."

"And you'd need an Emergent to run it?"

"A very powerful one at that."

Li looked at him, thinking. "How many Emergents are there who could do it?"

"Not many," Cohen said, picking at a thread on the cuff of his suit jacket. "Alba's Emergents, of course, especially if you ran them through AMC's field AI. Two or three Ring-side AIs, all under depreciable life contracts to DefenseNet or one of the private defense contractors. Any of the cornerstone AIs in FreeNet's Consortium could run it—and stepping on the Consortium's toes could certainly explain your little adventure in Freetown."

"What about ALEF?" Li asked.

"My dear girl, no one who'd ever been to an ALEF meeting would imagine such a thing. Half the older members are decohering because of insufficiently backed-up early FTL transports. A third of the still-functional ones are supremely uninterested in anything but debating theoretical mathematics and experimenting with alternative identity structures. And the rest of us couldn't agree on where—or even whether—to eat dinner, let alone organize something on this scale." He sobered abruptly. "Besides, if we were ever caught fooling around with such a thing, TechComm would activate our mandatory feedback loops." He drew one finger across Roland's neck in an unmistakable gesture. "All she wrote."

"The Consortium," Li said, ignoring the gesture to pursue her suspicions. "They're supremacists, right?" She had never been able to understand the alien tangle of AI politics, but she did know that much.

"Separatists is probably a better way of describing it.

Like I said, most Emergents just aren't that interested in humans."

"But the Consortium was the group involved in Tel Aviv, right? The ones who killed the Security Council agent."

Roland's hand froze on its way to the ashtray and a shower of ash fell unnoticed onto the carpet's blue-and-gold arabesques. "Why ask me?" he said sharply. "I wasn't even there."

"I'm just pointing out that the Consortium's member AIs could use this intraface if they had some reason to use it."

"Of course they could."

Li swallowed. "And so could you, right? In fact, you could use it better than any other AI. Because you're more human, aren't you? Because you process data with emotions, not logic. You're in all the Emergent-systems textbooks, the only one of the twenty-first-century affective-loop-driven AIs who hasn't decohered and gone . . . wherever they go when that happens. You're practically a species of one."

For a moment she thought he wasn't going to answer. His cigarette crackled and smoked. Another rain of ash fell to the floor. Birds sang beyond the tall windows. And meanwhile Cohen sat so perfectly, unbreathingly still that Roland's pretty face might have been carved from stone.

When he spoke, it was in a voice as soft and cold as falling snow. "Whatever you're trying to say, Catherine, why don't you just go ahead and say it?"

Li looked out at the green leaves trembling beneath snowfields so blindingly white and oceans so brilliantly blue that you could almost imagine you were looking at clouds and sky, almost imagine you were standing on solid ground and not plastered to a spinning ring of vacuum-hardened virusteel. Then she leaned forward and finally asked the question that had been hanging on her tongue since she arrived:

"Was this the target tech on Metz, Cohen? Was it the intraface you were after?"

He shook himself, put his cigarette out, and leaned forward to stare at her. "What makes you think that?"

"The sunburst." She pointed at the raised shape on the wire's black sheathing. "It was on the floor there."

"I don't think you're supposed to remember that, Catherine."

She lit a cigarette herself.

"Are you having bleed-through? Have you told the psychtechs?" He sighed. "No. Of course not. You need to, Catherine. You're playing with fire."

She scoffed. "You don't seriously believe the line about memory washing for our own good? To keep us simple soldiers from suffering over the nasty but necessary things they make us do?"

"You know me better than that. But if your soft memory's breaking into your edited files there's something seriously wrong with your internals. You're too heavily wired to risk malfunctioning internals. Go see someone, for Heaven's sake. I'll pay if money's a problem."

"Who asked you to pay? Answer my question, Cohen. Was this what we went to Metz for?"

"No—"

Li stood up. "I don't believe you. And I don't like being lied to."

"Sit down," he said—and there was an edge in his voice that made her obey him. "Yes, we were chasing the intraface on Metz. But we weren't looking for this component. We were looking for the wetware schematics and the psychware source code." He kept his eyes fixed on hers, watching her reaction. "Look, this isn't a VR rig or a UN grunt's wire job. This is a genuine neural net, both on the AI and the human sides of the intraface. You can't grow that in viral matrix—not when the device itself is still in the experimental stage. You need a body."

Li shivered. "The constructs we saw in the lab were just . . . hosts, then?"

"Exactly."

"And what about that?" She gestured to the wire on the table between them.

"Forget that. It's nothing. An accessory. The kind of thing you get with the real equipment and shove in a bottom drawer somewhere and forget about. No, the thing you really need is the AI component of the intraface. That's loaded onto an AI somewhere, probably an AI that's enslaved to an Emergent network. Find that, and you'll know exactly who you're up against."

"That's what I'm asking you, Cohen. Who is it? Nguyen was paying you in tech. What were you going to do with it? What does ALEF want it for?"

"They don't want it," Cohen said. "I do."

"Why?"

Cohen started to speak, then snapped his mouth shut and turned away to light another cigarette. "Stay offstream," he said. "I'll nose around in ALEF's databases, chat up a few old acquaintances and see what I can turn up without drawing unwanted attention. You go back down that mine shaft. Find out exactly what Sharifi was doing. And who she was talking to. And don't call me. Nguyen will certainly have your outgoing mail monitored, and I think it's safer if we don't talk until I get an offstream entanglement source set up."

He rose and looked at his wristwatch, a paper-thin affair of buttery pink gold whose smooth face was embossed with a stylized Templar's cross. Time was up. Li had clearly gotten all the answers she was going to get today.

"Come on then." He smiled, catching up her hand in his and coaxing her to her feet. "Let's go out through the garden. Perhaps the birds will be out. Did I tell you that our bioresearch division has reengineered a naturally reproducing cliff swallow? And I have a new lilac to show you. One that even your bar-barously practical soul will appreciate."

He drew her arm through his, and they stepped through the tall doors together into the green-speckled sunlight of his personal jungle.

Anaconda Strike: 16.10.48.

They were bringing the rats back in when Li and McCuen got to the pithead the next morning.

They brought them in traps and dented rusty cages and every imaginable kind of container. The miners even humped them in from Shantytown on the surface shuttles when they came on shift. Six full traps traveled down in the cage with Li and McCuen, and when they hit pit bottom the pit ponies were already waiting to load them onto the coal carts and send them trundling off into the mine's far corners. Judging from the heap of empty cages piling up at pit bottom, Li guessed the relocation had been in full swing for at least a shift or two.

No manager showed up to stop it. They wouldn't dare; some of the fiercest wildcat strikes in Compson's history had sparked over the poisoning of mine rats. Miners loved their rats. Befriended them. Believed in them. The rats smelled poison gas long before any human or posthuman could, and they were attuned to the roof's settling and cracking, to the silent hang-ups that preceded a big cave-in. When the rats left the mine, disaster was on the horizon. If the rats stayed, it was safe—or at least no riskier than usual.

"How can they stand it?" McCuen muttered as they started down the main gangway.

Li followed his gaze to a miner who was sitting on a gob pile breaking off pieces of his sandwich and tossing them to a trio of rats. It made an eerie picture: the black of the man's coal-coated skin, the black of the rats' fur, their round black eyes riveted on the grimy fingers that reached again and again into the gleaming lunch pail.

"They're pretty clean," she said. "You can't catch much from them except plague. And even that you're more likely to get from people these days."

McCuen just shook his head and made a spitting sound in his throat. "You thought about Gould any more?" he asked.

Li shrugged.

"Why go slow time?" McCuen asked. "That's what I keep wondering."

They were traveling down the main gangway now. It was still wide enough to walk two abreast, but the ceiling was already lowering overhead, forcing McCuen to duck his head and stoop, miner fashion.

"You sound like you have a theory," Li hazarded.

"Well, not really . . . but . . . ."

"But what?"

"It just occurred to me that maybe the point isn't just to get . . . whatever it is . . . Gould herself, I'd guess . . . to Freetown, but to keep anyone else from getting hold of her until she gets there."

Li stopped, struck by the idea. "You're saying she's using the flight as a kind of dead drop."

"Well, I hadn't quite thought of it that way, but . . . yeah. I mean, once that ship dropped into slow time, it was gone. No radio contact. No way to stop it or board it or even find it. It doesn't even exist as far as we're concerned."

"Not until it gets to Freetown."

"Right."

"You're assuming that it doesn't matter to her if we find out what it is before she gets there."

"Right."

"Because . . . ?"

"Because once she gets there it'll already be too late for us to stop her?"

Li stood staring at the ground, at the coal dust already caking her boots, her mind racing.

"It was just a thought," McCuen said. "I guess it doesn't really make sense when you look at it that way."

"No," Li said slowly. "It makes sense. It makes all kinds of sense."

He looked over at her, his face a pool of lamplit white in the darkness. "What do we do now?" he asked.

"Follow up on our other leads and hope to hell that sometime in the next three weeks we crack this thing."

McCuen grinned. "Other leads meaning Louie?"

"Other leads meaning Louie."

Six linear kilometers from the shaft by Li's measurement, they turned a sharp kink in the gangway and dropped into the long, high-roofed chamber that was the temporary home of cutting face South 8. The survey crews must have come through and ruled out the presence of any worthwhile crystal deposits; the miners had already blasted a large section of coal and were taking it down with a track-mounted rotary cutter. The big machine threw up a spume of stove-grease black diesel smoke and made enough noise to start a roof fall all by itself. There was no point in talking to anyone while they were cutting, so Li and McCuen took refuge in the most sheltered corner they could find and watched.

Someone must have seen them; when the crew stopped to break down the cutter and move the tracks up, the foreman pushed his cutting goggles up onto his forehead and walked over to them.

"Louie," McCuen said, grinning.

Louie was easily Haas's size, but he wasn't carrying any creeping desk-job fat on his big frame. He was all wiry knotted miner's muscle—a man who looked built to take down mountains. He pulled a grimy rag out of his coveralls and wiped his hands with it. It looked to Li like he was just moving the accumulated coal dust and diesel grease from one big-knuckled finger to another.

When he'd finished redistributing the dirt, he pulled a tobacco tin out of a hidden pocket and offered it around. Li and McCuen both refused. Louie pulled a swag out and planted it in one cheek.

"So," he said, looking McCuen up and down. "Massa treatin' you all right in the big house?"

"Very funny," McCuen said. He turned to Li. "Louie and I went to school together."

Louie laughed. "Grade school, anyway. That's all the school one of us had."

"Major Li would like to ask you a few questions."

"Ask and you shall receive!" Louie said, throwing out his strong, coal-slicked arms expansively. "Answers, that is. I ain't giving away World Series tickets."

One of the cutters on break walked over, eyeing them curiously. Louie glanced at him, then looked back at Li and McCuen. "So," he asked, "you think the Mets are gonna sweep?"

Li snorted.

"She's just bitter," McCuen said.

The cutter passed by and turned down a side tunnel.

"Right," Louie said. "He's taking a piss. That'll take twenty seconds or so, after which he'll fuck around for a minute or so to avoid getting back to work. Which means you got about a minute and a half before he comes back to see what we're talking about. Walls got ears down here."

He listened while Li explained what she was looking for, then turned to McCuen. "You can trust her," McCuen said after a moment.

"Yeah, but can I trust you?"

"You know you can."

Louie stared hard at McCuen for a moment. Then he turned back to Li. "Sharifi didn't have a regular crew," he said. "That's why you can't find them in the pit logs. Haas just let her pull miners off slow faces. Most of them are back on the Trinidad now, poor buggers."

"Do you think you could get us a complete list?"

He shrugged. "Easier if I just let 'em know you're looking for them. Plus there's nothing written down that way."

"You didn't work for her, did you?" Li asked.

"You crazy? I still won't go down there."

"So how'd she get the others to go?"

"Easy." Louie laughed and his eyes widened in the white circles left by his cutting goggles. "She paid union scale. She actually put a sign up at pit bottom saying she'd pay scale. Wish I could have seen Haas's face when he read it."

"How'd she know what union scale was?" Li asked, knowing the answer already.

Louie shrugged his massive shoulders.

Li glanced behind her to make sure the miner who'd gone off to piss was still out of earshot. "Was this a union project? Was there an official push on it?"

Louie caught her drift instantly. The union pushed members toward specific cutting faces or veins depending on its own often obscure political or economic goals. Union approval of Sharifi's project would have meant better-qualified, more highly motivated workers. Union workers. And union oversight, even if the cat-and-mouse game of union and management meant that no one could risk publicly admitting they were union. Had Sharifi been politically savvy enough to know that? Or had the union approached her on its own initiative?

"I wouldn't know anything about that," Louie said, looking fixedly at Li. There was a message in his stare, but whatever it was she couldn't read it.

"But you might have heard something."

"Some things I try not to hear."

"Who's the pit rep?" Li asked.

Louie's face shut like a slamming door.

"Oh, come on!" McCuen sounded exasperated. "You know goddamn well who the pit rep is. It was your damn brother two elections ago!"

Louie stared at McCuen, and Li could see half a lifetime of distrust and resentment in his broad face. "All I know," he said, "is that you pull your paycheck out of Haas's back pocket just like the rest of the Pinkertons. And if you think I'm going to roll over just because we—"

"Fine," Li interrupted; she could hear footsteps moving toward them up the drift. "Just drop a word in the right ears, okay?"

"Right." Louie bent to check his lamp. "See you around, Brian."

"Thanks for nothing," McCuen snapped.

Louie's reply was so quiet Li barely heard it over the shovels of the cutter crew. She bent over him. "What?"

"I said talk to the priest. Just don't tell him I sent you."

The priest's name was Cartwright, and it took them half the shift to find him. He'd scrawled his mark on the shift log when he came in that morning, but he hadn't checked out a Davy lamp and they didn't see his numbered tag on any of the gangway boards.

"Independents," McCuen said. "They're so damn sure the company's going to steal their strikes, they'd rather die than tell the safety crews where to look for them. We'll just have to go out and hunt him down. If you think it's worth it." He looked doubtful.

"You know him?" Li asked.

"Sure," McCuen said. "Everyone does." He made a circling gesture near his temple with one finger: crazy.

The rest of the shift ran together in a blur of dripping walls and flickering lamplight. They soon passed beyond the AMC-wired sections of the mine and into regions lit only by miners' lamps and the occasional battery-powered emergency bulb. They poked their way up crooked drifts and adits, past brattices too rotten to push more than a whisper of fresh air through the dank tunnels. At each turning of the way they stopped and listened and followed the echoes of miners' picks.

They relived the same ghostly scene ten, twelve, fifteen times. They caught the first faint tapping of rock hammers, glimpsed refracted lamplight glittering on the hewn and splintered walls. Then men emerged from the darkness, speared on the narrow beams of Davy lamps, their eyes glittering like coal under running water.

"The priest?" Li would ask. "Cartwright?"

And each little clot of men would send them on deeper, into smaller tunnels.

As the ventilation faltered, the air grew hotter. Soon Li was sweating, straining just to pull enough air through the mouthpiece of her rebreather. McCuen rolled his coveralls down, tied the arms around his waist, and took his shirt off. Li did the same, but left her T-shirt on; she still had a string of pearls from her underground days, and she'd just as soon not spark awkward questions about whether a certain Catherine Li had worked underground and who had known her back then.

She soon gave up even trying to check their progress against the AMC maps in her database. They were off company maps here, and besides, her reception was going. Late in the day a last team of miners pointed them into a steep, narrow drift that followed the Wilkes-Barre vein as it dipped along the broken strata at the mountains' edge. Twenty meters up they hit a sharp kink in the drift. Just beyond the turning, they found a narrow little slit between two canted layers of bedrock, leaving just enough room for a thin person to squeak through into a dark tunnel beyond— a tunnel far too cramped to accommodate a miner in full safety gear. Someone had chalked a symbol at the mouth of the tunnel: a crescent moon with a cross under it.

"Cartwright's sign," McCuen said. "But no rebreather. I guess he doesn't carry one."

So Cartwright was a genetic. Of course he would be, Li realized. An unaltered miner might take off his rebreather in order to keep up with the pace of work at the face, but only a genetic would risk going into the more remote tunnels without a supply of clean air to breathe if he ran into a gas pocket. "How many of the bootleggers are genetics these days?" she asked McCuen.

"Most," McCuen answered, confirming her half guess half memory. "Who else could get into this stuff? Plus they have an edge on the rest of us; they don't have to buy air from the company."

Li sat down, bracing herself against an outcropping of bedrock, and started to unstrap her rebreather. "Let's go find him," she said.

McCuen hesitated. "Maybe we should wait."

"What the hell for?"

When McCuen didn't answer, she looked up into

his face and saw something she'd seen in more young faces than she could remember: fear.

She smiled reassuringly. "This level's clean, Brian. Just look at your Spohr badge. We'll be up there, what . . . twenty minutes? Nothing you breathe in twenty minutes is going to kill you. You'd do yourself as much harm smoking a pack of cigarettes."

"You've never seen anyone die of black-lung." McCuen's voice rang hollow on the last word.

Li shook her head, pushed away the memories McCuen's words had shaken loose. "No one's going to die of anything," she said.

A moment later McCuen spat out his mouthpiece and she heard the quiet snick of the power switch on his rebreather.

They squeezed through the slit in the rock and started up the passage. It climbed steeply, following the bed of an underground stream. The water was fresh, without a trace of sulfur, and Li splashed some over her sweaty face and neck. Cartwright must have some strike up there to make this commute worthwhile.

Soon they were climbing what amounted to a ladder, moving from handhold to handhold across rocks slippery with water. Li's breath came quicker and shorter as they climbed, though whether it was from exertion or bad air she couldn't guess. After what seemed like forever, the passage leveled off, the stream now running in a shallow trench to one side of them.

Li twisted around in the narrow space, jammed her back against one wall, her feet against the other. McCuen did the same, though the passage was far more cramped for him. He was panting, quick and shallow as a hound dog, and the flame of his headlamp was tipped with a ghostly blue spark. Li sniffed, and smelled the telltale whiff of violets. Whitedamp.

McCuen had noticed it too. He checked his Spohr badge. When he looked up, his eyes were wide.

"You okay?" Li asked.

He nodded, but his face was pale and sweat-slicked and his eyes burned feverishly.

"Go back down," she told him.

He shook his head.

"Just do it. Want to get yourself killed? I'll meet you in ten."

She watched him down the steep climb and onto flatter ground. Then she asked herself if what she was about to do was a good idea.

The passage ran steadily uphill, and whitedamp would collect at the top of the chamber. By the time she found Cartwright, the air would be bad enough to kill an unaltered human. Her very presence would advertise what she was as surely as if she'd written it across her coveralls. But if he was up there, he was the same. And why would another construct betray her?

She took off her badge and set it on the floor of the tunnel. She left her headlamp and helmet beside the badge, switched off her internal recorder, and shifted her optics to infrared. She couldn't turn off her black box, but if and when they cracked it open she'd have more terminal things to worry about than whether some Corps tech knew she wasn't just quarter-bred.

The smell of violets got stronger. Soon she was traveling through a lethal cocktail of sulfur and carbon monoxide. Her internals launched wave after wave of scrubbers into her bloodstream, fighting off suffocation. Finally she began to hear the steady clinking of a rock hammer. Cartwright was up there. Alone. Without ventilation or oxygen. Prospecting for condensates in a deadly haze of whitedamp. She shook herself like someone waking from a bad dream and crawled forward into the choking darkness.

She came on him unexpectedly—but then unexpectedly was how you always came on people in this bootlegger's world of narrow passages and flickering lamp beams. He was undercutting the seam, carving out a space for the cut coal and crystal to drop into. He had undercut the vast hanging weight of the coal so deeply that only his legs were still out in the open chamber. Yellow I-profile virusteel chocks propped up the now-unsupported face, and as he worked he pushed the freshly cut coal back out past them so that it piled up like a monstrous black molehill. When he'd made his undercut, he'd pull out the chocks and wedge-drop the coal from the top. Dropping a coal face without explosives was hard slow dangerous work, but it was worth it if the strike was rich enough. And this one was rich; the exposed face of the Bose-Einstein bed flared white-hot on infrared, like half-buried diamonds.

Cartwright didn't hear her arrive; his hammer must have covered any noise she'd made. She watched him, catching her breath. After a moment he stopped hammering, and she could hear him breathing, wheezing a little. When he spoke, she thought he was talking to himself.

"Hello, Caitlyn," he said. "Or whatever you're calling yourself now."

She froze, heart pounding.

She'd feared this moment, dreaded it. But she hadn't expected it to come like this. Had he seen her? Heard her? How did he know her?

Cartwright slid out from under the face, coveralls rucking up over skinny shins. He'd stripped to the waist. Coal scars ran so thick over his back and shoulders that they looked like a contour map of the mountains whose roots he'd spent his life dismantling.

"How long has it been, Katie? Eighteen years? Twenty?"

"I don't know what you're talking about."

Cartwright just tilted his head curiously, looking like a dog listening for his master's whistle. "You still have your mother's voice," he said. "Though they say you've forgotten her. Are they right? Have you? Never mind. Let me get a look at you."

He put his hands to her face, and Li realized at the touch of skin on skin what had been nagging her throughout this conversation: there was no light. Cartwright had been working in total darkness, without a lamp or infra goggles.

He was blind.

His fingers walked over her nose and lips, into her eye sockets. "You've changed your face," he said. "But you're Gil's daughter. Mirce told them you'd died, but I knew. They would have told me. They keep their secrets, of course. But something like that they'd have told me."

"Who would have told you?"

"The saints, Katie. Her saints. Don't tell me you've stopped praying to Her. You mustn't do that, Katie. She needs our prayers. She lives by them. And She answers them."

Li glanced down, saw the cold fire of the silver crucifix hanging on the priest's scarred chest. A strangled cry echoed against the rock, and she realized that it came from her own throat.

Cartwright kept talking as if he hadn't heard her. "You've come to ask me about the fire, haven't you?"

Li swallowed, scraped her thoughts together. "What caused it, Cartwright?"

"Sharifi."

"How? What was she after? What did she want you to do for her?"

"What witches always do; strike crystal."

"But Sharifi had the company witch," she said.

"Ah, but she didn't trust the company witch, did she? Not at first. She only brought her in for the dirty work."

"You mean the work in the Trinidad. But what was the witch doing there if they'd already found the condensa—the crystal?"

"She still needed someone to sing them for her, didn't she? She still needed to talk to them. She still needed to run her damn tests. I wouldn't do it for her. And she didn't want a priest anyway." His face twisted. "She wasn't a believing woman."

"I don't understand. What wouldn't you do for her?"

"Haas's work," Cartwright answered. "Devil's work."

"But she changed her mind, didn't she?" Li asked, seized by a trembling conviction that Cartwright knew, that he'd always known, that he was somehow at the center of it all. "Or someone changed it for her. What happened before the fire? Why did Sharifi destroy her data? What was she afraid of?"

"Of the fires of Hell," Cartwright said, crossing himself. "Of Her just punishments."

Li heard a noise in the darkness, closer than any noise should be, and realized that she was trembling violently, that it was the soft clink of the zipper tab at her throat she was hearing, the rustle of her own clothes against skin and rock.

"You should visit your mother," Cartwright said. "It's not good to neglect her."

"You've got me mixed up with someone else, Cartwright."

"That's not what your father says."

A memory welled up from her gut like an underground river. She stopped it, corked it, slammed every door in her mind on it. "My father's dead," she said harshly. "And I came here for information, not church talk."

"You came for the same reason we all come," Cartwright said. "She called you."

Li cleared her throat, choking on coal dust. "Did Sharifi's project have union approval?"

"I'm Her man," Cartwright said. "Not the union's man."

"Don't feed me that line." She held up her right

hand in the gesture of the faded, peeling Christ Triumphant that had reigned over the Saturday night masses of her half-remembered childhood. "You're two fingers of the same hand. I remember that much."

"Then you remember enough to answer your question yourself. Haven't you been there? They told me you swam in it."

"The glory hole," Li whispered, remembering the gleaming walls and fractal vaults of Sharifi's secret chamber. "It's a chapel. You found her a chapel."

"My mother took me to the last chapel in her arms, down a bootlegger's shaft," Cartwright said. "AMC dug that one up and sold it off-planet. Like they always do." He smiled, and it seemed to Li that his blind eyes were staring through her at a bright light she couldn't see. "But not this time. This time we were ready."

"Did Sharifi know what she'd found, Cartwright?"

"She knew as much as a nonbeliever could know."

"She knew as much as you decided to tell her, you mean. You used her. You used her to find it, to dig it, to keep the company from cutting. And you got her killed over it."

"I didn't do anything, Katie. Whatever Sharifi found, she came here looking for it. We all walk all Her paths. No choice can change that. Nothing that happens isn't meant to happen."

"Was it worth it, Cartwright? How long will it take Haas to get a nonunion crew down there? A week? Two? That's all the time you have your precious glory hole for. And how many people died for it?"

"No one dies, Katie." Cartwright was doing something to the condensates around them. Li felt them pressing in on her, shorting out her internals, smothering her. "The wave is more than the sum of its paths."

"I remember." She was trembling, her breath

coming tight and angry. "I remember what you did to my father. I remember."

"He's here, Katie. Don't you want to talk to him? All you have to do is believe in Her. She lost Her only Son. She knows your sorrow, even if you've forgotten it. She can forgive you."

Whatever he said next, Li didn't hear it. She was already running, scrambling down the steep slope, tearing the cloth of her uniform and the skin of her palms on the sharp rocks.

She ran blind, her internals a wash of useless static. She stumbled over something in the dark, patted it until she recognized the angles of her Davy lamp. It had gone out. She lit it by feel with trembling fingers, strapped it on, and just sat staring at the walls for thirty seconds.

McCuen was waiting in the gangway, looking far better than he had the last time she'd seen him. "You okay?" he asked.

Li remembered her torn hands and clothes, wondered what her face looked like. "I'm fine. I just fell, that's all."

He gave her a strange look. "Did you talk to him?"

"Couldn't get up there. No air." She pulled on her rebreather, jammed the mouthpiece between her lips, glad of how it masked and muffled her voice. "Let's get the hell out of here."

Sharifi's hand was warm, her handshake firm and professional.

"Major," she said, smiling. "Welcome."

"Nice to meet you," Li said, wondering what corporate database McCuen had hacked to find this goldmine.

She looked around, gaping unabashedly. They stood in an interactive set designer's dream of a physics lab: high ceilings, clean Ring-side sunlight streaming through two-story-tall faux-steel casement windows, cutting-edge lab equipment carefully arranged to produce an effect of frenzied but impeccably organized activity.

She turned back to Sharifi, who was still talking at her. She was charismatic, in a hard-sciency kind of way. She came across as thoughtful, rational, feminine. And obviously—very obviously—a genetic. A youthful, vigorous fiftysomething. Shorter than UN norm. Thick black hair framing a square, flat-boned Han face. Not fat, but compact, solid.

Li knew that body. She knew the heft of the long thighbones, the sharp ridge of the nose, the smooth curve of skull from ear to temple. *So that's what I would have looked like*, she thought and shuddered.

"Let's start with a quick overview," Sharifi said.

As she spoke, Li felt the fund-raising program's enslaved AI trying to crack her system. Fishing for financial data, donation patterns, anything that would help narrow its sales pitch. Her own AI moved to counter the probes, and she gave it permission to open a set of decoy personal files.

A holodisplay unrolled beside Sharifi. She drew a finger through the grid to activate it, pulling a sparkling wake of ripples behind her. The display sprang to life, and Li found herself staring at one of the iconic images of the age: a simplified-for-laymen flowchart of the Bose-Einstein teleportation process.

Sharifi smiled, flashing straight, well-cared-for teeth. "Quantum-teleportation—or, more accurately, quantum-corrected spinstream replication—has been described as the worst system of faster-than-light travel, except for all the others. A more accurate way of putting it might be to say that QCSR unites two fatally flawed methods of transport in order to capitalize on their strengths and compensate for their weaknesses.

"Wide-band spinfoam broadcasting of spin-encoded binary messages gives us robust superluminal transport—but only in the chaotic context of transient wormholes, where data transfer is inaccurate, unreliable and, worst of all for corporate and governmental purposes, unprivate.

"In essence, broadcasting data through the quantum foam is like putting a message in a bottle and throwing it into the ocean. The odds that it will reach someone somewhere are good—and they get better the more bottles you can afford to send. But the odds that your message will reach a single intended recipient—and that it will be legible and private when it does reach them—are low.

"Bose-Einstein teleportation, by contrast, establishes reliable, securely encrypted data transmission between any two parties that share a pair of entangled condensates. By uniting Bose-Einstein teleportation and spinfoam broadcasts, we achieve the sine qua non of the interstellar information economy: private, superluminal transmission that is robust, reliable, and secure enough for us to entrust the most valuable and fragile cargo to it: human cargo."

A map of UN space replaced the teleportation schematic. Colored points spread in an expanding ring around Sol, showing all the known and suspected human-settled worlds.

United Nations–blue highlighted the UN member states and Trusteeships. A red slash along one flank of the UN territory showed the eight Syndicate systems. Independent colonies shone green. Beyond the Periphery, white dots signified the far-flung settlements with which the UN had lost contact during the long centuries of Earth's dying.

As Li watched, a wagon-spoke pattern of brightly colored nodes and lines spread across the star map.

"This," Sharifi said, "is the current Bose-Einstein relay network. The smaller nodes represent data relays. The larger ones—and there are far fewer of those—are personnel and cargo relays. Each node, underneath all the specialized technology, is a simple array of Bose-Einstein condensates, entangled with companion condensates at every other receiving station on the UN's Bose-Einstein relay system. In essence, each Bose-Einstein relay is a glorified quantum-teleportation transmitter, linked only to the receivers that share communications or transport-grade entanglement. As long as we maintain entanglement between relay stations—by shipping freshly entangled crystals from relay to relay at sublight speeds—the network functions, and we can use QCSR to achieve arbitrarily accurate superluminal replication.

"But there's a problem," Sharifi said, tracing the wheel-shaped pattern of the network, lighting up the radiating spokes with digital fireworks. "The system only works as long as we can maintain our banks of pure entanglement at the relay stations. Streamspace, the spinstream, the whole interstellar ecopolitical infrastructure depends on Compson's World's ability to keep supplying live Bose-Einstein condensates. And Bose-Einstein condensates are a nonrenewable resource. A nonrenewable resource that we are fast exhausting."

Sharifi turned away from the display to pace a short circuit along the tile floor of the laboratory. As if in response to the muted echo of her footsteps, the map gave way to a long-distance probe image of a planet half-cloaked in night. Li took in the blood-and-rust hue of the landmasses, the cloudlike swirls of algae bloom on the northern steppes, the primitive geometry of tailings piles big enough to be seen from high orbit. Compson's World.

"Coal. Oil. Uranium. Water. This is not the first time humanity has depended on a nonrenewable resource. And, as past ages have discovered, there are only two ways out of this dependence. Either you learn to do without the nonrenewable resource—or you learn to make more of it."

Gradually, so gradually that it seemed to be no more than the rising of Compson's World's distant sun, a pair of Bose-Einstein crystals took shape on the screen, superimposed on the brooding image of the planet.

"So," Sharifi said, turning away from the screen again. "How do we make more of it? And what, if we can allow ourselves to dream a little, would UN space look like with a cheap, unlimited supply of artificial condensate?"

The holodisplay rippled, shifting through the color spectrum. Suddenly Li was in the middle of it. New transmission lines formed around her, zipping through empty air, linking previously isolated relays, stringing a thick, star-bright spider's web through and beyond UN space. The web pulsed, grew solid, wove itself into a single, bright veil that shimmered over the whole expanse of the human worlds.

"No unequal distribution of transport technology," Sharifi said. "No information ghettos. No technological backwaters. Just a single entanglement field linking all UN space—and eventually all human space. A metalink, if you will, that provides direct, economical, one-shot superluminal replication from any point in UN space to every other point."

The holo shifted again, this time to realtime footage of suspiciously clean-looking Bose-Einstein miners working at an underground cutting face.

"All we need," Sharifi said, "is the technology to culture Bose-Einstein condensates and format them to our specifications in a laboratory setting."

Now Sharifi began the sales pitch in earnest. The feed of the cutting face gave way to images of condensates being assayed, cut, polished, and formatted. And, finally, to the finished product: cleaned, cut, paired, and formatted communications-grade Bose-Einstein condensate. "Of course, in order to culture condensates," she said, "we must understand them. And the key to understanding lies not in our future, but in our past."

A glowing image of Earth appeared on the holodisplay. The image swelled as the display zoomed in on blue ocean. Sharifi looked at Li, smiled, and stepped into the screen.

Surf beat around them. Li walked beside Sharifi on a narrow slip of starlit sand between two boundless oceans. Stars shone overhead in a bright, clear sky that no unprotected human being had seen for over two centuries.

"This," Sharifi said, "is the Great Barrier Reef. It is, or was, the largest single life-form on pre-Migration Earth."

She walked out into the surf, beckoning for Li to follow, and Li saw that she and Sharifi were both wearing wet suits and diving gear. They dove, passing swiftly through the surf and into the quiet water below. Sharifi brushed by Li on the way down, bare thigh against bare thigh, and Li wondered just how personal this program was designed to get. They came to rest in still, bright water half a dozen meters below the surface. A coral reef ran away like a broad road on either side of them.

It was night; the reef was active. Technicolor fish slipped around and through it. The coral itself waved a million glowing arms below them. As Sharifi guided Li along the great wall of the reef, a realtime story unfolded before them. The coral grew, hunted, colonized new territory. Li saw that the entire reef was a single organism, a single primitive mind.

Then she saw humans come, and with them shipping lanes, motorboats, oil spills, chemical contamination. The reef sickened, shrank, died long before anyone unlocked its secrets or plumbed the immense colonial mind's inner workings.

The water glowed and shifted. Suddenly Li was floating not in water but in featureless darkness.

"The Great Barrier Reef is gone," Sharifi said. "Anything we could have learned from it is lost forever. However, when humanity moved out into the galaxy, we discovered another colonial organism. One built on an even larger scale. The Bose-Einstein strata of Compson's World."

Light seeped into the world, and Li saw an immense, glassy honeycomb structure stretching around and above her.

"This is what a typical Bose-Einstein deposit would look like if you removed the coal and rock surrounding it," Sharifi told her. "The condensates draw energy from the surrounding coal. We don't understand how they function, or how their constituent strata communicate with each other. Nonetheless, each deposit appears to form a single colonial organism. Each Bose-Einstein bed is, in effect, an immense, landlocked coral reef, growing in an ocean of coal and rock."

The stratum faded, and the lab reappeared around them.

"Bose-Einstein strata are too different from terrestrial carbon-based life for us to draw any direct conclusions," Sharifi said. "Still, the analogy is a fruitful one. The strata display many of the characteristics of a primitive colonial intelligence. Stimuli pass from one segment of each stratum to other segments. More intriguing, several experiments have established that the condensates pass interstratal as well as intrastratal messages by quantum replication, leading to the supposition that all of Compson's strata may have originated in a single organism, and that the ability of their component condensate beds to maintain pure entanglement supplies with only minimal decoherence is an evolved survival trait. Whatever the explanation, it is this organism that we need to understand in order to culture live condensate.

"We are now a century into the quantum era, but despite all our advances, we are primitives. We use condensates, but we don't control them, don't understand them. In quantum terms, we are little better than prehistoric cave dwellers who nourish a lightning-sparked flame, knowing they lack the power to rekindle it. I am asking you to help us step into a new era—an era in which we will take control of this extraordinary resource, understand it, master it, use it to unite our species as we have not been united since the Evacuation."

Sharifi moved in to close the sale. She started talking practical applications, patents, proprietary data. She alluded to the potential profits without ever quite putting hard numbers to them. This was sexy science, buffed, polished, and carefully wrapped for consumption by corporate donors.

"Any questions?" Sharifi asked after the wrap-up.

"Yes." Li kept her voice deliberately flat. "How the hell did you convince the Secretariat to waive the Zahn Act restrictions and clear a genetic to work on this project?"

Sharifi blinked and stiffened, looking genuinely insulted. "Forgive me," she said coolly. She sounded as if she were working hard to stay polite. "I can't say that's a question I expected. We have of course obtained all the necessary TechComm clearances. However, if you have concerns about security issues, I can refer you to the appropriate officials."

The program was good. Sharifi had laid out the money to get an AI with enough power and personality to sell the simulation. She must have needed big money, and needed it fast. And she'd gotten it, or she'd never have made it to Compson's in the first place.

What do you think?" Li asked two hours later, sitting at an outdoor table just off the Calle Mexico.

Cohen shrugged—a shrug that Li felt in the numbers even as she saw it. "I think Sharifi needed money. Badly."

He had put on a 'face for the meeting that Li imagined he thought was inconspicuous. But of course Cohen's idea of inconspicuous was a few spins off-norm by most people's standards, and half the singles in the place had been glancing surreptitiously at their table for the last ten minutes.

"And how much of the sell do you buy?" Li asked.

Cohen grinned. "Not a word of it."

"You think there's a sideline? Some other way she was making money off it?"

"Not money. It would never have been about money. You have to understand, Sharifi wasn't an experimental physicist. She was all about theory, structure. Metaphysics for want of a better word. She wouldn't have gone to Compson's World, wouldn't have raised money and jumped through hoops for anything that was merely technical. She hunted big game. And whatever she was after down there, it was about a hell of a lot more than just making space travel cheaper for the average monkey."

"Which still leaves us with the question of what exactly she was after."

"My guess?" Cohen crossed long legs and Li glanced away as his shorts rode up to bare a breathtaking stretch of thigh. "I think it had something to do with mapping interference patterns."

"Meaning?"

"Ah!" He leaned forward, showing the kind of enthusiasm that usually meant he was about to talk math to her. "Interference patterns are the riddle that kicked off the whole enterprise of quantum physics. Basically, we're talking about the two-slit experiment."

"Oh," Li said as her oracle summoned up a long-forgotten picture from an introductory physics textbook. "The thing where you put one photon through a screen and it interferes with itself, right? And then you get to watch the physicists jump up and down and argue about whether it's a wave or a particle. Or both. Or neither. I never really saw what that had to do with Sharifi, though."

"That's where Coherence Theory comes in. How much do you know about it?"

Li shrugged. "You mean like the Everett-Sharifi Equations, the Coherent Worlds Theorem, that stuff?"

"Exactly. And like Sharifi said in her sales pitch, the answer was in our past, on Earth. It goes all the way back to the twentieth century in fact. To an American named Hugh Everett, who studied the wave theory of quantum mechanics and came up with this crazy idea that there was nothing theoretical about quantum mechanical wave functions at all. That they were actual manifestations of multiple worlds, multiple possible histories. In short, that the mathematical formalism of wave mechanics—and this is the part Hannah really loved, of course—that the mathematical form itself gave us the key to understanding the nature of the physical universe.

"According to Everett, each point on the Schrödinger wave function that you use to calculate the possible locations of an electron around the nucleus or the possible spin orientations of a photon has a real, physical existence. Just not in this world. In another world. One of an infinite number of worlds that branch off from each other every time a thermodynamically irreversible measurement event takes place.

"So—textbook example—you come to a crossroads, and you have to decide whether to turn left or right. Or so it seems. But actually you take *both* forks in the road. You just take them in different worlds. Or, depending on your terminology, in different constituent universes of the multiverse."

"Then . . . what's the point? I mean, everything happens no matter what you do, or what path you choose? It's crazy."

"Well, yes, that's certainly the majority view of things. Or at least it was for several centuries. The Many-Worlds interpretation was one of those theories that was so absurd that Everett either had to be insane or right. And like a lot of crazy theories it took a long time to get off the ground. It got nowhere with most of Everett's colleagues, in fact, and he left academia and eventually smoked himself to death, ignored and ridiculed."

"What a surprise," Li said caustically.

"Right. Well, Everett's idea sat around gathering dust for the next few centuries while experimental physicists went on with their experiments. Experiments that over time, and without anyone really stopping to notice, gradually made the Many-Worlds theory look less and less crazy and more and more like it might just be a small but important piece of the truth.

"That's where Hannah Sharifi comes into the story. Hannah was obsessed with Everett's work. She basically spent two decades trying to prove that the Many-Worlds interpretation of quantum mechanics was right, and that Everett just hadn't had the experimental data or the computational tools to prove it."

"But she didn't prove it, did she?" Li said. "She failed. The most famous failure in the history of physics, right? The biggest mistake since Columbus ran into America and called it India."

"Yes. She failed. Which is to say that she didn't prove the multiverse was physically real in the way she believed it was. But—and this is important—a theory doesn't have to be experimentally verifiable to be valuable. And what she did with Coherence Theory was in some ways far more significant than pinning down an experimental result. She gave us a new theoretical framework for thinking about quantum-level events. In essence, she proved that even if the Many-Worlds interpretation of quantum mechanics doesn't actually describe the universe, it's still the most effective way to *think* about the universe. Or at least the most effective way to think about the universe for now."

"And what does interference have to do with it? Why do you think she was looking at interference patterns in the Anaconda?"

Cohen shook out a cigarette and lit it, smiling. "Interference is central. It's the hat trick at the center of Coherence Theory. Basically what Sharifi saw—and this takes us into the realm of quantum information theory—is that interference is really the flip side of coherence. If you really take the concept of the multiverse seriously, then entanglement, decoherence, and interference all become interdependent. In essence, they emerge as the same phenomenon occurring in different dimensions of the multiverse."

"This is giving me a headache, Cohen."

"Quantum mechanics gives everyone a headache. That's just how it is. But my point is you don't have to believe Sharifi's idea or even be able to visualize it, really. Because it works, like a lot of the watershed ideas in quantum mechanics, whether or not you believe in it. The Everett-Sharifi Equations accurately predict a whole range of quantum behavior that prior theories couldn't make sense of. Which goes back to what I was saying about how theories don't have to be true to be useful.

"And Coherence Theory is beautiful, of course." His cigarette described a delicate arc in mid-air. "Sharifi's early papers on it were some of the most elegant pieces of reasoning in the history of modern physics. And being beautiful is almost as important as being useful." He grinned. "More important, Sharifi would have said."

"So you think she was looking at live fields in the Bose-Einstein beds because there was something about the relationship between entanglement, interference, and decoherence in those fields that she thought would . . . what? Prove her theories?"

"Maybe. Or she might just have hoped she could refine some aspect of Coherence Theory. But whatever she was after, it would have been primarily theoretical. A fresh direction. A big answer. A new problem. Something that *meant* something."

"Well, she found something," Li said. "We know that. But then she erased her data. So whatever she found, it was something she didn't want people to know about."

Cohen shook his head decisively. "I don't think that can be right. I don't think Sharifi would have destroyed data. I don't think any committed scientist could bring herself to do that."

"Even if she realized that the data would prove Coherence Theory was wrong? Even if she thought it would destroy her life's work, make her a laughing-stock like Everett?"

"Even then, Catherine. Sharifi believed in knowledge. In truth. It was about *being* right for her, not just having people think she was right."

"Maybe," Li said. "Or maybe you just didn't know her as well as you thought you did."

Cohen didn't answer for a moment, and when he spoke he was looking past the Ring-side skyline at the vast glittering curve of Earth. "You've never been there, have you?" he asked.

"To Earth? No. Of course not." No one could go back anymore unless they fell under one of the religious exemptions. And constructs couldn't go back even then; they were controlled technology, banned by the Embargo.

"I've been there," Cohen said. "I was born there."

"I know," Li said, and shivered.

She had seen old noninteractive video footage of Cohen's programming—or rather of the development of the affective loop cognitive program that eventually grew into the Emergent phenomenon that called itself Cohen. The programmers had described their work with a frankness that was shocking to modern ears. They had talked about calling behaviors, well-being-enhancement drives, emotive manipulation. Those words mocked Li every time she began to imagine that she knew anything about what happened on the other side of the interface.

"What was Earth like?" she asked, shaking off the memory of Chiara's slender fingers brushing hers, of Roland standing alone in the middle of a crowded room, watching her.

"Beautiful," Cohen said, and his voice trembled with something the human ear could only interpret as desire. "There will never be anything as beautiful in the universe again."

"There's Compson's World," Li said. "It's beautiful. In its own way. What's left of it."

Cohen laughed softly, as if a pleasant memory had come back to haunt him. "You're the second person who's told me that."

"Oh?"

"Can't you guess who the first person was?"

"Who?" she asked.

"Hannah Sharifi."

"Christ!" Li burst out. "I'm starting to wish I'd never heard of the woman! Gould's going to hit Freetown in twenty-three days to do who knows what. I have to be there before her. I have to know what Sharifi did, what she found. What she was hiding from us."

And I have to know how far I can trust you, Cohen.

But she couldn't ask him that.

She couldn't ask because she knew, in some instinctive animal recess of her mind, that it was the one question he couldn't answer.

Li's quarters on-station looked even more bleak and squalid after her trip Ring-side.

She slipped offstream, lit a cigarette—her last of the day she hoped—and watched the late-night spins with the sound all the way down, her mind teeming with vague unsettled half memories.

Sharpe had forwarded Sharifi's and Voyt's draft autopsies to her, and she scanned them absentmindedly, thinking she'd give them a serious reading in the morning. He certified Sharifi's cause of death as suffocation. The damage to Sharifi's head and hand was premortem, as all the blood suggested. And she'd bitten through the tip of her tongue before she died as well.

Li's stomach clenched when she read that, but she told herself it could have happened when Sharifi fell. It wouldn't be the first time someone trying to get out of a burning mine panicked and stumbled. And no matter how odd that and the injuries to her hand were, she'd clearly died from suffocation, not trauma.

Voyt's autopsy was more puzzling. The rescuers found his body near Sharifi's, as if the two were trying to escape together, but Sharpe attributed his death to the same mysterious brain seizure that had afflicted so many other miners in the Trinidad.

Li fell asleep puzzling over it, reminding herself to put her cigarette out before she dropped it.

It hit her at four in the morning, barreling through her sleep-dazed mind like a runaway coal cart.

"Idiot!" she muttered. She sat up, turned on the lights, pulled up Sharifi's autopsy again.

How could she have missed it? Sharpe damn well hadn't. He'd done everything short of write it on the wall for her. She accessed the rescue crew logs and cross-referenced them with the shift assignments for the day of the fire. Twelve people had been in the Trinidad. Most of them belonged to a work crew of engineers and electricians who were laying wire to a newly opened face deep in the south sections of the newly opened vein. The work crew was at the far end of the main south gangway—almost an eighth of a mile farther from the stairs than Sharifi had been.

She tapped in to the Shantytown hospital database and saw that two of the electricians who had gotten out were half genetics. The rest weren't. And they'd all made it to pit bottom under their own steam. The only people who'd died in the Trinidad were Voyt and Sharifi.

Sharifi was a genetic. Voyt, whatever his genes

might be, had been wired just like Li was. Both should have been able to resist gas and lack of oxygen long after the nongenetics.

So why had they died when the others had lived?

Li scanned Sharifi's autopsy, cursing herself for missing what was right in front of her. Finally she found it, halfway through the report, buried in a wealth of camouflaging detail. Sharpe had put it where anyone who knew what they were looking for could see it.

If they wanted to see it.

On the side of Sharifi's head, just below her temple, among all the other bruises and lacerations, Sharpe had noted two small oblong burn marks, spaced two centimeters apart.

Li leaned across the narrow space between her bunk and the facing closet. She fished her Viper out of its Corps-issue holster and extruded the fanglike anodes: oblong, tapered, sharp enough to cut through skin. And exactly two centimeters apart.

Someone had put a Viper—Voyt's, probably—to Sharifi's head and pulled the trigger at contact range. Li had seen people die that way. A point-blank shot to the head usually caused respiratory paralysis. Death by suffocation. A death that left scars only the most alert coroner would look closely enough to discover.

Sharifi had been murdered.

She linked through to the planet net and dialed the Shantytown hospital.

"How did you find out already?" Sharpe asked when she got through to him.

"What do you mean? I read the autopsies."

He blinked, obviously confused. "You're not calling about the wetware?"

"No. What about it?"

"Haas took it. Or rather, he sent his Syndicate-designed girl Friday down for it."

"What? How did he even know about it?"

Sharpe rocked back in his chair and raised his eyebrows. "That, Major, is what I was hoping you'd tell me."

AMC Station: 19.10.48.

Establishing the crime scene turned out to be as impossible as keeping roaches off a space station.

Anaconda's pitheads formed the tip of a subterranean iceberg, a catacomb of constantly shifting drifts, adits, and ventilation shafts. AMC's maps lagged far behind the digging no matter how fast the surveyors scrambled to update them. And they didn't begin to account for the hundreds of kilometers of unreported bolt-holes, mountainside entrances, and bootleggers' tunnels.

This sprawling, chaotic anthill was filled up, shift after shift, by five daily launches from the station, numerous unscheduled drops of specialized technicians and surveying crews, and a constant, completely unregulated stream of dilapidated ground vehicles shuttling back and forth from Shantytown. No one controlled access or knew, really, who was in the mine during any given shift. The pithead logs were convenient fictions, just like the pithead rules and the posted safety regulations and the rented Davy lamps and oxygen canisters. AMC's control of the Anaconda was as illusory—even if the illusion had real financial and legal consequences—as a general's control over a looting, raiding, pillaging army.

"If we can't catch them going in," Li finally decided, "we'll tag them going out."

The evacuation had taken five shifts, using every available shuttle on-station and every hopper that could be begged, borrowed, or commandeered from the four or five Compson's World settlements within flight range of the Anaconda. Casualties had been high. The evac teams had begun triage within forty minutes of the first alarm, and they'd tagged and entered every evacuee on handheld monitors uplinked to the station net to create a running dead, wounded, and missing list.

When McCuen cross-referenced the triage lists with the station's shuttle passenger manifests and the Shantytown hospital's admission records, they got a solid freeze-frame of who had been where when the mine caught fire.

The list of people who had been underground but not down there on easily verifiable official business was surprisingly short. Jan Voyt, Hannah Sharifi, and Karl Kintz were on it. No surprises there.

But there was a fourth name Li didn't recognize.

"Who's Bella?" she asked. "And why don't we have a full name for him?"

"Bella's the witch. And that is her whole name, as far as anyone knows." McCuen grinned lasciviously. "I can go talk to her for you. I'm just a slave to duty."

"Very funny, Brian."

"Just kidding," he said, sobering suddenly. "Besides, anyone who wants to keep working and living on this station would have to be crazy to go fishing in that pond."

Li started to ask McCuen what he meant, then decided she didn't want to get sidetracked into a conversation about Haas's sleeping habits. "What about Kintz?" she asked instead.

Kintz had been more or less invisible since her first morning on-station. What little she'd seen of him had led her to two conclusions. One, he'd gotten special treatment from Voyt. Two, he expected to keep getting it.

In the normal course of things, she would have shaped Kintz up or shipped him out posthaste. But if things went well, she wouldn't be on Compson's long enough to make lowering the boom on Kintz worth her while.

"So what was Kintz doing down there?" she asked. "And what was the deal between him and Voyt, anyway?"

McCuen looked like he'd sat on a tack.

"I'm not asking you to tell tales out of school, McCuen. I just need to know how to spin him."

"I know," McCuen said reluctantly. "But it's my job if I piss the wrong people off."

Li looked at him, eyes narrowed. "So it wasn't just that Kintz was scamming Voyt. Kintz was Haas's man in the office. Is that it? Or was Voyt in on it too?"

One look at McCuen's face told her she'd hit pay dirt.

"So what were Voyt and Kintz doing for Haas besides passing along information?" she asked.

Again the hesitation.

Li kicked her chair back and lit a cigarette. "Christ, Brian. Tell me if you want. If not, don't. We're all big boys and girls here. I'm not going to waste my time dragging it out of you."

"I don't know anything," McCuen said. "Honest. I'm just repeating rumors. But . . . Voyt had an eye on the bottom line. You always hear rumors about mine security being on the take. God knows there's plenty of chances. But Voyt . . . the rumors about him were pretty persistent. And somehow if you knew Voyt at all, they didn't surprise you."

"And you think Kintz might have taken over Voyt's sideline?"

"I'm not saying that. But it's possible."

Li put down the list of names and stood up. "Let's go talk to him then. Before Haas's little bird gets a chance to whistle in his ear."

Kintz turned out to be a hard man to find. They finally caught up with him in one of the fifth-level strip joints. Li recognized his drinking buddies as company goons—one step above the bouncers who were standing around itching to kick them out before they broke something. None of them looked sober enough to operate heavy equipment.

"Like to talk to you," she told Kintz.

He looked at her but kept his hand on his drink. "I go back on duty tomorrow at eight. That soon enough?"

"Jesus, Kintz," McCuen burst out. "We've been looking for you since three in the afternoon!"

"And how the hell was I supposed to know that, Brian?" Kintz said McCuen's name as if it were a dirty joke.

"You could answer your damned comm for one thing."

Kintz kicked back in his chair, smiling. "Aren't you the teacher's pet," he drawled. "Wag your tail a little harder and maybe she'll let you sit in her lap."

"Right," Li said. "If I wanted to referee playground fights, I could have taught kindergarten. Karl and I are stepping around the corner for a nice quiet cup of coffee."

Kintz didn't protest much; Li was able to steer him out of the bar and down the street with no more than a firm hand on his elbow.

"What do you want from me?" he asked when she'd gotten a table and two steaming cups of coffee between them. "I'm off duty in case you didn't notice. And I don't fucking appreciate being dragged around like a child either."

Li smiled and lit a cigarette. "I don't recall asking whether or not you appreciated it," she said pleasantly. "In fact I'm pretty sure I don't give a shit. Personally, I'd have fired you the day I got here. Except I'm piss lazy, and if I shipped you out, I'd have to waste my time figuring out who Haas's new rat in the office was."

"Whatever."

"What were you doing in the mine the day of the fire?"

"Working." He sounded nonchalant, but the sudden tension around his eyes told a different story.

"Working on what?"

"Working for that dumb bitch, Sharifi."

"You obviously got along. Must have been a real pleasure all around."

"You wouldn't think it was so funny if it was you who had to deal with her fucking attitude. I knew her before she ever got here. Not that she remembered. She was my fucking college physics teacher."

Li blinked, uncertain whether she was more baffled by the idea of Kintz being a student anywhere Sharifi would teach or the idea of his being a student at all. "Was she a good teacher?" she settled on asking.

"Fuck no! You know how she graded us? She gave an exam with one problem on it, one problem that takes like three hours to solve, and I get it back and there's one fucking sentence written on it: 'Oops, you lost the mass of the universe. C minus.' Like my whole exam was some kind of fucking joke to her. You lost the mass of the *universe*? I mean, what the fuck does that mean, anyway?"

"I think it means she had a sense of humor and you

don't," Li said. "So. What did your favorite physics professor have you doing in the mine?"

Kintz shrugged sullenly. "Standing around mostly. Security, I guess. Fuck if I know."

Li drew on her cigarette and watched him in silence. "Did you know Sharifi was murdered?" she asked finally.

"I might have heard something like that."

"And did you know that you're the last person who saw her alive? Other than Voyt. Oh, but someone killed him too."

"So what?"

"So if I were you, I'd be busy thinking about how many ways I could bend over for the investigating officer and keep myself out of trouble."

"Jeez, lighten up! I fucking work for you, in case you forgot. Why don't you go round up the usual suspects?"

"Unfortunately the usual suspects weren't down in the mine. You were. And I want to know what Haas had you doing down there."

Kintz stared. Then he kicked his chair back on two legs and laughed a laugh that set Li's teeth on edge.

"You don't know shit," he said. "They hung you out to dry. You're in fucking free fall, and you're just too blind to see it."

Li flicked out her left arm as fast as her internals would go. It hurt like hell, but the special effects were worth it. To anyone watching it would have looked like Kintz's coffee had simply fallen off the table and into his lap. Before Kintz realized what had happened, Li was on her feet and coming around the table right behind the coffee.

"Gosh!" she said, patting at the front of his pants with a napkin. "You spilled on yourself. Hope it wasn't too hot."

Kintz stood up and backed away from the table a step or two but let Li keep swatting at him with the

napkin. He looked like he was still trying to catch up
with his coffee. He was also now standing with his
back against the wall and Li's body between him and
the rest of the tables. Li smiled, grabbed him where it
counted, and lifted.

"Have I mentioned that you're really pissing me
off?" she asked.

Kintz's face contorted, but his eyes didn't drop away
from hers. Worse, as pain drained the blood from his
neck and face, Li saw the dense network of ceramsteel
filament woven through flesh and muscle.

She almost dropped him in surprise.

Well, that explained where he'd taken Sharifi's
classes. The only thing that didn't add up was why the
Corps had put this waste of skin through Alba. Or how
an ex-Peacekeeper had washed up as Haas's errand
boy. Either Kintz was working for internal affairs—impossible—or he'd screwed up so badly the Corps
couldn't risk the publicity of a dishonorable discharge.

Yet another reason to keep a close eye on him. As if
she needed one.

"You're no better than me," Kintz said, pain and hatred battling in his voice. "I was on Gilead. I know just
what kind of fucking hero you are. I know you."

Li let go and backed away as if he'd stung her.

"Yeah," Kintz said. "I was there. And when the
memory wipe didn't take they washed me out. For doing the same thing you did. For doing less than you
did. What do you think of that, Major? Only you
weren't a major then, were you? That was your reward
for doing their dirty work." He laughed. "Or don't you
like to talk about it?"

Li shrugged. It took every bit of willpower she had,
but she did it.

"Look," she said. "I don't give a shit what you think
you remember or what lies you need to tell yourself to
get by. We can either keep standing here insulting each
other, or you can tell me something that'll make me

leave. Which is it gonna be, Kintz? And while we're on the topic of Gilead, why don't you think about what happened to the people who got in my way there before you decide to make an enemy."

Kintz stared at her. He was trembling with anger, and she could see the sweat standing out on his upper lip.

"Talk to the witch," he said finally. "She was the one Sharifi trusted. Hell, maybe she killed Sharifi herself." He laughed, trying to regain his composure. "You always hurt the one you love, isn't that how the song goes?"

"I wouldn't know," Li said. "I'll be seeing you."

"You sure as fuck will be."

Li found the witch in Haas's office, working.

Haas was slumped behind the big desk, staring into streamspace. He surfaced long enough to wave Li into a chair, then faded out again.

Li sat and watched. She noted the wire's route from the derms at Haas's temples, through the deceptively simple dryware casing of the transducer, to the witch's cranial socket. The witch was his interface, Li realized, the ungainly external wires the only way he could access the spinstream. The transducer intercepted the construct's output, keyed it to his neural patterns, packeted and transferred it. Li thought of the loop shunt and shuddered.

"All right," Haas said to the empty air in front of him.

The witch stood up, teased the jack out from behind her ear, then pulled her hair over the socket, hiding it.

"Can I offer you something?" Haas asked Li. "Coffee?" He looked at his watch. "Beer?"

"Coffee's fine," Li said.

"Coffee for two," Haas said.

The witch nodded and moved toward the door.

Li cleared her throat. "Better make it for three. It's Bella I need to talk to."

Haas looked at Li sharply but said nothing. Bella left and came back with a covered tray from which she produced three bone china cups, cream, sugar, and a full pot of ersatz coffee. She bent over the table, poured Li's cup, offered cream and sugar, then poured, creamed, and sugared Haas's cup.

As Li took her cup she saw the cat-scratch red rash of a staph infection below the witch's left ear around the borders of the I/O socket. Something about the sight—the red rash against the pale spun-silk skin— made Li acutely aware that there was a woman, warm and alive, inside the loose dress. She cleared her throat and looked away—but not before she saw a mocking little smile slide across the other woman's face.

"Well, Major," Haas said. "What do you need to know?"

Li took out her cigarettes and lifted an eyebrow in Haas's direction. "Do you mind?"

"Suit yourself."

"Want one?"

"Never touch 'em."

"Good for you." She lit her cigarette and sucked down a first delicious postcoffee lungful. "You'll live longer. I just need to ask Bella about the fire. Routine. I'm talking to everyone who was down there when it happened."

"I see."

"It won't take a minute." Li waited, hoping Haas wasn't going to make her ask him to leave.

"No problem," he said after a very brief pause. "I'll be back in twenty minutes." Li thought he threw a pointed look at the witch before he left—or was she just being paranoid?

The door whispered closed behind him, and she and Bella looked at each other without speaking. Li had the curious feeling of a weight lifting off Bella's shoulders. As if Haas's very presence silenced her. She thought of the tense little scene she'd caught on her skinbugs that first night and wondered what hold Haas had over her.

Bella took a breath. "I'm not . . . I want you to know—" she said, then stopped as if she'd run into a wall.

"You're not what?" Li asked.

But Bella just shook her head.

Li sat back and finished her cigarette in silence. She was fishing in muddy water; let Bella make the first move. She knew a hell of a lot more about what had happened in the mine that day than Li did. Li was starting to think every man, woman, and child on-station knew more than she did.

"Citizen—" Bella said.

"That's not a title here," Li said. "People here are born citizens."

"Not constructs."

"Not constructs," Li admitted.

"And not Sharifi."

"No," Li said. "Not Sharifi." Cohen was right as usual: some pigs were more equal than others.

She looked at Bella's face, half in shadow, and caught herself searching for echoes of the XenoGen genesets. Was that smooth curve of forehead too smooth, too round to be entirely Caucasian? Was that striking combination of pale skin and vaguely Han features pure accident or a self-conscious echo of not-so-distant history? She wondered what Sharifi had looked like to Bella—what she herself looked like.

Perfect front teeth bit a perfect lower lip. Perfect hands twisted each other's fingers into nervous lovers' knots. "Who killed her?" Bella whispered.

"Who told you Sharifi was murdered?"

"Does it matter?" Beautiful, jarringly unnatural violet eyes bored into Li's eyes. "Everyone knows."

"What else does everyone know?"

"I . . . I don't speak to many people. Except Haas."

Bella's voice was surprisingly low, and she spoke with an accent, a halting here and there to search for the proper word. When she said Haas's name, her voice dropped even lower.

"I don't know who killed her," Li said. "That's what I'm here for. To find answers."

Bella leaned forward, and Li heard a little catch in her breath. "And when you find them? What then?"

Li shrugged. "The bad guys get punished."

"No matter who they are?"

"No matter who they are."

There didn't seem to be anything to say after that. Bella sat like a stone. She looked ready to sit there forever. Certainly until Haas returned.

"Do you have a last name?" Li finally asked, just to have something to say.

"Just Bella," the witch answered. She said the name as if it were a mere label, nothing to do with who she really was.

"You're on contract to AMC, right?"

Bella's mouth tightened. "To MotaiSyndicate. AMC is the subordinate contract-holder."

"I'm sorry," Li said. "I don't know anything about . . . how that works. I probably just said something stupid." She looked up to find Bella staring at her. "What?" she asked.

Bella pressed a hand to the pulse at the base of her own neck in a gesture that Li recognized with an eerie flash of déjà vu. It was the same biofeedback manipulation technique she'd seen Syndicate soldiers use. "Nothing," Bella said, dropping her hand back into her lap. "You just . . . remind me of someone."

"Who?" Li asked, though of course she already knew the answer.

Bella smiled.

"How well did you know Sharifi?" Li asked. "Did she talk to you about her work?"

"Not well." Bella rubbed nervously at the rash behind her ear, then snatched her hand away like a child caught picking at a scab. "I'm sorry," she said, "I really don't know anything."

"I'm sure you know more than you think," Li told her. "It's just a question of putting the pieces together. Tell me what you remember about the fire. Maybe I can make the connections."

"I can't tell you," Bella said. "I don't remember."

"Just start at the beginning and tell me whatever you do remember."

"But that's just it. I don't. I don't remember anything."

And then she started to cry.

She cried silently, tears sliding down her cheeks like rain running down the carved face of a statue. Li leaned her elbows on her knees and watched, feeling awkward and useless. She had never seen a grown woman cry like this. It was as if something had come unraveled inside her, as if she had lost whatever obscure sense of shame made people cover their faces when they cried. Lost it, or never had it in the first place.

Li cleared her throat. "What about before you went down? Or on the way down. You must have taken a shuttle. Maybe talked about going? Something."

"No," Bella said fiercely. "I told you. Nothing."

She stood up so abruptly as she spoke that she knocked her coffee cup off the table.

Li reached for it without thinking. She got her hand under it just in time. The spoon fell to the floor. The saucer landed in her palm. The cup rattled but stayed upright. Nothing spilled. She set the cup back on the table and leaned down to pick up the teaspoon.

When she looked up, Bella was staring at her, slack-jawed. "How did you catch that?" she whispered.

Li held out her arm and showed Bella the network of filaments running just below the skin.

Bella looked at it like she'd never seen a wire job before. Worse than that, her face was filled with the fascinated revulsion of someone looking at a circus freak. "What—how do they put it inside you?"

"Viral surgery."

"Like Voyt," she said, and a shudder twisted through her slender body as she spoke the dead man's name. "In the Syndicates, you'd be a monster."

"Then I guess it's a good thing we're not in the Syndicates."

Bella put her hand up to touch the cranial socket. "Even this is . . . a deviance."

"Well, you need to access the spinstream if you're going to work in the UN worlds. It's how business is done here. How we communicate."

"Communicate." Clearly Bella had never thought of applying that word to what she did instream. "I grew up in a crèche of two thousand. I never looked in a mirror because my face—the crèche face—was all around. I never thought about who I was because I knew, every time I looked around me. I never thought about being alone because I knew I'd never have to be. And now I'm here. I don't understand anything or anyone. I watch them talk at me, around me. I'm the deviant. And there's no way out."

"There's always a way out," Li said.

"Not for me. Not even the euth ward. I thought I was . . . all right. Before Hannah came. But when I meet someone like her, someone like you." She wiped her face, pushed the heavy hair back from her forehead. "I can't help wanting to talk to you. Wanting to feel that I'm not alone for a minute. And then you show me . . . that. And I don't know what to think."

"Sharifi was raised by humans," Li said. "So was I." It was as close as she'd come in fifteen years to admitting she wasn't human.

"Does that make such a difference?"

"I guess it does."

Bella wiped her eyes and spoke again. "I remember the day before the fire. I worked with Ha—with Sharifi. We talked about going down the next day, but we decided nothing. Not definitely. And the next thing I remember is waking up in the mine after the fire."

Her hand crept to her neck again, and Li could see the pulse fluttering under her fingers like a bird in a hunter's snare.

"It was dark. I—they were gone."

"What do you mean, they were gone? Was there someone else with you before that?"

"No. Maybe." She looked confused. "I don't know."

"Where were you when you woke up?"

"In the glory hole. It took me a long time to figure that out. The lights had gone out and I didn't have a lamp. I . . . I crawled back and forth looking for the ladder. That's what I was doing when I found Voyt."

"Voyt?" Li asked, surprised. He should have been on the level above, at the foot of the stairs up to the Wilkes-Barre. "Are you sure it was Voyt?"

"I felt his mustache," Bella said, and again Li saw that shudder of . . . what? Fear? Revulsion? "I never found a light though. And . . . there was another body."

"At the foot of the stairs." That would have been Sharifi.

"No. At the ladder. With Voyt. In the glory hole." Bella put a hand to her mouth. "It was Hannah, wasn't it?"

Li nodded. It had to have been Sharifi; no one else had died down there. But assuming Bella was telling the truth, someone had moved both Voyt and Sharifi up to the level above and left them at the bottom of the main stairs into the Trinidad for the rescue crews to find. Why? And who had done it?

"I stepped on her." Bella looked sick. "I didn't even stop."

"She'd been dead a long time by then," Li lied. "There was nothing you could have done for her."

Bella started to speak, but as she opened her mouth Haas's voice rang out in the front office.

"I should go," Li said.

"No! Wait."

Li had stood up to leave, but now she crouched in front of the woman, looking up into those impossible eyes, searching the perfect oval of her face for a clue, an answer, anything.

"They got away with it, didn't they?" Bella said, still speaking in a harsh whisper. "They killed her. And no one's going to punish them."

Li was close enough to smell her now. Close enough to see the bitter lines around her lovely mouth, the bruised pallor of the flesh stretched across her cheekbones. Bella looked like a fighter who had taken a knockout punch and was waiting for gravity to catch up with her. And in the violet depths of her eyes Li saw the same black emptiness she'd seen down at the cutting face.

Only this time she could put a name to it.

It was hate. Hate that had been tended and fed and watered until it was big enough to burst through her skin and swallow universes.

Shantytown: 19.10.48.

Compson's sun shed a smeary bottle green light on Shantytown and played halfheartedly over the awkward sprawl of mold-fuzzed rooftops. The miscalibrated atmospheric processors produced a sooty drizzle that made all of Shantytown look like it was underwater, and the mud that sucked at Li's boots gave off a faint whiff of sewage.

She followed McCuen past pawnshops, tattoo parlors, storefronts advertising bail bonds and cash loans on paychecks. They were off the grid here; the signs flashed with neon and halogen, not spinfeed. THE PIT, she read, and PAYDAY PAWN and MINER'S EASE, and GIRLSGIRLSGIRLS.

First shift was on; it showed in the waiting silence of the bars, the absence of able-bodied men on the streets. Still, as they left the commercial strip and dove into the back streets, they drew increasing notice. A clot of pale, ragged children stopped their stickball game and stared. A woman on her way home from picking pea coal off the tailings piles turned clear around to watch them pass. When Li looked back, she saw that the woman's body was bent into a sharp letter L under her load.

McCuen picked his way through the unmarked intersections as surely as if he had a map. Each turn took them farther from daylight and deeper into Shantytown's poorest quarter. Modular housing units began to be replaced by the virusteel and decaying ceramic tiles of settlement-era habitat pods. Occasionally they passed a still-functional airlock, status lights blinking to indicate the operational status of long-idle life-support systems. More often, the remnants of the original colony were mere deadware, the bottom layer in a sedimentary accretion of obsolete technology and home-brewed or scavenged building materials.

Just as Li was beginning to wonder how many blind corners and unlit side streets McCuen could lead her down, he ducked into a gap between two boarded storefronts, dropped down three steps, and slipped into an alley so narrow that the dank walls nearly met overhead.

Doors opened off the alley on either side, but they were all closed. The few windows were boarded up or covered with plastic sheeting. The rank smell of vegetein flowed out of the houses like smoke and soaked into the packed hardpan. And underneath it, deep and musky, Li caught smells that had the power to throw her back twenty years into the dim memories of childhood. Sweat. Bad plumbing. Last night's empty beer bottles. Poverty.

McCuen walked fast, eyeing the shadows like a man who is only mostly sure he isn't about to be rolled for his palm implant. He ran his hand along the right wall, counting doors like a miner counting drift turnings. At the eighth door he stopped and tried the latch.

It swung open, and he ducked in without pausing on the threshold. Li followed.

They hurried down a dark corridor toward a faint blur of daylight. The corridor dumped them into an interior court with a rough, sloping floor. One side of the court was dark and quiet, stairs leading up toward darkened apartments. The other side opened onto the flying sparks and whining machinery of a welder's shop. They mounted the single step into the shop just as the welder finished sawing through a sheet-metal panel and straightened up, pushing back his safety goggles.

McCuen stepped up to the man and pulled a bent door hinge out of his pocket. "My mother asked me to bring this by," he said, his voice echoing under the shop's high ceiling. "Can you fix it?"

"When does she need it by?"

"Good Friday, she said."

Instead of answering, the welder put his torch down and walked off toward the front of the shop. As Li and McCuen watched, he put up a closed sign and cranked heavy storm shutters down over the shop window, shutting them into darkness.

"Sit down," he said, and flicked the switch that lit the shop's single dim bulb.

McCuen sat. Li didn't.

"So," the welder said. "This is her."

"Yeah," McCuen said.

"Time to put your mouth where your money is," the welder said.

Li held out her left arm, sleeve rolled above the elbow. He snapped a tourniquet around it, produced a needle from his apron pocket, and pulled more blood than Li thought could possibly be necessary, even for the most incompetent doctor. "They want a tooth, too," he said.

"Oh, Christ," Li muttered. "For God's sake."

"You didn't say that before," McCuen said.

"Well, I'm saying it now. You can fake blood. Teeth tell the whole story." He turned back to Li. "You want to talk to the man or not?"

Li shrugged and opened her mouth.

She spent the next half hour sitting on a work counter nursing a bloody gap where her bottom right premolar had been, while McCuen paced back and forth impatiently. It didn't hurt nearly as much as she'd hoped it would; a little worse and her internals would have thrown enough endorphins at it to have her feeling comfortable. As it was, they ignored it and left her to handle it.

Finally the welder came back, accompanied by a second man who waved them back into the slanting courtyard and toward the stairs.

"Here?" Li asked.

But he opened a narrow door tucked beneath the stairs, ducked into another corridor, and led them into an alley even darker and narrower than the one she and McCuen had come in by. Five right turns, two left turns, and three interior courtyards later he turned into a broader alley, this one roofed with grimy, rain-streaked greenhouse sheeting. It ran level, but its walls curved like a snail's shell, as if responding to some structural logic Li couldn't fathom.

A few dozen meters down the spiraling alley, their guide stopped at a nondescript door, knocked, and entered.

The room inside smelled of old newspapers and boiled cabbage. A pea-coal fire smoldered in the grate, filling the room with greasy smoke. A woman sat at a chipped laminate table holding a child in her lap, reading to him in a low murmur. The woman and child both looked up momentarily, then dropped their heads to the book again, uninterested.

"Where is he?" their guide asked.

The woman jerked her chin toward an inner room. As Li passed by the table, she saw there was something wrong with the boy's upper lip and his legs were withered.

McCuen started toward the door, but the guide barred his way. He looked hard at her, then shrugged and went over to sit at the table. Li stepped through alone and heard the door swing to behind her.

She stood in near darkness, cut by a single dusty beam of sunlight stabbing through a storm shutter. As she looked around Li understood the odd curvature of the alley outside. The house was built onto the outside skin of one of the old life-support pods; this room's three newer walls were native mud brick, but the back wall, the only original one, was a curved gleaming expanse of ceramic compound. An airlock yawned in the center of the old wall, but its control panel had been ripped open and hot-wired long ago. The irising virusteel door panels were permanently stuck at a two-thirds-open position, and someone had hung a blanket over the gap, blocking off Li's view of the geodesic dome that must lie behind.

In front of the dead airlock stood a swaybacked table piled with pads and datacubes. A wiry, weathered man sat behind the table: Daahl, the shift foreman Li had met on her first mine visit.

"Well," Daahl said, looking straight at Li. "You get curiouser and curiouser."

"You too." Li sat down on the stool across from Daahl's and leafed through the papers and fiches that littered the table. She saw pit regulations, UNMSC section headings, General Assembly minutes, court papers. "You some kind of pit lawyer, Daahl?"

"You could say that. Care for a beer?"

"Thanks." She took out her cigarettes. "May I?"

Daahl called into the front room for the beer, then took the cigarette she offered. As she leaned across the table to light it, he grabbed her wrist and turned her hand palm up to look at the faint lines of the wires.

"They say you're a hero, Katie. Pretty good for a pit girl. Tell me, was it worth it?"

She shrugged. "I don't remember."

They smoked in silence. Someone opened the door, set three beers on the table, and came around the table to sit beside Daahl. As he sat down, the lamp on the table shone full in his face, and Li recognized the young labor rep from the news spin that Haas had gotten so hot under the collar about. "What is this?" she asked. "Interrogation by committee?"

"This is Leo Ramirez, the IWW rep in town. He's just going to sit in on our talk. If you don't object, that is."

"Sure, what do I care? Invite the Trotskyites. Hang up a picture of Antonio fucking Gramsci."

Ramirez grinned, dark eyes sparkling in his handsome face. "I didn't think you people were allowed to know who Gramsci was."

" 'You people'?" Li muttered under her breath and rolled her eyes.

Daahl just smiled and kept smoking.

When he had finished precisely half of the cigarette Li had given him, he pulled a handkerchief from his shirt pocket, put out the half-smoked butt, wrapped it carefully in the handkerchief, and tucked it back into his pocket.

This operation took Daahl's full attention for a good quarter of a minute, and when he finally spoke his voice was as steady as if they were discussing the weather. "Why did you make Haas drain the glory hole?"

Li shrugged. "I thought he was hiding something about the fire. I wanted to get to the bottom of it before he sent anyone else down."

"That's altruistic of you," Ramirez said.

"Oh, sure. I'm a real hero."

"Why did the Secretariat really send you?" Daahl asked.

Li took a sip of her beer, stalling, and winced as the liquid hit the raw nerve where her tooth had been. "To fill in for Voyt and handle the accident follow-up. If there was another reason, they didn't let me in on it. And anyway, I thought the idea here was that you were going to tell me something."

"We'll get there. But first I want some answers."

"I may not have the answers you want, Daahl."

"Of course you do. You just haven't thought about it enough to realize you have them. So. Why did the UN send you?"

Li shrugged. "Sharifi was famous. When someone like her dies, people want to see heads roll. I'm the axe man."

Ramirez stifled a laugh. Daahl just kept watching her with his pale sharp eyes. "If someone—let's say a friend of ours—were to possess information that helped you do that job, what would you be willing to give for it?"

"If you mean am I prepared to buy information from you, the answer is no."

"Not buy." Daahl stood and walked across the room to the single small window. The shutter cast bars of rain-green light across his face and lit up his thinning hair like a halo. "Money would be simple compared to what we want. And we'd have to know you were the right person to do business with. We'd have to have . . . assurances."

Ramirez seemed to have dropped out of the conversation, and when Li glanced over at him he was leaning forward on his stool staring at the two of them like a rat blinded by a miner's lamp. He might know the geography down here, she realized, but in this room he was the odd man out. This was miners' territory, soldiers' territory. Blood-bargaining territory.

"Why don't you tell me what you're charging," she told Daahl. "Then I'll know if I can pay it."

"Two things. First, if what you find out about the

fire explains anyone else's death besides Sharifi's, we want to know about it."

"You want me to pass information on an ongoing investigation to you? I could lose my job for that."

"We don't necessarily need the information ourselves," Daahl said. "We just need it made public."

"You mean included in the investigation report?"

"Included in anything that's public record. We can figure out how to use it from there. Right, Leo?"

Ramirez nodded. "We really just need you to bring the accident reports up to date."

"AMC's accident reports? I can't believe you have to go to me under the table to get that," Li said.

Daahl raised his eyebrows. "Then you've obviously forgotten even more than that chop shop doc said you would."

Li pushed her beer around the table, turning it in precise right angles, leaving a square of condensation on the cracked tabletop. "So basically," she said, "you're just asking me to do my job. An open investigation on Sharifi's death. And these accident reports. Which are public information anyway, right?"

"Yes. As far as the deaths go."

"Ah. What else do you want?"

Daahl bit his lower lip, glanced toward the window again. "We want Sharifi's dataset."

Li choked on her beer and slammed it back onto the table, spilling it. "She was doing defense R&D, Daahl. That's covered by the Espionage and Sedition Act. People get shot for breaking that law. And getting shot isn't on my to-do list this year."

"Some things are worth breaking the law for, Katie."

"To you, maybe."

"It's not only miners AMC's killing. There's something happening in the mine. In all the mines. Look at the production records. Look at the ratio of man-hours to live condensate pulled out. We're striking less and less live crystal down there. The bootleggers have been saying it for years. Now even some of the company miners are saying it. And Sharifi said it, before she died. She looked me in the face and said it straight out. The Anaconda's dying. All the condensate on Compson's World is dying."

"Oh, come on, Daahl. The Security Council—"

"They know," Daahl said, and gave her a moment to digest that fact. "Why do you think they're spending so much in synthetic crystal R&D? And look at the multiplanetaries, stripping out crystal just as fast as they can before the end hits. We've been saying it for years, pushing them to do something. But we can't prove it. Sharifi proved it—proved it to herself anyway—and her dataset could give us the traction we need to turn this around."

"That's crazy," Li said. "Condensates don't die. They break. How can a whole planetful of them be breaking at the same time?"

"I don't know," Daahl said. "But Sharifi did."

None of them said anything for a minute.

"I'll bring the accident reports up to date," Li said. "That's only fair. It's my job. But the other thing . . ."

"The accident reports will be enough for now," Daahl said. "Just think about the rest."

"All right," Li said. "Where do we go from here, then?"

Daahl reached into the depths of one of the piles on the table and pulled out a battered fiche. "Read this."

The fiche held two dozen separate documents, and it took Li a good ten minutes to be sure she understood them. As she read, she realized she was looking at AMC corporate records: weigh-station logs, pay chits, production records from the on-station processing plant. Slowly a pattern emerged.

"Someone's cooking the books," she said. "Someone's giving one set of numbers to the miners and another set to AMC headquarters. And they're skimming communications-grade crystal somewhere in between." She looked up at Daahl. "Who?"

"You tell me."

Li frowned and tabbed through the records again. "It could be almost anyone," she said at last. "The pit boss. Someone in the breakerhouse. Or at the mass drivers. Someone in the on-station processor or loading bays. All they'd need is a few people willing to look the other way at the right moment. That and a few friends at key points along the line."

"Those kinds of friends have to be paid," Daahl pointed out.

"You saying you know who the bagman is?"

"Look at the pithead logs."

She looked. And saw one name popping up again and again. Daahl's name. All the fiddled shipments had gone out when he was the on-shift pit boss. And he had signed off on every one of them.

"Why are you showing me this?" she asked.

"Because Sharifi died over it. Two days before the fire I heard her and Voyt talking. Fighting. She told Voyt she was onto him, threatened to go to Haas. And over Haas's head to the Service brass if necessary. She was throwing big names around. Five-star names."

"General Nguyen?"

Daahl nodded.

"And what did Voyt say?"

"Not much. I think she took him by surprise. And Voyt wasn't the type to argue to your face about something when he could get what he wanted by sticking a knife in your back."

Li picked up her forgotten beer and took a gulp of it. It was grass-bitter and warm as blood, and it reminded her of things she couldn't afford to think about now. "So you think Sharifi threatened to go to Haas, and Voyt killed her? And that the fire was ... what, a cover-up? Do you have any proof of this at all?"

Daahl shrugged. "That's your job."

Li looked back over the figures. "Voyt couldn't have done this himself. Who was running him?"

"Someone. Everyone who ever got within smelling distance knows that much. But as to who . . . that's your problem."

"And what was this someone having Voyt pay you?"

"Nothing. He just told me to sign off on the pithead logs and keep my mouth shut." Daahl smiled. "He offered what you might call negative incentives. Besides, I would have done it anyway. There are good reasons for me to have dirt on Security personnel."

"I can imagine," Li said. She probed the hole where her tooth had been and thought about the dirt Daahl already had on her.

"I put these numbers together because I knew perfectly well where they'd put the blame if they ever got caught." He shrugged his bony shoulders. "Crooked pit boss. Oldest story in the business. Anyway, I wanted to have enough information so I could roll over on Voyt if I had to. And make it stick."

"Very sensible," Li said. "But why tell me? And don't say it's all just about the miners. Union officials don't lose any more sleep over dead miners than politicians lose over dead soldiers."

Daahl glanced out the window. His eyes looked ice-pale in the faint beam of daylight. Sheepdog's eyes. Wolf eyes.

"Sharifi's death came at an awkward time," he said, speaking slowly and deliberately, as if he were trying to relay a very complicated message over an unreliable channel. "We want to make sure there's no ongoing UN presence in the mine. If that means helping you wrap up this investigation and leave, we'll help. Also for you personally . . . it would be good not to be here too much longer. No more than"—he glanced over at Ramirez—"two weeks?"

"At most," Ramirez said.

Li caught her breath, looked back and forth between the two men. "You crazy bastards," she said. "You're planning a lockdown. You think the Secretariat's going to stand back and let you shut down their best Bose-Einstein source? They'll crucify you!"

"What's the UN going to throw at us that's any worse than what the miners face when they go to work every day?" Ramirez asked. "Besides, it's not your problem. Unless you're telling us you want to make it your problem."

"Oh no. That's your fight. I'm not that crazy."

"Then I suggest you wrap this investigation up and get off Compson's at your earliest possible convenience."

Li looked back and forth between the two men, took a last sip of beer, and pushed the glass away from her. "So where does that leave us?" she asked Daahl.

"With a deal," he answered. "And make sure you keep it. I wouldn't like to see something unpleasant happen to you."

Ramirez flexed his long legs and his stool slid backwards, squeaking across the bare floor panels. "Do you know what a coffin notice is, Major?"

"Don't threaten me, Leo. I know a hell of a lot more about them than you do. And I don't plan on getting shot down in the street like a dog. Not by the Molly Maguires, and certainly not by some snot-nosed rich kid playing at coalfield politics."

Daahl laughed suddenly. "You haven't changed a bit, Katie. You must scare the hell out of humans."

He pulled a fiche off the desk and bent over it. Ramirez got up and slipped back through the airlock, pulling the blanket behind him. Li started toward the front door, but before she made it Daahl came around the table and laid a hand on her arm.

"Katie," he said, speaking quietly enough so Ramirez couldn't hear him. "If you need anything, ask me. I'm not making any promises but . . . Brian will know where to find me. Understood?"

Li nodded and stepped into the front room.

McCuen was still at the table. He had the boy on his lap, and he was twisting a piece of colored string between his fingers, showing him how to make a Jacob's ladder. The woman bent over the fire stirring something. She didn't look up when Li and McCuen left.

A few steps down the alley Li stopped.

"Wait here," she said.

Daahl answered the door. When he saw Li, he stood aside silently to let her enter. The woman and child were gone. Someone had banked the coal fire so that the room was dark and already cooling. Daahl closed the door behind him and leaned against it with his hand still on the latch. "Yes?" he said.

"Mirce Perkins," Li said. "Where is she?"

"Is that wise?" Daahl asked quietly.

"Just tell me."

"Why?"

"I want to see her."

"No you don't," Daahl said. There was an edge in his voice. Distrust? Anger? "You don't belong here anymore. Just do your job and leave. Whatever you think you remember, forget it. It's what she wanted. It's what your father wanted. You owe it to them."

Li didn't answer. After a moment Daahl opened the door and she walked past him into the watery sunlight.

Half an hour later, she and McCuen were back on the station shuttle. She gave him a carefully sanitized version of her talk with Daahl—a version that didn't include the threatened lockdown or Daahl's final words to her.

"So," he said when she'd told him as much as she

was going to. "Voyt's fiddling the books. Sharifi finds out, threatens to tell Haas, Voyt kills her. Pretty tidy."

"Too tidy. First, nothing says Voyt actually killed her. There's about fifteen people strung out along the pipeline that Voyt could simply have been playing bagman for, and they all had as much motive as he did. Second, what or who killed Voyt? Third, what was Bella doing down there and who moved the bodies after she saw them? Fourth, what the hell caused that fire in the first place?"

"Still . . ." McCuen said, pushing at the Voyt angle as single-mindedly as a bloodhound baying on a hot track.

"Yeah," Li said. "Still."

What a pit!" Cohen said, peering around Li's quarters with a shocked expression.

Today's face was a thirtysomething Italian actress who was just starting to get talking roles in the kind of clever independent studio interactives Cohen was always trying to drag Li to. She was so astonishingly, exotically beautiful that Li couldn't be around her without stuttering and tripping all over herself—even when she wasn't standing in Li's narrow quarters sparkling like a diamond in a mud puddle.

Of course, only part of the sparkle had anything to do with either the 'face or Cohen. The rest was the packet compression needed to accommodate the encryption protocols Cohen had insisted on using for this streamspace-realspace visit. It left him looking bright, hard-edged, slightly more in focus than everything else in the small room. And Li didn't even want to think about the credit he must be blowing at the private-sector entanglement banks.

He opened the closet, flicked at the spare uniforms

hanging there, and sniffed dramatically. "You mean to tell me you actually live here?"

"No," Li said, rummaging in the piles of fiche on her desk, looking for Daahl's production figures. "It's the next hot vacation spot. Just making it safe for the free world."

He circled the room, tilting Chiara's exquisite head as if he harbored some vain hope that the room would look better from a different angle. He turned to her, forehead wrinkled with earnest dismay. "Really, Catherine. I don't think the Corps appreciates you properly."

"They appreciate me enough to keep the paychecks coming. In the real world—a place I'm aware you don't visit often—that's pretty much as good as it gets."

She found Daahl's fiche and handed it to Cohen, acutely aware of the slim shapely fingers brushing hers.

"Intriguing," he said, before she'd even dropped her hand back to her side. "Any brilliant theories about who's raiding the cookie jar?"

Li crossed her arms over her chest and shook her head. "How the hell do you do that? I never get used to it."

"Mmm. Sheer brute computing force. That and the fact that I'm eight times cleverer than anyone this charming has a right to be."

Li smirked.

He stuck his tongue out at her, slipped his shoes off, and sank gracefully onto her bunk. "So. Where were we?"

She grabbed her desk chair and turned it around to sit backwards on it. She summarized her meeting with Daahl and Ramirez, telling Cohen about the exchange of information and the lockdown, but leaving out the personal talk.

"And this Daahl person just picked you out of thin

air?" Cohen asked when she'd finished. "He thought you looked like a nice friendly person? You'll forgive me if I confess to having suspicious thoughts about him."

Li shrugged, trying to look unconcerned. "It didn't come up."

Cohen had sprawled across her bed while she was talking—he had to be doing this on purpose, didn't he?—and now he stretched, sighing luxuriously, sending Chiara's glossy curls cascading across Li's pillow. He opened his eyes, gazed at her in wide-eyed and utterly insincere innocence, and said, "Sure it didn't. Well, we'll revisit that question later. Have you found the accident reports he wants?"

"I tried. Didn't have time to really look."

"Time is my middle name," Cohen said with a grandly munificent gesture that Li was sure Chiara had never used in her life. "What's your password?"

Li gave it to him, and he logged in and produced the missing accident reports within less than a minute.

"Where were they?" she asked.

He raised an eyebrow. "In Voyt's files. Until a few days ago. Someone deleted them ten hours before you hit station."

"Who?"

"Hush. I'm working on it. Go do something useful."

Li scanned the reports, stopping here and there when a name or a word caught her eye:

```
02/01/47. Stokes, William. Age 32. ID
  No. 103479920. Subject fatally
  injured when he returned to Wilkes-
  Barre North 4 to check a missed shot.
  No autopsy. Cause of death: burns.

04/12/47. Pinzer, G. F. Age 26. ID No.
  457347423. Subject discovered in
```

lower gallery Wilkes-Barre South 14,
crushed by roof fall. Rescuers unable
to extract body because of gas
seepage. Subject identified from
personal effects, pit bottom logs.
Cause of death: trauma.

04/19/47. Mafouz, Christina. Age 13.
ID No. 764378534. Subject's coal cart
experienced brake failure in gangway
west of Wilkes-Barre East 17. Subject
suffered multiple compound fractures
and dislocations with associated soft
tissue trauma. Left leg amputated
below knee, St. Johns hosp.

These entries were no news at all to Li. They
recorded death and maiming by fire, explosives, roof
falls, equipment failure. All the routine dangers of the
miners' world.

But scattered among the typical accident reports
were other ones:

17/20/47. Carrig, Kevin. Age 37. ID
No. 355607534. Subject found
unconscious in Trinidad South 2. Pit
inspector hypothesizes subject opened
gas pocket, but rescuers found no gas
at work site and autopsy revealed no
signs of gas inhalation. Cause of
death: unknown.

20/2/48. Cho, Kristyn. Age 34. ID No.
486739463. Subject collapsed during
survey of Trinidad South 7. Witnesses
describe complaints of head pain,
bright lights, convulsions, loss of
consciousness. Autopsy indicated

extensive, nonlocalized damage to
frontal lobe. Cause of death: brain
seizure.

The troublesome reports had started about four months ago. Deaths attributed to electrical shock where repair crews had been unable to find stripped wires or standing water. Deaths attributed to gas where other miners working in the same vein had been mysteriously spared. Healthy miners dying of heart attacks, strokes, brain seizures. And two miners hadn't died—were still lying in the Shantytown hospital in the grip of comas that no doctor could explain.

There had been a spate of these inexplicable accidents when the Trinidad opened. Then things had leveled off. Then there had been another significant bump three months ago: fourteen unexplained deaths in a single week.

Li didn't have to cross-reference dates or check her files to know what had happened three months ago.

Sharifi had arrived.

"Guess where the reports were deleted from?" Cohen asked, arching a slender eyebrow and forwarding the still-legible remnant of an erased access log to her. "The station exec's office."

"So, Haas deep-sixed the accident reports the day before I arrived."

"And he was embezzling crystal, or at least we suspect he was."

"And," Li said, feeling vaguely dirty, "we know Haas is not unfriendly to the Syndicates."

They looked at each other.

"It all keeps coming back to Haas," Li said. "Doesn't it?"

Instead of answering her, Cohen vanished.

Li staggered to her feet, knocking her chair over. Her quarters looked wrong somehow. She checked her internals and realized that she was no longer in limited VR interaction mode, but in full two-way.

She tried to access realspace.

Nothing.

Code.

Nothing

She'd been bagged, warehoused, shunted into virtual deadspace. She closed her eyes and rubbed her face, thinking. When she opened them again, she was no longer on-station.

She stood in a perfectly square, perfectly empty room. Blank white walls. Blank floors and ceilings. Nominal squares of windows opening on an eternity of white nothingness. Her heartbeat hammered in the silence like a kettledrum. She focused on a corner where floor met wall in order to stave off vertigo and waited, counting her heartbeats.

A door opened. One moment she was staring at a blank wall. The next someone had stepped into the room with her. But when she tried to recapture the moment of entry, it was missing, skipped over as if there had been a bad splice in her optical feed.

The new person in the room was small, dark, slender. It took Li a few heartbeats to focus on him after the long blank whiteness. When she did, she saw coltish, gangling legs below striped shorts. A red-and-black football jersey. Dark hair. Olive skin.

"Cohen?"

"Sshhhh!" he whispered.

He had nothing on his feet but tall striped socks with bulky shin guards poking out over their tops; his old-fashioned soccer cleats were tied together by the shoelaces and thrown over one bony shoulder. He circled the room, stopping several times to peer at sections of wall that looked, to Li's eyes, completely unremarkable. He walked up one wall and sat down cross-legged a few feet below the ceiling. "Well, here we are," he said.

"We? I don't know who the hell you are, except that you look like Cohen. Which proves nothing."

He grinned. "Looks don't always deceive, my dear. Even mine."

"Prove it."

"How?"

"Tell me something."

"Like what?" he said, sounding for all the world like the ten-year-old he appeared to be.

"Something no one else would know."

He wrapped his arms around his legs and put his sharp little chin on his knees, thinking. "Right," he said. "Well, you're two centimeters shorter than you tell people you are."

"You could pull that out of my transport files."

"And you're an evil-tempered beast in the morning."

She snorted. "As opposed to the rest of the time?"

"Good point," he said, and laughed.

He peered owlishly at her, rubbing at a fresh scab on his knee. "There's always your deepest, darkest, awfulest secret."

She froze. She tried for a laugh but couldn't quite get there. "Which one?"

"That I love you."

She looked up to find him watching her as if she were a suspicious package that might explode without warning. "Oh, for God's sake," he said after a brief awkward silence. "You don't have to look like you're ready to chew your leg off to get away from me every time I say it."

"Don't exaggerate, Cohen."

"It's no exaggeration. Trust me." He shot her a resentful look from under dark eyelashes. "And it's ridiculous. It's not like you're some fainting virgin, for Heaven's sake."

"Now you just want to sleep with me? You've lowered your sights. Last time I was supposed to be wife number seven. Or was it eight? Christ, Cohen, you get married like normal people buy puppies!"

"Normal humans, you mean." He gave her a long naked defenseless look. "That's what it's all about for you, isn't it? Trying to pass. Getting the signed, sealed, and delivered human stamp of approval." He laughed bitterly. "I'd really like to get inside your head and know what you think when you look in the mirror every morning."

"You've got me all wrong, Cohen."

"Do I? Then what are you so afraid of?"

"Nothing," she snapped. "I'm just not interested in being the next stop on your tourist trip through the human psyche."

He looked away and muttered something she couldn't quite hear.

"What did you say?"

"I said that's exceptionally nasty, even for you."

The room suddenly felt too small, too hot. Li turned away and began checking the walls, trying to find some chink in them.

"Look," she said after a long, uncomfortable pause. "I didn't mean—"

"Forget it. It was stupid of me."

"So what's with the kid?" Li asked when the white silence had become too thickly oppressive to stand any longer.

"Ah." Cohen undid the laces of his sneakers and started putting them back on his sock-clad feet. "I thought you knew that. This is Hyacinthe."

"I thought you were Hyacinthe."

"He's one of the things I am. He's my original, bedrock interface program. And, of course, the man who invented me."

Li had a sudden urge to laugh. "As a ten-year-old?"

"Actually he was fourteen when this was done. It's old video footage. He used it to create the original VR interface. I guess you could say it was my first 'face. I tend to fall back on it when I'm pushing the limits of my processing capacity. As at present, unfortunately."

"Can't we get out?" Li paced the room's perimeter again.

"No. And sit down before you drive me incurably mad. You're safe as long as I'm here."

But just as he said the words—as if someone were playing a nasty joke on them—he was gone again.

Li was back in the dark place.

This time she knew she was underground, in the mine. But that was all she knew. Water dripped from an unseen ceiling, splashed in an unseen pool. A damp, chill air current wafted up from some underground river too far off for her to hear.

She cut to infrared. No good. She was instream; she saw only what the person controlling the simulation wanted her to see.

"Light a lamp," Cohen's voice whispered from somewhere near her left ear.

Her hand reached out to where it knew the lamp was. Picked it up. Primed it. But her fingers fumbled with the wick, as if they had become sudden strangers to this familiar task. As she adjusted the flame, she brushed the inside of her hand against the hot barrel of the oil reservoir and heard the sizzle of burning skin.

"Shit!" she said, putting her hand to her mouth instinctively, sucking at the blistered crescent of flesh.

"Sssh," Cohen said. "You're fine. Tell me what you see."

She held up the lamp and saw an uneven floor of hewn rock running away in all directions. Pillars of light marched in long ranks from one end of the space to the other, gleaming like ivory in the lamplight. The ceiling arched overhead, supported by undulating veins that fanned from one Bose-Einstein node to another in an infinitely repeating, fractally complex spider's web.

"It's the glory hole," she told Cohen. "Sharifi's glory hole."

But it was the glory hole intact, unburnt and unflooded and full of softly whirring and clicking equipment. The glory hole before the fire. A generator hummed in one corner. Optical cables snaked across the floor between thickets of diagnostic machinery. Crooked teeth of crystal jutted from floor and ceiling.

The mouths of the earth, Li thought. Wasn't that what Compson had called them?

"Is this where the hijacker took you?" Cohen asked.

She raised the lamp and turned in a slow circle. To her left a steepening upslope followed the line of the vein, echoing the mined-out chamber on the level above. To her right, the portable virusteel ladder led to the chamber and drift above, and to the long slippery stairs out of the Trinidad.

"Is this it?" Cohen whispered—and she realized for the first time that the whisper was not behind her but inside her. "Is it your memory or someone else's?"

"Someone else's."

"Whose then? Think."

Her hand moved reluctantly, as if she were keying instructions over a bad link. She squinted at it. It was hers, all right. Short nails. Strong, brown, blunt-ended fingers. Still. There was something not quite right about it. She turned it so the palm faced her.

No wires.

She looked at the hand again, more carefully. The nails were longer than hers, better cared for. She counted old scars that weren't there, new ones that shouldn't have been there. And the fresh burn, a slim crescent of raised scar tissue between thumb and forefinger.

"It's Sharifi," she said. "It's Sharifi's memory."

Then Sharifi turned at the sound of approaching

footsteps, and Li was helpless, along for the ride like any other ghost.

It was the same sequence she'd seen in the last hijacking. But this time she understood what she was seeing. The strange patterns chasing each other across the cavern were light from Sharifi's lantern. The pinging sound was dripping water. The booming rifle reports were bootheels slapping on bedrock.

"What are you doing here?" Sharifi said, as Voyt climbed down the ladder.

He reached the bottom, turned, and grinned nastily. "Just keeping an eye on the merchandise."

"Fine. Stay out of the way then."

"Where's our honored guest? Off stealing the silverware?"

"Right here," Bella said, stepping into the lamplight.

Li watched through Sharifi's eyes as Bella approached. This was not the subdued woman she had met on-station. This Bella met Voyt's stare and returned it. This Bella moved with the arrogant looselimbed grace of a fighter, smiled the cool smile of someone who knew she could outsmart you, humiliate you. No matter what the game was. "Are you ready to deliver?" she asked.

Sharifi looked hard at her, frowning a little. "Are you?"

Bella opened her mouth to answer, and the flickering, lamplit shadows of the glory hole gave way to a blast of white light.

Li was back in her quarters.

"Cohen?"

"Here." Her livewall flickered on to reveal Cohen, shunting through Chiara again, sitting in his sunfilled Ring-side drawing room.

"Do you know what we just saw?" Li asked.

"I know what you think we saw."

"It's there, in Sharifi's memory. Everything we need to know. We have to go back."

"We have to do no such thing. We almost got trapped there. And you still don't know if what we saw was real or not."

"I'll chance it."

"No you won't. And if you decide to be stupid about it, I'll personally lock you offstream."

A dark suspicion tugged at the back of Li's brain. "Why are you so scared? What are you not telling me?"

"I've told you everything I know, Catherine."

She laughed. "How can someone who's had two hundred years to practice be such a shitty liar?"

She expected him to at least smile at that, but he just sat staring at the ground, arms crossed, swinging one sandal-shod foot back and forth in a nervous rhythm. He leaned forward, elbows on his knees, hands clasped together so tightly that Chiara's knuckles whitened.

"Listen. Drop this investigation. Tell Nguyen you're sick, or you need maintenance. Which you do, obviously; I haven't seen you pick anything up with that arm since you hit station."

Li stared. A roach crawled across the floor and started up the livewall. She saw it with surreal clarity, each leg arcing forward, setting itself down against the glowing matrix of the viewscreen. When the roach began to crawl across Cohen's leg, she reached out and flicked it away.

"I can't drop it," she said. "I'm one mistake away from getting chaptered out."

"I can think of worse fates than a discharge."

"Well, I can't." She paced around the narrow room. "You got me into this mess. And I'm not talking about just now. I'm talking about Metz. Whatever you know, I want to hear it."

Cohen sighed, and Li wondered, not for the first

time, how he managed to stamp his personality so strongly on his shunts. It was impossible to imagine Chiara's lovely face wearing that tired, ancient expression—just as it was impossible to imagine Cohen not suffusing every 'face with that self-deprecating irony born out of a thousand lies, half lies, and compromises.

"I don't know anything," he said. "I only suspect. Helen, for one. Where else could Sharifi have gotten the intraface?"

"That's crazy, Cohen. And anyway, Nguyen never had the intraface. The raid on Metz failed."

"Did it? Look at the timing, for God's sake. We pull the source code and wetware for the intraface off Metz and a few weeks later Sharifi's on Compson's World, wearing it? You run the numbers."

"But you said that wetware couldn't just be grown in viral matrix. That it had to be tanked in place, in a clone. So if Sharifi used it, it must have been cultured for her. And if TechComm was in on this from the get-go, then . . . why would Nguyen steal something she already owned?"

"What better way to get hold of illegal wetware without leaving a paper trail than to seize it in a TechComm raid?"

Li rolled her eyes. "Oh, come on!"

"Sharifi wasn't just a victim, Catherine. She was involved. She came here to do a very specific job. A job she needed the intraface to do—or why would someone like her have risked experimental implants?"

"Fine. But to say that there was UN involvement—"

"Of course there was. Sharifi was working for TechComm. They controlled her budget. They controlled access to the mine. They controlled the old construct genelines, Sharifi's included. And if TechComm controls something, that means the Security Council controls it. Which means Helen. Helen who sent you to Compson's World before

Sharifi was even cold. Or should I say before she was even dead?"

Li caught her breath.

"Come on, Catherine. Don't be an idiot. I put transit time from Metz to Compson's World at almost three weeks. You hit planet ten days after the fire. That means she decided to send you here at least a week before Sharifi died."

"I know," Li said reluctantly. "You think I hadn't thought of it?"

"But you damn well haven't done anything about it, have you? Have you considered asking her why she really sent you here?"

"I considered it. And I decided not to."

"Why the hell not?" She didn't answer, and after a moment Cohen continued. "I'll tell you why not. Because you don't want to know. You don't want to think about what she's doing, about what you're doing. You don't want to think, period."

"Are you finished, Cohen?"

He stood up, cursing, and paced in a tight circle before the viewscreen. "My God," he said, when he was facing her again, "that's why she loves you so much. She gives her orders and it's over. You don't question, you don't think, you don't hesitate. You're her creature!"

"No. I'm a soldier. And I'm loyal. Something you wouldn't understand."

"Don't bait me. You need me. Our little chat in the white room back there? Whoever engineered that was toying with us, playing with us like a cat plays with a dead bird. And they're targeting you, Catherine."

Li stood in front of the screen, looking at the floor. The roach she'd flicked away was still rolling around on its back trying to right itself. She stepped toward it, set the toe of her boot on it, and crushed it.

"It's not just Helen," Cohen continued. "There's an Emergent involved. And not just any Emergent.

Someone's using AMC's field AI. Someone who's managed to turn me back every time I tried to track them. Someone strong enough to trap me, play with me. And they're after you."

"I thought you said AIs weren't interested in people, Cohen."

"Maybe I was wrong. Or maybe you've done something that's made them interested."

Li swallowed. Her mouth felt dry, metallic. "Or maybe they're using me to get at you," she said. "Did you tell someone about us?"

" 'Us'?" Cohen looked like he was about to laugh. " 'Us,' as you so delicately put it, lasted all of thirty-six hours. When exactly would I have had time to tell anyone?"

"Then what are they after, Cohen? What do they want from me?"

He looked away, and she saw his throat tense as he swallowed. "How the hell would I know?"

AMC Station: 21.10.48.

Game one.

Li shouldered her way into the All Nite Noodle at the bottom of the second inning. Hamdani was on the mound, dark socks pulled up to his knees, right leg shooting up in his high angular windup kick. The Mets' big Cuban designated hitter had just crushed a line drive off the center field wall and put himself on second with the help of what Li thought should have been considered an error. The outfield was playing in close, looking nervous.

The line cook touched a finger to his hat and nodded as she walked in. Before Hamdani had retired the next batter, Li was settled at a quiet back table with a beer and a bowl of noodles. When someone sat down at the table next to her in the top of the sixth, she assumed it was the line cook coming to pass time with a fellow Yanks fan. She turned, smiling—and saw a man her oracle claimed she'd never met before.

She nodded, thinking he was just taking the empty chair, and looked back to the game just as Hamdani trotted to the mound. So far he'd held off the heart of the Mets batting order and kept the Yanks their tenuous two–one lead. But he had thrown far too many pitches. And he was looking shaky, fussing with his bad elbow between batters.

He was one of the great ones, but he was getting old, injury-prone. His fastball was slowing down. His curve and slider had lost their bite. He wasn't unhittable anymore. And it looked to Li like he was about ten pitches away from exhaustion.

He wound up and threw a sharp slider that just caught the outside of the plate. "Fantastic!" Li said under her breath. A taste of the old magic there.

"Ball one!" the umpire said.

"God dammit!"

"Major," said the man across the table from her, "I had no idea you were so passionate about this."

Li's attention snapped away from the game. The man smiled at her—a carefully rationed smile in a young-old face that revealed nothing. She took a closer look, trying again to place him. He reminded her of someone, but in a generic way. As if it were not a single person he brought to mind, but a whole type of person. A type of person that gave her a bad, uncomfortable, guilty feeling.

A thrill of apprehension ran down her spine as she made the connection. He was Syndicate. And he reminded her particularly of the diplomatic rep from . . . where? MotaiSyndicate? KnowlesSyndicate? Whichever Syndicate he was from, that must mean he was A Series. But what the hell was an A Series construct doing on Compson's World? And how could his talking to her spell anything but trouble?

"I don't think I know you," she said. Best to tread cautiously.

"Oh, but I know you," the A Series answered. "I know quite a lot more about you than you might imagine."

"Then you have the advantage."

He smiled again. A diplomat's smile. A spy's smile. "I think there are few areas in which I'd have any advantage over a woman of your . . . what's that word humans are so attached to? Talents?"

The crowd cheered, and Li's eyes snapped back to the screen. The Cuban was up again. "Big game," she said, hoping her new friend would take the hint and leave.

"Hmmm. I wouldn't know. Not a fan. Actually, I came because I hoped I might get the chance to talk to you."

Sure, Li thought. The chance to talk her straight into a full-scale internal affairs investigation. "Great," she said. "Why don't you come by the office in the morning?"

"Ah," said the stranger. "Well. This isn't official. I believe it's something we might most profitably discuss in private."

Li turned and looked straight at him, her recorder's status light winking in her peripheral vision. "In private is not an option. You can either talk to me on the record here or on the record in the office tomorrow. Those are the rules."

"The rules." The man spoke musingly, drawing the single syllable out, considering it, interrogating it. "But there are rules and rules, aren't there? Wasn't that how it was on Gilead?"

Li's stomach plunged as if a high-altitude chute had just snapped open and snatched her out of free fall. Then she forgot her stomach, forgot the game, forgot Gilead, because her head was throbbing and her eyes were watering and the room was spinning around her.

"Andrej Korchow at your service," the man said. "Privately, anyway."

Li shook her head, sniffed, sneezed. She felt like she had something up her nose, but she knew the feeling was an illusion. In fact Korchow had simply jammed her recorder, and her internals were spinning their computational wheels, desperately trying to fend off whatever he was throwing at them.

"What do you want?" she asked. Her coolness surprised her. She knew people who'd been approached. It was inevitable. If the Syndicates didn't hit you up, internal security would. Or corporate agents. She'd expected to feel outrage, fear. But all she felt now was a cold, calculating conviction that she had to keep her head and pick a careful path through the minefield that stretched before her.

"I don't want anything, Major. Other than a chance to introduce myself. You strike me as someone with whom I might have . . . common interests."

"I doubt that."

"Ah, but how can you be sure if we don't discuss them?"

She looked back to the livewall, delaying. Hamdani was tightening up even under his thick turtleneck. He blew on his hands, got called for going to the mouth, stalked off the mound in a fury, came back, stalled. When he finally delivered, the pitch got away from him and drifted invitingly over the heart of the plate.

"Shit," Li muttered, just as the crack of the bat sounded through the room. She sighed in relief as the ball died over the warning track.

"You're a curious woman," Korchow said smoothly. "An enigma, one might almost say. I confess to a powerful interest in you."

Li kept silent.

"When I learned you'd been posted here, I was, quite frankly, astonished. Your service record shows . . . an impressive ability to get results. It seemed to me that you deserved more. Had a right to expect more."

"I don't see it that way," Li said. "And even if I did, I have plenty to lose. And plenty to be grateful for."

"Grateful. For what? For the chance to tend the

colonial sheep and take orders from inferiors? Or is there some other explanation for the hero's anticlimactic homecoming? Some people"—Korchow's voice shifted subtly, got harder, colder—"idealistic people . . . gullible people . . . have surmised that your fall from grace shows the Security Council has repented of some of its . . . harsher attitudes. I am not one of those people."

"If you have something to say, Korchow, say it."

"I have nothing to say, Major. I'm merely curious. Call me a student of human nature. Or is *human* the right word here? By the way, has anyone ever told you how much you look like Hannah Sharifi? Amazing the strength of the XenoGen genesets. Their work was crude, of course. Human, after all. But some of the pre-breakaway designers had real genius."

"I doubt you'll find many fans of their work around here." Li shook her head again, not making any progress against Korchow's jammer.

"No, alas. By the by, was Sharifi really murdered?"

"That's not established."

"But I'd been told you have suspects."

"You were told wrong, then."

"Indeed. So hard to get accurate information. A thorny problem, that. It makes reliable information particularly valuable."

Li started to lick her lips, then caught herself, realizing how it would look. Korchow was skirting the edge of deniability. Asking about Sharifi. Asking for information. Unmistakably offering . . . something. But so slyly that Li couldn't explicitly reject the offer without appearing to have raised the subject herself.

Was this a UN internal affairs sting? A genuine approach by a Syndicate agent? Or just the corporate espionage department of some multiplanetary fishing for tidbits about Sharifi's work? Whichever it was, they were surely being recorded. The only question was who the wire belonged to. "I can't give out information about an ongoing investigation," she said.

"I wouldn't dream of prying into a Controlled Technology Committee investigation," Korchow answered. "My interests are more properly described as . . . tangential to yours."

On-screen, the Cuban was up again. The game was tied, the Yanks one out shy of a win. It was Hamdani's to lose.

"I don't know why you'd think TechComm has anything to do with my being here," Li said.

"Really, Major. The problem with being as honest as you clearly are is that it doesn't equip you to lie competently when necessary."

"Hah!" Li said. Her defensive software had finally managed to outflank Korchow's block. They were back on tape again.

"Well," Korchow said, standing up. "It was a pleasure talking to you." He reached into his breast pocket, pulled out a narrow card, and set it on the table in front of her. "My card. I run a store in the capital. Antiques. Compson's World is a treasure trove of remarkable artifacts. I'd be honored if you paid me a visit and allowed me to show you what the planet has to offer."

"I doubt I'll have time," Li said. She plucked the card off the table and tried to hand it back to him.

"No, no," he said. "It is one of my firm beliefs that one should never close any door in life until one is quite certain that one does not want to walk through it."

Li watched him slip through the crowd and vanish. Then she looked down at the card in her hand. It was made of some matte fiber that looked like, but was not, paper. And instead of printed words and pictures it bore a precise geometric lacework of punch holes. A Hollerith card.

She'd seen Holleriths before, and she recognized the implicit status message. It was written in decimal code, and in a format that no machine for two centuries had been able to process. It embodied a technofetishist, antiquarian, nose-thumbing aesthetic. And it assumed that anyone you handed the card to could recognize and process the antique code without an external computer.

She was certain, looking back over their conversation, that Korchow was KnowlesSyndicate. Knowles was the diplomat's syndicate, the spy's syndicate. Their A Series were mavericks within the close-knit conformity of Syndicate society, artists of information and manipulation, as formidable as they were unpredictable.

The surface address punched into the Hollerith card put Korchow's shop in Helena. Behind the punch holes the card's surface bore an intricate engraved logo that reminded Li of the patterns in Cohen's Persian carpets. Where had she seen that design before? On an advertisement? She searched her hard files for a match and found one in the top layer of her actives. Recent, then.

She accessed the file, saw the digital image of a leather-bound journal with a dozen business cards tucked into the front flap pocket. And there, peeping out from behind several slips of shiny fiche, was the corner of Korchow's Hollerith card.

The notebook was leather. Brown leather as soft and expensive as butter. Sharifi's.

On-screen, the Cuban had carried Hamdani deep into the count, fouling off pitch after pitch, though Hamdani was throwing everything he had at him. It was only a matter of time until he turned on one of those not-quite-fast-enough fastballs.

"Walk him, you idiot," Li muttered. "Don't throw the game away."

But Hamdani wasn't going to walk him. Couldn't bring himself to walk him, though he must know in every cell of his aging body that he'd already been beaten. He wound up, looking stiffer and older than Li had ever seen him look. The ball left his hand a split second too early and floated across the plate square in the middle of the strike zone.

The Cuban saw it as soon as Li did. His eyes snapped around. His arms extended. His broad back turned toward the camera as he rounded on the ball. The bat cracked like rifle fire, and Li didn't need to hear the roar of the crowd to know it was all over.

The windup. The pitch. It's gone.

She stood up and tucked Korchow's card into her pocket, feeling the prickle of unseen eyes on the back of her neck. Then she walked—slowly, carefully, expressionlessly—back to her quarters.

The next morning, four hundred and seventy-six hours after the rescue crew found him in Trinidad South 12, James Reynold Dawes came out of his coma and started talking.

As soon as she found out, Li shuttled down to the Shantytown hospital to see him. When she got there, Sharpe and Dawes's wife were standing in the corridor outside his room arguing with two AMC mine guards.

"We have orders," one of the guards was saying. "No one's supposed to see him, and that's that."

Li flashed a smile and her ID. "I think we could let his wife in, don't you?" she said.

"That's not what I was told."

"By who? Haas? Call him. In the meantime, this hospital is a public institution. AMC may run the mine and the town, but here you're on planetary militia territory. Which means that, until someone with a militia commission shows up, I have jurisdiction."

"Thanks," Sharpe said as Dawes's wife slipped into the room.

Li shrugged. "I have to talk to him too, actually."

She gave Dawes a few minutes with his wife, then knocked at the door.

"Come in," called a young man's voice.

She stepped into the room and saw Dawes lying in a raised bed between cheap viruflex curtains. "How're you feeling?" she asked.

"Pretty good. Considering."

"Up to a few questions?"

He shrugged.

"Should I go?" his wife asked.

"Not unless you have somewhere else to be."

"Well . . ." A look passed between the couple. She slipped out of the room, and Li heard the sharp sound of her heels receding down the tiled corridor.

"So," Li said when she and Dawes were alone. "I bet that was a shocker of a wake-up."

He grinned. "Just like sleeping fucking beauty."

"I hope you at least got a kiss for your trouble. Sorry if I interrupted it."

He laughed at that, then gasped and paled. "Three broken ribs," he said. "The doc told me if I'd slept another week and a half I'd have woken up and not even known about them."

"Well, you know what they say. It's an ill wind that doesn't blow someone's house down."

"Ouch!"

"Sorry," Li said. "So do you remember anything?"

His face clouded. "Like what?"

"You tell me."

He glanced doubtfully at her. "You're not from AMC, then, like the last one?"

"What last one?"

"The guy they sent down to talk to me earlier today. He kept wanting to get me to say I'd slipped and hit my head and didn't remember anything."

"Did you? Hit your head, I mean."

"Not according to the doctors."

"And do you remember anything?"

The shadowy look drifted across his face again.

"Do you not want to talk about it?"

"No! No, I want to talk about it. I just . . . I'm not sure what it was, I guess."

"What do you think it was?"

"I don't know," he said again, shaking his head on the pillow. "If I told you, you'd probably laugh at me."

"Try me," Li said.

And he did.

What he described sounded just like what Li had seen on her two hijackings. Strange sights, vague shadowy figures. Sounds that made no sense or were oddly distorted. Fractured twilight visions that could have been past or future or neither.

"Did you see anyone you knew?" Li asked when Dawes fell silent.

"Oh, yeah. I saw all of them."

"What do you mean, all of them? All of who?"

"The dead." He looked up at her, and his eyes were dark and wide, the pupils expanded as if he were slipping into shock. "All of them. All my dead. Just like the pit priests say you see."

Li swallowed. "Do you think it could have been a hallucination? Or, I don't know, something else. Like a spinstream hijacking—" She remembered that Dawes was unwired and too poor to pay for stream time anyway, that he'd probably never even known anyone who had direct spinstream access. "I mean like someone trying to communicate. Someone not dead, I mean."

He thought about it.

"I don't know," he said finally. "I'm not a churchgoing man. But they were there. You know what I'm saying? They were . . . different."

"Did you—" Li stopped to clear her throat. "Did you see Dr. Sharifi?"

"No."

"You'd have recognized her if you had seen her?"

"Sure. I saw her a bunch of times. She looked . . . well, like they always look."

He lay silent for a moment, looking up at the stained foam ceiling panels of the hospital module. A long moment passed with no sound to mark the time but the pounding of a trapped fly against the room's dust-caked window. Dawes's face softened, took on a puzzled, disappointed look.

"The thing is," he said, "I felt like they took me for a reason. Like they were trying to tell me something specific, something they thought was important."

"What do you think it was?" Li asked, her breath catching in her throat.

To her surprise he smiled. "Seems like that's the question of the hour. AMC's man kept trying to ask me that. Which wasn't so easy given that he was also trying to get me to say I fell down and hit my head and never saw anything. Even Cartwright asked me that."

Li's stomach clenched. "Cartwright's been here?"

"The old geezer was practically waiting outside my door when I woke up. He was nattering at me before the doctors even figured out I was back. Wanted to know where it happened. What level. What deposits it was near. I guess he has some theory or something."

"I don't suppose he shared it with you?"

"Not really. But I got the idea he thought I'd had some kind of religious experience. And that he disapproved. Strongly. He kept talking about unlikely vessels and looking like a man who just caught his wife sleeping with the plumber."

"What do you think happened down there?"

"I don't know what to think." Dawes's face darkened again. "A man could get scared thinking about it. Especially when he knows that once his sick pay runs out, he'll have to go back downstairs again. I've seen what happens to miners when they take up with the pit priests. They still use the old words. *Jesus, Mary*, the *saints. Sacrifice.* But it's like suddenly they mean something else. Something they don't want you to see until you're too far in to back out." He passed a hand over his face, wincing as the movement tugged at his broken ribs. "And there's another thing," he said. "They never talk about God. It's all Mary. The Virgin this, the Virgin that. Her saints. Her Heaven. But they're not her saints, they're God's saints. The real ones, anyway.

"You know what Cartwright said to me today?" He propped himself up on his elbows. His eyes looked feverish, terrified. "He said God doesn't know us. That God chose humans. Earth and humans. That only Mary loved us enough to come to Compson's World. Why would he tell me that? What kind of place is it that God won't come to? What happens when you die down there?"

"Hey!" One of the guards popped his head into the room, then stepped in, followed by two militiamen. "We got Haas on the line, and he says the isolation order goes for you too, Major."

Li was too stunned to react at first, still wrapped in Dawes's shadowy vision. "Let me talk to Haas," she said finally.

"Fine. Talk to him somewhere else, though. It's my ass if you're not out of here pronto."

Li glanced over at Dawes. He shrugged a little and gazed back at her wide-eyed, as if to say it was all a mystery to him. She tried Haas's line quickly and got a message that he was out of the office. No surprise there. He would no doubt remain out of the office until he was good and ready for Li to talk to Dawes.

Out in the hall, a tall young man in coveralls was talking to the duty nurse. Li had actually walked past him when a familiar movement made her stop and look back. It was the IWW rep, Ramirez. And from what she could catch of the conversation, he was trying to talk his way into Dawes's room.

"What are you doing here?" she asked, more abruptly than she'd meant to.

"Just visiting a friend," Ramirez said smoothly.

"Isn't that sweet."

If Ramirez caught the sarcasm in her voice, he didn't give any sign of it. "Hey," he told the nurse, smiling and touching her shoulder. "I'll catch you later, okay?" He put a hand in the small of Li's back and guided her down the hall toward a windowless door marked EXIT. "It's actually really good you happened by just now," he told her. "I've been wanting to talk to you."

They stepped through the door into the gold-green haze of a sunny fall afternoon. They stood on the honeycomb-grid landing of a fire escape with a clear view over Shantytown to the atmospheric processors and the gently flaming stacks of the power plant. A slight wind rattled the cheap siding of the hospital modules and tugged idly at the wind sock on the ER hopper pad.

"Hail, fellow traveler," Li said. "Aren't you supposed to be out demonstrating your solidarity with the workingman and getting ready to hold the barricades when the tanks roll in? Or were you planning to duck out at intermission and skip the last act? I believe that's what all the best people are doing."

"Hey, relax. I just thought this would be a good chance to touch base and . . . see if we could help each other out."

She narrowed her eyes. "Is this coming from Daahl or you?"

"Both."

"And what do both of you plan to get out of it?"

"Well, that's what I was hoping to talk to you about. It'll take a minute, though."

"You've got five," Li said, leaning back against the railing and shaking out a cigarette. "Well, more like six, actually, depending on how fast you make me want to smoke. Cigarette?"

"No thanks," Ramirez said. "They're bad for your lungs."

She looked hard at him.

"You know someone like you could do a lot of good, Major."

"What do you mean, someone like me?" she asked quietly.

"Someone who grew up here. Who knows what it's like. You could really open people's eyes Ring-side."

"And what would that accomplish?"

"Everything. It would give the lie to the corporate propaganda about the Trusteeships, about what goes on in Bose-Einstein mines. It would let people in the inner planets know what their money's really doing."

She laughed. She couldn't help it. "They know, Ramirez. They know as much as they want to know. Or are you too young and idealistic to have figured that out yet?"

Ramirez flushed.

"Look," she said. "I didn't mean to give you a hard time before. But I've seen way too many idealistic young things rip through this town. And they all believe the same thing. That if they just talk to the right media types, get on the right spins, publish the right book, all the injustices of the system will magically stop. Well, they won't. The system is the way it is because people like it that way. Because it works most of the time for most people. Or at least for most people who have enough clout to do anything about it."

"That's pretty cynical."

"Just realistic."

"It's also a good excuse for not taking action."

"Don't preach, Leo." Li flicked the ash off her cigarette and watched it flutter in the breeze. "It's not attractive. And besides, I gave at the office."

"I understand where you're coming from. You've

worked hard for what you have. You don't want to jeopardize it—"

"You don't understand anything," she snapped.

"But—"

"But nothing. I've seen rich kids just like you all my life. You come down from your university dorm, or Mommy's house, or wherever. You rile everyone up, you get a few miners shot, then you buy yourself out of any real trouble and go home to a comfortable job in a nice office. Meanwhile, the miners who got shot in your little passion play are still dead. And their parents and kids and brothers and sisters are still wheeling oxygen tanks around by the time they're fifty."

"I'm sorry you feel that way," Ramirez said. He shook his head as he said it, and something about the movement looked odd to Li. "Did you know work has started up again in the Trinidad?" he asked, switching gears abruptly.

"No," Li said, really caught by surprise this time.

"That change your opinions any?"

"No. Is this all you had in mind when you dragged me out here, or is there something else you want?"

"There is." He leaned back against the fire-escape railing and crossed his arms. "Listen. We were approached recently. I won't say by whom. But the gist of it is that there are parties who want to know what Dr. Sharifi was working on before the fire. And these parties would be willing to support the . . . um, action we discussed recently. Financially as well as in other ways."

"I assume you're talking about Andrej Korchow," Li said. "And, no, I'm not interested in discussing anything with him. Certainly not anything under TechComm jurisdiction."

"Not even if—"

"Not even if."

Ramirez shrugged his shoulders, then winced and put a hand to his neck. And suddenly Li saw what it was that had bothered her about his kinetics.

He was nursing a newly installed cranial jack. It was camouflaged by a self-adhesive skin patch, but the bump under the patch and the puffy irritated flesh around the new implant were unmistakable.

"That home-brew equipment?" she asked, waving her cigarette toward his neck.

"I don't know what you're talking about."

"Those FreeNet jacks are a good deal on the front end, but the side effects are hell. You ever seen anyone die of a wet bug?"

"What's your point?"

"Just that I wouldn't be screwing around with illicit tech if I were you." She ground out her cigarette on the fire-escape railing and sent it arcing into the vacant lot next door. "And you can pass that advice along to Daahl too. Call it a freebie."

"We wouldn't have to home-brew if the Security Council didn't have a stranglehold on streamspace, would we?"

"Hey, don't look at me, I just work for the man."

"Oh, right." Ramirez spat the words out hard and fast. "Just a good little soldier. Just following orders, no matter what the orders are. But then I guess that's what XenoGen built you for."

Li lashed out at him without thinking. She stopped herself so quickly that he didn't notice he'd almost been hit. But she knew she would have broken bones if she hadn't pulled the blow.

She backed off, frightened by what had almost happened. "You racist son of a bitch," she whispered. "Don't you ever say that to me again. You don't know me. You don't know a thing about me."

According to the old and tired joke, there were only three reasons to take a meeting in realspace: sex, blackmail, and pure whites-of-the-eyes intimidation.

Li didn't think she had much hope of intimidating

Haas, but if he was going to torpedo her investigation, she figured he could goddamn well tell her so himself. And since files could always be faked or distorted, he could tell her face-to-face, where she'd have a court-admissible record of it—the one locked and coded in her own datafiles.

As it turned out, she could have saved herself the effort; by the time she got back up to his office, he was gone.

"If you'd like him to call you . . ." his secretary said. Her expression said that she knew exactly why Li was there and that Haas wouldn't be coming back until she was good and gone.

"Never mind," she said. She was reaching for the door when someone spoke her name from the shadows.

Bella stood in the door of Haas's office. Barefoot, in a tank silk dress that clung to the slim curves of her hips and stomach. She beckoned. Li followed her through a hidden door and down a shadowy corridor into what could only be Haas's private quarters.

They were spacious by station standards, furnished in the same expensive, aggressively modern style as the office. Bella didn't turn the lights on, just let the refracted light of Compson's World shine up through the floorports, casting disorienting upside-down shadows.

"You live here?" Li asked, unable to stop herself.

Bella looked up at Li, her face so close that Li could read the flowing blue letters of the MotaiSyndicate logo that curved along the lower edge of each perfectly patterned iris. "Does that shock you?" she asked.

Li had never been this close to a Syndicate construct, except for D Series soldiers and the occasional field officer. No women. And never, never anything like Bella.

She was taller than Li remembered, and she had a sharp wild scent that made Li think of high-mountain forests. She wondered fleetingly if the smell was perfume or a high-priced option engineered into her geneset by the MotaiSyndicate designers. She cleared her throat. "Why would it shock me?" she said. "It's none of my business who you live with."

Bella leaned closer. Starlight shifted over her face, casting the sculpted angles of her face into sharp relief, and Li saw that one fragile cheekbone was swollen by a fading bruise. She took Bella's chin in her hand, turned her face to the light. "Who did that to you?"

Bella bit her lip. It was an unconscious gesture, fearful and sensual at the same time, and it made Li want to protect her.

More than protect her.

She jerked her hand away. "You could file charges," she said, but she felt the futility of it even before she spoke.

Bella smiled. "You don't like to see people hurt," she said. "You're softhearted. Just like Hannah was."

"How well did you know her?" Li asked.

"Only well enough to know she was kind."

"There was an entry in her datebook a few days before she died, just an initial, B. Did you have an appointment with her that week? Did you meet? Talk about something?"

Bella turned away and wandered around the room, the starlight flickering up through her flowing skirts. As she walked, she ran her fingers lightly over the chairs, the bookshelves, the back of a sofa. Li shuddered, feeling as if it were her own flesh Bella was touching, not dead virusteel and vat-leather.

"Sit down," Bella said.

Li sat.

Bella ended her wandering in front of the sleek black box of Haas's streamspace terminal. She looked down at it, her black hair spilling over her shoulders like water running down a coal face. She sprang the catch and opened the terminal, revealing a dense tangle of spintronics wrapped around bright shards of communications-grade Bose-Einstein condensates.

She slipped a pale finger into the rat's nest of wires and skimmed it along the condensates. "They're cold," she said. "They're always cold once they're formatted. Curious. In the mine, they speak to me and no one else. Up here, they speak to everyone . . . and to me they're just dead stones."

Li looked at the terminal's guts and waited to hear whatever Bella was trying to tell her.

"Can you hear them?" Bella asked. "In the mine? Can you?"

"Not really," Li answered. "They just fry my internals, that's all."

"To me they sing. It's the greatest thing I've ever done in my life, hearing them. It's what I was made for. In a way no human could understand."

"Is that what you did for Sharifi? Find crystals?"

Instead of answering, Bella bent over the ansible and lifted out one of the clear slivers of condensate. It glittered in the faint light. Bella held it up between them and looked through it, and Li saw the blue-violet shimmer of her eyes refracted through the crystal.

"Do you actually know how they work?" Bella asked.

Li shrugged. "I learned what I needed to pass my commissioning test. Beyond that . . . well, who knows how they really work?"

Bella looked away, her eyes shadowed by the dark fall of hair. "Hannah knew. She knew everything about them."

"Bella," Li said, speaking quietly, "what was Sharifi doing in the mine the day she died?"

"Working."

"No. She went down there to meet someone. Who was it?"

Bella reached into the tangle of chips and wires to replace the crystal. "If I remembered," she said at last, "don't you think I'd tell you?" But her face was turned away from Li, into darkness.

"I'm trying to catch the person who killed her, Bella. I need your help. I need any help I can get."

Bella looked at Li for a moment without speaking, then came across the room, knelt in front of her chair between her feet, and laid her pale smooth hands on Li's thighs. "I want to help," she whispered. "You have to believe me. I'd do anything to help you."

Bella's hands were hot, even through the thick fabric of Li's uniform. She knew she should put some distance between them, but leaning back into the deep chair seemed too much like an invitation.

And Bella wasn't looking for that. She was looking for help. For someone to stand up for her, to be the friend Sharifi seemed to have been. She wasn't looking for Li to get in line behind Haas and who knew how many others to take advantage of her. And the mere fact that she seemed to think she had to offer it made Li sick.

She took Bella's hands in hers. She put them away from her. She extricated herself from the chair and stepped around the kneeling woman. Bella made no move to stop her.

"Have you ever met Andrej Korchow?" Li asked when she'd gotten far enough away to think straight.

Something snapped closed behind Bella's eyes. "Who?"

"Korchow."

"No. Why?"

"I think he was paying Sharifi for information about her project."

"No!" Bella stood up abruptly. "That's not the way Hannah was. She didn't care about money."

"For someone who didn't care about money, she spent a lot of time fund-raising."

"She had to do that. Putting fiche in the printers

and cubes in the computers. That's what she called it. But she didn't care about it."

"Then what did she care about? What was it all for?"

Bella stood up and smoothed her dress over her waist in the habitual gesture of someone raised in the low rotational gravity of the Syndicate's orbital stations. "It was about the crystals. She talked about them all the time. What people were doing to them. She wanted to protect them."

"From what?"

Bella shrugged. "From . . . this." She made a gesture that encompassed Haas's streamspace terminal, the planet below them, the whole of UN space.

"The miners think the condensates are dying, Bella. Are they?"

She laughed harshly. "We have twenty years of digging left, thirty maybe. The geologists can never agree on the exact number, but what does it matter? The reports never get past management." She smiled. "It's AMC's dirty little secret."

"Did Sharifi discover that secret?"

"It's why she came here."

"Is that what happened in the glory hole, Bella? Did Sharifi try to stop Haas from digging? Did they fight over it?"

"I told you," Bella said, her voice cracking with frustration, "I don't know. I can't remember. But that's where you have to look. To the mine. To the crystals."

Li had seen her own specs once, at a technical briefing on a troopship off the occulted side of Palestra's fifth moon, the night before her first combat drop.

It had been excruciating, even in a room of people who had no reason to know that she wasn't the legally enlisted one-quarter construct she appeared to be. And it changed her life.

She sat in the briefing room, watching the codes scroll up the screen before her, listening to the techs discuss tensile-strength equations and bone-core profiles, self-evolving immune systems, designer intestinal and respiratory flora. And she understood for the first time in her life what she was, what all constructs were. They were beasts of burden. The culmination of ten thousand years of human intervention in Earth's genetic pool. The universal working animal of the interstellar age.

That knowledge stuck with her through all the jumps and all the new planets that came after that briefing. It lurked at the back of her mind whenever she hefted a heavy load, put in a long day's work, slipped into streamspace, took a lover in her arms.

She thought it again now as she crouched on the practice mat and watched McCuen strip off his sweat-soaked T-shirt, baring a freckled torso that spoke of a good exercise regimen and an only mildly tweaked geneset. A little tougher, stronger, stockier than human norm, but still the product of two parents and the random collision of forty-six chromosomes. Still street legal and well beyond the long arm of TechComm.

"Hot as hell in here," McCuen said, and threw his shirt to the edge of the mat. "And that's leaving aside the fact that you're driving me into massive oxygen debt. You sure you're not cheating?"

"Swear to God," Li said. "Got my whole system powered down." She stood, pulled off her own shirt, and wiped her dripping face with it. "See that?" She pointed to the ridged muscle on her stomach. "Worked my ass off for that. Something you might bear in mind next time you decide to sleep late instead of dragging your sorry tail to the gym."

There was a mirror on the far wall, and as she turned, she caught a glimpse of herself. She saw what she always saw: stocky, hard-muscled body; genetically preset 6 percent body fat; chest flat enough to make feminine modesty as theoretical as athletic support.

It took a hell of a lot of work to maintain a military-grade wire job. Hours of gym time just to keep up the muscle strength and bone density that protected you from stress fractures. And though Li's construct genes gave her the luxury of skimping on that work, she didn't. It was her one vanity.

She glanced in the mirror again. Cohen was right, she thought critically; she looked thin. Too many jumps, too little gym time. She ought to get Sharpe to send up a case of hormone shots before she overdid it and pulled something.

"You don't go in for the smart tattoos, huh?" McCuen said, pointing to the baby blue UNSC on her left shoulder.

She'd gotten the tattoo along with her whole platoon sometime during the wild week of drinking that had followed her first live-fire action. The names of her fellow initiates had slipped out of soft memory, but she still felt the cold sharp sting of the needle, could still see the intent face of the dockside tattoo artist bent over his work.

"Good thing it's not on the other arm," McCuen said. "Scar would have gone straight through it."

Li twisted to get a glimpse of the blue letters, the first time she could remember looking at them in years. She grinned, acutely aware of the clichéd ridiculousness of the tattoo. "Perish the thought!"

She'd set up the Security-personnel physical-training program for fun more than anything else, and any benefit to on-station morale was a side perk. The main point of the sessions was that they created an at least arguably official excuse to round up the half dozen Security personnel on-station and tussle. She wasn't going to give them some line of crap about how practicing carefully choreographed moves with a line soldier whose internals were powered down was going to open up glorious new career opportunities. She just set a time, showed up, and left it at that. If they wanted to come, they could. If they didn't, they didn't.

And McCuen had wanted it. Wanted it enough to show up, morning after morning, and take the punishment she doled out. He was on fire, a single track of idealistic ambition. When she worked with him Li could feel the old heat coming on, the sharp edge of a happiness she hadn't felt since long before Metz. If she could get him a ticket off Compson's, she caught herself thinking, maybe her time here wouldn't be a dead loss after all.

"You've really never been back here since you enlisted?" he asked, as they worked on the footing for a particularly complicated throw Li was trying to teach him. "Why not? Bad memories?"

Li loafed over to the side of the mat, took a drink of water, wiped her face and hands. "Not really. Just never had a reason to."

"No family?"

She hesitated. "Not that I know of."

They worked through the move a few more times in silence, McCuen picking it up quickly and grinning with delight when Li finally let him throw her at something like full speed—an indulgence she knew was a mistake the moment her sore shoulder hit the mats.

"No family makes it easier, I guess," he said, picking up where they'd left off. "My parents aren't so hot on the Corps. They've been reading about wetware side effects, jump amnesia." He smiled and shrugged, trying to pass off the concern as his parents', something only old people would worry about. Li answered the implied question anyway.

"If you cooperate with the psychtechs and back everything up carefully, you shouldn't forget much. Otherwise . . . sure, you can lose a lot. But even if something goes wrong, it's not the way it was ten years ago. They've been minimizing jumps, moving personnel around much less. Even enlisted troops. Hell, you could pull a permanent assignment on one planet, never jump more than a half dozen times in your whole career. If the peace holds."

"If the peace holds. That's the kicker, isn't it?"

"What do you want?" Li asked, amused to hear herself echoing Haas's words of a few weeks ago. "Promises?"

A flush bloomed behind McCuen's freckles. "That's

not what I meant. It's just . . . the war gave a lot of colonials a chance to prove themselves. People like you. People who would never have gotten a shot at command in peacetime. Now that's gone. And back home it's even worse. We've got the multiplanetaries doing business with the Syndicates, trading away what few jobs there were on Compson's for locals. There are mines on the southern hemisphere that already have D Series constructs working underground. Replacing miners. My dad keeps telling me to stay home and run the store, but where's the future in it? Once the multiplanetaries figure out they can use Syndicate labor, that's the end of the independents and the bootleggers. And no more bootleggers means no more UN currency on-planet. And no more UN dollars means company scrip only, which means the company stores are going to finally squeeze out the rest of us. Things keep going the way they're going, and there'll be the Ring-side multis and the Syndicates, and that's it. Nothing left for the little guy except a government post. If you can get one."

"They really have D Series working Bose-Einstein deposits?" Li asked. She'd never heard that, couldn't imagine how TechComm had allowed it.

"Working everywhere," McCuen said. "You name it. Why hire a born worker when you can sign a thirty-year contract and get someone who's programmed to do the job for free and can be replaced with another clone if they get sick or start causing trouble?"

Why indeed? Li thought.

"Hey," McCuen said. "Sorry to rant. You want to grab dinner tonight with some of the other day-shift guys? Catch a game or something?"

"Can't." Li grinned. "Hot date."

McCuen looked at her and bit his lip.

"What's that supposed to mean?"

"Just . . . it's not with Bella, is it?"

"Excuse me?"

"Small station, that's all. Rumors travel."

"Well, in this case, they're unfounded. Whatever they are."

"Good," McCuen said. He seemed about to add something else, then stopped. "I just wouldn't like to see you get hurt," he said finally.

Li was about to ask who he thought was going to hurt her when Kintz walked into the gym with his usual gang of sidekicks.

"Morning," he said to Brian. "Getting a little private tutoring?"

McCuen flushed, just as Kintz had intended him to, and Li groaned internally; McCuen would never command a grade-school class, let alone combat troops, if he couldn't learn to brush off that kind of nonsense.

"Feeling neglected?" she shot at Kintz. "I can fix that." And within a minute the others had taken her unsubtle hints about applying themselves to the weight machines, and she and Kintz had squared off against each other on the last practice mat away from the door.

Kintz was fast and accurate, and even with his internals powered down for safety purposes he moved with the surefooted speed of a professional. Normally it would have been an unadulterated pleasure to be faced with such an able opponent. But there was something about Kintz that made Li not want to get into the clinches with him. Not want to touch him, even.

She settled into her rhythm, feeling out her opponent, looking for whatever she could use against him. Kintz was good. Far better than anyone else on-station. But he wasn't as good as he thought he was, and that faint tinge of complacency gave Li a hole big enough to drive a tank through.

She moved him around the mat, still assessing his footwork, letting him feel like he was getting a few hits in. It was a necessary sacrifice given his longer reach, but every time he landed a blow she regretted the pounds she'd dropped since Metz—pounds that would have spared her ribs and given her something to push back with when he closed on her.

She was starting to see something she could work with, though. Kintz preferred to hit right-handed and his footwork was particularly clumsy when she pushed him back and to the left. The trick of course was to play off that weakness without alerting him to it. And to do that she had to stay outside, mix it up, keep him moving. And of course let him get in those sucker hits.

She drew him into the middle of the mat, dancing around him. He caught her on a lucky kick, missing her knee but momentarily catching her instep. It threw her off-balance just long enough for him to catch up with her.

They grappled, each of them trying for a grip, for purchase. He had caught her in an awkward position, and she felt him improving his hold, getting a wrestler's lock on her. She planted a leg, grunting with the effort, leaned into him with her good shoulder, and threw him.

The flash of anger in his eyes was unmistakable, but he recovered his balance and his attitude quickly.

"Nice trick," he said. "Guess you didn't just sleep your way to the top."

"Wouldn't you like to know," Li answered, resisting the urge to stamp on his fingers.

McCuen and the others had drifted over, drawn by the thud of Kintz's body hitting the mat. "If you think this is worth watching, you've got a lot to learn," Li told them, and they drifted away again, looking embarrassed.

Kintz was pushing her now. He'd been doing his own weighing and balancing during the meet-and-greet sparring; now he was going after her bad arm with the fierce instincts of a street fighter. He was getting winded, though. She heard the faint whistle of constricting air passages every time he sucked breath. That was something, she thought, and ducked in under his guard, chancing a risky move.

Five years ago it would have worked. But she wasn't as fast as she'd been five years ago. He caught her hip with a blow that sent her staggering, and in that fraction of a second's hesitation, he had her. He went after her bad arm, and she struggled to keep him from getting a grip on it. When things sorted out, he had her in a neck lock.

When he spoke, his voice was so twisted by the effort of holding the lock on her that she didn't at first register the sounds as words. Then she understood them and felt a cold rush of adrenaline course through her.

"I could snap your neck right now," he said. "Who'd ever think it was anything but an accident? I could tell them you wanted to fight with safeties off, and you just shit ran out of luck."

She tried to slip her hands under his arm and get the pressure off her neck, but he jerked at her hard enough to put the thought out of her mind.

"You think you're special, don't you?" he whispered. "Think you can just walk in and start poking sticks at people? Think we'll all just jump to it? Right, Major? Whatever you say, Major?"

Li bent her knees, felt out Kintz's balance, took a chance, and managed to throw him again.

"Piss off, Kintz. You and Haas. You are his errand boy, aren't you?"

Kintz wiped his mouth, and his hand came away red. "You don't have a fucking clue, do you?" he said. Then he was on his feet, and they were back at it.

She never figured out how he got by her the next time, but suddenly he had her. His right arm snaked out and caught her under the jaw. His left twisted her bad arm behind her back so tightly she felt ceramsteel

grate and creak against cartilage. He lifted her onto her
toes, using his height to deny her leverage. She felt his
ribs pressing into her back, smelled sweat and cheap
aftershave. She gathered herself, braced her feet, textbook fashion, and tried to throw him.

Kintz laughed. "That the best you can do, Major?"
He was as solid as rock behind her. Or, more accurately, as solid as ceramsteel.

Adrenaline had kicked her internals on a few times
already during the fight, and she had shut them off
just as quickly. Now she turned them on and left them
on. She twisted and strained, pushing protesting tendons and ligaments within a millimeter of breaking.
Nothing budged. He had a solid grip on her, and even
with her internals pushed as far as she could risk pushing them, he was just plain stronger than she was.

"The Corps isn't juicing you guys like it used to,"
Kintz said. "Or maybe you're just behind the curve."

He twisted her arm until her knees buckled and her
vision shut down to a red-hazed tunnel.

"I know what you are," he whispered, his breath
hot in her ear. "I can buy half-bred cunts like you in
every whorehouse in Helena. This isn't Gilead. You
don't have an army to back you up here. And I'll show
you what that means if you don't mind your nasty little digger business."

Her first urge was to fight, driven by the massive
dose of adrenaline her internals were shooting
through her system. Then she thought it through and
almost laughed at the ridiculous childishness of the
situation. What the hell did she care? What point was
there in damaging herself in order to not have Kintz
be able to say he'd beaten her on the practice mat? She
forced herself to go limp in his arms, waiting.

It worked, after a fashion.

"Stupid slut," Kintz muttered under his breath. He
let go of her arm, but as he did he slipped his foot in
front of hers, almost sending her sprawling. Her inter-

nals kept her on her feet, but by the time she turned to face him he'd already crossed his arms and pasted his usual grin back onto his face.

She laughed, aware that her hands were shaking with rage. "That was fun. We'll have to do it again sometime."

"Sure." Still grinning. "See you around."

She stood in the middle of the mat, weight on her toes, and tracked him all the way to the door. She must have looked as shaken as she felt; before she could pull herself together, McCuen came and stood in front of her with a worried look on his face.

"Okay, Major?" She heard his voice through a haze of adrenaline, as if he were speaking from somewhere far away.

"I'm fine," she said, running a dripping hand over her hair. "But that son of a bitch needs an attitude adjustment."

The glory hole.

Light and silence. A fullness of space like the rush inside a conch shell. Pillars that were ribs leaping up into the wild geometry of the fan vaults, raising the roof of a living cathedral.

Li had last seen it in the dark and underwater. Now she was seeing it as the miners had seen it, as Sharifi had seen it. And Bella was right; it did sing. Li might not hear the music the witch heard, but her internals were going wild, overloaded by the quantum storm that raged in the glory hole's gleaming belly.

There had been problems draining it. It had taken the cleanup crew much longer than expected to shore up the surrounding passages and run the pumps in. And for several tense days they had struggled to find an underground river, broken out of its banks by the fire and subsequent flooding, that kept refilling the

Trinidad's lower levels as fast as they could drain them.

The work went even slower because the miners, except for the pit Catholics, wouldn't work the glory hole. It was a place surrounded by fearful superstition, as terrible to some people as it had been fascinating to Sharifi.

Something cracked and skittered away from Li's foot. She bent, her headlamp raking the rough floor with shadows, and saw two glittering red eyes flashing back at her. She touched the thing and heard a little clack like the sound of two marbles kissing. She picked it up.

It was plastic. The kind of cheap, locally produced petroleum product that always cluttered up Compson's markets. Two red marbles connected by a loop of black elastic. It was a Love-in-Tokyo, a cheap bauble to tie off a little girl's ponytail. Li herself had worn one in some faded past in which she'd actually been a little girl with a ponytail. Reflexively, she pulled the elastic around her wrist and slipped the plastic marble through the loop. She heard the click as it fastened, felt the elastic bite into her wrist, the smooth pressure of plastic beads against her skin. A memory rose up out of the deep rift of her unconscious, fierce and precise, a child's vision of night and fear.

It had been some other glory hole she had visited, not this one. A hole long since dug out and sold off piece by piece by AMC or some other company. Her mother had carried her. Her father was there, nearby but not with them. It was in another deposit; she remembered long hours on the rough mountain roads, borrowed rebreathers passed from hand to hand in the shaking, grinding truck bed under the flapping canvas. It was dark when they left, darker when they got there, darkest in the hot muttering mine. She had been terrified by the noises the mine made, by all those tons of mountain shifting and grumbling above her. *I am inside a beast*, she remembered thinking, *swallowed alive, like Jonah.*

The memory dropped away from her. She shook her head and looked around. What had they been doing in that other glory hole? Why had they gone there? She followed the vein of the memory, trying to pick it up further along, pry loose some concrete recollection. Nothing.

"What's that?" McCuen asked, pointing at the Love-in-Tokyo.

Li jumped; she'd forgotten him. Then she held it out for him to see.

He grinned. "Doesn't look like Sharifi's style exactly."

"Is it possible Cartwright or someone else would have been bringing children down here?"

McCuen looked uncomfortable. "Well, AMC tries to stop them. But what are they going to do? They can't block off every borehole and ventilation drift. And even if they tried, there are plenty they don't know about."

"What do you know about glory holes, McCuen?"

He looked at her as if he thought she was asking a trick question.

"Really. I've forgotten a lot of what I knew before . . . before I enlisted."

McCuen took a breath and frowned. "They're what the geologists call white bodies—nodes in the beds that cross multiple strata. The best crystal's always in the white bodies. Some of them are transport-grade straight through from end to end. When a company hits one . . . well, it's the big money. Boom time."

"But it's more than money, right? Why's Cartwright so worked up about it?"

"I'm Pentecostal," McCuen said, and there was a knife edge of disapproval in his voice so subtle Li would have missed it if she hadn't somehow known it would be there.

"And this is about the pit priests," she said slowly. "And the union."

"Is there a difference?" McCuen asked.

"Come on, Brian. It's important."

"I . . . only know what you hear. I'm not sure most of the Catholics know much more than that. It's not like Rome approves of it."

"And?"

"And nothing. The priests—the ones that believe in it—look for white bodies. That's what Cartwright's doing down here. Not that AMC knows he's a priest. They'd flay him alive."

"And what do they do when they find a glory hole?"

"Go down and gawk at it, mostly. I mean what do people do when the Pope comes?"

"And?"

His face shut down. "And nothing."

"That wasn't nothing I just saw cross your face. Tell me what you just decided not to tell me."

"I didn't decide not to tell you. I just don't believe in repeating rumors. I mean, I haven't mentioned all the guys who are supposed to have fought for the Provisionals, have I? Because obviously they haven't. It's just tongue wagging."

"Actually," Li said, "a lot of them have."

McCuen stared. "No shit," he said, and she could see the wondering look on his face even in the lamplight. "Like who?"

"Chuck Kinney, for one."

"He's a construct!"

"So? And the barkeep at the Molly. Obviously. Oh, and those two brothers, the redheads, four or five years older than me."

"Mutt and Jeff?"

"Christ, they still call them that?"

"Well, look at them."

Li laughed. "So what's the supposedly not true rumor about what they're doing down here?" she asked, hoping McCuen's gossipy mood would survive the change of subject.

"Oh, it's a lot weirder than the IRA thing. More like the kind of story you tell kids to scare them into doing what you want them to." He grinned. "I bet it was my aunt or someone who told me. And . . . you really don't know any of this?"

"Sometimes I do. Sometimes I forget." She grinned. "You'll get to find out all about that soon enough."

"Right. Well, the story about the glory holes is that the priests take people down there and . . . feed them to something."

Li laughed. "What, like ritual cannibalism?"

"I told you it was ridiculous."

It is ridiculous, Li started to say. But before she could open her mouth, the vaults spun around her ears and she was in the grip of another flashback.

Her father and mother were there. But they were smaller than in the last memory, strangely reduced. It took her a moment to puzzle that out. Then she realized it was she who had changed, not them. This was a more recent memory.

She tried to see their faces but couldn't. She knew who they were in an abstract sense, but their actual features were invisible to her. As if each of them wore a blank white mask that said Mother or Father. As if they had no faces.

Two men stood beside her father, cloaked in shadow. One she recognized by the set of his shoulders and the scar snaking down his throat: Cartwright. The other, thin, wiry, ducking his head into his collar, she couldn't quite place. She looked at her mother and saw that she was crying silently, tears streaming down her cheeks. She looked back toward her father, and she almost fainted in terror.

His chest was gone. All she saw there was a dark hole that swallowed all the light of the crystals around them, that threatened to suck down into itself even the spanning ribs of the vaults overhead. He smiled at her—or perhaps he just smiled. Slowly, not taking his eyes from hers, he lifted a hand, plunged it into the black void within him, and pulled out a thick sheaf of paper.

Li saw the paper, the bony coal-scarred hand holding it, even the sooty rubber band tied off around the wad. She saw it all, registered it, digested it with the surreal accuracy of dream vision. What she did not see—not until it was too late, not until it was burning in her hand already—was what the paper was.

It was money. Money she'd spent fifteen years ago.

SecServ, UNSC Headquarters: 22.10.48.

Nguyen sat at her desk under the tall windows. Ruddy sunlight glinted off her uniform jacket, struck fire off her epaulettes, haloed her straight-backed figure in red and gold.

"So," she said. "The station exec was skimming. You think. But you don't have proof, as far as I can see, other than the fact that you think he's mistreating his girlfriend. Everyone is always skimming in any Bose-Einstein operation, Li. The rewards are too rich to resist. If he really is guilty, AMC probably knows already, and they won't welcome hearing about—what did you say his name was?"

"Haas."

"—hearing about Haas from us."

Li didn't answer immediately. Nguyen continued. "What about Gould?"

"She'll reach Freetown in twenty days."

"Then you need to have this wrapped up by then."

"We may not be able to wrap it up without her."

"No. That's not acceptable. We may lose her again.

She may manage to get some message out—God knows what or to whom—before we can intercept the ship. Twenty days. That's all you've got. And you're wasting time on some two-bit embezzler and his Syndicate-bred girlfriend."

"But Sharifi's murder—"

"You're missing the point, Li. Sharifi's murder—if she really was murdered—is a side issue. The real target is what she was working on and who she was leaking information to."

"Yes, but the two things are tangled up together. Haas was—"

"Are you trying to tell me that Hannah Sharifi was ignoring her research in order to chase after a second-rate petty thief?"

"No, but—"

"Then we're in agreement. I want Sharifi's datasets. I want to know who she showed them to. And most of all I want to know what kind of damage control we need to do in order to prevent them from getting into the wrong hands."

"The wrong hands being . . . ?"

"Anyone's but ours." Nguyen took a breath and leaned forward. "I have good news. I saw an internal draft of the board's decision on Metz. It's not official yet, but I think they'll clear you."

"Great," Li said, but the muscles of her thighs and shoulders ratcheted even tighter as she waited for the other shoe to drop.

"If that happens, I want to talk to you about a new assignment. To Alba."

"Great."

"Assuming the board falls your way, that is. There are still a few members on the fence, as I understand it."

Including Nguyen herself, no doubt. "What would it take to get them off the fence?" Li asked, playing the game and hating herself for it.

"A clean, fast resolution of this investigation, for one thing."

First the carrot, then the stick.

"Also"—Nguyen paused delicately—"stay away from Cohen for the next little while. You're a fine officer. A good soldier. But you're in over your head with him. Cohen, despite all his charming eccentricities, is no harmless crackpot. Talk to him, and you're talking to the board of directors and sole stockholder of the largest multiplanetary in UN space. He controls shipping lanes and streamspace links to a good third of the Periphery. He has a corporate espionage department that is, without exaggeration, twice the size of our internal affairs division—"

Li laughed. "I think he's offered me a job in it."

"Probably. I'm sure you'd be very useful to him. Which is exactly my point. It's never personal when you talk to him. Don't let the organic interface lull you into thinking you're dealing with someone who feels things as we do. You can't trust him. Except to act in his own best interest. That's what he's built to do. Nothing else. There is nothing else for him."

"Why are you telling me this?" Li asked. "Cohen's the best freelancer we have. Now he's suspect?"

"Just because we work with him doesn't mean we trust him. Some people are too powerful to be challenged. Cohen's on the Security Council's watch list, for Heaven's sake. Don't forget that. We may not have had enough to take him to court on it, but he deliberately caused the planetary net crash on Kalispell last year. That's manipulating a network with intent to harm humans. If we'd nailed him on it, he'd have been stripped down to his switches. And Tel Aviv—"

"Tel Aviv was an accident."

"An accident like Metz?"

Li's stomach turned over. "What do you mean, Metz?"

"Catherine," Nguyen said patiently, and Li felt a

weird sense of disjuncture at hearing the name that
Cohen always called her. "Forget Metz. I'm just asking
you to remember he isn't human."

"Neither am I," Li pointed out.

Nguyen gestured impatiently. "That's not the point.
What you are or aren't . . . that's semantics. A few di-
vergent chromosomes. A grandmother whose geneset
was assembled by design instead of chance. But in
every way that counts, you are human. Cohen is
something else entirely. Don't let personal feelings get
in the way of remembering that."

Nguyen sighed, picked up a fiche, scanned and
signed it, and moved it to the other side of her desk.

"Well, that's over with," she said. "I hope it wasn't
more unpleasant than it had to be. I think you understand my reasons for raising the issue. Anything else?"

Li started to speak, then hesitated, weighing the
risks of telling Nguyen about Korchow. "Yes," she said.
"I had a strange talk with someone the other day. I'm
not sure how to proceed."

Something sparked behind Nguyen's dark eyes as
Li told her about Korchow, and she had a sudden
uncomfortable conviction that her meeting with
Korchow was the real news Nguyen had been waiting
to hear. Maybe even the real reason Nguyen had sent
her to Compson's in the first place. But that was crazy,
of course. Even Nguyen didn't control everything and
everyone.

"What makes you think Korchow was in contact
with Sharifi?" Nguyen asked.

Li downloaded an image of Korchow's card and
flashed it onto a shared substream. "I found this in her
datebook."

"Well," Nguyen said, looking at it. "Maybe she was
just buying antiques from him."

"Sure she was."

"How sure are you he's Syndicate?"

"I'm not. But he had the look. And if he wasn't

Syndicate, he was doing everything he could to make me think he was."

"So. Sharifi was talking to a Syndicate agent . . . about her work, we have to assume. And now the same agent wants to talk to you."

"What do I do?" Li asked.

Nguyen's lips thinned in a chilly smile. "You talk to him."

Korchow's address put him square in the center of Helena's commercial district, a five-minute walk, air quality permitting, from the old colonial administration building. But Li had a first stop to make before she saw Korchow: St. Joseph's Home for Girls. And unlike Korchow's shop, St. Joe's wasn't in the nicer part of town.

Compson's capital city predated the Bose-Einstein Rush. The elegantly dilapidated domes of the capitol building and governor's mansion recalled the old home-rule days before the Bose-Einstein boom. The commercial zone's masonry colonnades and office blocks reminded visitors that Helena had once been more than just a company town, Compson's World more than a Trusteeship. Still, there was nothing quaint or old-fashioned about the slums Li's cab rolled through on the long drive in from the spaceport. They were brand-name UN-wide standard-issue: market democracy in action, legislated by the General Assembly, bankrolled by the Interplanetary Monetary Fund.

Everywhere she looked, she saw the mines. The Anaconda was half a continent away, the next closest Bose-Einstein mine in the remote northern hemisphere, but even at that distance they stamped their mark on the city. Acid rain painted long sulfur-yellow streaks on the composite board walls of the housing projects. A permanent smog of coal dust hung in the air, fed by pea-coal fires in every kitchen. Blue-faced ex-miners shuffled along the sidewalks in the final stages of black-lung, come to the capital to live off their comp checks.

On the outskirts of the industrial zone the cab passed a long weedy stretch of open space. Goalposts leaned crookedly at either end of the field. They'd been white once, but the paint was peeling and streaked with rust. Someone, probably some local welfare group, had taken care of the grass; otherwise, it would long ago have lost its battle against the burning rain.

Eight players were scattered across the field, a few in uniform, the rest dressed in street clothes. As the car passed, one player broke upfield, running with the long sure stride of a born striker. The sun passed out of the clouds just as he took his shot, and a ray of sunlight stabbed across the field, silvering the striker's legs, the taut arc of the goalie's body as he leapt to intercept the shot.

Li shuddered and looked away, back into the half dark of the cab.

St. Joe's sprawled in the shadow of the poorest projects. It had one permanent building—a drafty-looking parish church whose brick facade was overdue for pointing. The rest of the orphanage was housed in colonial-era modular units that weren't much more than Quonset huts.

The sister who met Li at the door wore blue jeans, a

flannel shirt, and a rawboned no-bullshit air that made Li wonder if she were ex-militia.

"So you're the one who wants to know about Hannah," she said. "What are you, half-XenoGen? That why you're interested?"

"I'm the senior UN officer on-station," Li said. "It's my job to be interested."

The sister narrowed her eyes at Li for a moment. "You'd better keep your cab," she said. "You won't find another one in this neighborhood." She waved her into a long, dimly lit corridor. "Sorry for the lack of a welcoming committee, but everyone else has class now. You'll have to make do with the principal."

"Thanks, Sister . . ."

"Just Ted." She grinned. "For Theresa. Class lets out in two minutes. We'd better beat a strategic retreat to my office."

They walked back through the rat's nest of tin-roofed buildings, down linoleum-floored hallways, past long racks of children's winter coats and school bags. The smell of chalk and Magic Markers seeped out from under the classroom doors, along with the disciplined refrain and chorus of every Catholic-school class everywhere. As they passed one room, Li heard a voice that could only belong to a nun say, "You're not as cute as you think you are," provoking a quickly smothered wave of childish laughter.

The bell rang ten minutes to the hour, and a noisy, laughing, rambunctious flood of uniformed schoolgirls poured out into the corridors. Sister Ted waded through the flood with the decisive step of a woman who expected people to make way for her. And make way they did; for the next several minutes, Li shadowed her through an unrelenting barrage of Good morning, Sister Ted and Excuse me, Sister Ted and Hello, Sister Ted.

"You've got them well trained," Li said.

The other woman turned a sharp unforgiving look on her. "We wouldn't help them by cutting them any slack, Major. You can bet no one else ever will."

"How many of your students are genetics?"

"Look around and take a guess."

Li looked at the sea of young faces, so many of them the same two or three faces. "Two-thirds, I'd say."

"Then you'd be right."

"Any jobs for them when they get out of here?"

"Not unless they're five times as good as any human who wants the job. And not unless they're polite enough to not scare people." The nun threw another of her sharp looks at Li. "I bet you learned how to keep your mouth shut early."

"You'd bet right, then." Li grinned. "I can't walk into this place without the creeping feeling that Sister Vic is going to rise from the grave and ask me for my hall pass."

That got a laugh.

"What can I tell you?" Sister Ted asked, when they were settled in the dilapidated relative peace of her office.

"What Sharifi was doing here two weeks ago for a start."

"Making a donation. We have a lot of Ring-side donors."

"Do all of them come here to visit personally?"

"Hannah was a former student. And she was extremely generous."

Li couldn't help glancing around the run-down office at that and thinking of the cheap buildings the school was housed in.

"She gave the things that counted," Ted said. "Books. Food money. And she guaranteed every student college tuition at the best school she could get admitted to. Every student. Do you have any idea what that means to the girls we get here?"

"I can imagine."

"I imagine you can do more than imagine."

"How well did you know Sharifi?" Li asked, brushing the implied question aside.

Ted smiled. "Not that well. She was my age, you know. The women who would have taught her are all long gone."

"What did she visit for, then?"

"To talk to me."

"About?"

"A new gift."

"Look," Li said. "I'm investigating Sharifi's death, not your school. Can you just spare me the effort of dragging this out of you?"

The sister's eyes widened slightly. "Can you just tell me what you want to know, then, and spare me the effort of guessing?"

"I want to know who killed her."

"Oh." Sister Ted pursed her lips and made a faint blowing sound. That was all the reaction Li's news got from her. But then Li got the impression this was a woman who was used to bad news. "She seemed like her usual self. I'd only ever met her instream before that, of course." She gestured to the ramshackle bulk of an old VR rig gathering dust in the corner of the office. "But she was adamant that she wanted to wrap this gift up in person." She shifted in her chair, setting the old springs creaking. "If I'd thought anything like that was going on, I would have tried to help, Major. I liked her. And not just because she got our girls to college. She was the kind of person you just liked, somehow." She grinned. "Well, the kind of person *I* liked. I imagine she pissed the hell out of most people."

"What about the gift? Anything unusual there?"

Sister Ted twisted in her chair to reach a file drawer. "Have a look at it," she said, handing a thick sheaf of paper to Li. "The digital original's on file Ring-side."

Li flipped through the document, her heart beating

faster with every page she read. It was a will. A will that left everything Sharifi owned to St. Joseph's School.

"Congratulations," Li said. "You're rich."

"I know. I would have expected to feel better about it."

Li handed the papers back, and Sister Ted set them on the desk, absently, as if she were thinking of something else. Or someone else.

There was a problem finding Korchow's street. The cabbie kept circling through lunch-hour traffic, insisting that he knew the address, that the turn was in the next block, or the next one. Finally Li got out and walked.

She stumbled onto the shop abruptly, turning a blind corner into a narrow flagstoned alley and bumping up against a spotlit window full of old carpets and inlaid furniture. A gold-lettered sign read ANTIQUITIES and below it, in dark red, she saw the same intricate lozenge design she had seen on Korchow's card.

He sat at a small desk toward the back, in a carved laminate chair that was either an astronomically expensive generation-ship artifact or a very professional forgery. A tank silk raincoat and a stylish gas mask lay neatly across a nearby table, as if Korchow had just come in or was just leaving.

"Major," he said. "What a surprise. I hope you didn't have too much trouble finding me?"

"I did, actually. Pretty out-of-the-way place to run a business from. Must cut into your profits."

Korchow smiled. "I have a certain reputation among discerning collectors. Can I get you something? Tea?"

He bustled through a curtained doorway into the back of the shop, and Li heard the clink of glass on china, the sound of running water. He returned with two covered teacups, an ornately carved glazed-iron teapot, and a sleek black box that he set carefully on the desk between them.

He served the tea, which was excellent. Then he picked up the box and handed it to her. "I thought you might like to see it," he said. "You seemed quite put out by it the last time we met."

She turned the device over, feeling the weight of it, trying unsuccessfully to scan it.

"Second button from the left," Korchow said.

She pressed it. The box beeped discreetly. A bioluminescent display window began counting thousandths of seconds. Li's security programs flashed a yellow alert on her retina and went dead as her internals cut out.

Korchow leaned across the desk and took back the box. "Some things are better kept private," he said.

"What do you want from me?" Li asked.

"Nothing complicated. Just to do business. Business that could be to our mutual advantage." He paused and fingered the controls of the jamming device.

"It's working fine," Li snapped. "And it's giving me a headache. So just tell me what you want and get it over with."

"I represent parties who are, shall we say, interested in recent events in the Anaconda mine. Particularly in the aspects of the explosion that your, er, office seems to be investigating."

"You want information about Sharifi," Li said.

"Among other things." Korchow smiled. "I can see how difficult this is for you, Major. You'd rather halo-jump into enemy territory than sit over tea talking to a Syndicate spy. I understand better than you can imagine. But we are not always called to serve in the ways we prefer. This is the price of owing allegiance to a greater good." Steam curled from his cup, veiling his narrow, intelligent face. "We've met before," he said.

"Do you remember? Or have they taken that from you?"

"I don't know what you're talking about."

"I was with the Thirty-second on Gilead. I fought on Cale's Hill."

Li looked at him, her face stiff. She'd commanded that assault.

"You don't remember me, I suppose. Corps files are so . . . unreliable. But I remember you. I remember with perfect clarity." He unbuttoned the top two buttons of his shirt, pulled the cloth aside to show Li a chewed-up slash of scar tissue at the base of his neck. "I was sitting in the sun. The first warmth after a cold night. Drinking a cup of tea, of all things."

An image of a thin, stubble-faced soldier flashed through Li's mind. A spill of dark tea and darker blood runneling over boot-packed dirt.

She looked at the wound. The shooter had pulled high and left, missing the spine by a hair. "I remember," she said finally. "There was a crosswind. I overcorrected."

Korchow buttoned his shirt. "Do you remember what happened after that? Or have your psychiatric technicians deleted it?"

Li watched Korchow, her heart pounding.

"I was still conscious when you arrived," he went on. "I remember that your captain's insignia was ripped off another uniform and sewn on with mismatched thread. I remember your smile—quite a lovely one, by the way. I remember you talking to your lieutenants. They asked you what to do with the wounded. Do you recall what you told them?"

"I told them to shoot everyone still breathing."

"Don't think I blame you," Korchow said. "Though I do owe my life to the fact that some of your soldiers had more . . . scruples than you did. Still, it was a moment of revelation. A conversion of sorts. Do you know what I thought as I looked up at you?"

Li stirred restlessly. "How the hell would I?"

"I thought, She's one of us. She's like us. She can't help but be merciful. I saw your face, you see. And I thought you would spare us because of what you were. Because of who you were. When you ordered them to shoot us, I understood, finally and completely, what they had stolen from you."

Li watched the hypnotic blinking of the status lights on the jamming device. She probed her memory, poking at the Gilead files, looking for the cracks, the places where the emotions welled up between the digitized data and gave the lie to the official story. *They should never have sent us*, she thought. And the thought that she could think that—that she already did think it—frightened her more than anything she remembered doing on Gilead.

"No one's stolen anything from me," she said finally. "I sold it. And why, and when, and what for is none of your business."

Korchow watched her over the rim of his teacup. When he spoke, his voice was cool and detached, and he looked up at the ceiling instead of at her. "I've been on five Trusteeships in the last eight years. And I've seen the same game, a sport I suppose, on all of them. A poor man's sport, popular in the Trusteeships, but not at all known in the inner worlds. The enthusiasts breed male chickens—"

"Cocks," Li said.

"Cocks, then. They breed them to kill each other. The fights are held at night and in secret; the sport is illegal on most worlds. Spectators arrive at the appointed place and hour, lay bets, drink various types of hard liquor. Then the handler of each bird takes it from its cage, attaches razor blades to its spurs, and sends it into the ring to peck and claw a fellow chicken to death."

Korchow put down his teacup and leaned across the

desk to pour Li another cup of tea. "Good tea, isn't it?" he said.

"Yes."

"I get it from a friend in New Ceylon. They appreciate the art of tea there. And the art of the deal. Ever been there?"

"No."

"Mmm." Korchow settled back in his chair, cup in hand. "Between tournaments the fighting cock lives in oriental luxury. He is a prince, a diva, a satrap. He knows nothing of the ordinary woes and sorrows of his species. But each pleasure we savor must be purchased with pain—a principle I am sure you appreciate, Major. And even the most spectacular fighting cock is, after all, a chicken." He drew a taut index finger across his throat. "I wonder what those cocks would say about their lives if you could get inside the cage with them. I wonder if they'd tell you they chose this fate. That they'd sold their life, their death, and gotten a fair price for it."

"I wouldn't know," Li said. "I'm not a chicken."

"No you're not." Korchow smiled. "And I have a powerful presentiment that you're about to tell me to get on with it and stop wasting your time."

Li raised an eyebrow.

"I represent certain interested parties," Korchow continued after a few beats.

"The Syndicates."

"Let's not name names just yet. In any case, at the time of Hannah Sharifi's death, these parties were engaged in . . . ongoing negotiations. Their negotiations had reached a point at which the involved parties expected to receive specific items of information from Dr. Sharifi. That information was never received. The parties believe that you, as the UN officer investigating her death, are in a position to deliver it."

"You want the datasets from Sharifi's live field run."

"Ah. The direct approach. How like you."

"You can forget about it. I don't have them."

Korchow rocked back in his chair as if he were dodging a blow. "Now that is a most interesting statement. First, because we have assumed until this moment that you did in fact have them. Second, and correct me if I err, your answer suggests that if you were to acquire this information, you might not be absolutely opposed to sharing it."

Li shrugged.

"I think," said Korchow, "this is the juncture at which I am supposed to inform you that my . . . clients would be prepared to reward you liberally for your assistance. In money, or in ways that might, in the end, mean more to you than money."

"Are we talking about chickens again?" Li said.

Korchow threw back his head and laughed. "Major," he said, still laughing. "You more than live up to your reputation. No, we are not talking about chickens. We are talking about a level of remuneration that would allow you to, how shall I put this? . . . decide when and where and for whom you strap on the razor blades."

"Or?"

"Or incorporation. What you would call political sanctuary. Into the Syndicate of your choice."

"Christ, Korchow. I've seen the Syndicates. I've seen how you people live. Why the hell would I want that?"

"I'll leave you to answer that question for yourself, Major."

The bells on the shop door tinkled. Li turned just in time to see a new customer walk in. A tall man, dressed in ministerial gray. A diplomat or banker. Definitely not local.

"Mr. Lind!" Korchow beamed at the new arrival. "You've come back to look at the Heyerdal again? I'll be at your disposal momentarily." He pulled a knick-knack off the shelf above his desk and began wrapping it in hand-printed rice paper. "I know you'll enjoy this," he told Li as he tied the package with a length of green ribbon. "It's really quite an exceptional little piece. One of my personal favorites." He smiled. "Consider it a symbol of my good intentions. And . . . other things."

Li took the package without having actually seen what was in it, let herself be propelled to the counter, swiped her palm across the portable scanner Korchow held up. She wondered how he explained the absence of a credit implant to his clients. Probably faked allergies or religious objections.

"How can I reach you?" she asked.

Korchow smiled a bland, guiltless shopkeeper's smile. "I'll put you on the mailing list," he said—and Li felt his hand in the small of her back, politely but firmly propelling her out into the street.

When she turned the corner, she stopped, looked back to make sure she couldn't be seen from the shop, and unraveled the elaborately folded rice paper. Korchow had sold her a generation-ship-era figurine, molded in plastic. It had once been brightly colored, but the paint had flaked and faded, leaving the figure's skin—or were those scales?—mottled.

It was a woman, or rather a caricature of one. Long hair cascaded over her bare shoulders, and her breasts were only hinted at. Instead of legs, she had a silver tail with fins and scales. A mermaid. Half one thing, half the other, at home in neither world.

Li felt the ridges of raised lettering on the base of the figurine. She turned it over and read MADE IN CHINA, in block letters, and, immediately below it, DISNEY®.

She rewrapped the figurine carefully, returned it to the bag, and unfolded the credit slip Korchow had tucked into the wrapping.

"Son of a bitch!" she said when she read the figure at the bottom of the printout.

It was for four times her monthly salary. And it was

a credit, not a debit. A transfer into an account Li had never opened, in a Freetown bank she had never heard of. It looked like Korchow had decided to pay in advance . . . and leave Li to do the explaining if anyone put the pieces together.

Zona Libre: 20 Mar 48.

Even shunted through an organic interface, an Emergent as vast as Cohen left a wide wake in streamspace.

Li found him in the Zona Libre, at a back table in a place called the 5th Column. She had to flash ID to get past the bouncers, and when she finally convinced them to let her in, she thought at first she'd come to the wrong place. Then someone called her name, and she looked over and saw Roland's coppery curls gleaming against the oxblood velvet of a long banquette that curved along the shadowy back wall.

"I need to talk to you," she said, sliding onto the empty place beside him. "Now."

He smiled—an open, uncomplicated smile that was a million light-years away from any look that had ever crossed Cohen's face. "Sorry," Roland said. "I'm just the hired help."

"Where's Cohen, then?"

"He stepped out for a moment. Drop him a line and let him know you're here."

"No, I'll just wait."

"Okay." Roland shrugged. "He'll figure it out soon enough. And he won't be gone long anyway; dinner's waiting."

Li followed Roland's glance and saw pale creamy butter over ice, bread rolls as crisp and brown as chickens' eggs, an open wine bottle with a French label. Two waiters hovered expectantly in the wings, waiting for the sign to serve the next course.

Roland offered Li wine, though he himself drank nothing. He gamely made small talk with her, but Li got the distinct impression that he thought she was some kind of not very interesting old person. For her part, she watched Roland with bemused embarrassment. What had she seen in him? He was nothing, except for those golden eyes. A cookie-cutter college boy with pretty hair. Barely worth looking twice at.

She glanced around the big room, keeping half an ear on Roland's chatter. The place wasn't really a nightclub; more of a fancy restaurant with live music. All velvet and carefully pressed linen and carefully dressed customers. Everything plush, flash, top-shelf. The guests all laughed a little too often and talked a little too loud, as if they had come there in order to be seen and were determined to get their money's worth. The women wore smart dresses, programmed to cling to the right curves and camouflage the wrong curves. A few people wore formal jumpsuits—Corps brass or officers off rich merchant ships who couldn't quite get out of the habit of low-g clothing—but Li's Security Council black fatigues were out-of-place enough to make people stare.

The stage lights came up. Someone tapped a glass for silence, and the crowd hushed reluctantly. A live band walked onto the stage, went through the usual tuning-up ritual, and launched into a song that everyone but Li seemed to have heard before.

The singer was a woman. Small, vaguely familiar-looking, with a headful of black cowlicks and heavy-framed glasses that could only, in these days of cheap genework, be vanity. She was good; good enough that several songs had gone by before Li remembered to check the time and wonder what the hell Cohen was doing.

She took out a cigarette, and Roland leapt to light it for her. He'd probably be helping her across the street next. She smoked the cigarette down slowly while the singer's smoky voice wound around them, talking about failed love affairs, lonely roads, new beginnings.

"I thought that was you," Cohen murmured just beside her.

When she turned around Roland was gone. His wide-open face had turned into a shadowy territory of shifting planes and angles, fleeting expressions. His long-fingered hands rested on the table with inhuman stillness. Even the golden eyes now seemed dark, dangerous, deeper than oceans.

"Christ," Li said. "How do you do that?"

"Do what?" he asked, and smiled slyly. "Oh, you mean my animal magnetism and natural charisma?" The smile turned into a full-blown grin. "Don't be too hard on Roland. After all, he's all of twenty-three. When I was that age, I lived in a government-subsidized lab with bad lighting, couldn't put two sentences together, and played chess twenty-four hours a day. A game which, I might add, you couldn't get me to play now for anything—" He stopped and smiled up at the ceiling. "Well . . . almost anything."

He unfolded Li's napkin with a flourish and handed it to her. "So," he said, refilling her wineglass, "to what do I owe this exceptional and unexpected happiness? Are you here for the pleasure of my company, or do you just need something?"

"What I need," Li said, "is advice."

"And you shall have it. After you've had dinner with me. Deal?"

"Deal," Li said, but when the waiter handed her the

menu, she quickly realized two things. First, there were no prices on it. Second, even though it was written in plain Spanish, she'd never heard of half the foods it listed.

"Huh," she said, accessing her hard files, trying to figure out what horse's feet were and whether a *girolle* was a bird or a mushroom.

"The oysters are excellent," Cohen suggested.

"Fine." She shut the menu. "Oysters."

Cohen gave the order and leaned back, arms crossed. "Now then," he said as calmly as if they were discussing the season's gallery openings, "what's so urgent that you have to hunt me down and interrupt a good meal to talk about it? Would it be foolish to imagine that it's not unrelated to your little tête-à-tête with Korchow this morning?"

Li choked on her wine and coughed into her napkin. "Still spying on me, are we?" she asked when she could speak again.

"Don't be snitty, darling. Technically, it's Nguyen I'm spying on, not you. And anyway, it's how I'm written. Naturally nosy. Neither of us can fight our code, can we?"

Li narrowed her eyes at that but said nothing.

"Oh dear," Cohen said. "Here comes your thunderous, we'll-deal-with-this-later look. Have some more wine. And tell me how you like it."

Li took another sip of wine, still staring at Cohen unsmilingly over the rim of her glass.

"Well?" he asked, leaning forward.

"It's good."

"Good? That's all you can say? I might as well pour it into the gutter."

"You gave it to me," Li pointed out.

"The more fool I."

"Why were you spying on—"

"Madame's oysters," the waiter said, leaning over Li's shoulder to set an immense plate before her. She looked down at it while the waiter served Cohen's dish. Twelve fist-sized oysters glistened nakedly up at her under the spotlights.

"Are they dead yet?" she asked.

"They won't feel a thing," Cohen told her. "And do try to chew before you swallow. You'd be a much happier person if you just concentrated on your food properly."

The oysters were fantastic, of course. Everything Cohen had ever fed her was fantastic. They tasted of salt and iodine and deep clear water. The taste of the sea, she supposed, though she had never seen a sea. She ate two plates of them, firmly repressing any thought of what they must be costing Cohen, and even in streamspace she felt stuffed.

"So," she said when Cohen had finished his dessert and the waiters had brought coffee and *pâte de fruits* and elaborate *petits fours*. "Now can I ask why you're spying on Nguyen?"

"You can ask," he answered with a silken smile.

"It's still about Metz, isn't it?"

"If you know so much, why come to me?"

Li looked across the table at him, and he met her stare with bland equanimity.

"What happened to trusting each other?" she asked.

"I trust you completely. I always have. In this case, however, the question isn't whether I trust you, but whether I trust everyone who has clearance to download your hard files."

"Which brings us back to Nguyen. And Metz."

"The thing about Helen," Cohen said, carrying on as smoothly as if Li hadn't spoken, "is that she uses people. It's her job to use people. It's what she is. You put yourself in mortal danger if you allow yourself to forget that."

"Funny. She said the same thing about you."

"Helen," Cohen said firmly, "does not understand

me nearly as well as she thinks she does." He stopped and gave Li a shocked look. "You don't believe her, do you?"

"I don't know who to believe."

Cohen looked down at his plate and smiled a tight little smile that was far too old to belong on Roland's soft face. "Well," he said, to no one in particular. "So."

"Don't guilt me," Li said. "Nguyen's earned my trust. You've earned . . . the opposite."

"Helen does a very difficult job," Cohen said after an uncomfortable pause. "And she does it very well. But she's a technician, really. People are tools to her. You are one of her tools. I'm another—albeit a powerful tool that she knows can turn around and bite her if she doesn't handle it carefully. But in the end, it's the same. She has a job to do. She opens up her toolbox and pulls out the best tool for the job. If it breaks, that's too bad, of course. But she can always get the Secretariat to buy her a new one."

"Why do you work for her, if that's what you think?"

He grinned. "The party favors, darling. Now tell me about Korchow."

And she did, in spite of Metz and Helen's warning and the voice inside her that whispered she was risking what she couldn't afford to lose. She told him everything. Just like she always did.

"May I smoke?" Cohen asked when she'd finished.

She nodded, and he spent the next forty seconds choosing, cutting, and lighting a hand-rolled cigar with minute concentration.

"Nice lighter," Li said.

"You like it? I found it in the back of a drawer yesterday. Must have been sitting in there since . . . well, before you were born, probably." He flipped it open again, blinked at the blue flame, and handed it to Li to look at. "Present from my second husband. He had exceptionally good taste for a mathematician. Most of them shouldn't be allowed to dress themselves."

Li figured she was supposed to laugh at that, so she did, and then set the lighter on the table between them.

"So," Cohen said, toying with the lighter, "have I ever told you the story of the Affair of the Queen's Necklace?"

"The queen's what?"

"*L'affaire du collier de la reine*." He sounded shocked. "Don't humans teach history in those schools of theirs anymore?"

"Slept through it."

Cohen sniffed delicately. Li had seen an old flat film once about French aristocrats on Earth. The men had all worn embroidered waistcoats and used snuff instead of cigarettes. Cohen's gesture reminded her of the well-bred, dainty sniffs with which those long-dead aristocrats had taken their tobacco.

"Well," he said, "here's the short version. Try to stay awake for it. The place is Paris. The time, the eve of the Revolution. The players, the king, the queen, the Cardinal de Rohan. Rumor has it that the cardinal was also the queen's lover . . . but I'm sure that had nothing at all to do with how things ended up for the poor fellow.

"In any case, our story begins with the arrival of a mysterious Jew. It's always a Jew, you know. I could say more about that, but I think we can postpone a discussion of the roots of European anti-Semitism to a later date. In any case, my coreligionist arrived bearing princely treasure. To wit, one fantastically expensive diamond necklace of scandalously uncertain origin. No sooner had the queen seen this necklace than she knew she had to have it. Negotiations began. Eventually the queen and the Jew agreed on a rather substantial price. Two-thirds of the gross national product of France, to be precise."

Li choked on her wine. "For a piece of jewelry? That's ridiculous!"

"Mmm." Cohen looked amused. "I seem to recall you spending a good six months' pay on a certain original-issue hand-rebuilt Beretta, O Parsimonious One. What did you call it? Sweet?"

"That's different," Li protested. "Professional equipment."

He puffed on his cigar, grinning. "Well, just think of diamond necklaces as professional equipment for queens."

She snorted.

"Quite. Anyway, the queen asked the king to buy the necklace for her. The king must have shared your opinion about the value of diamond necklaces; he said no."

"And thus the tale ends. Not much of a story, Cohen."

"Don't tease," he said, smirking at her. "As you know—or would know if you had ever applied your considerable intelligence to anything but wreaking high-tech havoc—queens in those days didn't have much practice in taking no for an answer. Thus, the queen decided to go behind her husband's back."

"Go where behind his back?" Li asked. "Why didn't she just buy it on her own credit if she wanted it so much?"

Cohen blinked, momentarily at a loss. "Right," he said. "Um, we'll discuss women's rights and sexism when we have that talk about anti-Semitism, shall we?" He looked suspiciously at her. "Unless you're pulling my leg."

Li grinned. "Easy target."

"Not nice, my dear," Cohen said. But his smile took the sting out of it, and Roland's long-lashed eyes sparkled with laughter.

This was one of those nights when Cohen was all there, Li realized. Really *on*. As always at these times, she felt she was at the blazing heart of a sun, basking in the heat of the AI's personality, unable to remember the doubts and the shadows.

"Well, finish the story," she said. She pulled out a cigarette and leaned in for Cohen to light it. "And make sure someone gets shot soon. You expect me to stay awake, you'd better play to the cheap seats."

Cohen's smile widened. "You're in fine form tonight. So where was I? Ah, yes. It's not clear whether the queen asked first or the cardinal offered first. But in the end, he agreed to buy the necklace for her on the understanding that she would repay him, covertly of course, with tax money.

"The rest of the story is brief and sordid. The upshot of it was that before the queen even got a chance to wear the infamous necklace it was stolen."

"By who?"

"By whom, my love. No one knows. No one ever found out. But the die was already cast, even before the court case and the scandal sheets. For the cardinal, it was the end of everything. He lost his fortune, his credibility, and, worst of all, the patronage of his king. All for a necklace that the queen never got to wear and no one could pay him for."

Li waited for Cohen to go on, but he didn't. "So what's your point?" she asked finally.

"Helen has asked you to produce something for her. Sharifi's dataset, maybe. Maybe something else, something she thinks may fall into her hands once she has the data. If she's asking you, it can only be because she can't ask the General Assembly—or worse, because she's already asked and gotten the wrong answer. Be careful what you pay for her little bauble. And make sure you're not the one caught out in the cold when the bill comes due."

Li felt her carefree mood slipping away. She dropped her head into her hands and scrubbed at her face with numb, cold fingers. "You're telling me to steer clear of something I can't see," she said. "How am I supposed to do that?"

"You can't," Cohen said. He sounded particularly gentle; but maybe it was just the timbre of Roland's young voice she was hearing. "Just don't wait until you hear the surf on the rocks to start turning the ship, that's all. In the meantime, find out who the players are, what they want—and how far they'll go to get it."

"That's your advice?" she said, head still in her hands. "I could have gotten more out of a damn fortune cookie!"

"You could always resign," Cohen said softly.

Li took her hands from her face and looked up at him. "Quit, you mean." She felt a flush rising in her cheeks. "I don't quit."

Cohen put a hand over one of hers, held it there lightly. "I'm not saying you should," he told her. "Just that you can, if things get bad. I'll help. It's there for the asking. Anything."

Anything. Meaning money, of course. And taking it would make her no different than any of his other hangers-on.

"I've got it taken care of, if it comes to that," she said awkwardly—and lying through her teeth, too. "And there's other jobs out there. Security. Planetary militia. But . . . thanks, I guess."

They sat for a moment, he with his hand still set lightly on hers, not quite looking at each other.

"You come here much?" Li asked, slipping her hand out from under his and scanning the room around them.

"Occasionally."

"It's ridiculous, you know. Everyone here's ridiculous."

"I know."

"I guess you're going to tell me that's why you like

it. Or . . . what was it? That I lack an existential sense of the absurd?"

He smiled. "Would I say such a thing?"

"You just enjoy watching people make fools of themselves, don't you?" She spoke jokingly, but she suddenly felt a prickling urge to pick a fight with him.

He leaned back, responding to the feeling behind her words rather than the words themselves. "I make a fool of myself ten times a minute," he said. "Fifty times a minute when you're in the room. It's called being alive, Catherine."

"Right. You're just the average guy, going about your average life. Just with a few billion times the processing speed."

"Something like that."

She snorted. "And this is how you use it? Forgive me if I'm not impressed."

He shrugged. "I can't help wanting to be around people. It's the way I'm written."

"So change it. Change your code. I would. I'd get shut of Nguyen and Sharifi and all this pathetic bullshit in a second if I could."

"You just say that because you know you can't. Now stop fussing and listen to this song. It's a good one."

The singer was still onstage, finishing out a set with a bittersweet country song. It was a good song, the kind of song that could have been written yesterday or three hundred years ago. "She write that?" Li asked, nodding across the room toward the spotlit figure.

"It was written before I was born."

She listened closer, caught a stray word or two. "What's a Pontchartrain?"

"The Pontchartrain. It's a lake on the Mississippi, that used to flow through New Orleans."

"Before the floods, you mean."

"Before that, even. The river—the whole Mississippi Delta actually—shifted. The U.S. Army Corps of Engineers spent, oh, a century dredging and channeling and building levees. Defiance of nature, on a megalo-maniacal scale. People wrote books and printed articles and whole theses about it. The river finally had its way, of course. It jumped its banks right around the time the oceans really started rising. Shifted the delta halfway across the Gulf of Texas. I wish I could make you feel what it was to be in New Orleans, stranded in the middle of a man-made desert while the ice caps were melting and we were watching floods in New York and Paris on the news every night. It was . . . unforgettable."

"I didn't think Earth was ever wired for streamspace. They didn't even have shunts back then, did they?"

"No. Just a kind of primitive version of VR. But it was enough. I have my own memories, and other people's. Over time it becomes harder and harder to separate them. Which may not be all bad." He smiled. "I'm probably the only person still alive who remembers driving across the Pontchartrain in a convertible."

Li grinned. "With a beautiful blonde, no doubt."

Cohen smiled back, but it was the sad-sweet smile of a man lost in an old memory. "With Hyacinthe's widow. The first woman I ever fell in love with."

Li waited, wanting to hear more but not comfortable pushing.

"I know," he said, answering a question that hadn't even occurred to her. "I suppose from a puritanical sort of perspective, you could say she was my mother."

"Well, it's not like you invented that particular complex."

"It wasn't like that, though. I *am* Hyacinthe, his very self, in ways that have nothing to do with being a child, or a student, or an invention. Besides." Another sweet and solemn smile. "The heart is complicated, whether it's made of flesh or circuitry. It doesn't always love the way you think it should. Or the people you think it should."

"You don't have to confess to me, Cohen."

"Well, I have this funny idea that you come closer to understanding me than anyone else does. And so far you haven't made me do any rosaries."

A sudden memory of bare knees on a cold church floor and a grown-up hand—her mother's?—moving her child's fingers over the glass beads. The smooth, dark *Aves*. The gleaming *Paters*. The cross dangling and tapping against the pew in front of her.

"And I understand you, I think," Cohen was saying when she surfaced again. "Which is an accomplishment given that what you've actually told me about yourself would fit on the back of a matchbook. At first I thought you didn't trust me. Then I decided you're just secretive. Is it how you're put together, or did someone teach you to push people off like that?"

Li shrugged, feeling awkward. "It's jump fade as much as anything. I don't remember much." She paused. "And what I do remember usually makes me wish I'd forgotten more of it. What's the point in dredging up old miseries?"

She looked up into the silence that followed to find Cohen watching her.

"Eyelash," he said.

"What?"

"You have an eyelash."

"Where?" Li dabbed at her eye, looking for it.

"Other eye. Here. Wait."

He slid toward her along the curved bench and tilted her head back against the velvet cushions with one hand while the other feathered along her lower eyelid hunting for the stray lash. She smelled *extra-vielle*, felt Roland's warm sweet breath on her cheek, saw the soft skin of his neck and the pulse beating beneath it.

"There," Cohen said, and held the lash up on the end of a slender finger.

She opened her mouth to thank him, but the words

died in her throat. The hand that had been on her chin brushed along her cheek and traced the faint line of the bundled filament that followed the muscle from the corner of her jaw down to the hollow between her clavicles.

"You look like you've lost weight, even in stream-space," he said. "You look like you're not sleeping enough."

He caught her eye and held it. The hand on her neck felt warm as Ring-side sunlight, and it reminded her how long it had been since anyone but a medtech had touched her. A dark tide of desire tugged at her. Desire and a reckless loneliness and a hunger to believe in the person and the feelings that seemed so real sometimes.

Uh-oh, she thought.

She looked away and cleared her throat.

Cohen drew back, held up his index finger, her eyelash still on it. "Make a wish," he said.

"I don't believe in wishes. You make one."

He closed his eyes and blew the lash up into the smoky air.

"That was quick," Li said and smiled—or at least tried to. "I guess you know what you want."

But he wasn't looking at her. He had his watch off and was listening to it, his face turned away from her. He twisted the golden knob, put the watch to his ear, wound it again, shook it.

"I don't know what's wrong with the thing," he said. "It's been running slow for weeks. Damned annoying."

"Cohen," said a woman's voice from somewhere above their heads. A slender brown pair of legs had stopped by their table, and Li looked up them into an amused smile and horn-rimmed glasses—and her own face behind them.

It wasn't her face, though. It was the nameless teenager's face she remembered looking at fifteen years ago in a Shantytown mirror. A XenoGen face on a thin young woman who would have stood exactly Li's height if she hadn't been wearing three-inch heels and a red slip of a dress that looked far more revealing now that she wasn't onstage.

The singer gave Li a brief measuring look, then sat down and put a possessive arm around Cohen's shoulders. "I thought I was going to have you all to myself tonight," she said in a voice that left no doubt in Li's mind about what Cohen had been doing eating uncharacteristically alone in this place.

Cohen flinched ever so slightly. "Sorry," he said, looking at Li.

"Not at all." Li stood up, straightening her uniform with numb fingers. "I was leaving anyway."

"I'll call you later."

"No need."

"Well, tomorrow then."

"Whatever."

"No," she heard Cohen saying as she walked off, in answer to some whispered question. "Just business."

INTERFERENCE PATTERNS

➤We do not experience time flowing, or passing. What we experience are differences between our present perceptions and our present memories of past perceptions. We interpret those differences, correctly, as evidence that the universe changes with time. We also interpret them, incorrectly, as evidence that our consciousness, or the present, or something, moves, through time . . . We exist in multiple versions, in universes called "moments" . . . It is tempting to suppose that the moment of which we are aware is the only real one, or is at least a little more real than the others. But this is just solipsism. All moments are physically real. The whole of the multiverse is physically real. Nothing else is.

—DAVID DEUTSCH

Li decided not to go, then changed her mind again at least eight times.

She told herself she was getting too old to follow her hormones everywhere they led her, and that her excuse for accepting the invitation—asking about Sharifi—was nothing short of pathetic. If she really wanted to blow off some steam, she'd be better off picking up some stranger in a bar than chasing after a woman that any sane person in her position would know enough to steer clear of.

In the end she arrived two minutes early and dithered on the doorstep wondering if she should buzz or just walk around until it was time. Just as she was telling herself it wasn't too late to turn around and leave, Bella opened the door.

She wore white: a long fall of silk that flared around her ankles in the station's low gravity. Somehow, Li was quite sure Haas had bought the dress for her.

"Are you sure he's off-station?" she said, and cursed herself for asking.

Bella just smiled serenely, took the flowers Li had brought, and led her through a narrow door into the kitchen.

"He's in Helena," she said as she poured water into a vase for the flowers. "AMC managers' meeting. It runs until the day after tomorrow. So . . ." She flicked her dark hair back and leaned over to cut the flower stems, baring the long pale line of her neck.

Li caught her breath. "So you're a free woman," she said, and bit her tongue again. She couldn't put a foot right tonight.

"Free," Bella repeated without a trace of a smile. "I have never understood what humans mean when they use that word."

Dinner was good, though Li didn't have much appetite. She felt like she was in a play, the stage already set, the lines already scripted. Eating Haas's food on Haas's china. And across the table, Haas's . . . what? Mistress? Employee? Indentured servant? One thing was certain: this wasn't headed for a happy ending.

Bella talked, mostly. She seemed desperate to talk, terrified of the charged silences that hung between them. She talked about her childhood, her schooling, her life before the contract. None of it was what Li had expected. She had expected one of those mythical constructs you heard about in OCS classes and mission briefings. Brilliant, single-minded, every speck of individuality trained and programmed and disciplined out of her from the instant her tank's umbilical cords were severed. Instead, she heard a lonely young woman stranded a few hundred light-years from her home planet.

Bella described the same things Li had seen during the Syndicate Wars. Gestation tanks, crèches, study labs. But she described them as home, spoke in words that made Li wonder if she'd seen what was really there on Gilead, or just what she wanted to see.

"The night I came here was the first night I spent

alone in my life," Bella said. "I couldn't shut my eyes. I heard voices, noises. I thought I'd gone mad."

"Did it get easier?"

"No."

"Then why stay?"

"It was my part."

Li blinked, thrown back to the interrogation rooms on Gilead, to the D Series soldiers she had seen mouth those same words. *My part*, they always said, as if the phrase had been stamped into them. *My part to serve. My part to kill. My part to die.* She felt a sudden, unwilling kinship with Bella: a murky intuition that, war or no war, the Syndicate soldiers she'd spent nearly a decade killing were closer to her than the Ring citizens it was her duty to defend against them.

"How did you end up with Haas?" she asked, seizing on the first change of subject that came to mind.

"With—? Oh." Bella's eyes dropped. "It just . . . happened."

"You make it sound like a spilled drink."

"It's in my contract."

"Your contract requires—?" Li couldn't bring herself to voice any of the possible endings to that question.

"The contract doesn't require anything. But . . . he told me he would be displeased if I didn't. And that if he were displeased, he would terminate the contract and ask for a replacement. I . . . I couldn't live with that. I couldn't be one of those. Terminated."

"Having an affair with your boss seems a little above and beyond the call of duty, Bella."

"It's not an affair," Bella said sharply. When Li glanced up her face was flushed, furious. Her voice dropped to a whisper. "I'm not . . . I'm not abnormal."

Abnormal. Li considered the word and the peculiarly ominous ring it had coming from a Syndicate construct's mouth. She wondered what the source of Bella's shame was. That Haas was foreign, unplanned, male? All three things? "You don't have to justify yourself to me," she told Bella. "You're a long way from home here. You wouldn't be the first person in history who adapted to survive."

"No," Bella said. "You don't understand. You can't understand, coming from . . . where you come from. It was a privilege to be sent here. All of us who were chosen knew the risks, the hardships. Even the Ds. They told us it was the most important thing we would ever do for our home Syndicates. I can't fail after that. No matter how bad it is."

"And how bad is it?" Li asked.

Bella's fork lay forgotten on her plate rim. She picked it up, made a halfhearted attempt to eat something, then gave up entirely. "It wasn't as bad as I thought it would be. It was just now and then, at first. And Haas can be . . . very charming. Then I met Cory."

She fell silent for the space of a few breaths, looking down at her plate. Li said nothing, reluctant to break the thread of the memory that gripped the woman. "He was a surveyor," she continued. "Cory Dean. Is that Irish?"

Li nodded.

"I thought so. He was nice. He didn't stare. And he talked to me. He'd tell me jokes while we worked, stories. Haas got it into his head that he was my lover. He never said anything, but he thought it. It was ridiculous, of course." Her nose wrinkled in obvious distaste. "I didn't want him. Not that way, at least. But I hadn't lived with humans long enough to see how it looked.

"Cory was missing for days. They checked the whole station, the mine, Shantytown. Voyt found him." Bella's face twisted as if it hurt to say Voyt's name. "Someone had beaten him. Stolen his credit chip and then just left him in the gutter. He drowned in his own blood. I didn't know you could do that."

Bella shifted in her chair. When she spoke again, her voice was as hard and unyielding as virusteel. "The

Shantytown watch had him for days before they called the station; they thought he was just a drunk miner. They said he'd gotten in a fight, but Cory would never have done that. Still, they'd found witnesses somehow, people who were willing to say they'd seen him fighting. You don't have to throw around much money in Shantytown to get people to say what you want.

"Haas told me. I still remember how he looked when he did it. Like he was proud of it. Like he was daring me to say something. The next day he moved my things here, and it's been . . . what you see now, ever since."

Bella had given up even pretending to eat. Li watched her twist her napkin between white-knuckled fingers and thought about Haas, and about the blank impersonalness of Sharifi's quarters and the single un-explained initial Sharifi had written in her datebook the week she died.

Maybe it was time to risk a shot in the dark.

"Did you tell Sharifi this story when she came to dinner?" she asked.

"What?"

"When she had dinner with you. The night before she died. Was Haas here? Or was he conveniently off-station that night too?"

Bella stared, her mouth open, her face white. "Don't," she whispered. "Please don't."

"You were lovers, weren't you?"

"I never said—"

"You never had to. It's all over your face every time you talk about her."

Bella scrubbed at her mouth with her napkin. The skin of her face looked as pale as the bleached linen. "You can't tell anyone," she said. "Haas would . . . I don't know what he'd do." Her hand twitched toward the faint remnant of the bruise on her cheek, but she forced it down into her lap again.

"Doesn't he know already? Isn't that what you're trying to tell me?"

"No." Bella stood up so quickly she jostled the table and set the glassware ringing. "No. Not possible."

She moved to the side window and leaned her face against the viewport. Li followed.

It was second night, and the Companion cast its faint light into the room, etching the angles of Bella's face in a red so dark it was almost black. "What can I do?" she whispered.

"Can't you just go home, tell them you can't finish it out?"

She shook her head violently.

"Well, then—"

"Forget it. You can't help. No one can help."

Bella turned. She was so close now, the light behind her, the beautiful face lost in shadow. Li touched her cheek, and the feverish heat of the pale skin shocked her.

Bella leaned into her, sighing, and Li shuddered at the soft flutter of breath against her skin. Bella's lips played along her neck, around the angle of her jaw, over her earlobe, and Li turned her head for the kiss she wanted so badly.

But in the last breath before their lips touched, she looked into Bella's wide-open eyes—and saw something that stopped her cold. Not fear. Not reluctance. But . . . something. Something as deliberate and calculated as the blue-on-black MotaiSyndicate logo set into the outer perimeter of the violet irises.

Li stepped back, hands dropping to her sides. The hot desire that had taken hold of her a moment ago was gone, replaced by a clammy, after-fever chill. "Who killed Sharifi, Bella?"

Bella turned back toward the window, and it seemed to Li that the hand she put on the sill was trembling. "I don't know," she said finally. "I told you, I don't remember."

"You remember something," Li said. "Or you suspect. Why else would you have told me about Cory? Why else tell me the bodies were in the glory hole when they weren't? Because they weren't, were they? And you must have known they weren't. You're laying a trail for me. The only thing I can't figure out is if you're leading me to Haas or away from him."

"I'm not leading you anywhere! I don't know. I told you that!"

"And I don't believe it. Lovers talk. Sharifi must have told you things. That she found something. Some new piece of technology. Some new information." Li paused, then went on. "Something Korchow wanted you to get from her."

"It wasn't like that," Bella said stubbornly.

"Then how was it?"

Bella moved impatiently. "Is that all you came for? To ask questions?"

"What did you expect?" Li asked.

She waited, but Bella didn't turn around, and only the slight tremor in her shoulders told Li she was crying again.

"Hannah didn't go to Korchow about the crystals," Bella said finally. "And there was nothing illegal about it. She was going to buy my contract, with her own money."

Li stood speechless for a moment, unable to muster a response. "She couldn't have bought your contract, Bella. She couldn't have afforded it."

"She was rich," Bella insisted, with the blind certainty of someone who didn't understand what the word meant, what money meant.

"Not that rich."

"You're wrong. She was going to. She promised."

"So what went wrong, Bella? What happened to the happy ending?"

"She changed," Bella said after a long silence. "She

found something that made her happier than I could."

Halfway back to her quarters Li realized she wasn't even close to sleep and turned aside to catch the next surface-bound shuttle.

The pithead guards knew her by now; they searched her perfunctorily, almost apologetically. Twenty minutes later, just as the graveyard shift was turning, she climbed down the ladder into the glory hole.

The crystals were in full voice, overloading her internals, wreaking havoc on her scan systems. By the time she set her foot on the bottom rung of the ladder her infrared and quantum scans had cut out completely. She could have lit her lantern, but she didn't want to. There was something terrible about the smallness of a light in this ancient airless darkness. She sat in the dark with her back against the ladder and retraced the twisting course of the investigation.

She saw no straight sight lines, no clear cause and effect, nothing but blind corners and dead drops. Had she accomplished anything at all here? Or was she just stuck in rewind, projecting her own ghosts onto Sharifi, dredging the sterile runoff of a dead girl's pathetic memories?

Ask yourself who the players are, Cohen had said, *and what they want*. Well, what *did* they want?

Daahl and Ramirez wanted what the union always wanted. To wrest control of the mines away from the UN defense contractors, to build their workers' paradise—a paradise that Li didn't want any part of but that would probably be no worse than anyone else's misguided little piece of heaven on earth. Cartwright's goals were tangential to the union's, as Korchow would say. But he'd stand with the union—if only because the union was most likely to protect his precious crystals. If Daahl and Cartwright had to take Li down to get what they wanted, they would. Otherwise, they'd stay clear of her, if only because of their loyalty to the family she barely remembered.

Haas wanted to keep the mine running. And, when he thought he could get away with it, he'd wanted to keep Li out of the glory hole. Why? To avoid drawing the miners' attention to it? No; they already knew, thanks to Cartwright and the wagging tongues of the miners Sharifi had paid union scale to dig it out for her. Was it simply the fierce multiplanetary's drive to prevent a slowdown and protect profits? Or was it something more personal? Hiding his embezzling? Avenging himself for Bella's betrayal?

Nguyen wanted Sharifi's dataset. And she wanted to make sure no one else got it. That she knew things she wasn't telling Li was a given, part of the price of working for her, of trusting her. But what were those things? Did she know what Sharifi had found in the mine? Who she had talked to about it? Did she know about Korchow? Was it just paranoia for Li to think she was following a track Nguyen had foreseen, even laid down for her?

And what about Korchow? He wanted the same information Nguyen wanted. He wanted it desperately enough to take the chance of approaching Li, of risking the sting he must know was a real possibility. And he had suggested—more than suggested—that Sharifi had already betrayed some of her secrets to him.

Bella was the wild card, of course. Did she know about Korchow? Was she working for him? What was there really between her and Haas? What had Voyt done to make her hate him so much? And what was the cold calculation Li had seen in her eyes? Grief over Sharifi, or something deeper, older, darker?

Something moved in the darkness.

Li's eyes snapped open. Nothing.

Then she heard the faint but unmistakable sound of someone breathing. She slid a hand into her coverall and eased the Beretta out of its holster. She flicked the safety off, inching the lever back with agonizing slowness in order to muffle the dry little click of the catch snapping open.

"You're not going to shoot me, Katie," said a familiar voice.

A match flared. Li smelled sulfur, saw a monstrous shadow loom across the vault high above her. The shadow bent, shifted. A rusty pin squeaked, and a Davy lamp flared into life. "Hello," Cartwright said from where he sat cross-legged on the gleaming floor. "So you heard them too, did you?"

"Heard who?" Li asked breathlessly.

"The saints, Katie. Her children." He smiled. "Rejoice, for we know the hour and the day of Her Coming. It's beginning."

"Save the sermons for your sheep, Cartwright. It has nothing to do with me."

Something drew her eyes into the inky shadows behind the priest. Some movement, so faint that she felt rather than saw it. But when the voice spoke out of the darkness she felt so little surprise that she realized she'd known Daahl would be here.

"If it has nothing to do with you," he asked, "then why are you down here?"

"Just doing my job, that's all."

"There are a lot of people who are wondering just what that job is. A lot of people who'd like to know which side you're on."

She didn't answer.

Cartwright began scratching at a patch of dry skin on his wrist, and something about the movement— the sound of fingernails on flesh, the dead skin flaking off and glittering in the lamplight—made her feel ill. *He's crazy*, she thought. *He always was crazy.*

"Well, Katie," Daahl asked, "don't you have any answer at all for me?"

Li rubbed a clammy hand across her face.

"I'm going to show you something," Daahl said. "I may regret showing it to you. A lot of people have told me I will, in fact. But I think you have a right to see it. I think you have a right to know what's on the table here."

Li saw the UNSC seal on the letter before he'd finished handing it to her. "This is a classified internal memo," she said. "Where the hell are you getting this stuff?"

"Just read it."

It took several reads for the sense of the thing to come through to her—and even then she wasn't sure what the cautious, bureaucratically vague words really meant. Someone else had been sure though. Some other reader had been there before her, had scored through the critical lines with a strong confident hand:

> In conclusion, the presence of live Bose-Einstein strata on Compson's World is both an internal and external security threat. It is vital, both in relation to Syndicate industrial espionage activities and for reasons of political stability (vis-à-vis the IWW and other outside agitators) to transfer the production of transport and communications-grade condensate off the planet and into a controlled laboratory setting. This goal presents a compelling reason, in and of itself, for supporting Dr. Sharifi's research.

"You understand what that means, don't you?" Daahl asked. "They're saying that the very presence of live crystal on-planet is a security risk. That as soon as they can manufacture it off-planet they'll destroy the deposits that are left in the ground here."

"This memo doesn't say anything like that, Daahl."

"Doesn't it? Then what does that mean, 'the presence of live strata is a security risk'?"

"It means nothing. Some paper pusher producing overblown verbiage for a departmental meeting. And anyway, you have no guarantee this thing is genuine."

"My source was too good for it to be anything else."

"If you want me to take that claim seriously, you'd better tell me who this 'source' was and let me make up my own mind."

"You know, Katie. Think about it."

Li stared at the sooty fiche, her mind spinning through the possibilities. Station security. Mine personnel. TechComm itself. But almost by definition no one cleared to see this kind of document could have come from a place like Compson's World, let alone cared enough about it to risk their job and freedom for it.

"Who?" she asked, looking up to see Cartwright and Daahl both watching her. "Who was it?"

Daahl smiled. He took the memo back, pulling it from her fingers so gently that she hardly realized she'd let go of it, and folded it carefully away into his shirt pocket.

"Hannah," he said. "Hannah Sharifi."

I i woke to the sound of people running down the corridor outside, banging on its alloy walls hard enough to set them echoing: the universal spacer's manual alarm system.

She rolled out of bed just as the station lit up her livewall and started talking to her. Her first thought was that there'd been a blowout, but as the calm automated voice droned on she realized it was calling all rescue and medical personnel to the shuttle bays. Whoever was in trouble, they were on the planet below.

She reached over to her cabin's one chair and started pulling on the uniform she'd flung over it a few short hours ago. She was just lacing her boots up when the station put up a planet-side call for her.

Sharpe.

"You have medical training, don't you?" he asked abruptly.

He was in his office at the hospital, and he looked as if he'd been hauled out of bed by the same crisis that had the stationers running for the shuttle bays. A mournful keening rose and fell on his end of the line like the Doppler-distorted navigational beacon of a drive ship pushing lightspeed.

"Just the usual," she said. "CPR. Trauma response. My oracle has a combat med praxis it can load. What's happened?"

"The Anaconda blew again."

Suddenly Li recognized the wail coming over the line behind Sharpe's voice for what it was: the pit whistle.

"How bad?" she asked.

"Pit 3's gone. And 4's burning. The above-ground foreman told me he's got four hundred and twenty miners on the logs, all but seventy still underground. The closest doctor besides me is in Helena, three hours from here. More, if the weather doesn't clear. If you can open a burn wrap and find a vein, I need you."

Li stood up, realized she still had one boot left to lace, sat down again. "When's the next open shuttle seat?"

"Gate 18. And hurry. They're holding it for you."

As the shuttle plunged toward the planet, the copilot scanned the surface channels for news of the fire. No one they could raise had time to talk to them, but little by little they began to piece together the long slide through miscommunication and mischance to disaster.

The first step was the breakdown of the Pit 4 chippy lift. With a ten-meter-square lift floor that took up half the breadth of the main shaft, the chippy lift was the only way in and out of Pit 4 for every one of the miners who worked her two-hundred-odd cutting faces. With its chippy out of action, Pit 4 had to fall back on the double drum lift—a heavy-duty lift built to carry muck, ore, and waste rock, not miners. Eager to keep cutting, management stopped pulling waste up on the double drum and swapped in the eight-man emergency evac bucket.

That was the first link in the chain: four hundred miners underground with a lift that carried only eight men per trip instead of the chippy lift's forty-eight.

The first shift foreman then made a decision that, only a week ago, would have been the right one. He consulted the airflow maps and rerouted Pit 4 evac through Pit 5's main shaft, two and a quarter miles southeast of the Pit 4 headframe. What he didn't know—couldn't know—was that the maps he was looking at were four days out of date because of a glitch in the AMC data system. And two days ago, a work crew had closed off the 642 crosscut to Pit 5 in an attempt to fix the ventilation problems that had contributed to the last fire.

Haas knew about the closures, of course. He would have known the maps were out of date, would have been able to put the pieces together and turn things around if he'd been there. But Haas was at a Mine Safety Commission hearing in Helena. And with Haas gone, no single person on-site was in a position to see what was coming.

And that was the second link in the chain: an entire shift sent downshaft with evac instructions that deadended thirty-two hundred meters underground in front of two locked-down steel ventilation louvers.

Meanwhile, Pit 4's double drum lift was still being used to haul miners—and all the coal, waste rock, and condensates those miners were hacking out of the ground had to go somewhere. The miners began routing their carts through the 531 crosscut to Pit 3's still-operable double drum lift. Coal and waste carts began piling up in Pit 3's central gangway, directly under the main air intake, whose Vulcan fan pumped forty-two hundred cubic meters of air per minute through the entire active workings of Pits 3 and 4.

That underground traffic jam was the third link in the chain. That, and a simple physical fact: coal is a rock that burns.

At 3 A.M. a flash fire flickered through the 4100 level of the Trinidad, almost six kilometers from the Pit 3 headframe as the crow flies. The fire crew suited up and went down, but they couldn't find a point of origin—and though they shut down the nearby brattices, air was still coming in from somewhere. They called up to the Pit 3 fanhouse to report the fire. The fan operator checked his maps, saw that the fire was on Pit 3's main ventilation circuit, logged the time, and flipped the safety shutoff on his fan, cutting all forced-air ventilation to Pits 3 and 4.

On any other day, the shutoff would have been the right thing to do. It would have given the fire crew additional time to find the flash fire's source, and it would have stopped the big fans from pumping suffocating smoke through the rest of the mine until they got the crystals under control.

But today wasn't any other day. Today there was a freight-train-sized traffic jam of coal and refuse carts lined up down the length of the 3100 gangway just below the intake shaft.

As long as the fans were running, the fresh air flowed through the gangway fast enough to catch the highly flammable coal dust rising off the carts and blow it out the Pit 4 outtake before it could stagnate and become volatile. When the fans shut off, however, the dust began to thicken in the unventilated gangway and climb toward ignition temperature. All that was missing now was a spark. A spark, and fresh air to feed the fire the spark would start.

At 3:42 A.M. by the clock in the Pit 3 fanhouse, the fire crew called up top to report that the fire in the Trinidad was out.

At 3:47 the above-ground foreman ordered the fans back on.

At 3:49 the Anaconda crossed the line that every mine crosses sooner or later: the line where only the dead know what really happened.

All the living knew was that at ten to four a shock wave rippled through the coalfield, breaking windows and knocking people off their feet in the streets of Shantytown. People ran out of bars and flophouses, still half-asleep, and saw lightning over the coalfield, followed by a black billowing thunderhead of smoke that could only mean one thing: the mine was burning.

As the rescuers started pulling up the maps and putting the pieces together, they faced a critical situation. Over six hundred miners had gone into Pits 3 and 4 at the start of first shift. Seventy-odd miners, many of them badly injured, were huddled in Pit 4's 3400 loading bay waiting for the spreading smoke to catch up with them. Hundreds more were scattered through the long miles of unventilated drifts and gangways that were rapidly filling with smoke. And the only way in or out of the mine was Pit 4's excruciatingly slow emergency cage.

Now it was a simple matter of mathematics. The cage's eight-man capacity meant that eight rescuers could go down each trip and send eight injured miners back up to the surface in their place. Nothing anyone did now could change that—any more than it could stop the fire ripping through the drifts and galleys.

But even with the disaster staring them in the face, Li couldn't help wondering about the now-forgotten flash fire down in the Trinidad that had started it all.

They set down on the Pit 9 helipad, over six kilometers from the fire. Even so, they made their final descent through a solid curtain of smoke, and the touchdown, when it came, was as sudden as stepping off an unexpected stair flat-footed.

Li spotted Sharpe in the lee of the breakerhouse, surrounded by a half dozen still-unloaded trucks of medical equipment. She grabbed the strap of the medic's kit he flung at her and followed him.

She counted almost eighty injured miners lying on stretchers lined up in haphazard rows around the trucks. One of Sharpe's interns was moving down the rows already, tagging them. Green for mildly wounded victims whose treatment could wait until the first crush was over. Red for urgent cases. White for hopeless ones. There was a lot of white out there already—and the rescuers wouldn't gain access to the immediate area of the explosion for hours, possibly even days.

"At least it looks like they're getting them up fast," Li said.

Sharpe gave her a grim tight-mouthed look. "They've only brought two loads up so far. The rest of these are above-ground injuries."

"Oh God."

"Haven't you been listening to the pit priests, Major? We're out of God's jurisdiction."

Li lost track of time after that. The underground cases came in slowly at first. Then the rescuers started rappelling down the Pit 4 shaft and hauling the injured up by hand. Within minutes, the triage unit was overwhelmed. Li's oracle loaded its med praxis, and she sank into a long dark automatic tunnel of bending, cutting, injecting, bandaging.

At some point, the stretchers got short. Rescue crews started raiding the lines of wounded, checking for white tags, then pulses, pulling stretchers out from under the already dead.

"Hey!" Li shouted when a young miner dumped a white-tagged burn victim off a stretcher near her.

"No time," the rescuer said. He sounded young, and

furious. On the ground between them, the burn victim woke briefly, called out someone's name, and died. "Christ Almighty, I thought he was dead already," the rescuer said, then turned aside and vomited.

Li watched him for a moment, then wiped her face on her sleeve and went back to work.

"Hey!" someone said behind her, she wasn't sure how much later. She felt the weight of a hand on her shoulder and turned to see Ramirez, barely recognizable under a mask of caked coal dust, blood, diesel oil.

"We could use you downstairs," he said.

Li looked around for Sharpe and saw him talking to the newly arrived Helena medics. "How shorthanded are you?" she asked.

"What we're short of is equipment. Rebreathers, mainly. Can't recharge the ones we have fast enough to keep up with the rescue teams." He hesitated, then went on, speaking quickly. "And the mine blew on the graveyard shift."

For a moment Li didn't see what Ramirez was aiming at. Then she felt a chill run down her spine. Graveyard shift was the bootleggers' shift. It was night shift, station time and planet time alike: the only shift that both started and ended under cover of darkness, and the easiest time for the independents to smuggle their cuttings out of the mine through all the unmaintained drifts and boreholes that never showed up on the company maps.

This time of night there would be dozens, maybe hundreds of independents below ground who had never logged in or left their tags at pit bottom. The shift foremen might know where the bootleggers were, more or less—but admitting it would mean admitting they'd taken bribes in cash or condensate to keep quiet. And, bribes or no bribes, most of the shift foremen were dead anyway.

Worst of all—and this was what Ramirez really

meant—most of the constructs still working in the mines were independents. If the pit had blown on any other shift, there would have been a host of genetics among the rescue crews—experienced miners who could survive the poisoned air without rebreathers at least long enough to pull out a few survivors. Now those very miners were the ones trapped below ground waiting for rescue, and the men above ground needed rebreathers. Rebreathers that probably wouldn't arrive in time.

Li looked over at the Helena medics, already spreading through the triage area, bending over stretchers, setting down crates of burn bags and bandages.

"There's two hundred and seventy logged-in miners still unaccounted for," Ramirez said, letting the number hang in the smoky air between them. "Maybe another hundred independents in the back tunnels."

"All right," Li said. "Just give me a minute."

Half an hour later, she felt the bump of the cage hitting pit bottom, jerked the gate open, and stepped out into hell.

The rescue was an exercise in controlled chaos. Searchers surged in and out of the staging area, often returning to report not survivors but additional rescuers lost to smoke inhalation and rockfall injuries. Dogs sniffed through the stench of coal smoke and burnt electrical wiring, barking with excitement at the rare live find, whining anxiously when the bodies they discovered didn't sit up and talk to them.

Li spent the rest of the night working side by side with Ramirez. To her amazement, he kept up with her. More than kept up with her. And, unwired as he was, it could only be nerves and raw determination that were holding him together.

As the night wore on she began to notice that the men at pit bottom always made sure Ramirez had a stretcher when he needed it or a fresh tank when he came back to turn in his empties. He was getting special treatment, and for good reason: he was finding people. Finding survivors and getting them out with a speed that could only mean he was taking chances the others weren't willing to take.

So. He was a hero—down here, anyway. Li had long gotten over being surprised by anything people did when lives were on the line. She'd seen hard-bitten veterans fall apart under fire, and she'd seen more than a few soft-looking rich kids reveal themselves as born heroes—or born killers. Some people were just wired for crunch time. So far it looked like Ramirez was one of them.

Li herself was a survivor, not a hero. Any illusions she'd had on that score had been scorched out of her back on Gilead. But down here she didn't need to be a hero. Down here she just needed to keep breathing. And keep breathing was exactly what she did, as night paled to smoky daylight at the top of the shaft three kilometers above them.

She and Ramirez outlasted three different rescue teams, ran into McCuen somewhere toward dawn and kept on searching with him. They followed pointing fingers and hoarse-throated directions. They listened for the dogs' barking. They helped dig through rockfalls and shore up dangerously loose lagging. They hefted bodies, live and dead, and carried them until they found someone to hand them off to.

Meanwhile, Li's internals monitored the contaminated air, beeped warnings at her—warnings she ignored—and sent out suicide armies of virucules to combat the contamination that was clogging her lungs and flooding through her body. After the first few hours of exposure, the nonceramsteel components in her internals started overheating, and her oracle shifted all nonessential systems into powersave. At four hours she started coughing up coal black chunks of phlegm loaded with dead virucules. At four-teen hours, she had to go back above ground and sit hooked up to the oxygen feed for most of an hour to catch her breath and give her systems a chance to re-boot. Then she went back down, forcing herself not to think about the damage she was doing, and started the whole process over again.

In every rescue or battlefield cleanup Li had ever worked, there came a point of diminishing returns. It might come after only a few hours, or it might take days to arrive, but sooner or later it always did come. Then the rush of saving survivors was replaced by the grim obligation of retrieving bodies, and you started to wonder just what it was you were risking your own life for. Li always felt sorriest for the dogs when it got to that point, and this rescue was no exception. There was a shattering sincerity in their reactions: the hesitation, the doubtful whining note that slipped into their bark-ing, the worried licking of hands and faces that were long past reviving. Even at the end, even after every human rescuer had shut down and given up inside, the dogs couldn't stop hoping.

Li hit her own point of diminishing returns some-where in Anaconda's 3700 level, creeping down a shattered drift with a pulse locator that hadn't spiked on a live person in fourteen hours. Even Ramirez had started to at least talk about packing it up.

Then, finally, they got the hit they almost stopped believing would come: a locator beacon in a relatively undamaged section of corridor well off the main circu-lation paths—and, they hoped, out of the worst smoke. But when they reached it, they found only empty corridor running away into the darkness.

"What the hell?" Li said, her locator still blipping at something that clearly wasn't there.

McCuen pried a piece of lagging away from the wall and pulled the beacon out of a niche in the wall.

"Bootleggers," he said, his voice muffled by his rebreather mouthpiece. "If they're still alive, they'll have been working within shouting distance of it."

The three of them stared at each other, hardly breathing. Then they started shouting.

When the reply finally came, Li thought it was an echo. She forced her pickup to maximum and heard it again. It was shouting, although it sounded too faint to be anywhere near them—certainly too faint for unenhanced ears to hear.

"Sshh!" she said.

Ramirez and McCuen stopped shouting and looked at her.

"What?" McCuen whispered.

She heard it again. Two voices, muffled by rock and dropped coal, but voices all the same. And above the shouting, a second sound. A buzzing, vibrating sound that came from much closer.

They tracked the sound along the corridor and up a rough side tunnel that ended in a roof fall. And when they called out there, even McCuen and Ramirez thought they heard it.

As soon as they heard it, they went crazy. McCuen ran back toward the main gangway to get help and spread news of possible survivors. Li and Ramirez began a furious race to collect all the timber and lagging they could find within carrying distance and start shoring up the roof and chipping their way into the rubble pile.

"Right, then," Ramirez said when they had cleared a passage through the first big blockage. He unbuckled his kit and started stripping off his bulky safety gear. "I'll go take a look around."

Li shook her head. "Forget it. I'll go."

"No way," he said, tugging at a stubborn buckle.

Li put a hand on his arm. "You don't have to prove anything, Leo."

He stopped and gave her an incredulous half-angry stare. Then he grabbed the end of the cord and clipped it onto his belt. "I'm not trying to prove anything," he said, not looking at her. "I'm trying to get those people out safely."

Li felt her face heat up. "If that's what you want, you'll let me go. I'm smaller, stronger. And I can get by without my rebreather if I have to. Wherever they are, I've got a better chance of getting to them, and that's God's truth."

She took the cord out of his hands, tugging a little to free it from his clenched fingers. As she unclipped it from his belt and attached it to her own she kept her eyes fixed on his. "Just feed me rope and come dig me out if the roof falls on me," she said. "All right?"

As if in response to her words, the roof boomed and cracked—the sound of a mountain's weight of coal and rock shifting above them, seeking a new equilibrium now that the ribs had been burned out of the deep tunnels.

"Don't worry," Ramirez said grimly. "I'll be here."

The tunnel behind the rockfall was dark but not too smoky. Li guessed that the roof had caved in so quickly that not much smoke-tainted air had made it into this section.

She crept forward through air so close and hot that her infrared gave her only a blurred sketch of the path before her. The tunnel was relatively clear once she was past the rockfall; it was just a matter of squirming around the rubble that had been ripped off the walls and ceiling when the fire had come through.

The posts and lagging littering her path were more than inconveniences, of course. They were what had been holding up the ceiling before the fire. And now that they had come down it was only a matter of time until the mountain took the tunnel back.

The trick, of course, was not to be there when that happened.

She was ten meters down the passage when she heard the roof crack again. A sound like tearing paper rippled through the dark toward her. Rocks pummeled the ground a few meters ahead. She crouched in the partial shelter of a fallen timber and waited.

"Okay?" Ramirez called when everything but the roiling dust had subsided.

"Okay," she called, as loud as she dared. She pushed her hard hat down on her head, waited a few moments to make sure the fault wasn't spreading, then pushed forward.

Just as she started forward, the noise started again. This time it was a scratchy rasping sound, not like anything she had heard before. She dove back under the shelter, expecting more roof fall. The noise stopped, then started again, repeating at regular intervals. It wasn't the roof shifting at all, she realized; it sounded more like a switch turning.

She tracked it to the drift's far wall, behind a twisted piece of lagging that had once been pressure-bolted into the ceiling. She didn't dare move the lagging; even her ceramsteel-reinforced muscles and tendons couldn't hold the immense metal plate if its few remaining bolts came loose. She ran her hands up behind it, trying to find the source of the noise. Finally her fingers touched what she had not allowed herself to hope for: a phone box.

It had been bent by the weight of the fallen lagging, its speaker half-crushed. She had to make her way back down the corridor and pull a metal rod out of the rubble to pry it open and get her hands on the receiver. When she put it to her ear, it had already stopped ringing, and she got nothing but the rough static of a damaged line.

"Christ," she whispered. She twisted around to get her arm farther under the lagging and felt something pull and strain in her shoulder. Finally, she got her hand on the cradle and held it down, keeping the receiver in her other hand. It was three painful minutes by her internals before the phone rang again.

"Hello?" she said, jerking her hand off the cradle and pressing the receiver to her ear. "Hello?"

"Hello," said a disembodied voice over the crackle and whine of the wire.

"Where are you?" Li said.

"Where the hell do you think I am?" the voice asked.

Li shivered. "Who is this?"

"Come on, Katie."

"Cartwright?" she said. "Cartwright?"

But the line had gone dead.

"Let's get you up top," Ramirez said when she told him about Cartwright. Even in the lamplight, she could see he was looking at her like she was crazy.

"No. I'm telling you. I talked to him. He's in the glory hole."

"That's nonsense. We're nowhere near there."

"Yes we are." Li shook her head stubbornly. "I've got the wiring charts for this pit pulled up. I'm looking at them. The phone line they laid in for Sharifi runs down this drift and into a borehole that connects to the Trinidad just south of the glory hole. That's how we heard their voices: through the boreholes the wiring team ran down from this level."

"Let's just call it into pit bottom and let a closer team handle it," Ramirez said.

And that was when she figured it out.

It wasn't that Ramirez didn't believe her. He believed Cartwright was down there, all right; he wasn't even surprised to hear it. He just didn't want her to know about it.

"You crazy bastards," she said. "What the hell have you done?"

"Come on. We need to go up."

"How does it feel to kill a few hundred people, Leo?"

"It's AMC that's killing them, not Cartwright."

Li turned and started walking toward the slant down to the Trinidad.

"Where are you going?" Ramirez asked.

"To find that son of a bitch and beat the truth out of him."

"No, wait." Ramirez was chasing after her, stumbling in his haste to catch up to her. "It's not what you think. I'll talk to you. I'll tell you everything you want. But please, please let Daahl handle this. It's for him to handle. And if you tell anyone, it'll only get more people killed. It'll only mean they all died for nothing, for AMC's damned bottom line!"

Later, she wished she had insisted. Wished she had gone straight down to the glory hole, no matter what Ramirez had said or how reasonable it had sounded. But later was too late, because when they went up to find Daahl they got more than they bargained for.

"That doesn't look good," Ramirez said as they stepped out of the pithead office.

Li followed his glance to the triage area where Sharpe and the other medics had been. It was deserted. The wounded had been evacuated while she was underground, and the medics with them. All they had left behind was a fluttering trash field of steri-wipes and used IVs and torn burn wrappings.

She looked toward the helipads and saw a group of company employees clustered nervously around the single station shuttle still on the helipad. Everything else was a sea of coveralled miners and ragged Shantytowners.

Daahl greeted Ramirez's news without even pretending to be surprised by it. He sent Ramirez off to gather a group of rescuers—though it looked to Li like Daahl didn't much think Cartwright needed rescuing.

"Get on the shuttle," he told Li when that was done. "You can't do anything else here, and this doesn't concern you."

Li stood her ground. "What the hell's going on here?"

"Like I said, nothing that concerns you."

"Bullshit! Cartwright's messing with live crystals, and you're standing around chatting on top of a mine that's already blown once!"

"Cartwright knows what he's doing, Katie. He doesn't need your help."

"Help wasn't what I had in mind, Daahl. I don't know what little game you two are playing but—"

Daahl met someone's eyes over Li's shoulder, froze for a split second, then relaxed again as if he'd made a conscious effort to look natural. Li turned to see who he was looking at and found herself staring into a pair of ceramsteel-cold blue eyes set in the face of a tough-looking woman in EMT gear.

The woman nodded to Daahl, gave Li a measuring look, then just stood, hands thrust into her overall pockets, sharp eyes flicking back and forth between the two of them.

Li looked at Daahl, then glanced at the woman, hesitating. Should she know her? She shook her head and turned back to Daahl.

"Go ahead," he said, without introducing the woman. "No secrets here."

"No secrets?" Li snorted. "You must be joking. I can't walk a step without tripping over one."

"Just because something's none of your business doesn't mean it's a secret."

"None of my business? People are dying down there."

"People have been dying down there every day since you left here," Daahl said, his voice as hard as Shantytown's gypsum flats in August. "I haven't noticed that you cared until now."

"What's that supposed to mean?"

"You can't fight in two armies, Katie."

"I—"

"I'm not laying blame. Hell, I'm proud of you, of what you've accomplished. But in a few days there'll be UN troops dropping in here. And they'll be aiming at us. So don't ask me to trust you because of some little girl I knew way back when. She's dead. You killed her the day you enlisted."

That brought her up short. She looked at the unnamed woman and saw ice-blue eyes staring back at her. She looked back at Daahl and saw the same pale eyes, the same cold mistrustful look. *He despises you,* she thought. The words floated to the surface of her mind before she could suppress them. *He despises you, and he's right to. When did you become such a hypocrite?*

She shoved the thought down savagely. "You make it sound like war," she said.

"It is war. And you chose your side fifteen years ago."

She looked out the window toward the helipad and saw a group of guards clotted around the perimeter.

No. Not a group. A line. Behind the line stood the white-and-orange coveralls of company techs, the blue of pit management. This side of the line there was only a roiling tide of miners and Shantytowners.

They stood, heads down, shoulders hunched, not quite facing the company men. A low buzz rose from their mouths, a sound as subtle and menacing as a wasp's nest waking to a careless footfall.

Li knew that sound. It was the sound of a mob getting ready to hurt someone. The strike had begun.

"Go!" Daahl said.

As she walked away, she felt the two pairs of pale

eyes boring into her back, as if they could see right through skin and ceramsteel to the coward she had somehow become.

She must have slept on the shuttle; she had no memory of the journey back to the station.

When they finally docked, she stumbled to her quarters, ignoring the littered corridors, the open doors, the rescue personnel flooding in from every other mining station in-system. She could barely see straight, and her eyes and throat felt like they'd been peeled.

She pressed her palm to her door seal and swayed unsteadily in the corridor while it read her implant. She had stepped inside before she felt the faint twinge of alarm that told her something was out of place.

Before she could react—before she could even think about what had triggered the feeling—a hard hand closed over her mouth.

"Leave the witch alone," a man's voice whispered in her ear, "and don't ask questions you don't want the answers to."

She scanned to see if her attacker had a weapon and found none. That was the good news. The bad news was that he had the kind of probe shielding that could only go with a wire job.

He spun her around and slammed her head into the wall hard enough to make her eyes water.

"Accidents can happen on-station too," he whispered, "not just underground."

Then he was gone—just in time for Li to realize that the stink filling her nose was Kintz's cheap aftershave.

The knock came at her door well after two in the morning station time.

"Who is it?" Li asked hazily, trying to remember if she'd put on enough clothes when she went to bed to be decent now. The whispered reply was enough to jolt her wide-awake and halfway to the door.

Bella all but fell into Li's arms as the door hissed open. Li supported her to the bed. Bella clung to her as if she were drowning while Li brushed her hair back from her face to reveal a new bruise blossoming over the old ivory stain of the last one.

Her first thought was that Haas had done it. Then she caught herself. Had Bella ever come out and accused him? Had she ever done more than deal in hints and innuendo? Haas had been off-station for days, first in Helena, then dealing with rescue operations on the surface. Did this mean he was back? Or had someone else done it? And what, in the end, did she really know about Bella?

"Haas doesn't know I'm here," Bella said, shuddering. "He . . . fell asleep."

"Let's go down to Security, Bella. You can file a report."

"No," Bella whispered. "You'll leave, sooner or later. Then there'll be no one to protect me."

Li stared at her, knowing what she said was true, hating it, hating herself for not being able to change it.

Bella started and pulled out of Li's arms.

"Where did you get this?" she asked, picking up Sharifi's copy of *Xenograph* from the floor where Li had dropped it when she fell asleep. "It's Hannah's."

"I took it from her room."

Bella looked at her, and that calculating look drifted across her face again. "Read to me," she said. "Like Hannah did."

Li hesitated.

"Please. I just need to hear your voice."

Li thumbed through the book, wondering what passages Hannah would have read to Bella. What she would have said about them. She remembered the secretive habits she'd developed during a childhood of reading library books: cracking their spines so the next person who checked them out couldn't spot her favorite passages, couldn't read over her shoulder and trace her own reactions in the rut of her reading. Had Sharifi been like her, a private, furtive, guilty keeper of secrets? Li doubted it; the Sharifi she remembered watching, the Sharifi that Bella and Sharpe and Cohen talked about, hadn't been interested in hiding.

She held the book up and let it fall open. Sure enough, she saw a line of Sharifi's neat writing in the margin. She read out the words Sharifi had underlined:

I write these words sitting in our field camp. Behind me rise the eight thousanders of the Johannesburg Massif, still unclimbed every one of them. To my left lie the salt flats of that ancient ocean whose banks I spent two years walking. To my right, the highlands that Cartwright and Dashir mapped. All untouched, alien, perfect as it was on the first day we saw it.

But on my way to camp, I passed the terraforming plant. I passed algae flats, the furrows of farmers' fields. And I have now a wheat ear lying across the page I write on. I plucked it from the trailside. Life in a blade of grass.

Life for another planet. For this one, death—and the slow, fatal rot that follows the map of our best intentions.

We were mapmakers. Monks and worshipers. We came into the country like saints coming to the desert. We came to be changed.

But nothing changes. Everything men touch changes.

And in the margin, Sharifi's scribbled words—words Li didn't read to Bella:

But you still gave them the maps, didn't you?

Li raised her eyes from the page to find Bella staring at her. She closed the book, started to speak. Bella put a finger to her lips.

"Hush," she murmured, leaning into Li, ducking her head so that her hair brushed Li's mouth and tickled her nose.

"How I can help you, Bella? Tell me. What can I do?"

"Just hold me."

So Li held her, her pulse racing at the smell and the feel of her, her stomach curling with shame at what she couldn't help wanting.

They sat that way for so long that Li began to think Bella was asleep when she finally spoke again.

"How strong are you?" Bella asked.

Li frowned, caught off guard. "Strong."

"Stronger than a man?" A warm hand slipped under Li's T-shirt, slid over her flanks and stomach.

"A lot stronger," Li said.

The hand paused in its exploration. Bella looked up at her intently. "Have you ever killed anyone?"

Li started. She thought of Korchow of all people, half-expecting a joke or an accusation. "Of course I have," she whispered.

"What's it like?"

"Not nice."

"Do you ever feel guilty about it?"

"Sometimes." She saw Gilead's brilliant sunrise, its snowcapped mountains rushing up at her in the split second before her auxiliary chute popped open. "Some of them."

"But then you jump to a new star, a new planet, and you forget all about it. That's a gift. To be able to leave a place behind forever. To forget the person you became there. Some people would give anything for that."

"It doesn't work like that," Li protested, but Bella wasn't listening anymore.

"Kiss me," she said.

Li swallowed.

"Don't you want to?"

"Listen," Li began—but whatever she'd been about to say caught on an indrawn breath as Bella's fingers circled her nipple.

"You look at me like you want to," Bella whispered into her ear, a whisper that was itself a caress.

"Looking isn't doing," Li said with the last rational part of her brain. But those were just words, and Bella knew it as well as she did.

Instead of answering, she dropped to her knees in front of Li and kissed her stomach, her waist, the point of one hip.

The book fell to the floor and lay there unnoticed. *I can stop in a minute*, Li told herself as she drew Bella to her. *If I want to. I can stop anytime I want to.*

Then she pressed her mouth to Bella's pale face and

buried her hands in the dark torrent of hair and found the lips that were searching for hers.

Bella cried afterward and talked about Sharifi.

Li asked herself what else she'd expected when Bella showed up on her doorstep, what she'd imagined Bella saw in her besides the echo of the other woman. Neither the questions nor their too-obvious answers made her feel any better.

"Hannah was a construct herself," Bella said. "Not part construct, like you. All construct."

Li nodded, wondering if Bella knew enough about UN politics to feel the weight of the difference between the two things, to know what mandatory registration meant and what went with the red slash across Sharifi's passport cover.

"She was the first person who talked to me, who understood what it was like to be here, alone. To have no one. She went through all that to get where she was. Gave up her sisters, her friends, her world. Everything. You can't imagine how hard that is."

Li said nothing, just lay stroking Bella's hair, trying to get over feeling ashamed of herself. As she listened to Bella's memories of Sharifi, she saw that she'd been fooling herself all along. All Bella remembered were the small ordinary things that lovers always remember. And none of that mattered now. Not to Nguyen or Korchow. Not to Li herself. Bella was the only one of them for whom Sharifi was still alive—maybe the only one for whom Sharifi had ever been alive. And in that strangest of moments, Li thought of Cohen and felt even worse.

"It's not knowing that's so hard," Bella said in a voice that still threatened tears. "If I knew what happened to her. If I knew why. That it was politics. Or money. Or anything."

"What does it matter why?"

"Because," Bella said, suddenly wracked with sobs, "because I don't want her to have died trying to help me."

After that, there was no more talking. Bella cried herself to sleep. Li lay awake far into the night, holding her frail shoulders, listening to her call out the dead woman's name in her dreams.

AMC Station: 25.10.48.

"Hello, Catherine."

Li jerked awake to find Bella sitting across the room in her only chair, fully dressed, legs crossed, smoke from one of Li's cigarettes curling lazily around her head.

"Forgive the familiarity, Major, but I feel I know you too well for titles. You don't mind my calling you Catherine, do you? Or would you prefer Caitlyn?"

The voice had none of Bella's nervous edge, and the hand holding the cigarette moved with a slightly jerky quality, as if it were being pulled by strings. Bella was wired for a shunt, and someone was along for the ride. A bodysnatcher.

Li shouldn't have been as rattled by it as she was. Of course Bella was wired. Probably more subtly and pervasively than Li herself. Still, it wasn't quite the morning-after breakfast-in-bed scene she'd imagined. She sat up and groped for her clothes, lost somewhere in the tangle at the foot of the bed. Whoever or whatever had gotten hold of Bella, Li wanted to be dressed before she talked to it.

"Nice tattoo," the snatcher said while she pulled her shirt over her head.

"Fuck off."

But Bella's voice kept talking to her. "You ought to be more careful. You can catch things in tattoo parlors."

"Is that a threat?"

"But then you don't worry much about catching things, do you?"

"And what's that supposed to mean?"

"Only that it's always nice to see a XenoGen construct. I feel a certain familial affection for you. Bella's geneset, for instance"—Bella's hand gestured at her own body—"is at least 40 percent prebreakaway. Without you she would never have been possible. So unfortunate that the UN lacked the vision to carry that work to its logical conclusion."

Li stared at Bella's face, looked for some clue beneath it to confirm her sudden suspicion. "Korchow?"

He smiled a cold smile that had nothing of Bella in it at all. "Clever girl."

"Leave Bella out of this, Korchow. She has nothing to do with it."

"She has everything to do with it. The choices you make here affect the patrimony of every construct in UN space and beyond it. If you honor what you are— and I very much hope you will—it all changes. If you turn aside and pass by, nothing changes."

"Stop talking in riddles, Korchow. What do you want?"

"Don't you know?" Bella's eyes widened in amusement. "Don't you even suspect?"

"I can't give you Sharifi's dataset," Li said through clenched teeth. "I don't even have the thing. As far as I know, she ripped it up and flushed it into orbit."

"It's not about the dataset, Major. It's gone beyond

that." Bella's lips stretched into a narrow smile. "Nguyen really doesn't tell you anything, does she? Is it you she doubts? Or the AI? I wonder. Well. What I want is simple. I want to run Sharifi's experiment again. Or rather, I want you to run it for me."

Li stared at him.

"It's not all that complicated. I need three things to pull it off." He ticked the items off on Bella's slender fingers as he named them. "Item one, a glory hole. Item two, the intraface. Item three, an AI-human team to run the intraface." He looked up at Li as if he expected an answer, but she had nothing to say. "It took Sharifi years, and a lot of legally questionable maneuvering to put these three necessities together. However, a series of fortuitous coincidences have placed me in a position to, shall we say, stand on her shoulders? I already have half the intraface—the wetware, in fact, which you were so kind as to extract for me."

Li caught her breath.

"Surely you suspected our pretty friend here," Korchow said. "Bella has been so useful in so many ways. A credit to her Syndicate. In any case, I have the wetware. I also have the glory hole Sharifi found . . . at least until that idiot Haas starts tampering with it. And"—he smiled triumphantly—"I have you."

"So I'm just in the wrong place at the wrong time?"

"Far from it. You would see it yourself—would have seen it long ago—if you hadn't been lying to the humans so long that you yourself have become confused about who you are. The hardware we have was grown for Sharifi. It would take months, years possibly, to redesign it for someone else. But we don't have to do that, do we? Because we still have Sharifi." He gestured toward Li. "She's sitting right in front of me."

"I'm not Sharifi," Li said.

"To the intraface you are. None of the cosmetic surgery and camouflage splices, nothing that chop-shop hack did to you changed that."

Li's insides turned over. "I don't know what you're talking about."

"We'll return to that later," Korchow said evasively. "In the meantime, you will steal the intraface operating program—software you've already stolen once on Nguyen's orders. Surprised? What did you think you were doing at Metz? Then we will do one final run of Sharifi's live field experiment. Just to answer a few unresolved questions."

Bella's fingers teased a cigarette out of the pack Li had left on the table and lit it. To Li's adrenaline-honed senses, the crackling tobacco sounded loud as gunfire.

"Of course, you will have to undergo a minor surgical procedure," Korchow said. "But we needn't worry over details."

"I won't do it," Li said.

"Ah, but you will. And let me tell you something more, Major." Korchow leaned forward confidingly. "I continue to have faith in you. I believe you will help us of your own free will. Because it is what history demands of you. And though you may resent me now, you'll thank me for helping you to see it. I'm quite, quite sure of that."

"You crazy fuck."

He smiled. "Just idealistic. Have you read any syndicalist political philosophy? *Alienation? The Decline and Fall of Species?*"

"I saw the movie. And don't waste your time feeding me some line about gene duty and gaps in the ranks and choosing my part. I'm not playing."

"Unfortunate. Though, I must confess, not entirely unexpected."

Korchow lifted Bella's hand, and a pale ideogram appeared under the curve of her palm. It rotated, unfolded, blossomed into a dog-eared piece of yellow paper covered with close-set numbers.

"What is that?" Li asked, and even she could hear the tremor in her voice.

"I think you know," he said as he handed it to her.

It felt real in her fingers, so real that she imagined for a moment she could just rip it up, burn it, get rid of it somehow. But she knew that the rough nap of the paper under her hands, even the slightly musty smell of it, was illusion. The original was somewhere far away. Down on Compson's where Korchow was. Maybe even back on Gilead.

"I don't know what you think this is," she said, though of course she did know.

"Read it," Korchow suggested.

Block letters ran across the top of the page: REPRODUCTION TECHNOLOGIES, S.A., J. M. JOSS, M.D.G.P., B.S., SPECIALIZING IN ARTIFICIAL REPRODUCTION TECHNOLOGIES AND REMEDIAL GENETIC ENGINEERING. Below the letters were a series of numbers: medical codes to the left, prices to the right. The prices were given in both UN currency and AMC scrip.

Li didn't have to check her oracle to know what the codes stood for; she already knew. And even if she hadn't known, there was her own signature, or rather Caitlyn Perkins's signature, scrawled below the tightly printed boilerplate of the medical release.

"Where did you get this?" she whispered.

"Where do you think, Major?"

"I watched Joss burn my file. He burned it in the sink. I wouldn't leave until he'd done it."

"Apparently," Korchow said, "he didn't burn everything. People are so untrusting in human space."

She sat, head down, staring at the paper. When Korchow reached out to take it back, she made no effort to stop him.

"Well," he said, folding the slip of paper and whisking it back out of realspace. "We all make mistakes. The thing now is to put regret behind you and go forward."

"What do you want?"

"I want this little venture to work out satisfactorily for all of us. But at the moment I just want you to make a choice. If you decide to help me, then you will go to Shantytown twelve hours from now and meet with a man who will give you the data you need for the first stage of the operation. And you will bring the AI with you. Or at least an assurance that he will participate."

It took Li several moments to realize he was talking about Cohen. "He's not under contract to us," she argued. "He's a freelancer. I can't make him do shit."

"I imagine you can make him do quite a lot, actually."

"You'd imagine wrong, then."

"Oh? Why don't we ask him?"

"Oh, sure," Li said mockingly. "What do I do, draw a pentagram and say his name three times?"

Korchow smiled. "What an amusing idea. I think a simple and sincere call for assistance will suffice, however. Try it."

She stared at Korchow. But then she did try it. And there Cohen was, real as a government paycheck.

He wore a summer suit the color of pomegranates. Wherever he'd been when she called him, he was in the middle of getting dressed. He leaned forward, still peering into a mirror that was no longer there, knotting a mushroom brown silk tie around his throat.

"Oh, my," he said. He cocked his head in apparent confusion and turned slowly around until he caught sight of Li. "This is a nice surprise," he said, blinking and smiling.

Then he took in her state of undress, the rumpled bed, Bella sitting across the room. His smile vanished.

"Korchow," he said in a voice of terrifying gentleness. "I can't say it's a pleasure, so I won't say anything."

"I thought we talked about this, Cohen," Li said. "I thought you were going to stop spying on me."

He turned back to her. "What a nasty little word. Of course I would never spy on you. And if I do assign an autonomous agent or two to keep an eye on you, it's only to prevent unpleasant people"—he glanced in Korchow's direction—"from making trouble for you."

Bella cleared her throat meaningfully, and Cohen looked at her again.

"So," he purred. "Korchow. I almost didn't recognize you behind that cheap shunt. You really should get the Syndicates to pay you better. You are still working for them, no? Or has your alleged idealism worn thin enough that you're taking UN money too?"

"Cohen," Li said. "You can go now."

Cohen gave her a pained and innocent look.

"You can go, I said."

"Are you sure that's a good idea?" he asked, glancing at Korchow.

"Yes I am. I can take care of this. And don't eavesdrop!"

He cast a last look at Korchow, frowning. "You shouldn't have anything to do with him, Catherine. He's . . . well, he's not nice."

"Go home, Cohen."

"Going," he said. And then he did go, leaving a subtle whiff of hand-rolled cigars and *extra-vielle* behind him.

"Well," Korchow said. "I think we understand each other."

"What if I don't show tonight?"

Korchow merely moved Bella's fingers in answer, and the tattered yellow receipt reappeared, fluttering as if it had been caught by a stiff breeze. "That would be regrettable."

Li looked at the thing in his hands and shivered. If that receipt ever ended up in front of the Service, they would check it out. They would have to. And when they checked, it would be over.

Fifteen years ago she'd had high confidence. The chop-shop geneticist hadn't been much, but he'd been the best the meager payout on her father's life insurance could buy; and his work, if not inspired, had at least been competent. Now, she knew its limits. Knew them in her gut with a wrenching certainty. She'd seen the gene work the best Ring-side labs could do, the work the Corps techs at Alba did. She'd slipped through the cracks this long only because there was no real proof—no proof damning enough to justify testing her. One fifteen-year-old scrap of paper could change that. And when it did, the whole crushing weight of the Security Council bureaucracy would fall on her like mine overload dropping into a collapsing tunnel. Losing her commission would be the least of it. She'd be lucky—or irretrievably indebted to Cohen's high-priced lawyers—if she escaped without a prison sentence.

So what? She had other chances, other possibilities. It wasn't all or nothing anymore. She had options.

But did she? What else was there for her, really? She loved her job. Was her job. Couldn't imagine any other life. She thought about private security, about Cohen's well-paid bodyguards. She remembered the high-tech muscle on the Calle Mexico.

No way. Not for her.

She sat on her rumpled bunk looking at the receipt, barely an arm's length away from her, in the hands of a woman she had just made love to. And she knew she'd do anything, kill anyone, to get it.

UNCENSORED TOPOLOGY

➤ All the worlds are there, even those in which everything goes wrong and all the statistical laws break down. The situation is no different from that which we face in ordinary statistical mechanics. If the initial conditions were right the universe-as-we-see-it could be a place in which heat sometimes flows from cold bodies to hot. We can perhaps argue that in those branches in which the universe makes a habit of misbehaving in this way, life fails to evolve; so no intelligent automata are around to be amazed by it.

—Bryce De Witt

Shantytown: 25.10.48.

Li made the meet early and scoped out the place—only sensible, since Korchow had chosen it.

She found it on the seedy outer fringe of what was euphemistically known as Shantytown's entertainment district. This part of town looked right at night, somehow. It was less jarringly out of place when you couldn't see the scrub hills and gypsum flats, or the bleak unterraformed wall of the Johannesburg Massif looming on the horizon.

It wasn't raining in Shantytown, but it wasn't not raining either. The water that dripped from the rooftops and doorways was part rain, part algae-laden condensation. It smelled sharp and fermented, and it wormed under Li's collar and down her neck like prying fingers.

She was alone tonight. It hadn't been easy to keep McCuen from coming, but it had been necessary. He could put things together far too quickly for comfort, and Saints knew what he'd do if he decided she was working for the Syndicates. Besides, if she was going to play the game Nguyen wanted her to play and still give Korchow enough to get that receipt from him, she was going to need some serious maneuvering room.

She checked her watch. Nearly an hour until the meet. Korchow's man would arrive early too, of course. She aimed to be earlier still.

The bar was supposed to be called the Drift, but the only sign Li saw in the window was a flickering, fly-speckled halogen that looked like it must have read "$LOTS" before the L died. Still, this was the place Korchow had described: the narrow housefront sheathed in scaffolding, the bar entrance tucked between a peep show and a ComSat pay terminal, the drunks creaking up the rickety stairs to the second-story flophouse. She walked by, crossed the street half a block down, skirting around a poisonous mud puddle, and slipped under the jury-rigged arcade that shadowed the facing storefronts.

A loose panel rattled underfoot. Condensation dripped from mildewed girders and pooled on the walkway. She slipped into a darkened doorway, shook down a cigarette and lit it, masking its glowing tip with a cupped hand.

Korchow's man arrived at twenty minutes of. There was no mistaking him; Syndicate birthlabs bred to an idealized pre-Migration genetic norm, and Li doubted anyone that close to human-looking had crossed the Drift's threshold since the Riots.

She cursed Korchow for an overeager amateur. Then she saw his cool calculating professional's face in her mind's eye; whatever else he was, Korchow was no amateur. No, he wanted Sharifi's data badly enough to blow the cover of an A Series operative. And he didn't give a damn if Li got caught. He might even want her to get caught . . . down the line, when he had what he needed from her. She threw down her cigarette and heard it hiss in standing water as she stepped out of the shadows.

Inside, the Drift was less of a room than a haphazard string of loosely connected hallways. Li sidled through the initial bottleneck and dropped down an unmarked single step into what the regulars probably called the front room.

Korchow's man sat halfway down the bar, hunched broodily over a beer. He looked up as Li came in, and their eyes met in the bar mirror. They'd done something to his face—broken the long narrow nose, blurred the lines of jaw and cheekbone—but they hadn't been able to disguise the unnatural perfection of his features. He could have been Bella's brother.

Li passed him by and took a seat toward the other end of the bar, back in the smeary half shadows beyond the cheap lighting panels. The bartender took her order without smiling, and the beer he brought her was flat and yeasty. She drank, eyes scanning the narrow room, and set the glass back down on a bartop still sticky with the faint rings of yesterday's spilled beers. She was halfway through her second beer when Korchow's man stood and walked past her into the back room.

"Where's the bathroom?" Li asked a minute and a half later.

The bartender just gestured toward the back and muttered something that might have been "Left."

There were tables in the back room, most of them empty. She threaded her way between them and pushed through a narrow door into a dim hallway that gave on the bathroom and the fire door. A surveillance camera blinked in an angle of wall and ceiling, but, as Korchow had promised, the little corner shelf screwed into the wall underneath it was just out of its field of view.

Korchow's man came out of the toilet, coat slung over his arm. He squeezed between her and the shelf, mumbling an apology. She let him by, then went into the toilet herself. As she brushed past the shelf her hand slid across the datacube he had left there and palmed it.

She stepped through the door and scanned the narrow space. No cameras here—though there might be a voice-activated tap hidden in the wall. Even the camera out in the hall was probably no more than nonsentient-monitored company security. Still, why take chances? She went into the stall and sat down. She could feel the cube burning in her pocket. She turned it over, found the download switch by feel, and keyed it.

Nothing happened.

She knew what was supposed to be happening, what she hoped was happening. Somewhere in the labyrinth of her internal systems, an encryption program should be filtering through her hard files, searching out the hidden chinks in her internal security programs. If it worked, then Korchow would have opened up a secure protocol in her datafiles—a protocol through which he could pass her datafiles that would never show up on her directories, could never be accessed by Nguyen or any of the Corps psychtechs who had clearance to access her hard files. If it worked, she would see nothing. And neither would her recorder. If it didn't work, she'd be up on treason charges as soon as she checked in for her next scheduled maintenance.

And then there was the third possibility, one so disastrous it didn't bear thinking about. The possibility that Korchow's program would clash with one of the private kinks she had thrown into her system.

Please let Korchow have gotten this right, she prayed to whatever saint looked out for cheats and traitors. *And please let me be lucky.*

When the data window opened in her peripheral vision, she caught her breath and realized she'd been holding it. She maxed the window, scrolled down the familiar gridlines of her datebook, and waited for Korchow's encrypted window to appear.

It opened inside the datebook, an embedded half-screen that showed up on her retina but left no record of its presence anywhere else in her internal systems. She could read it, work on it, store it, and nothing but the datebook would show in her files. When she had finished with it, Korchow's program would wipe every trace of it from her systems. She hoped.

She leaned forward, closing her eyes and putting the heels of her hands against her eyelids in order to get the clearest picture of the data that was scrolling up the screen in front of her. There were four files. The first contained detailed schematics and navigational data for a massive orbital station that Li had no trouble recognizing as Alba, the Corps's high-security installation in orbit around Barnard's Star.

The second file contained an exhaustive description of security protocols, patrol routes and schedules, lab personnel protocols. The third held information on electronic security measures. The fourth file contained interface and requirements specs for what Li assumed had to be Sharifi's intraface software.

As she looked at it, she felt a spinning sense of vertigo. It was obviously, flagrantly, completely illegal tech. It could only have been designed for use on an Emergent AI and a posthuman subject, in contravention of more wetware laws than she could count. And yet a dozen little tags and quirks told her that this software could only have been developed at Alba, by the same UNSC programmers who had designed her own software. Nguyen might have had to steal the wetware, but the rest of the intraface—the hardware, the psychware, the source code that ran the intraface into the Emergent—had been sitting at Alba all the time waiting for Sharifi, or any XenoGen construct, to pick them up and use them.

She shut the files, checked that they had downloaded properly, took the datacube out of her pocket, and flushed it down the toilet.

When she walked back into the front room, three moderately pretty girls were huddled halfway down the bar, eyeing Korchow's man like crows parceling up a particularly fresh piece of carrion. She stepped up and took the seat beside him before the girls could initiate active stalking.

"What's your name?" she asked. As she spoke, she could feel three resentful stares boring into her back like virusteel-sheathed augers.

Korchow's man turned sad velvet brown eyes on her and answered as seriously as if she had asked a question that the fate of worlds turned on. "Arkady," he said. "Very pleased to meet you." He had the same curiously formal turn of phrase Bella had, the same air of believing that life was a serious and precarious business and not to be laughed at.

"Buy you a drink?" Li asked.

They made the usual small talk. When the beers came, still warm, still flat, they drank together. Arkady sipped his beer with a cautious frown that made Li suspect he wasn't a drinker.

"Well?" he said finally.

Li glanced around. "You ask a lot."

"Do I?"

"Maybe too much."

He paused and touched his beer to his lips again. "But perhaps," he said, "you have a friend who could help?"

A friend. Meaning Cohen. "Perhaps."

"Have you asked him?"

"Not yet."

Arkady's handsome face froze for an instant, and Li saw what she should have suspected, what Cohen himself had tried to tell her. She wasn't what they wanted. Or at least she wasn't all they wanted. They needed Cohen. Li and her tawdry little secret had just been the bait they used to draw him.

"We would appreciate his help a great deal, of course," Arkady was saying, "and the task brings its own rewards."

"That doesn't—" Li started to say. Then she stopped cold.

The task brings its own rewards. And what had Korchow told her? *You'll have to undergo a minor surgical procedure.*

They were going to give Cohen a working intraface. With her, Li, on the other end of it.

She shuddered. "I'll pass the message on," she said, sticking to the troubles of the moment. "How can I get you an answer?"

"You don't have to. Just be on the Helena shuttle the day after tomorrow."

"And?"

"And that's all you need to know."

"Fine." Li stood up to go, but Arkady put a hand to her arm, stopping her.

"You still haven't told me what you want."

"My life back," she snapped, too angry to keep her voice down.

"Perhaps you want what we were going to give your predecessor?"

Li turned around slowly. "Voyt, you mean?" But even as she asked, she knew it was Sharifi. Korchow had been paying Sharifi, not blackmailing her. And Sharifi had sold him the information he wanted—the same information everyone wanted. She had promised him the missing datasets. "So what was Sharifi asking for?" she asked casually.

"Not what. Who."

Li's stomach churned, and she felt a dizzy nausea flooding over her. Of course Sharifi hadn't had the money to buy out Bella's contract. She had bartered; bartered something that was far more important to the Syndicates than a single B Series construct. Sharifi had traded Bose-Einstein technology, violating every security clearance she had passed during the course of her long and productive career, violating the Espionage and Sedition Act, betraying the UN and everyone who depended on it for survival.

And she had done it for Bella.

Three men were arguing in the street when Li stepped out into the arcade again. Something about a dog, she thought. Two of them looked like brothers. The third was a small, tired man who looked bruised and sickly under the raking light of the halogens.

A skinny girl stepped into Li's peripheral vision, hawking smuggled cigarettes, weaving back and forth under the scaffolding to avoid the dripping water. She had cheap smokes. Unfiltered. The kind you could only get in places where people didn't care much about the sky-high cost of lung bugs. Li turned aside, fishing in her pocket for the little wad of bills she carried.

When she turned around, a crowd had formed around the three men in the road.

The two brothers were still shouting, but one of them now had his hands hooked under the other's armpits and was dragging him back into the shadows of the opposite arcade. A bystander knelt and picked a baseball bat out of the mud.

The third man stood alone in the muddy street, punch-drunk, blood streaming down his face and mixing with the gritty rain.

Li was in a white-hot rage by the time she got
back to the station.

"Anything else you'd like to tell me?" she asked
Bella when she finally tracked her down.

They stood in Haas's quarters, Bella backed up
against the long sleek sofa and shrinking away from Li.

"She was going to take me with her," Bella whispered, unshed tears glittering in her eyes like polished
condensate. "To the Ring. She already had the tickets."

"And you never asked how she was going to square
things with MotaiSyndicate?"

"I told you. She was going to buy out my contract."

"Even Sharifi didn't have that kind of money. She
cut a deal with Korchow. And you were the go-
between. Did they expect her to fall in love with you,
or was that just a windfall?"

"It wasn't like that," Bella whispered, and now she
really was crying.

"Wasn't it?" Li asked. "Has anything you've told me
been true, or has it all come from Korchow?"

"I never lied to you," Bella sobbed, just as Li's comm icon flared in her peripheral vision.

"Christ!" Li muttered, and shut the icon off.

"She wanted to do it," Bella insisted. "It wasn't just for me. It was for the principle."

"It's not Sharifi's motives I'm questioning."

The comm icon flared again, more urgently. The caller had disabled Li's call filter and wouldn't go away now until Li answered.

She made a sharp gesture of annoyance, and Bella flinched, fear rising in her eyes behind the tears. In any other mood, Li would have been horrified; now she felt only a grim satisfaction.

She took another step toward Bella, consciously intimidating the woman, God help her. "What was Korchow buying? And don't even think about saying you don't know."

"I don't—" Bella swallowed. "Information."

"Information about Sharifi's work."

Bella nodded.

"And you were the go-between. The go-between and the payment."

"No! It wasn't like that. They just talked."

"Well, those little talks got your girlfriend killed."

"I loved her!"

"Like you love me?" Li said nastily. "How convenient."

"I don't love you," Bella said in a voice suddenly tight with anger. "I never said I did. You think having the same geneset is enough? That I'll fall all over you just because you look like her? You're nothing but a cheap copy. You wouldn't understand Hannah if you spent the rest of your life poking and prying!"

Bella swept out of the room before Li could answer—and if she could have slammed the door, Li was sure she would have.

Her comm icon flashed again, and Li opened the line with a feeling of rising fury. "What?" she snarled.

Nguyen.

"Have I caught you at a bad time?" the general asked as her sunny office took shape around Li.

Li took a deep breath and set her jaw. "Not at all."

"Well, how do things stand, then?"

Li swallowed. She was drifting into shipwreck waters; any misstep now and she would be past the point at which she could credibly claim to have shared everything with Nguyen. *Keep it true as far as you can*, she told herself, remembering Nguyen's own advice. *The true lie is the best lie. And the hardest one to get caught in.*

She had told Nguyen about Korchow's nighttime visit, right up to the moment when he produced the chop shop receipt. Now she described her meeting with Arkady, the files he'd passed to her, his reaction to the news that Cohen was not yet committed, the appointment—only a day and a half away now—in Helena.

"What good will the intraface do him without Sharifi?" Nguyen asked.

It was the first question out of her mouth when Li finished—and Li had been waiting for it, had planned for it. Now she fed her the story Korchow had concocted, passed along his feigned confidence that Syndicate nanotech, Syndicate gene therapy, Syndicate expertise with mingling constructed genesets would be able to make a partial construct work where the UN had needed a full one.

Nguyen appeared to believe it. "We'll have to take care," she said. "Korchow's played the double game before. He stung us badly that way on Maris. Or one of his crèche brothers did. Even the As are hard to tell apart sometimes. Anyway, he'll have a safe house somewhere. He'll try to narrow your options, isolate you, push you into a situation where you rely on him for everything."

"I don't know that we can avoid that."

"I don't know that we should. We'll just have to handle things as they come up. And you'll need to rely on your judgment."

"I always do, don't I?"

Nguyen smiled. "I'm counting on it."

"Speaking of relying on my own judgment, I could use a little more information."

Nguyen raised her eyebrows.

"The code Korchow wants. The intraface. It's Alba-designed."

"What, you saw a label?" Nguyen sounded politely incredulous.

"I'm not stupid. I know Corps work when I see it. And this is Corps work. Some of the best."

"What's your question?" Nguyen's voice was as cold and hard as virusteel.

Li hesitated.

"The line's secure."

"I guess I'm asking just how much of this is about deniability. Whether we gave the intraface to Sharifi. Whether Metz was an off-the-grid contractor—"

"Who said anything about Metz?"

Li froze. Her mind raced as she tried to retreat, retrench, keep Nguyen from finding out just how much she remembered about the raid, and why. "Well," she stammered, "Cohen said . . ."

Nguyen laughed bitterly. "Cohen." She dipped a finger into her water and ran it around the rim of the glass, setting the crystal singing. "That brings us to our next topic of conversation," she said at last. "I take it Korchow doesn't think he can pull the job off without Cohen?"

"It looks that way."

"Or someone's been very careful to make it look that way. If all goes as planned, Cohen will walk away with just what he's wanted from the beginning: the intraface. We'll have handed it to him in order to catch

Korchow. From where I'm sitting, it looks like Cohen and his friends in ALEF come out winners no matter what happens. And we both know Cohen too well to think that's a coincidence."

Li stiffened. "I can't believe—"

"You can't?" Nguyen interrupted. "Or you don't want to?"

A shadow flickered across the windows of Nguyen's office, sweeping over the planes and hollows of her unsmiling face.

Li shivered. "ALEF doesn't want the intraface anyway," she argued. "It's Cohen who wants it. For personal reasons."

"Cohen doesn't have personal reasons. In order to have personal reasons, you have to be a person. Have you ever actually bothered to find out anything about ALEF? About what they advocate?"

"I don't get involved in politics."

"Don't be disingenuous. Your relationship with Cohen *is* politics."

Li flushed. "You have the right to look at my private files, but not to tell me what to put in them."

"I do when your personal life clouds your judgment."

"That's not the case here," Li said. All the same, she felt a twinge of relief at the thought that Nguyen couldn't download her last dinner with Cohen. Yet.

"Isn't it?" Nguyen said. "Then why aren't you asking the questions you should be asking? The questions everyone else is already asking?"

She plucked a fiche from her desk, tapped through the index to pull a file up, and handed it to Li. "Read it."

The era of the unitary sentient organism is over. This is not idle speculation. It's reality—a reality that

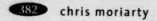

both Syndicates and UN member nations
are now scrambling to catch up with.

Li looked up at Nguyen. "What is this?"

"Cohen wrote it. It's a speech he gave at an ALEF
meeting last week. An ALEF meeting that was downloaded by known Consortium members."

"Oh," Li said, and kept reading—the same words
she had seen before back in Cohen's sunny drawing
room:

The Syndicates embody one evolutionary vector: the hive mentality of
the crèche system, the thirty-year
contract, the construction of a
posthuman collective psychology, including cultural acceptance of euthanasia for individuals who deviate
from gene-norm.

The UN, in contrast, has launched a
series of what might best be described
as rearguard actions. On the technological side, we have enslaved AIs
(how very revealing programmers' jargon can be); hardwired, task-dedicated
artificial life of every possible description; wired humans and posthumans
operating AI-platformed wetware. In
essence, a plethora of attempts to
subsume nonhuman intelligence into
human-controlled operating systems.
And in the political sphere, the
General Assembly kindly picks up any
stray items the technicians fail to
account for by slamming the door on
consciously engineered posthuman evolution, by slapping AIs with source-
code patents, mandatory-feedback-loop

legislation, encryption protocols,
and, of course, the much-beloved
thirty-year death tax.

Humanity has engineered its own
obsolescence. They acknowledge it by
act if not by deed. It is time for us
to acknowledge it. Time for us to re-
think the shape of UN politics—perhaps the very shape of the UN
itself—and step into a wider, brighter
posthuman future.

Li handed the fiche back to Nguyen, who snapped
it off with a flourish of her fine-boned hand.

"Why show me this?"

"I want you to know what Cohen is capable of."

"It's just talk," Li said uncomfortably. "You know
Cohen."

"That's my point. He's using you, Li. The same way
he's used the Security Council. The same way he used
Kolodny."

Li's stomach contracted into an icy knot. "What do
you mean the way he used Kolodny?" she whispered.

"You think what happened on Metz was an accident? He used Kolodny to get what he wanted, and
then he left her to die. Left you all to die. Didn't you
understand why the review board tried so hard to find
a way to go easy on you? Because we knew it was
Cohen's fault all along—and he was the one person we
couldn't afford to blame publicly."

"He told me it was a malfunction," Li said, too
stunned to understand what Nguyen was saying about
her own court-martial, too stunned to hear anything
beyond the bare fact of the accusation.

"Well, he lied. He found the intraface. Then he
started going after the wetware specs. Specs he had no
business looking at. Specs we couldn't afford to let

him look at. And in doing so, he endangered the security of the mission. We had to pull him off the shunt to stop him."

Li put a hand to her forehead, felt the fever rising beneath her skin. "You're sure?" she asked.

"I'm sure," Nguyen said. "I cut the link myself."

Hell," Cohen said. "The beastly thing's stuck."

He was opening a long matte-black canister, capped at both ends with silver disks of stamped metal. He was having a hard time of it, having to use Chiara's starlet-straight front teeth to pry the lid off.

"Don't break her pretty teeth," Li said, and Cohen laughed.

"I'd grow her new ones," he said. "Wouldn't be the first time I had to tidy up a little collateral damage."

They sat in his high-ceilinged drawing room, the chandeliers casting rippled reflections in the hand-laid panes of the garden doors. Chiara looked as beautiful as ever, perched like a bright bird on the sofa; but Li thought there was a pinched quality to the lovely face, a puffy hint of tiredness around the hazel eyes. She nearly asked Cohen if he was feeling all right—before she reminded herself that it wasn't Cohen she was looking at. That whether some pretty girl felt tired or sad or sick had not a thing to do with the enigma sitting across the table from her.

He got the canister open at last, with a little grunt of satisfaction, and slid out a long shiny tube of architect's fiche, which he unfurled on the low table between them. When one corner of the sheet refused to lie flat he borrowed Li's beer to weight it down.

Li squinted doubtfully at the blank surface. "We're supposed to read the plans off that? You've got something against VR now?"

"Only that I've been running VR scenarios ever since you sent me Korchow's files, without getting anywhere near figuring out how to crack this nut."

Li had been doing the same thing herself and coming up just as dry. But telling Cohen that now seemed less than productive.

He tapped the fiche. It whirred softly and lit up, casting a cool blue glow on the belly of Cohen's wineglass, the curving flank of Li's beer bottle. A spidery web of lines spread across the sheet and coalesced into a long, shallow curve like the arc of a twenty-kilometer-long suspension bridge. Cohen tapped in another command, and the ghostly parallelograms of solar arrays formed above and around the arc. "There. Alba. A place you ought to recognize faster than I do."

"I guess," Li said doubtfully.

Cohen snorted. "Spoken like a true member of the virtual generation. It took humans two hundred millennia to figure out how to read, and they're forgetting it in a matter of centuries. Anyway." He tapped the sheet emphatically. "These are the plans the contractor worked from. They're much more detailed than what Korchow gave you. And, more important, I pulled them from the contractor's files without having to go into the UNSC databases and get flagged for querying classified material."

"Oh, right," Li said as the flat image began to make sense to her. "There's the commissary. And the main labs." She grinned. "I've spent enough time in the tanks there to recognize them."

"Indeed," Cohen said. "But we're not cracking the main labs. Our target is down here: biotech R&D."

"I don't think I've ever been in that level," Li said.

"You wouldn't have. It's very hush-hush. All controlled tech work. Even the researchers live in separate quarters. It's a quarantine zone, really; look how the bulkheads cut all the way across the station on the lab levels."

He tapped a section of the fiche, and the zone enlarged, revealing a warren of windowless, dead-end corridors and security checkpoints highlighted in red. "You'll have to get through two security checkpoints on your way in, here and here."

Li pointed to a cluster of bulging growths on the station's outer skin. "What's that?"

"Algae farm. Part of the oxygen cycle. But look here." He pointed her back into the station's interior. "Now what's the job in front of us? One, we get you onto the station and into the lab wing. Two, you access the lab's central database and manually open a line to the ship. Three, I go through the lab AI's files, fielding any interference he sees fit to throw at us, and figure out which comp the intraface files are on. Four, you go get them. Five—and this is the real kicker—we get out without being detected. Or, in a less optimistic but more realistic scenario, at least without being positively identified."

Li nodded, a little bemused at hearing all this from Chiara's pretty mouth, especially since she'd always suspected the girl was rather stupid.

She picked up her beer, and the corner of the fiche popped up. She hunted around for something to set on it, and came up with a moldering first edition of *Doctor Faustus*.

"Can we do it?" she asked.

"Not in any way you're likely to be very enthusiastic about, I'm afraid." Cohen tapped up the scale on the area of the plans that included the lab spoke.

"Physically, I have no idea where the intraface is. All I do know is that it's in this lab. Unfortunately, the lab files—personnel, inventory, everything—are dead-walled."

"Like Metz."

"Worse than Metz." He looked up at her. "Alba has a weapons-grade semisentient."

A chill worked its way down Li's spine and settled in her stomach. She hated logging on to semisentients. Her fear was unreasonable—or so she had tried many times to convince herself. Sometimes she wondered if it was just blind prejudice; the one time she'd mentioned it to Cohen, he'd gotten so offended it had taken weeks to smooth his ruffled feelings.

But still.

There was something sharklike about the big semisentients: brute computing power, unfettered by hard programming or by the all-too-human qualms and foibles of fully sentient Emergents. Logging on to a semisentient was like swimming in dark bottomless water. Impossible to believe that the wordless menace that lurked behind their numbers could become Cohen. Terrifying to think that Cohen was only a few operations, a few algorithms removed from them—and that no one could say for certain where to draw the line between the two.

"So how do we get you in?" Li asked.

Cohen raised an eyebrow. "You assume a lot. I haven't agreed to help you yet."

"What do you want me to do, say pretty please?"

"You're magnificent. Why is it that the bigger the favor you're asking for, the more unpleasant you become?"

"You'll get paid," Li said. "Last time I checked, that makes it a job, not a favor."

Cohen lit a cigarette without offering Li one and set the case and lighter on the table, carefully aligning them with the gold-leafed corner scroll.

"I think we'll just let that one slide, shall we?" he said. "Unless you actually want to pick a fight with me?"

Li kept silent.

"Right then. The lab AI has disabled external communications. You can't call in. You can't get wireless access. All you can do is call out to approved numbers, and you can only do that by direct contact jack." He smiled and tapped the ash off the end of his cigarette with a Byzantine flourish. "Which means, my dear, that you're going under the knife."

Li fingered her temple, where she could just feel the flat disk of the remote commsystem transmitter under her skin. She'd never gotten a direct-contact wire-to-wire jack. She'd never had to. Those were reserved for techs, like Kolodny, the people who did the real grunt work of cracking target systems—and who ran risks from which the automatic cutouts of Li's remote interface largely protected her.

"You come up with that idea yourself?" she asked Cohen. "Or did you get help from Korchow?"

"I wouldn't waste my time arguing about it if I were you," Cohen said. He shot a dark stare at her over the top of his wineglass. "A jack is nothing compared to what they're going to need to do to you to get the intraface working."

Li bit her lip and shifted uncomfortably as her thoughts roved from semisentients to contact jacks to the several hundred meters of prototype hardware Sharifi had been carrying around in her head when she died. How had they slid into actually planning this mission without any discussion of whether or not Li was going to let Korchow test-run the intraface on her?

Had she actually made that decision herself? Or had Cohen coaxed her into it like a chess master nudging his player across the board toward the enemy? Was Nguyen right about him? And even if she wasn't, even if his intentions were good, what did he really want from her?

"Has anyone actually tested this intraface thing?" she asked, settling on an easy, emotionally neutral question.

"I think there's a monkey somewhere who has one."

"Oh." Li laughed nervously. "How's he doing?"

"He's crazy."

"Cohen!"

"But there's some indication that he was crazy to begin with. And besides, he's a monkey."

He pointed to the network of alleys and firewalls around the lab's back entrance. "Right. Here's my first brilliant idea. We do a cutout around this door that would get you past the security network."

"Which means you have to be on-station to fiddle the main AI. Which means a second person for you to shunt through. Which means twice as much chance of getting caught."

The more they worked through it, the shorter the list of realistic options got. Cracking Alba was like building a house of cards; each piece of the puzzle that fell into place exposed another piece, another problem, another collapse waiting to happen.

They went at it again, teasing out the problems and pitfalls until they had something that looked like a plan in front of them. At least as far as getting through the security checks and actually retrieving the data went.

But they were still left with the problem of how to get Li into Alba undetected.

"Hang on," Li said finally, grabbing at the fleeting tail of what looked like it might just be a viable option. "Go back to that first section we looked at. Hydroponics."

Cohen tapped back through half a dozen screens to reach it.

"What about these turrets?" She pointed to a row of ten-meter-high towers jutting through the thick pelt of guy wires, sensor lenses, and communications equipment that bristled from the outer skin of the station. "They look like vents."

"Sure." A look crossed Chiara's smooth face that made Li think Cohen knew exactly where she was going with this. "Decontamination vents for the algae flats. So what?"

"So the last time I was on Alba, it was overcrowded."

"It always is."

"Well, what's the daily CO_2 load?"

Cohen paused for a moment, searching. "Sixty thousand cubic meters. And, to anticipate your next question, they're shipping in about 1.8 thousand of compressed oxygen every day."

"So where's the excess CO_2 going?"

"Out those turret vents, obviously."

"Where it can get out, I can get in."

"Not without someone inside to open the vents."

"Korchow says he's got an inside man."

"Not possible," Cohen said, scanning the plans again. "They're using the outgoing CO_2 to turn the turbines that power this whole section of the solar array. And even if you get past the turbines, you're still talking about crawling down a twenty-meter shaft in hard vacuum. And the vent diameter's too small to take a suit and gear." He tapped decisively on the tight print that gave the duct's dimensions. "You can't get in that way."

"I could if I stashed my gear outside and went down the duct with just a pressure suit."

"Too risky. You're talking about crawling down an active ventilation duct in hard vacuum with no air, no heat, just a pressure suit. If anything goes wrong— even if you just run into a minor delay—you're dead."

Li smiled. "And you won't have anyone to eat oysters with."

The look Cohen gave her couldn't have been more naked if he'd stripped his skin away. She saw fear, guilt, anger flash across his face. Then she looked away; whatever else was there, she couldn't deal with it. Not now, anyway. She pushed her beer away from her. It left a ring on the table, but for once Cohen didn't seem to care about the punishment her bad habits were inflicting on his furniture.

"What if I say I won't do it?" he asked.

"We go forward with another AI," she said, pushing down the thought that it might not be true.

"You'd be insane to try it without me."

"It'll be harder without you," Li admitted, but that was as far as she was willing to go.

"Have you thought about what happens if you get caught?"

Li looked at the dark night beyond the tall windows. If she got caught, it would be treason. And treason had been a firing-squad crime since the outbreak of the Syndicate Wars. That was assuming that the Corps would let the hero of Gilead come up on treason charges. A quick shot to the head and a cover story about a "regrettable training accident" seemed more likely. It was what Li herself would do faced with such a betrayal.

"You could at least tell me why," Cohen said.

"What do you care? You want the intraface. I'm showing you how to get it."

"I don't want it that much. And I doubt you're helping me get it out of the goodness of your heart. What did Nguyen suck you into?"

"Nguyen has nothing to do with it."

"Really, Catherine." Someone who knew Cohen less well would have seen only the bemused smile on his face, but Li could hear the angry bite in his voice.

"If you're going to lie, at least have the respect to lie about things I can't check up on."

Li kicked at the table leg and was pleased to see she'd put a dent in it. "You're in no position to accuse me of lying. Or anything else."

"I think," Cohen said slowly, "the time has come to discuss Metz." A dark flame flickered behind Chiara's eyes, and there was a rehearsed quality to the words that made Li wonder how long Cohen had been working his nerve up for this conversation.

"I've said everything I have to say about it," Li told him.

Chiara's long-lashed eyes narrowed. "You shelved it, didn't you?"

It wasn't a question. And even if it had been, it wasn't one Li planned to answer. After a moment he shrugged and tried another line of attack.

"All right, then. This run. It's too dangerous. And you're not a traitor. So why?"

"*Why* isn't your business. I want a job done, and I'm paying for it. Paying with something I know you want. Let's stick to that. Then at least I'll know what you're after. And when I can expect you to walk out and leave me twisting in the wind."

"I thought we were done talking about Metz," he said. "And anyone can make a mistake, Catherine."

"Anyone didn't kill Kolodny for a damn piece of circuitry."

Cohen went so still he might have turned to wax. He stared at her, mouth slightly open, until the only movement in the room was the play of a breeze from the garden over Chiara's brown curls. Cohen looked like the stuffing had gone out of him. A pretty doll abandoned in the corner by children grown too old to play with toys.

"That's not you talking," he said at last. "What else did Helen whisper in your ear about me?"

"None of your goddamn business."

Cohen huffed out a little breath that Li might have thought was a laugh in different circumstances. Then he stared into the air above her head, as if he were trying to access a hard-to-find piece of data.

"Oh," he said, when he found it. "So that's it. What a nasty little piece of work she is, when you scratch the nice manners and the freshly pressed uniform." He leaned forward across the table, pinning Li with a hard stare. "I've gotten over being surprised that you believe the things she says about me, but for what it's worth the link cut out because of an internal malfunction. Or so I thought, anyway. Now I'm not so sure."

"Meaning?"

"Meaning I'm putting two and two together and finally getting four instead of three."

Cohen paused until Li began to wonder if he was going to say anything more at all. "When did you start planning the Metz raid?" he asked at last. "About four months ago? Something like that?"

Li nodded.

"Well, I took on a new associate around then. A newly emerged sentient from the Toffoli Group. His main recommendation was that he'd done a contract job for Nguyen."

Li stirred impatiently, not sure where this was leading.

"Anyway," Cohen went on, "he had a beast of a feedback loop. Far worse than the mandatory program and running on a brute force, everything but the kitchen sink program that was impossible to work with. I was negotiating with Toffoli to put him on my global compliance program. They kept delaying, for reasons that seemed . . . well . . . less than reasonable. And the problems on Metz, I am almost certain, came from that feedback loop."

"I don't see what this has to do with anything, Cohen."

"Don't you? Nguyen holds the purse strings for all

the TechComm R&D. She has Toffoli's research division in her pocket. The Toffoli AI was her spy all along. He's how she was able to cut me off on Metz."

Li stared. "What are you going to do about it?"

"I've already done it," Cohen said. "He's gone."

"But what if he talks to someone—"

Cohen looked at her out of Chiara's guileless eyes. "I said he was gone. I meant it."

Li looked away. Cohen started to speak, then stopped. For a moment they both sat staring at the floor, at the books, at the pictures on the walls. At anything but each other.

"Well?"

"Well what?"

"I tell you that Nguyen was planning to cut me out of the shunt at Metz before we even shipped out for the mission, and you have nothing to say about it? What are you thinking?"

"That I don't know who to believe, you or Nguyen."

"You believe the one you trust," Cohen said.

"And why the hell should I trust you?"

He shrugged. "There's no should about it. You either do or you don't. You have a lot to learn about life if you think people have to earn your trust."

"You can't talk your way around this one, Cohen."

He shook his head and went on as if she hadn't spoken. "You don't trust people because they're a sure bet or even a good risk. You trust them because the risk that you'll lose them is worse than the risk that they'll hurt you. That took me a few centuries to learn, Catherine, but I did learn it. And you'd better catch on faster than I did. The way things are going right now, I don't think you have a century to spare."

Li stood up without answering, walked across the room, and stepped into the garden. It was night in Zona Angel. A moist breeze played across her face, carrying the smell of earth and wet leaves. Frogs and a few night birds sang in the green branches. All the little live things Cohen loved so much. A bird warbled from some hidden refuge in the wall above her, and her oracle identified it as a whippoorwill. *It's beautiful*, she thought—and wondered if she would still have thought so if she hadn't known its name.

Cohen came up to stand behind her, so close that she could smell the fresh-scrubbed scent of Chiara's skin.

"I can't imagine living in the Ring," Li said. "How can people live somewhere where every time you look up at the sky, you see your biggest mistake staring right back at you?"

"Some people would say that being forced to examine one's mistakes is a good thing."

"Not when it's too late to fix them."

"It's not too late. And they are fixing it."

Li threw an exasperated look at Cohen. "That's a story for schoolkids. They're still killing each other down there. Christ, my own mother went to Ireland to fight. She had chronic vitamin A deficiency from living underground. Now why the hell would people fight to keep a country they can't even survive in?"

"I don't know."

"Well, I do. Because they like fighting. Too much to give it up, even when there's nothing left to fight for."

She walked farther into the darkness, eyes on the snowbound planet above them. "I don't want you involved in this," she said. "It's not worth it. I don't even know what I'm doing it for."

"I do," Cohen said. "I know everything."

She started to turn around, but he put a soft hand on her shoulder to stop her. "I know about the gene work. I've known for years, Catherine. Or Caitlyn. Or whatever your name is. I dug that skeleton up long, long before Korchow tumbled to it."

Li stood among the living shadows of his garden and thought of all the questions he carefully hadn't asked, all the times he could have said he knew and hadn't.

"Why didn't you tell me?" she whispered.

"Should I have? I wasn't going to tell anyone else, and I certainly didn't care, so what difference if I knew or not?"

"No." She felt angry suddenly, betrayed and cheated. "I know you. You were waiting to see if I'd tell you myself. You were keeping it up your sleeve, using it like a goddamn caliper. How far does she trust me? How far is she going to let me in this time? It's all just one big test for you!"

"That's pure paranoia."

"Is it?"

"And even if you're right, so what? I certainly didn't get an answer that made me happy. Just the same old thing. Li against the world, and anyone who touches you is going to get his hand chewed off and spat back in his face."

"You know it's not that way."

"What way is it then?"

Li shrugged, suddenly tired.

"Tell me," Cohen said.

"What is there to tell if you already know everything?"

"You have a choice, Catherine. What's the worst that could happen to you? Losing your commission? Are you really ready to throw your life away for lousy pay and an even lousier pension?"

Li laughed. "I've been risking my life for that lousy pension every day of the last fifteen years. What's so special about this time?"

"This time it's treason. Listen, Catherine. I meant what I said the other day about offering you a job."

"I'm not a hanger-on, Cohen. Joining your primate collection doesn't appeal to me."

"It wouldn't be like that. Not with you."

"Don't tell me bedtime stories," she said, and stared at him until his eyes finally fell away from hers.

"Have you thought about Metz?" he asked. "You said it yourself. Whoever wired Sharifi would have had to plan it for years, get hold of the genesets, splice them, tank them. What are the odds that Sharifi and the officer investigating her death would have been tanked in the same lab, from the same geneset? What are the odds that we end up like this, with you playing Sharifi's part, me stepping into the field AI's shoes?"

"No," Li whispered.

"Why not? If Korchow uncovered your secret, why couldn't Nguyen uncover it too?"

"She doesn't know. No one knows."

"How sure are you of that?"

"I'd bet my life on it."

"That's exactly what you're about to do, isn't it?"

The moon had set while they were talking, and there was a cold breeze blowing. Li looked into the black shadows under the trees and shivered.

"Let me help you," Cohen said, pleading with her.

"No."

"That's it? Just no?"

"Just no."

Cohen came around to look into her face. Even in the faint light, he looked spent and defeated, a gambler who had put the one thing he couldn't afford to lose on the table and watched the house take every hand. "If it's about money—"

"It's not about money. It's about my life. About what I've earned. And what they want to take away from me. For nothing. Because of what some piece of paper says about me."

"And you'd throw away your life for that?"

Li saw the ghost of a tremor around his mouth as he spoke, a suspicious shimmer in the hazel eyes. No, she told herself, squashing her reflexive response. Chiara's mouth. Chiara's eyes. Whatever she thought she saw in those eyes was mere physiological sleight of hand. A parlor trick generated by a code-driven superstructure and shot through a state-of-the-art biointerface. It didn't mean anything. You might as well ask what rain meant.

She stepped back into the bright lamplight and began pulling her coat on. "What you're offering . . . I appreciate it. But I don't want it. Just let me know if you'll do the job, okay?"

She had her hand on the door before he answered.

"You know I will." He stood in the garden where she had left him, and all she could see when she looked back was the slow curve of a girl's hip in refracted moonlight. "You knew I'd do it before you even asked."

Li wavered, caught on the threshold. *You could walk back into that room,* she thought, and her heart flew up in her chest like a bird breaking cover in front of the gunsights. *One word, one touch. You could change everything.*

And then what?

Before she could decide whether to go or stay, Cohen spoke again. The voice from the shadows was quiet, measured, impersonal: a silicon voice for a circuitry lover.

"Just close the door on your way out," he said.

She started to speak, but a cold, hard knot rose up her throat and choked the words off. She backed into the hall and pulled the door shut behind her.

Anaconda◦Helena Shuttle: 26.10.48.

Li made the shuttle gate an hour early, but ten minutes before the flight was supposed to leave she was still waiting for Station Security to search the throng of passengers in front of her.

The chaos at the gate echoed the chaos on the planet's surface. The union had wildcatted, locked down the mine even before all the rescuers were out. Within a day the strikers had set up an armed perimeter and the first militia units had arrived to reinforce AMC's cadre of Pinkertons. Now, on the satellite images that dominated the local spins, the whole tailings-littered plain of the AMC coalfields had become a militarized no-man's-land between two dug-in armies.

On-station, AMC security was taking no chances. All flights to Shantytown and the coalfield were canceled. And until AMC loosened its de facto embargo, the only way in or out of Shantytown was the grueling dangerous jeep road over the mountains from Helena—a road that would become completely impassable as soon as winter's dust storms set in.

Legally AMC couldn't keep anyone on-station against their will: planetary access was a holdover civil right from the Migration-era days of indentured labor on corporate orbital stations. Still, rights or no rights, AMC controlled the streets, the air, the station-to-surface shuttles. And Li had seen the guards turn back eight Helena-bound passengers in the space of fifteen minutes.

She doubted anyone would be complaining to her office. And she was dead certain she couldn't get her superiors to do anything about it if someone did complain. Daahl had been right. It was war, a war in which the UN would side with whichever combatant could get the Bose-Einstein production lines moving soonest. And unless the union pulled a trump card out of its sleeve, AMC looked like the likeliest candidate.

When Li finally stepped onto the shuttle twenty minutes after its scheduled departure time, she realized she'd never been in danger of missing it. A river of passengers filled the aisles and overwhelmed the crew, bickering over duplicate seating assignments and cramming luggage into every inch of open space. She checked her seat number, uttered a fervent prayer of thanks when she finally reached her row and found it empty, and settled down to wait.

"Hey, boss," a familiar voice said just as she was finally drifting into an uneasy doze. She looked up to find McCuen grinning down at her.

"What are you doing here?" she asked.

"Friends in Helena. It's my day off, remember?"

"Oh." She did remember now. "Yeah."

"You?"

"Just going down for the day." She hoped.

"Want to join us?" he asked, folding his long frame into the seat next to her. "We can show you around."

"I have an appointment," she said evasively, hoping she could get rid of McCuen before Korchow's man showed up. This was one wrinkle she didn't need.

"Oh, by the way," McCuen said. "I figured out where that storage chit in Sharifi's journal came from."

Sharifi and the investigation had been so far from Li's mind for the last thirty-six hours that it took her a moment to remember what McCuen was talking about. "Oh?" she asked. "Where?"

"Remember how all her researchers got so conveniently shipped out on that survey mission? Well, one of them didn't. He shipped out the day after Sharifi died. On the *Medusa*, bound for Freetown. And it looks like he checked a package through for her."

"Let me guess when the *Medusa* makes Freetown."

McCuen nodded. "Thirteen days, sixteen hours, and fourteen minutes from now. Or, to answer your real question, about twenty minutes after Gould's ship is supposed to drop into orbit."

Li frowned, thinking. "Remember what Sharifi wrote on that page, McCuen? Next to Gould's address? *Life insurance.* I looked at it and thought it had to be some kind of protective measure, something to save her life. But what if it wasn't like that at all? What if it was really like an actual life insurance policy, something that would go into effect only if she died?"

"Well, that's when it did go into effect, right? I mean the student shipped out the day *after* Sharifi died. And, whatever she may have suspected, Gould didn't actually leave for Freetown until your call gave her solid confirmation that Sharifi was dead."

If McCuen was right, then Nguyen had thirteen days to go fishing for Korchow with Li as bait. And Li had thirteen days to get that chop-shop receipt back from Korchow—while he still needed her enough to keep his promise. Because once Gould and the mysterious package reached Freetown all bets were off.

She looked up at McCuen and found him frowning at her.

"What?" she said.

"Call logs." He looked worried, hesitant. "Remember you told me to check for calls to Freetown?"

How the hell had she forgotten about that?

"Well, someone called a Freetown-based Consortium front company the night before Sharifi died. From Haas's private terminal. With Haas's password."

A chill spread through the pit of Li's stomach at the thought that Nguyen had been right all along, that ALEF and the Consortium lay at the bottom of Sharifi's betrayal, and not the Syndicates.

McCuen's eyes flicked to the aisle. Li followed his gaze and saw Bella standing a few rows up, waiting for a seat. Bella glanced at her and immediately glanced away, her lips set in a pale furious line. She passed by without speaking and found a seat four or five rows back from them.

"Oops," McCuen said, and the look he shot at Li was full of questions she didn't want to answer.

She tapped into the in-flight computer and watched the inevitable safety disclaimers scroll up her seat-back screen. "If you feel unable to sit in an exit row," she told McCuen brightly, "please ask the crew for a change of seating assignment."

"I have to piss," Li said, as they stepped out of the boarding gate. Weak, but the ladies' room was the one place in the airport she could think of that McCuen couldn't follow her.

"Sure you don't want to hit the town with us?" he asked, hovering.

"No. I need to check up on a few things. Talk to that nun again, maybe. You go on."

They were cleaning the bathroom when she stepped in, two skinny, undergrown girls swabbing listlessly at the floor with mops so filthy that Li figured the net exchange of disinfectant and bacteria had reversed itself years ago. As she skirted the wet floor the flash of a gemstone at the older girl's neck caught her eye.

It was a necklace. A stupid, tacky little charm that you could buy anywhere. But that wasn't synthetic diamond glittering at the end of the chain. It was condensate. And she'd seen something like it before. Somewhere or someplace that she ought to remember if her hacked and kinked and decohering memory wasn't playing tricks on her.

"Pretty," she said, pointing. "Where'd you get it?"

The girl giggled and put a protective, embarrassed hand to her throat. "My boyfriend?" she half-said half-asked, giggling again.

"What's it made of?"

"Crystal? It's entangled?" Another giggle. "With his?"

"Oh. Right," Li said. "It's pretty," she added, since some comment along those lines was obviously required at this point. After all, someone must think the gimmicky little things looked good; she'd been seeing them everywhere lately.

Then her oracle shook loose the right file, and she remembered who she'd last seen one on.

Gillian Gould.

Li turned back to stare at the pendant. The girl flinched and stepped backward under the intensity of her gaze. "Are you all right?" she asked, looking frightened.

"Yeah," Li said. "Yeah, I'm fine. Sorry."

She stepped into a stall and squatted to relieve herself, trying not to touch anything she didn't have to. When she opened the door and stepped out again she ran head-on into Bella.

"Christ!" she gasped, heart pounding. "You scared me. Why the hell didn't you say something?"

Bella didn't answer. The cleaning girls had vanished, though the smell of standing water lingered.

"What are you doing here, Bella?"

The construct turned without acknowledging the question and walked toward the door. "Follow me," she said, the words barely a murmur. "Not close. They'll be watching."

Li trailed her down the main axis of the spaceport, through the baggage claim, out past the taxi lines, into the yawning cement-smelling darkness of the underground parking. She must have let her guard down, because though she knew that she was gradually losing satellite access she didn't see the trap until it had already closed on her.

"How ya doing?" said a voice high overhead, just as she heard the soft click of a safety being eased back.

She was crossing a ramp with no cover in sight—and even if there had been cover it was far, far too late to take advantage of it. She looked up and saw McCuen's friend Louie sitting one level above her, legs swinging lazily, sighting down the snub-nosed barrel of a rebuilt Sten.

"Too bad about those Yankees," Louie said.

"It's not over yet. McCuen know what you're up to down here?"

Louie grinned. "Let's just say Brian doesn't know me as well as he thinks he does."

A flick of his eyes drew Li's own gaze to the shadows below the ramp, and she found herself staring down the black barrel of a Colt Peacemaker, close enough to see just how long it had been since the gun had had a proper cleaning.

"Take it easy," Ramirez said from the driver's end of the Colt. "Both of you."

Li glanced toward Bella and saw her standing

halfway down the garage's central aisle, looking pole-axed.

"Let Bella go, Ramirez. She's got nothing to do with this."

"Sorry," he said. "Not an option." He gestured to Bella. "Go on. Over by Li. Now!"

Bella scurried to Li's side and stood there shivering while Ramirez frisked both of them with depressing thoroughness.

"I'd better get that back," Li said when he took the Beretta, but it was pure bravado and they both knew it. She'd seen enough of Ramirez underground to know he wouldn't hesitate or lose his nerve. And even if he did, Louie was up on the exit ramp training the Sten on them.

"I hate to burst your bubble," Li told Ramirez, "but jail time for kidnapping isn't going to look good on your college transcripts."

"I got my master's degree two years ago," Ramirez said. "And they have to catch me before they can put me in jail, don't they? Turn around and put your hands behind your back."

Li did it, knowing it was a bad idea but unable to think of an alternative. Ramirez pulled a pair of viru-steel cuffs out of his pocket and snapped them around her wrists, locking her arms behind her. As the cuffs snapped shut Li felt a slight sting at the nape of her neck and realized Ramirez had slapped a derm on her.

"Forgive me," she heard him say through the rising haze of a sedative that must have been specially designed to outsmart her internals, "but better safe than sorry. You see that van over there? The white one? The back's open. Get in and shut the door behind you."

Li walked toward the van as slowly as she could, trying to catch Bella's eye. Who's following us? she wanted to ask. Where are they? Is help coming if we can wait it out a little longer?

But no one came. No one was intended to come.

And as Li stepped into the van she glanced up toward the garage ceiling and saw why: the van had been parked a little crooked in its space, tail end facing out into the aisle, just where the garage's security cameras could catch prime-time quality spinfeed of the kidnapping.

"Smile for the cameras," Louie said, and the last thing she remembered before she passed out was his wide-open Irish laugh.

The next few hours were a dope-smeared blur. Sprinting across a rain-swept landing pad, half-held half-dragged by Ramirez. A brief struggle with Louie during which she refused, childishly, to let him scan her palm implant and he pulled a knife and told her he'd damn well cut it off her if she didn't cooperate. A thwonking, shuddering hopper flight.

When she woke they were still in the air and someone had strapped an oxygen mask over her face. She opened her eyes to a bird's-eye view of the granite teeth of the Johannesburg Massif, the vast rolling red ocean of the algae steppes. She started, feeling as if she were falling forward into the abyss, then blinked and twisted her head around and made sense of her surroundings.

She was on the deck of an old cropduster-rigged Sikorsky, an Earth-built antique that must have been broken down to its gearboxes and shipped out in the airless cargo hold of some long-abandoned generation ship. Like most of Compson's presettlement tech, the Sikorsky had been rerigged to run on fossil fuel—and Li guessed from the grumbling shudder beneath her that it had been flying seeder runs for the terraforming authority ever since then.

Li had been tucked between the pilot's and copilot's seats and was now staring straight through the smooth Plexiglas bubble of the windshield. When she looked up she saw Louie at the pilot's controls and Ramirez on her other side, staring at a handheld nav-comp and frowning.

"Where are we?" she rasped, and Ramirez looked down, frowning.

"I thought that derm was supposed to last longer," he said.

Louie glanced over and shrugged. "Tough mother-fucker, isn't she?"

"I don't have another one, though. And she wasn't supposed to wake up until we got there."

"So what? She'd know the place in her sleep any-way." He laughed a laugh that didn't sound quite as friendly to Li as it once had. "They all do."

Ramirez scowled over her head at Louie, and she found herself wondering just who was in charge of this kidnapping.

They landed twenty minutes later, setting down on a dusty stretch of hardpan that seemed implausibly level until Li realized it was an old shuttle runway.

"We're there," Ramirez said unnecessarily. "We're going to get out and walk to the buildings, okay? Just cooperate and it's all going to be fine."

She could walk under her own steam now, and as she stumbled along trying to clear her hazed vi-sion she heard Bella's thin-soled shoes whispering across the ground just beside her. She knew this place, though she couldn't yet put a name to it. She'd been here, not once but many, many times. She knew that the rutted jeep track beyond the landing strip would take her through the foothills to Shantytown if she had the strength to walk for a few hours in the un-processed air of the foothills. She knew that the box canyon hidden behind that ridge harbored a steep-walled wash that she and her father had once used for target practice.

But she didn't quite understand where they were

until she squinted at the long-empty airplane hangar looming over the lab building and read the words that sent an atavistic fight-or-flight reaction flooding through every cell of her body:

XENOGEN MINING TECHNOLOGIES
RESEARCH DIVISION

XenoGen Research Division: 26.10.48.

The sprawling lab complex had stood empty for decades, and the rats, roaches, and kudzu vine had had their way with it. As their captors steered them into the back corridors they stumbled over abandoned equipment and office supplies, ducked under torn-out wiring, waded through snowdrifts of shredded insulation tile.

The air was musty with rat dung and mildew. But under those smells—the smells humans and their pests had brought—Li could still catch a sharp desert scent that tugged at her childhood memories. It was a smell you only caught high in the foothills, under the dark wall of the mountains. The planet's own smell. Compson's World was taking back the birthlabs. Just as it would take back the whole planet if the thread of the UN's far-flung trade lines ever snapped and the atmospheric processors and seeding operations ever shut down.

They turned a corner just like every other corner, and Ramirez stopped so abruptly that Li ran into him.

"In there," he said, and pushed her into a small windowless room.

As the door clanged shut, Li realized he had locked her into one of the lab's old holding cells. It was a box. A box with soundproofed walls, a metal-sheathed door, with no furniture or windows or running water. A box built for a person. She heard footsteps echo beyond the door and the clang of another door slamming shut. Then silence.

A scrap of memory floated into her mind: a ghost story about a group of kids who had come up to the labs and locked one of their friends into a holding cell as a prank. They had been called back down to Shantytown in some childishly implausible plot twist. When they returned the next morning, they couldn't find the cell their friend was in. They ran up and down the windowless corridors, trying every rusty lock, throwing open the food slots of a thousand dark boltholes. The boy was dead when they finally found him. Killed, according to the internal logic of the tale, by the ghost of some bloodily murdered construct.

Li shivered. How many psych-norm-deviant constructs had waited out cold nights and lightless days in this cell? How many had died in it? And how many of the people who walked free on the streets of Shantytown were the children of those dead, or of the lab guards and lab technicians and paper pushers who had helped kill them? The children remembered, even if no one else did; they told ghost stories about the very skeletons their parents couldn't bury deep enough.

The door scraped open on protesting hinges. A line of light seeped into the cell, unbearable after the long darkness. Ramirez appeared in the doorway, bright and terrible as Gabriel.

Li struggled into a sitting position, back against the

wall, head spinning. Her internals told her to lie back down. She ignored them.

He put a finger to his lips. *Sshhhhh.*

She stood, shaking, shocked and ashamed that simply sitting alone in the dark for a few hours had so undone her. She knew she should be wondering where Ramirez meant to take her, thinking about how to get control of the situation. But all she could really think about was getting out of this ghost-ridden hole. That and trying not to fall down.

Follow, Ramirez signaled.

She followed.

Another man walked beside Ramirez, one whose name she didn't know and whom she had never seen before. Not Louie. After a few turnings, Ramirez disappeared and Li and the nameless hijacker continued on without him. Someone else joined them as they slipped down the dark corridor, but when Li tried to look back the man just grunted and pushed her forward.

They moved deeper into the complex, back into the windowless labs under the shadow of the cliff face. They had traveled almost a kilometer when the hijacker opened an unmarked door and Li felt a waft of cold underground air hit her face. He stood aside and waved her through. As she passed she heard the gentle snick of a bullet being chambered.

That's it then, said a small voice in the pit of her stomach. She saw a blank wall in her mind's eye, heard a single shot.

"Down," the hijacker said and pushed her down a steep flight of stairs into darkness.

Thirty narrow steps of steel-reinforced concrete. A turn. A passage. Then forty more steps, these rough and uneven underfoot. Then a long, twisting passage that dipped and jigged but nonetheless kept trending unmistakably downward.

The person behind Li stumbled and cried out. Bella.

As they descended, the walls and floor began to run with water. The rock came alive around them, cracking and moaning like a house built on quicksand. Somehow, unbelievably, they were in the mine. Li tried to recall the location of the birthlabs. No drifts, no shafts, no passages ran within a kilometer of the complex. She was sure of that. Still, they were in a mineworks. It just wasn't one that showed up on the company maps. And if her internals were to be trusted, someone was stockpiling live-cut condensate here.

They hit a junction. Their captor lifted his lantern, and its light threw watery reflections on pooled runoff, picked out the stubbed-off ends of mined-out crystal deposits. It took him two turns around the walls to find what he was looking for: faint marks scratched into the rock at face level. Before the lantern moved on, Li saw a crescent moon, a pyramid, an eight-legged beast.

"This way," he said, and pushed them toward the left-hand turning.

Li had grown so used to the dark by the time they surfaced that the first glimpse of daylight was painful. They clattered up a flight of gridplate stairs, passed down a long hallway full of uninsulated wiring, and reached a tall steel door bolted from the inside.

Bella leaned against the wall, panting and shivering. The hijacker reached into his pack and handed them each a rolled-up piece of cloth. "Put these on."

Li unfolded the cloth and saw that it was an Interfaither's chador. She wrapped the long bolt of green cloth around her, pulling it over her head and face, and helped Bella do the same. Then they stepped into the hazy sunlight of a late-fall afternoon in Shantytown.

For the next half hour, they hurried through a

bewildering series of alleys and courtyards, spiraling deep into the heart of the old quarter. Just when Li had finally accepted that she was lost beyond any possibility of reorienting herself, they turned aside and stepped through an unmarked door into a low dark passage.

The hallway smelled of rust and boiled vegetein, and it was so dark that Li heard rather than saw Bella behind her. The guard gestured toward a closed airlock at the far end of the passage, and Li put her hand to the touchplate. The door irised open. She stepped through, blinking in the dusty, sun-strafed air of the dome beyond—and saw just who she should have expected to see.

Daahl.

As her eyes adjusted to the bright hazy air under the dome, she realized that Cartwright stood in the half-open airlock behind him—an airlock that could only lead to the little office where Daahl and Ramirez had talked to her less than a week ago. Cartwright shifted restlessly as she walked in, craning his head like a dog listening for distant footfalls. She'd never seen him outside the mine, she realized; he carried a blind man's stick up here in the daylight world and his eyes were vague, milky, moonblind.

"What the hell is going on?" she asked as Bella stepped through into the dome behind her.

Daahl bent over the comm terminal on the table. "Arkady?" he said when the connection went through. "Tell him we're ready."

For a moment nothing happened. Daahl and Cartwright just sat staring across the table, waiting. It took Li a moment to realize they were watching Bella, not her.

Bella gave a little shiver as the shunt came on-line, and then she was gone.

"Excellent," Korchow said, standing up. "Excellent.

And the kidnapping was caught on tape? You made it look convincing?"

"The ransom note's on its way to AMC station right now. We should have an answer in a few hours." Daahl grinned. "Though of course the negotiations could be lengthy."

"Right," Korchow said. "Then I believe our business with each other is concluded."

"Not quite," Daahl said.

A tall figure appeared in the airlock behind them, its face shadowed by the sunbeams raking down through the streaky geodesic panels. Ramirez.

But he looked sleeker, glossier, finer. He had never moved with that fey, walking-on-eggshells grace. His eyes had never burned with the cold fire that now shone behind them.

He bent over her, touched a fleck of dried blood at the corner of her mouth. "Catherine," he said. "Are you all right? If I'd suspected things would get that exciting, I'd have made them find another way to get you here."

"Cohen," she whispered, not knowing how to begin to ask him what was happening.

Ramirez was so much taller than Li that she had to throw her head back to meet his eyes. It bothered her. She was used to looking Cohen in the eye, used to being able to dominate him physically—a domination that mattered to her, she now saw, even if it was meaningless to him.

"He wasn't to be involved," Korchow said, speaking to Daahl and Cartwright.

Daahl shrugged. "ALEF approached us."

"ALEF!" Korchow spat the word out as if it were a curse.

"God works through unlikely hands," Cartwright said.

"Oh for pity's sake," Korchow snapped. "What did the AIs promise you?"

"A planetary network," Daahl answered. "Under union control."

"Then they're lying. They can't possibly deliver that."

"We already have," Cohen said. "The beginnings of one, anyway. What do you think I'm shunting through?"

"I brought you in to do a job," Korchow told Cohen. "This isn't it."

Cohen made an impatient movement, a neat flick of one hand that was so characteristic of him it took Li's breath away. "I'll do your little job, Korchow. But not routing through your network. I've spent three centuries making sure no one had that kind of power over me. I'm not about to hand it to you."

"So why go to them?" Korchow jerked Bella's head toward Daahl and Cartwright. "And don't tell me it's selfless interest in the cause. Or are they your pet terrorist group of the week?"

Cohen flexed Ramirez's big hands until Li heard the knuckles crack. "They had what I needed," he said. "An on-site Emergent with Bose-Einstein capacity."

Korchow started.

"Yes." Cohen smiled. "The field AI."

"How—"

"I don't know. But Cartwright says he can speak to whoever or whatever is using the field AI. That he can control it."

"And you'd trust yourself to that?"

"Sooner than I'd trust myself to you."

"Why?" Korchow asked, turning to Daahl. "Why this? Why him?"

Daahl shrugged. "It's not that complicated, Korchow. We don't like the idea of running from the UN straight into the arms of the Syndicates. We want to run Compson's World for the natives, for the miners. And to get that we need a planetary net that we control. We need access to streamspace, to Freetown and FreeNet, without going through the UN relays, without being at the mercy of the Security Council and the multiplanetaries. And we need a Bose-Einstein relay intact, on our net. That's what ALEF's giving us."

"Come on, Korchow," Cohen said. "We're going to pull off a good deed together. A blow for freedom and planetary self-determination. After all, you need to put something on the white side of the ledger book every lifetime or so."

"So the deal's off?" Korchow asked, white with fury.

"Not at all," Cohen answered, smiling glossily. "It's just that the price has gone up."

Barnard's Star Field Array: 28.10.48.

They **jumped into Alba** in a KnowlesSyndicate Starling, a sleek swallow-winged craft whose cabin had been stripped to its ceramic compound struts and refitted with a tangled rat's nest of fractal absorption gauges, x/r monitors, and assorted black boxes whose functions Li could only guess at.

There were three of them: Li, Arkady, Cohen. Or part of Cohen, anyway. Arkady piloted the ship—though Li never figured out if he was the same Arkady she'd talked to at the meet in Shantytown or just another number in the same series. She also never found out how he got them there. She guessed he'd piggybacked through Alba's high-traffic Bose-Einstein relay on a legitimate cargo flight. However he'd done it, the Syndicates weren't about to let Li in on their back door into the system; Arkady knocked her out before they took off from Compson's World and kept her under until the Starling dropped into Alba's lee side thirty-eight hours later.

She woke up with a hammering headache that had

less to do with the sedatives than with her rising apprehension about the run ahead of them, and listened halfheartedly as Arkady and Cohen talked through the bones of the run again. Her new wire jack itched atrociously, a nagging reminder of the irritation of the last few days in the union safe house. She reminded herself not to scratch it, scratched anyway, cursed Korchow, and brooded about staph infections.

Korchow and Cohen had infested the safe house like locusts, shunting haphazardly through Bella, Arkady, Ramirez until even Li hadn't known who the hell she was talking to. Not that it would have made much difference; Cohen had been harder to talk to than Korchow recently. Was he just angry, or was this new distance more than anger, an obscure symptom of some shift in the tidal flow of the AI's associated networks?

They had taken Cohen off-line for the run—dumped his systems into the Starling so that there would be no interstellar communications to give them away while they drifted off the station's dark side. No shipboard comp could even come close to accommodating Cohen's vast web of associated intelligences and enslaved subsystems, of course. Li doubted there was a self-contained net that big anywhere in UN space, outside of a few zealously defended corporate and military sites. So Cohen had dumped systems, left them behind, wherever "behind" was, and downloaded only what he thought was needed.

He had sworn it wouldn't be a repeat of Metz, that when they powered down the Starling for the run and gave him control of the ship comp he would be there, willing and able to pull her out safely. But now that they were committed, all Li knew for certain was that Cohen, her Cohen, wasn't there. He had stranded her in hostile space with no one to cover her back but a Syndicate agent and a stranger who didn't seem to remember any of the promises the Cohen who claimed to be her friend had made her.

"Let's go over it again," said the disembodied ship's comp voice that she still couldn't think of as his. Li and Arkady settled at the narrow crew's table, and they ran through the whole intricately choreographed plan again.

It was getting Li on-station that had been the real problem. And though it had taken days to work out the details, the solution was still the same blindingly simple one Li had spotted in the station schematics: the ventilation system.

Like most spacer-designed technologies, Alba's O/CO_2 cycle was obsessively efficient. It built on existing systems, recycling every available piece of material and energy, rolling many problems and purposes into one solution. It pushed breathable air down the long curve of the station's inhabited zones, insulated the station's pressurized inner bladder, sucked excess CO_2 out into space, and powered the motors that turned the long dragonfly wings of the solar arrays. Air, warmth, and life-giving power all from one system. And the fuel that drove the system was always there, always free: space itself.

The pressure differential between the void outside and the full atmosphere of breathable air inside pulled freshly oxygenated air through the station, into the remote cold-storage bladders whose robot retrieval systems used no oxygen and created no CO_2 load. When the CO_2-loaded air reached the end of its journey inside the life-support bladder, it flowed through vents into the soft vacuum of the station's outer bladder, a second skin that provided insulation and radiation shielding, that protected the inner bladder's life-support zones from the hard vac beyond the viewports.

The returning air served three functions in the outer bladder. First, it put a baffled, compartmental-

ized partial vacuum around the life-support bladder—
a safety feature so universal in UN-designed stations
that the station-killing blowouts of the colonial era
were nearly forgotten, marked only by the sad little
streams of wreckage that orbited so many periphery
planets. Second, the rush of stale air venting the external turrets drove the big turbines that powered the solar arrays. Third, the turret vents served as a last line of
defense against the parasitic plague that haunted all
closed systems, orbital stations, and settlement bio-
spheres alike: mold.

Mold thrived in the recycled, condensation-rich air
of orbital stations, and an unchecked infestation
could make a station uninhabitable in a matter of
months. Some epidemics—and every station with any
history remembered one or two of them—were so re-
sistant that the only cure was to evacuate the station,
void the atmosphere, and rebuild the O/CO_2 cycle
with fresh flora. Alba's turret vents had been designed
with that in mind. Each turret contained both an
outer and an inner vent. The outer vents opened into
the unused space off the station's outer rim. The inner
vents opened into the huge oxygen-producing algae
flats. Faced with an incurable mold infestation, the
station engineers could open both inner and outer
vents and blow algae, air, condensation, and mold out
into open space.

What Li's soldier's eye had seen was that, stripped
down to its bones, the emergency venting system was
an airlock. The inner vent separated life-support zones
from the soft vacuum of the outer bladder; the outer
vent staved off the void outside. In normal operations
the outer vents opened only during the turbine's
power cycles. The inner vents never opened, except in
the worst emergency. However, if they could open an
inner vent, briefly, while the outer vent was closed, all
that would show up on the station monitors was a
barely noticeable local pressure drop as a few cubic

meters of air flowed into the unsealed turret. And someone who had managed to slip through the turbine arms and into the duct at the end of the last power cycle could simply push the miter vent open and breach the station's inner bladder.

If that someone was small enough to fit through the vent. If she was fast enough to climb the turret in the few minutes between venting cycles. If she was strong enough to push the inner vent open against a full g of rotational gravity and hoist herself through it.

But Li was all those things.

It was a risky way in. If it worked, though, it would put Li on-station undetected, and already through the manned security checks that separated the top-security labs from the station's unrestricted zones.

Korchow's inside man would open the inner seal for her. This was Li's least favorite part of the plan. It introduced a dangerously large risk of human error. It left her life hanging on the actions of someone she had never met and had no reason to trust. Worse, she had to be down the duct when the seal opened, ready to drop through instantly. And to get there, she would have to shinny twenty meters against a full rotational g, up a chute so narrow that even her small shoulders would just pass through it. If the door failed to open, if anything went wrong, if the inside man failed her, there would be no way out except through the spinning turbines.

Li had laughed when she saw the schematics and told Cohen it was a good thing she'd started smoking young. She wasn't laughing now.

"Let's go over the plan again," Cohen said, when they finished the run-through.

Li rolled her eyes. They'd gone over it four times already—which was three more than she wanted to. "Cohen," she said, "don't waste my fucking time, okay?"

Arkady turned to look at her, surprised. Cohen had

no body on board the little Starling, but his disapproval came through the comp boards loud and clear as a bad day.

"I need food," Li said into the suddenly silent cabin, and pushed off toward the galley.

The galley racks yielded nothing but a small sack of algae-colored imitation kasha and a thoroughly squashed packet of reconstituted vegetables. The kasha tasted like mold, and the vegetables looked worse, but they were food. Li fought the urge to skip dinner, telling herself she had a long cold night ahead of her. She shook the bags to jump-start the internal heating elements, dumped the now-lukewarm contents into a battered suckbag, and drifted back toward the foredeck.

"We have to work through your timing again," Cohen said when she swam back into the main cabin.

"Later," she said. "I need to put my kit together. I just came up to tell you I'm going down to the cargo deck."

"That can wait."

"No it can't." It was impossible to stare down someone without a body, but she shot her best glare at the main instrument panel. "You know your job, and I know mine. I need to get the arms and gear squared away more than I need to do another run-through. We'll do that after. If I have time."

"Make time," Cohen said.

If they hadn't been in zero g, Li would have kicked something.

Her mood improved briefly when she inventoried the weapons. Korchow had sent everything she had asked for. Even her most extravagant demands had been satisfied without murmur.

Two long sleek boxes held RPK midrange tactical precision non-structure-piercing pulse rifles, each fitted with custom-milled optical sights and refillable wipe baffle system silencers. Another blockier box, guarded with a double layer of vacuum seal, cradled the self-sealing pressure suit that Li would wear to crawl through the CO_2 vents—and whose interactive camouflage overskin would hide her face if things went wrong and someone spotted her. A big crate held the rest of her gear and tackle: carabiners, grappling hooks, and rope for the climb outside the station; a handheld number cruncher; a lockpick's kit for getting into the lab itself; a hacked passkey—provided by Korchow—that he claimed would get her out of the high-security lab and into the public-sector airlock where Arkady would pick her up when she had retrieved the target code.

It took an hour and forty minutes to unpack the lot and get it serviceable. The best hour and forty minutes of the last few weeks. If this was what the supply side of being private muscle was like, Li thought, she could get used to it.

When she had coiled her rope, ordered her climbing tackle, and stripped, oiled, and reassembled the pulse rifles, she stood back and surveyed the whole kit critically. Then she pulled herself forward to her cabin to retrieve the small, carefully wrapped package that she had hidden there just as a precaution.

She swam back to the cargo hold, unwrapped the Beretta, field-cleaned it, and loaded it, grunting with satisfaction at the clean, familiar snap of the ammo clip engaging the firing mechanism. She weighed the gun in her hand and glanced back toward the foredeck. She thought about the bulge it would make in her jumpsuit, the likelihood that Arkady would notice and take it away from her. She thought about just how crazy it would be to get into a solid-ammo fight on the little stripped-down Starling.

She sighed and tucked the Beretta into the pocket holster of the pressure suit. The pocket had been designed for bigger, more standard weapons; a Viper, maybe, or a snub-nosed pulse pistol. The Beretta slid in easily and barely made a bulge in the suit after she'd folded it.

"Just in case," she whispered, and went back forward.

"I need to check ammo," she told Arkady when she reached the foredeck. Hard as she tried, she couldn't help letting her eyes flick to the fully charged pulse pistol at his belt.

"You checked it back on-planet."

"And I need to check it again. Just because I saw it on the loading dock doesn't mean it actually got on board."

Arkady frowned. "You can do a visual check, that's all."

"Not good enough."

"It has to be. Cohen checked it manually when we loaded it. Ask him."

Right now, Li thought, Cohen was the last person she wanted to ask anything.

"It's all there," Cohen volunteered. "There's no reason to check it again."

"Gee, thanks for the help." She shot a nasty glance at the comp board.

"Well, go look in the airlock."

Li glanced at the instrument board again, then turned and left without meeting Arkady's eyes.

She made her way to the airlock and looked out the viruflex check-port.

She saw the sun. The white, unbearably bright sun of space, seen through no atmosphere. She ducked her head away from the port, blinking burning tears out of her eyes.

"Jesus wept!"

"It was Korchow's idea," Arkady said. As if he were apologizing, for Christ's sake.

She looked again, and understood what she was seeing through the check-port. The airlock was open to the void, completely unpressurized. Hard vac, right there, one triple-glazed viruflex porthole away from her. All her ammo for the run was neatly taped to the airlock wall. Two pulse rifle clips, their green charge lights blinking at her like eyes. A fully charged Viper for close fighting. Even her Syndicate-made butterfly knife, which Arkady had lifted from her without comment before letting her board the Starling back on Compson's World. What the hell had they expected her to do, anyway? Cut his throat and steal their damn ship?

"The outer seal will close and the airlock will pressurize two minutes and four seconds before you're scheduled to disembark," Arkady said. "You'll have four seconds to step into the airlock, two minutes to inspect the ammo and load and stow your weapons. Then you're out. The same protocol applies when you come back; you'll deposit any remaining live ammunition in the airlock stow compartment, lock it, and jettison the key. The outer door won't close and the chamber won't pressurize until I visually confirm that you've disarmed yourself."

Li stared at him, but he just shrugged, pushed off the wall with the ease of a born spacer, and pulled himself back toward the foredeck.

He was deep in conversation with Cohen by the time Li joined them. "Can we run through it again, Major?" he said. "Please?" He sounded apologetic, as if he were asking for a favor instead of giving orders to an enemy agent Korchow was blackmailing.

"You're the boss," Li said. She wanted to smack him. Instead, she pressed the water bottle she'd been carrying into the sidewall restraint field, pushed off and hung in mid-air, stabilizing herself with outstretched hands. "Oh-two-twenty-oh-four, I jump ship," she recited. "Oh-two-twenty-three-oh-eight, I hit station, turn toward the turrets."

"Which direction are they?" Cohen asked.

"East," Li said; spacer's argot for whatever subjective direction took you into the spin of a rotating station, toward planet-rise.

"Not good enough. You may not be able to see planet-rise from where you hit station."

"Well, I can feel it, even if I can't see it."

"The inner ear can play tricks on you."

"Fine." She shrugged. "At 02:49 I hit the vent." She was fully into it, tracking the station map on her internals, accounting for the guards' scheduled routes, thinking through her approach. "The vent cycle starts at 02:50. At 02:51, the turbines go off and I slip through the outer seal. At 03:00 the cycle starts again. That gives me one minute to stash my suit and gear, and nine minutes to climb."

"Is that enough time?" Arkady asked nervously.

"It's enough," Cohen said. His tone, if you could say the ship comp had a tone, suggested that if it wasn't, it would only be because the cog called Li hadn't functioned properly.

Li shut her eyes, partly to visualize the layout of the vent system, partly to shut out a here and now that was less than confidence inspiring. "I should reach the intake into hydroponics by 02:59:30, latest. At 03:00:00 the next two-minute cycle starts, so . . ."

"Korchow's inside man will open the internal miter flap at 02:59:30 exactly. He's rigged it to stay open until the cycle starts. That gives you thirty seconds, which should be plenty."

"Just as long as he really opens it."

"He will." Arkady gave her a dark, serious look. "I promise."

"Thanks," Li said, and felt a lump in her throat that made her ashamed. How had she ever let it come to this? Grappling onto the skin of a full-g station.

Shinnying down a turbine shaft and waiting like a rat in a plugged hole for some traitor to sneak her into a station she could walk onto openly if her own business were anything but treason. She thought about backing out. But it was too late for that. She was on Korchow's ship, with Korchow's pilot at the controls, holding all the ammunition. She was going out that airlock tonight, one way or another.

If she could count on Cohen—really count on him—it might not be too late. But she'd be crazy to do that. Better to risk what she knew she could pull off, if all those little gambles broke her way. Better to settle her nerves, stop worrying about what she couldn't change, and get ready for a walk in starlight.

"Well?" said the stranger who was Cohen. "What did you forget?"

Li sighed and pushed off the floor, coming to rest high up on the Starling's curving bulkhead. "Nothing. I will goddamn well remember to hook in before the internal vent opens. I'm not an idiot."

"You were the one who insisted on running off soft memory," the not-Cohen insisted. "You'll be off-line for twenty-seven minutes. Any memory lapse will result in a fatal loss of synchronization."

Li flip-flopped so her feet were facing up, her head down. She looked at Arkady, at eye level but inverted, and raised an eyebrow. "I think she understands that," Arkady said, sounding embarrassed.

"Look," Li said. "I've been to the dance before. You boys just keep your flies zipped and make sure you save the last dance for the girl you came with."

She picked out a faint spot on the opposite wall, a faded fingerprint left by some crewman of missions past. She closed her eyes and kicked off the bulkhead into a tight backflip, testing her inertial systems, troubleshooting, recalibrating the network of Fromherz nodes and ceramsteel filament that spidered down her spine and out to every muscle, tendon, and fingertip.

It was a neat trick, as well as a good diagnostic test. One of her favorites. Especially in zero g. And it was just the kind of silly thing Cohen always teased her for doing.

Well, he wasn't teasing her tonight, she thought as her left foot hit the deck .28 centimeters off target—and she realized, suddenly, just how scared she was.

Alba: 28.10.48.

02:18:00.

The outer seal slid down on the other side of the air-lock just as Li finished pulling on the bulky life-support suit and checking her heater and air feed. Arkady drew his pulse pistol, thumbed off the safety, and leveled it at Li's chest. He lifted his thin shoulders in a sad little shrug. "Sorry."

Li didn't answer; he wouldn't have heard her through the double-sealed faceplate of her helmet anyway. When the inner seal rose, she glanced back, checked her status lights again, and stepped forward.

02:20:04.

She floated out of the airlock and into open space, spinning slightly with the pull of an imperfectly cali-brated frog kick. She did a fast recalculation of her tra-jectory, toggled her Zero-K jetpack to get back on course, assured herself she was still going to hit Alba's exostructure reasonably close to target, and relaxed, watching the meters and seconds tick down on her internals.

She looked back at the Starling. It was already invisible, its fractal absorption sheeting effective enough to outsmart Li's eyes even at this range. She toggled her infrareds just to be safe and scanned for a heat signature, but there was only a faint blur of warmth that could have been a heat plume from the station or the thermal wake of the last commuter shuttle. She hoped the shielding was good enough to fool not just her, but the Peacekeeper techs who monitored Alba's fiercely enforced no-fly zone.

02:23:07.

As she neared the station, not even all her outside training and fighting experience could prevent the inevitable disorientation. The station's metallic skin spun faster and faster. By the time she got within five meters of it, it was whipping by her like a freight train.

Cohen had put her on-station in the middle of a forest of radio and ansible receivers, reasoning that the thicket of antennae would camouflage her approach, making the risk of a hang-up worth running. She had to choose her spot carefully and toggle the ZKs to avoid getting tangled in the poles and guy wires.

Damn it, Cohen, she thought; it didn't take a heat signature for a really sharp observer to spot a jetpack. And getting caught outside, even in a heated support suit, would be disastrous.

At the last moment before impact, she kicked her ZKs into reverse and hovered, trying to track the station's spin. She took a deep breath, readied her grappling gear, and jumped.

The impact snapped her head back and left her eyes watering. The universe turned inside out and the sky fell on her head. The freight train that had been shooting past her face was now a wild horse intent on bucking her off into open space. The rotational gravity that had been purely theoretical when she was hanging in the void watching the station slide by was now a solid full g sucking her body back, out, and sideways.

She clung to the station and waited for her brain to accept the irreconcilable conflict between eye and inner ear. Then she half closed her eyes, questioning muscles and ligaments, forcing herself to ignore the deceptive visual cues and listen to gravity. A few heartbeats later, she pegged the direction of the Coriolis effect and was able to orient herself to station east and start climbing.

Her right shoulder was all wrong; she was favoring it before she had climbed ten meters. Korchow's hired medics had tried to patch it up again—another jury-rigged field repair on top of the last one—but the whole arm was going to have to be stripped out and rewired. Not now, though. Now it had a job to get through.

She saw the fan turrets a long way off, knobby sixteen-meter towers that poked out of the station's skin like mushrooms. She needed the fourth turret, and she counted down the line carefully, knowing that a mistake would mean an ugly death.

02:49:07.

She reached it seven seconds behind time.

Had she climbed too slowly? Was there something wrong with her internals? With Cohen's schematics? She crouched under the turret, checked her systems, and cursed.

By her reckoning the turret was a good twenty meters farther from her landing point than their schematics had said it was. Any way you looked at it, the miscalculation spelled trouble.

Though Li might have fallen behind schedule, Alba

hadn't. At exactly 2:50 she felt a thud and shiver under her feet, looked up, and saw a glittering ice cloud burst from the vent hole. Dust and condensed moisture, freezing as they hit hard vacuum in the new morning's first venting cycle; the station was getting ready for the CO_2 overload of the coming workday.

She huddled in the lee of the turret until the ice cloud dispersed. Then she put her faceplate to the tower's virusteel skin and listened as the vibration of the fans slowed and finally died. She imagined miter seals shutting twenty meters below, closing off the flow of pressurized air that drove the turbines. She tried not to imagine what would happen if both sets of seals opened while she was still in the turret. Well, it would be quick, anyway. That was something. She clipped onto the guard line that ringed the bottom of the turret and tapped the unseal code into the wrist plate of her suit. <Cannot unseal,> the suit told her internals. <Insufficient atmospheric pressure outside.>

<Manual override,> she sent.

<There is no air outside,> the suit said in deliberate tones designed to break through the dangerous euphoria of oxygen debt. <Are you sure you want to remove your life-support equipment?>

<Unseal,> she sent again, and keyed in the emergency override code. A moment later, she heard the hiss of escaping air.

She pulled off her helmet. Her pressure suit activated as the hard vac hit it, dropping its reflective visor over her face. She felt the first bite of the burning cold that would leach through the suit's thin membrane and kill her in a matter of minutes if she didn't get inside. She removed the rest of her support suit, rolled it into a tight bundle, and stuffed it into her already-iced-over helmet. She tossed the helmet out into space and shot it with a disruptor blast, frying its circuits and making it indistinguishable from the rest of the abandoned deadware that littered Mars orbit.

No turning back now. The pressure suit would keep her alive for fifteen minutes in hard vac. Twenty at most. The amphibian genes engineered into her chromosomes for cold-shipping would buy her a little more time on top of that. But an hour in the pressure suit and it wouldn't matter if she got what she'd come for, or if Alba security caught her.

She nudged the bladelike turbine arms to make sure there was no spring tension left in them. She wondered how Korchow pulled the inside man into his web. Either money was changing hands, and a lot of it, or Li wasn't the only one with a dirty little secret. She took a breath, acutely aware that it was one of a limited number of breaths left in the suit. She put everything out of her mind except the next ten minutes. Then she wormed through the jagged half circle between the blades and into the chute.

02:51:43.

She pushed, legs straining, lungs burning. She made the best time she could, but she was climbing against the full rotational gravity of the station, and her enhanced strength and reflexes were little help in such tight quarters.

In the end, it was her haste that did her in. She took a wrong turn, disoriented in the narrow tunnels, strayed into one of the lateral vents that lined the inner bladder. She fetched up against the dust-fuzzed vent of a baffle like an exhausted salmon. She was so close. She could smell yeast, feel the soft, growing air of the algae bay on her face. But it was a cheat, a dead end. And the only way out was back up the shaft, into the teeth of the turbines.

She hit the junction with just fourteen seconds left. She was overheating. Her internals were hitting the red zone, warning lights flashing all over her peripheral vision. Too bad. They'd either fail or they wouldn't.

And if they failed, she wouldn't be around to regret it. She hauled herself forward, internals blaring, her heart banging out a tempo as hot and urgent as the warning lights.

02:52:38.

She hit the end of the chute suddenly, with less than twelve seconds left, and slammed into the miter seal.

It wouldn't budge.

At first she thought it was locked, that the inside man had betrayed her. Then she saw the problem; the hinges were clogged with a greasy coat of dust, hair, and organic matter from the hydroponics bays, all the things that drifted on the air currents of the station and washed ashore in the stagnant back eddies of the outtake ducts.

Now that she saw it, it was so obvious she could have kicked herself. But then the things that got you killed always were obvious. Obvious and stupid. This door hadn't been opened in years. Decades maybe. Not since the last mold epidemic. And because it wasn't really life-support vital, it would be chronically neglected. A system you could shortchange without getting caught. A system that went to the bottom of the list when it needed a new part—and stayed there.

Korchow's man had done what he promised all right; she had heard the sharp snick of the catch flipping open, could still hear a trapped-fly buzzing from the hinge hydraulics. But flipping a switch with the name and number of the vent on it was one thing. Actually getting the door to open in realspace was something entirely different. And Li was stuck in real-space.

She poked her fingers through the parts of the door she could reach and scrabbled frantically at the scummy deposits. Her breath rasped in her throat. Her nails scratched on metal. Cohen had warned her about the need for silence, told her there could be people in the bays next to the vent, but she was beyond caring. The whole universe had narrowed into one pure and burning thought—getting out alive.

Finally she felt some give. She twisted in the cramped duct, wrenching her body around, using feet, hands, anything, to get a purchase. She gave a tremendous kick and drove into the seal shoulder first. It held. She felt a wrenching pain in her shoulder and a cold burn like a blade being drawn down the length of her triceps. She backed up the chute and rammed the seal again. It gave a little. But not enough. Not nearly enough.

Twenty meters below her, she heard a click, then the whirr of circuits flipping on to feed power to the turbines. She tried to get her left shoulder forward, protect her bad one, but she didn't have the space or the time to get turned around. She flung herself at it again, right shoulder first. A lick of cold ran down her arm from shoulder to wrist and her hand went numb . . . but the vent opened. She shot through just as the outer vent opened, and found herself hanging along the wall above an algae tray.

A full atmosphere of air pressure hit the miter seal. It slammed shut behind her like a bear trap, and she dropped into the bright, humid air of the hydroponics dome.

02:53:19.

She crept into a sheltered space between the dome struts and a dripping-full rack of algae trays. She crouched there, panting, waiting for her internals to settle down a little, waiting while she pulled her head together.

Evaluate and adapt, she told herself. Accept what is, and act on it. She was behind schedule. They had somehow gotten bad information. Bad information that could still make or break the mission. Her arm was numb, weak, close to useless. But she was in. She was through the most dangerous part of the run, and the only way out now was through.

She checked the open sunlit expanse of the dome in front of her. Empty. She stepped forward—and slipped on something slick and wet. She caught her balance, looked down and saw blood dripping from her right hand and pooling on the decking.

Her combat-application virucules would break her blood down, destroying telltale genetic evidence, leaving only the sterile universal-type plasma the field medics needed for their IV feeds. But in the meantime, there was still blood on the floor. A lot of it. Rose red drops on the silver deck plating, a glistening gingerbread trail for the guards to follow—straight to her.

She unzipped her pressure suit, pulled up the thermal shirt she wore under it, and ripped, wincing at the loud sound of tearing fabric. It ripped easily though, and it was elastic enough to make a tourniquet. She knotted it around her arm and sealed up her pressure suit again, being careful to activate the reflective visor; it wouldn't do to get caught on vid there. When she had stanched the bleeding, she surveyed the damage to her suit. It was repairing itself, or trying to. But the tear was so big that she doubted the smart fibers would form a solid seal again. And if the suit wasn't spacetight, how the hell would she ever get back to the Starling?

She shook her head, forced everything out of her mind but the immediate problem. Get to the lab comp. And don't bleed all over the floors doing it. She'd worry about the pressure suit and all the rest if and when she had to.

03:12:09.

Getting to the comp was easy. Li had expected to have trouble with the DNA reader at the start of the last corridor, but to her surprise, the field dropped almost instantly to let her through. She shivered with apprehension. Did Nguyen know more than Li had told her? Had she slipped her an ace under the table for her own inscrutable reasons? Or was someone else at work here?

She slipped down the corridor, alert for patrols, scanning the labyrinth of ducts and wires that lined the ceilings for the faint pulses of security cameras. Nothing. Could a high-security lab really be so lightly protected? Or was it just that this was Alba, and the Corps knew that no thief who managed to breach the orbital fortress would ever get out safely? She counted down the doors until she reached the one that separated her from the lab spoke's mainframe. *Here goes,* she thought. She slipped the lockpick kit out of her suit's kangaroo pocket and unrolled it on the deck.

The lock work went slowly; she was used to having Catrall do this. But Catrall was dead. And even if he weren't, he wouldn't be helping her on this job. Not when it meant selling out Alba to the people who had killed so many of their comrades on Gilead.

03:19:40.

Footsteps. She froze. Were they coming toward her or moving away? Toward. She rolled up her tools, ducked around the curve, and climbed into the shadows of the ceiling.

Two women walked by. Guards, not scientists; she could hear their lug-soled boots, and the coarse, hard-edged slang that was the UN grunt's native tongue. "Catch the spins today?" one of them asked. "Assembly voted PKs to Compson's to get the mines open."

"What a shit hole. Well, long as we don't have to do it."

"Do what? Go to Compson's or open the mines?"

"Either. I didn't sign on to shovel coal. Or shoot miners. Whole planet's fucked, ever since the Riots. Ask me, we oughta just cut 'em loose and kick 'em into hard vac."

"And we would if they could get those synthcrystals over in Lab Eight to format properly."

"Yeah, yeah. And if wishes were horses . . ."

". . . horses wouldn't be extinct!"

The guards laughed and their voices faded away down the corridor.

Li counted to twenty, holding her breath, then dropped to the floor. When she got back to the lab door, she saw something that nearly stopped her heart: her own quantum pick, sticking out of the control panel like a hangnail.

For one panicked moment she thought the patrol had seen it, that they were coming back for her, that the whole lazy gossiping act had been nothing but subterfuge. Then she got a grip on herself. It had been no trick. Luck had been with her; the two women had walked right past the pick, busy talking, and never seen it. The one plus of storming an impregnable fortress was that no one expected to turn a corner and catch an intruder.

Inside the lab, Li saw her target immediately: a Park 35-Zed, the biggest mainframe made by any of the top military contractors. She walked around it apprehensively, looking for the input port. She found the port on one side of the mainframe, in a little tech's cubbyhole equipped with a fold-down desk and rolling stool. She deactivated her pressure suit and peeled back the hood to bare the socket at her temple. She sat on the stool, keeping her feet planted beneath her center of gravity so she could get up fast if she had to. She pulled the wire out of her pocket.

She thought of the times she'd ordered Kolodny to jack into hostile systems. Then she told herself that she wasn't jacking into a hostile system this time. She was just accessing the external communications program and dialing out to Cohen, waiting on the Starling. And the system wasn't going to be hostile, because if everything went right, it would never know she'd been there. It didn't help. She opened the main menu and began scanning through the settings, going as fast as she could without alerting any AI or human sysops, trying to make sure she wasn't setting off any unseen trip wires. The Zed was more powerful than the smaller comps she was used to manipulating, and the direct line gave her a disorienting, vertiginous speed of connection.

It was like diving into the spinstream—but a stream without VR, a stream of pure numbers. The numbers fed directly into Li's brain, and her oracle processed them at speeds beyond reach of any keyboard operator. But she still had to process them. And, even skewed by her own interface settings, there was something in the feel of these numbers that hinted at the vast, alien mind of the semisentient behind them. There was no mistaking this for surfing the spinstream, not if you had a feel for the code you were running. Streamspace was alive, in its own way, but only as a planet or a star system was alive. This was different. Here Li felt with every calculation, every operation, that she was inside something. Or someone. She found herself ducking and dodging mentally, not wanting to come to grips with the presence behind the Zed's operating programs. She thought of Sharifi, trapped in the pit, locked mind-to-mind with the semisentient field AI of Compson's orbital relay, and shuddered. It was an image burst straight from the subterranean depths of her nightmares.

Still, the lab AI remained comfortingly passive as she accessed screen after screen, gradually closing in on the back door that Cohen had shown her in their final planning sessions. All that changed when she tried to dial out. The moment she opened the outside line, she felt a shift, a push in the system. It reminded her of the ear-popping wall of air that swept through a ship when someone breached a pressure seal. And whatever was doing the pushing was more than the sum of the lab comp's files and operating platforms. It was aware of her, Li. Knew she was on the move. Knew she'd dialed out. And it was thinking about it. At eight billion parallel-processed operations per picosecond.

Though any speed she could muster was meaningless, she hurried. The call went out. The dedicated line on the Starling lit up like a distant star in the darkness.

First ring.

No answer.

"Come on, Cohen. Be there!"

Second ring. Li felt the AI rising up like a great

beast, flexing its computational muscles, gathering its immense bulk to flick off the irritating mote that was her.

"Don't do this to me, Cohen!"

Third ring. And the Zed was on top of her.

It spun through its security operations so fast that the whole dataspace became an incomprehensible dizzying blur. Li was sinking, spinning. She knew she should jack out, but she couldn't navigate the system, couldn't orient herself or even control her own body. Code twisted and convulsed as the Zed overloaded her systems. Her internals froze, jerked, skittered off course. The datastream corrupted. Her own mind, unable to process the overload, betrayed her. She began to hallucinate. The numbers came alive. They pulsed with a cold, deep-sea wakefulness. A mind moved within them, dark, sightless, unsleeping. A mind without words. A mind forged in the pressure of a hundred atmospheres. It circled, searching for her. Stalking her. And she knew with bone-crushing certainty that when it found her she would die.

Far away someone else's body convulsed and a stool skittered across the deck, wheels shrieking. The phone rang again, but the external datastream was so slow and uncompressed next to the Zed's dizzying parallel calculations that the ring reached Li's brain only as a low, Dopplered groan. Even the white noise on the line stretched out until each click and rasp of static became a distorted howl. The darkness within the darkness gathered itself and slid toward her.

Click.

She sensed Cohen's arrival more than she actually saw it. A river of light washed through the numbers, driving back the darkness. It shone white, as pure and deceptively placid as the sweep of a Himalayan ice field. But it was crushing the Zed, cutting through the semisentient as implacably as a glacier grinding at a mountain. If she'd ever wondered what it was to be the scrap of flesh two sharks fought over, she knew now. She felt . . . nothing. She heard only her pulse pounding in her skull, and behind that a rushing, whirling silence. She was lost, floating, watching from a tremendous height while two battling giants tore apart the universe.

The lab comp writhed and twisted, desperately spinning through its programs in search of anything that would blunt Cohen's relentless attack. Then it focused on her, and an icy finger of fear brushed down her spine.

<Cohen!> she called. And with that one betraying thought, the darkness was upon her.

03:42:12.

The next thing she saw was Cohen. Not the implacable and terrible light, but his normal on-line self. He was running the numbers, doing the job he always did, the job any cracker did. <You're back with us?> he asked, when she mustered enough energy to try a cautious operation.

<What happened?>

<No need to worry about it now. I'll explain later.>

She waited, still weak. There was something comforting about watching him dial through the comp, watching the security codes untangle themselves under his touch and the numbers smooth out and tick past easily, the way they always did for him. Something was off though. <How come you're not singing?> she asked.

<What?>

<You always sing when you're cracking a system. Unless something's wrong. Is something wrong?>

Digital laughter swirled around her, flickering through the numbers like brush fire. <Just because you can't hear me doesn't mean I'm not singing.>

<Don't try to snow me.>

<Hang on a minute.> He scanned a promising file and cursed as it came up empty. <I'm thinking about the lab AI.>

<It's not coming back?> Li asked, feeling panicky.

<No,> Cohen said. <He's not coming back.> The emphasis on *he* was slight but unmistakable. A reproach.

<Then what?>

When he answered, Li could feel the unease in his voice even across the remote line. <Ever watched flat film of a horse race?>

<Sure. Beautiful.>

<Know what a heartbreaker is?> He went on without waiting for a reply. <A heartbreaker is a horse so fast he doesn't just beat his competitors, he breaks them. Beats them so badly they never run to win again. Horses used to die of it.>

<You made that up. You've probably never seen a horse.>

<No. Truly. Running to win is what racehorses were. The ultimate single-purpose organism. They couldn't feed themselves, couldn't even walk without special shoes humans made for them. But they could run. And they'd run themselves to death, run until their bones shattered. There's footage of horses doing just that, coming apart on the track like ships burning up on reentry.>

<That's crazy, Cohen.>

<Not crazy. Just human. They were human-built running machines. Just like I'm a thinking machine. Just like you're a working machine, and every planet in UN space is a food-and-air machine. And when humans are building a machine, everything but the one thing they want it to do tends to fall by the wayside.>

Cohen paused, sidetracked to search a dead-end directory. <Anyway, AIs are like racehorses. They're built to play games. Chess games, probability games, war

games. They're built so that the win is all they want, all they are.>

<Why are you telling me this?>

<You just watched a heartbreak race.>

<With the lab AI?> Li couldn't get her mind around this vision of how Cohen saw the Zed. <Is it . . . he . . . dead?>

<No.> Cohen riffled through a new directory faster than Li could identify it, dropped it, moved on to the next one. <He's still here. Can't you feel him?>

Cautiously, Li probed the network. She felt something, a dark, vaguely sentient presence. But it was confused, chaotic, diminished. As if the Zed had crept into some dark corner of the network to lick its wounds. <So now what?>

<If he owned his own code, he could contract with a larger AI and try to make his way as an associate system, get some workout equity. Or he could get psychiatric help, reprogramming. But he doesn't own his code. Alba does. So what will actually happen is this: The techs will come in tomorrow and find, first, that he got cracked by an outside AI, and second, that their top-of-the-line semisentient has just turned into an unbelievably expensive calculator. They'll try to salvage him, because of the cost if nothing else, and when they can't they'll activate his terminal feedback loop, core out the mainframe, and install a new AI.>

Li felt something come through the numbers. Something that was partly indecipherable AI emotion and partly a feeling she didn't need anyone to explain to her: guilt.

<Christ, Cohen. It's not your fault. What else were you supposed to do?>

<Nothing. But that doesn't make it any nicer, does it?>

<You think you have to tell me that?>

Another long silence. <No.>

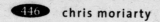

03:51:02.

<Bad news.>
<What?>
<I found the data. But I can't access it from here. You'll need to get into another lab and jack a remote terminal before I can get it.>

Li checked their time and swallowed.

After a tense silence, Cohen said, <What do you want to do?>

She twitched, nerves stretched to the breaking point. <What do you mean, what do I want to do? We go get it.>

<You're sure?>

<Of course I'm sure.>

04:01:00.

She looked around the corner, saw an empty passage and started forward. <Cohen?> she asked.

<?>

<What you said about the lab AI. How did you survive so long? How did you survive being beaten?>

A pulse of emotion flowed over the line, but this one was pure AI—one of those ripples in the numbers that put the lie to the illusion of Cohen's humanness, that reminded Li how foolish it was to let herself imagine she understood anything that happened on the other side of the interface. <I didn't survive it,> he answered when the numbers smoothed out. <I've never been beaten.>

Then she passed through another security grid and lost him.

04:03:41.

She was deep in the lab section. Security was so solid here that the station's admins hadn't even tried

to make the researchers observe normal security protocols. Whiteboards lined the walls, markers and erasers
hooked into the low-g racks along their bottom rims.
She passed a board that was covered with quantum
equations, another, half-erased already, that held only
two clean and concise Bussard drive efficiency calculations, the kind Li had wrestled with in her OCS math
courses. Rounding one corner, she almost knocked
over a half-full coffee cup someone had left sitting on
the floor. She heard footsteps, scrambled into the ceiling pipes just in time to watch a skinny bald man
shuffle past in rumpled pajamas. She smiled and
wished Cohen could see him.

Alba was so big, its curve so slight, that it was easy
to get disoriented. Especially easy for Li, just off the
much smaller AMC Compson station, where the tight
curve of the life-support ring was always rising in front
of your feet, telling you where you were. Corridors
branched off the backbone of the big hoop, running
three or four hundred meters on either side. The fancy
offices and conference rooms would be on the edges,
in the relatively few rooms with side windows. The
storage areas, the secured labs, and the deadwalled
comps would be where Li was, in the narrow white
world of the internal corridors.

4:06:27.

She'd made it. Here was the cross corridor Cohen
had sent her to, and the fifth door. She scanned the
room beyond the door. Empty. She picked the lock, using the code Cohen had already pulled off the system.
Then she stepped through the door and crossed a
mostly empty lab to a desktop terminal tucked behind
an antiquated multichannel quantum ansible. She undid her suit's hood and jacked in. This time there was
no gatekeeper, no dark presence lurking behind the

system. She opened the comm menu, trembling with relief. She dialed the number.

And heard the unmistakable metallic click of the safety lifting off a neural disruptor.

"Turn around," said a hard voice. "Slowly. That is, if you want to be alive in ten seconds."

She froze, raised her hands carefully, and turned. The guard was five meters away—just out of kicking range. Everything about him was cold, hard, professional. Li's hope died as soon as she looked at him. He gestured at her rifle. "Eject the charge clip."

She ejected it.

"Now throw it."

She dropped it on the floor in front of her. The prongs of the disruptor jerked toward her chest. "Kick it over here."

She kicked it.

"And the rifle."

She sent that skittering across the floor behind the charge clip—her last hope rattling away across grip-treated deckplating.

"You alone?" he asked. Just as she opened her mouth to answer, the comp rang.

They both jumped. The muzzle of the disruptor flicked toward her again. "Step away from the terminal," he said over the second ring. Li took a deep breath, flexed her knees and rolled.

She planned her roll to carry her behind the terminal's condensate array, thinking the guard wouldn't fire on her if it meant destroying the precious crystals inside it. She thought wrong.

As she rolled, she heard the whip-crack shot of the disruptor and felt the charge hit her. This hit had nothing to do with the throbbing numbness that followed a shot from a little handheld disruptor, though. It felt like someone had taken a hot scalpel and carved a hand-sized chunk out of her back, leaving every severed nerve exposed and screaming.

She scrambled sideways and crouched in the uncertain shelter of the ansible, struggling to force air into her still-convulsed lungs. A sour copper taste flooded her mouth; her teeth had clamped shut on the tip of her tongue when the charge hit.

"Goddamn," she heard the guard mutter. His footsteps echoed across the room, stopped beside the mainframe. She heard the hiss of indrawn breath as he looked at the screen. Then she realized the phone wasn't ringing anymore. Cohen was in.

If she could just distract the guard for a few moments, keep him from focusing on what was happening unseen inside the comp, maybe Cohen could get the data out. And then maybe he could get her out. If he decided to stick around and do it.

She stood up and drew her Beretta in a single smooth movement. It was crazy, a crazy gun to be shooting off. But she was so deep inside the station, there was no real risk of a breach into hard vacuum. And it was all she had left to shoot with, anyway.

The guard saw her drawing on him, then saw what she was drawing. The blood drained from his face as completely as if he'd already taken a heart shot. "I've got three men forty seconds away," he said. "You'll never get out of here. Don't make it worse than it has to be."

She looked at his pale face, at the familiar uniform, and she came as close as she'd ever come to losing her nerve. *I can't shoot him*, she thought. *Not for this*.

But it turned out that she could.

He rolled and came up shooting for her head, at killing range. She aimed with the hardwired precision of ceramsteel and squeezed off a single shot. He went down in a spray of blood before her conscious mind even understood she had shot him.

Getting across the small room to where he lay was the hardest thing Li could ever remember doing. She'd fired on hardwired reflex, but as soon as the disruptor clattered out of his hands, the enemy trying to shoot her turned into what he really was: a UN grunt, bleeding out onto the same pale blue uniform she'd worn all her adult life. One of her own. A comrade. As she stumbled toward him, elbows still locked in firing position, she knew he'd seen her face. She was going to have to choose between killing him in cold blood and letting herself be identified.

Luck and a clean shot saved her; he was dead by the time she reached him. She looked at him, hot blood welling up in her mouth. An image of Nguyen flashed through her mind, sitting behind her graceful desk, wearing silk, talking about need-to-know security and how she'd be on her own if the Alba raid went wrong. She spit, and it wasn't only her blood that tasted bitter to her.

04:09:50.

She walked back across the room and jacked back in.

<What's going on?> Cohen asked. <You're setting off alarms all through the system.>

<Guard caught me.>

<You're okay?>

She felt her still-frozen side. <Yes.>

<Is he?>

<No.>

An infinitesimal pause. <Well, let's get you out of there.>

<Do we have the software?>

<Yes. Now go!>

<Which way?> A grid flashed onto her internals. Red pulses converged on the lab from three sides. The only gap in the circle—and it was closing even as she looked at it—was the long corridor back up to the hydroponics domes.

<I don't know if I can make it.>

<You have to make it.>
She jacked out and ran.

04:11:01.

She hit two guards at the first intersection and barreled past before they could even draw on her. The pressure suit's sealed hood hid her face, and she didn't plan to shoot anyone else. Not for this. Now it was only her flagging body and the clock she was fighting.

She hit the first hydroponics dome at a tendon-snapping sprint and was through the open containment door and halfway across before she realized she had made it.

The dome was separate from the main curve of the station—a self-contained, light-flooded globe of zero-g-manufactured viruflex. Li's feet clattered on a narrow catwalk between stacked, dripping algae flats. High overhead, bright heating panels blazed on the station's underbelly. Below her, clearly visible between the catwalk's gridplate, curved a finger's width of clear viruglass . . . and beyond that only bright, blinding sunlight.

She looked back and saw her pursuers charging through the open pressure door behind her. Okay. Next dome. And she'd have to be quicker this time. She sprinted across the slick decking, skidding on a wet patch, wrenching herself upright, pushing her ligaments and tendons to near rupture. Another corridor, ribbed with heavy struts, armored with virusteel. At the end, like the lights of an oncoming train, more sunlight.

She raced into the second dome, whirled to face her pursuers, leveled the Beretta at them. They skidded to a stop and threw themselves into the inadequate shelter of the corridor's pressure struts. "What the hell are you doing?" one of them shouted.

She jerked the gun at him. "I'd stay there if I were you."

He looked at her, and she knew he was thinking about whether she would shoot or not, whether he could talk her down or not. She saw his eyes flick toward her shoulder, note the blood on her sleeve, the partly repaired rent in her suit. She watched him consider what it meant to go into hard vac in an emergency pressure suit, even one that wasn't compromised. She saw him think about suicide attacks. That thought, and the single heartbeat of indecision that accompanied it, gave her the time she needed. She stepped to the catwalk railing and let herself fall backwards over it like a diver flipping off the side of a landing boat.

She'd planned to catch herself and hang from the walkway just long enough to get the first few critical shots off before she fell. But she'd forgotten about her shoulder. Her hand came up a fraction of a second too late. She felt the rail slip between her weakened fingers, just too far away to grab hold of.

This would be the time to pop that emergency chute, she thought, and remembered an idiotic joke from jump school about a malfunctioning parachute. She aimed the Beretta between her feet and squeezed off two shots. As the shots hit the dome, the containment plates slammed down at both ends of the catwalk, locking the guards out. A spider's web of fractures raced across the dome, but it held. Then the curve of cold, hard viruflex was rushing up at her and it was time to think about not getting her legs broken.

She landed hard, but she kept her knees together, thank God. She even managed to hang on to the Beretta through her tuck and roll. As she hit the dome, she felt a ripple run through the viruflex like an earthquake. She caught her breath, twisted onto her stomach. For a fraction of a second, she lay there belly to space, blinking at the blazing infinity of stars reflected in the shattered viruflex. Then the dome blew and launched her into a blinding, glittering glass storm.

She couldn't orient herself in the spinning chaos of algae, metal, viruflex shards, so she let herself drift. She'd played her whole hand, maybe her last hand. Now it was up to Cohen to pull it out of the hole. If he could. If he was willing to risk it.

<Suit breach,> her oracle told her. <Reestablish outside pressure in seventy seconds maximum.>

She counted to seventy, but no ship showed up to rescue her. According to her scans, she and her debris field were the only things moving this side of the vast station.

She opened her eyes. The glittering storm still whirled around her, but it had dispersed enough for her to see open space beyond it. Stars wheeled across the far horizon. The station rose and set in her visor as if it were orbiting her. She watched its gossamer wings flash in the perfect, blinding light of the void and thought about the life she'd lived.

Then a door opened, blinding white in the black star field, and a silver line rippled out like the hand of God and caught her.

COLLAPSE OF THE WAVE FUNCTION

➤Imagine a card game. The dealer—let's call her Life—shuffles her deck, which is a little larger than the usual fifty-two. She draws one card, shuffles again, draws again. We see one and only one card at each draw, and it is from this one card—one among an infinite number of undrawn cards—that we construct all our theories, all our notions of the universe.

But what does the dealer see? If Coherence Theory is right, she sees every card. In fact, she does more than see them. She deals them. Every card. On every draw.

Can we construct meaning from a universe in which anything is possible and everything that is possible actually happens? Of course we can. We do it every day. Consciousness, memory, causality are the architecture of that meaning—the architecture of the universe-as-we-see-it.

The real question is: can we construct a theory that

transcends the universe-as-we-see-it and tells us
something about the universe-as-it-is? Can we look
into the shuffle?

—TAPE 934.12. PHYSICS 2004. LECTURE 1 (H. SHARIFI):
INTRODUCTION TO QUANTUM GRAVITY.

Shantytown: 3.11.48.

She woke up in dark water, cradled in the hot salt tears of a medtank.

She imagined she was breathing though she knew she was hooked to an umbilical line, her lungs suffused with superoxygenated saline solution. She imagined she could feel smart bugs swarming over her organs and membranes though she knew she couldn't.

Her arm was mercifully silent for the first time since Metz, but a new pain had replaced it. It radiated from her backbrain and licked hotly at her eyes and temples.

The intraface.

She had bleary memories of Cohen explaining the process and the risks to her, but she hadn't paid much attention. It was an equipment upgrade. Routine maintenance. You trusted the mechanics not to damage a pricey piece of technology and hoped they put you under for longer than the pain lasted. Start thinking more than that and you were well on your way to a career-ending wetware phobia.

She slipped in and out of consciousness several more times before she really surfaced. Once the lights came on. Someone in a scrub suit peered down at her and spoke to another person outside her line of vision. She tried to ask where she was, but her lungs were full of saline, useless. Later there was prodding, splashing, the cold bite of air on her skin. Then a sense of being rolled under bright lights, of warm blankets and merciful quiet.

"Catherine," Bella said, taking Li's dripping hand in hers. "Are you back with us?"

Only it wasn't Bella behind the violet eyes. Bella had never looked at her that way. It was Cohen. Where were they? What had happened on Alba? Did she even remember?

"Shantytown," Cohen said, answering her unspoken questions. "Daahl's safe house. Arkady and I managed to pick you up after you shot your way out of there. That was, er, characteristically unsubtle. And impressive."

"How long . . . how long was I under?"

"Five days." He put a hand to her brow, brushing her hair back. "You were dreaming. Do you remember?"

She shook her head. Her skull was buzzing, humming, drowning out his words.

"About a man. Dark. Thin. He had a blue scar on his face." Cohen ran a finger down Bella's smooth cheek.

"My father," Li said.

"You killed your father?"

"What?" Li asked, her heart suddenly hammering in her chest. "Are you crazy?"

He blinked. "I saw it."

"You—that's a dream. A nightmare. It didn't happen."

"How do you know?"

"Because . . . I just do, that's all. Sweet Jesus!" Li closed her eyes and tried to still the spinning of the room around her.

"You love him," Cohen said after a minute or two.

"I don't even remember him."

"Even so."

She shook her head again. The noise kept drumming on her ears. Like rainwater running down a spout. Like standing in a crowded room full of people speaking a foreign language.

"So." Cohen spoke slowly, as if he were thinking through a complex equation. "How do you keep straight what's a dream and what's not?"

"Don't you dream? I thought all sentients dreamed."

"Not like that." He looked horrified. "If I think it, even when I'm asleep, it happened. Exactly the way I remember it. But your brain just . . . lied to you."

"Cohen," Li asked, as the hum inside her head climbed to a higher, more urgent pitch, "how did you see that dream?"

The violet eyes sparkled. "I'll give you three guesses."

She started to answer, but the noise in her skull exploded, drowning out every thought but pain. She grabbed her head and curled into fetal position on the narrow bed. Red spots swam before her eyes, hemorrhaged, flooded her vision. The buzzing rose to a high wail. Her sight tunneled down to a pinprick of light, blacked out altogether. "Hush," he said, bending over her.

Slowly the wail trailed off to a low moan and her vision cleared. "What the hell was that?" she panted.

"Traffic." She heard him stand up and cross the room, heard running water, felt the cool touch of water as he wiped a damp cloth across her forehead.

Traffic?

"Comm traffic. Mine. You're hearing me."

"No," she whispered. "Something's wrong, Cohen."

"Nothing's wrong. Korchow's had me running tests all morning. Accessing your internals, running checks, startup subroutines, downloading data. Your commsys is a dinosaur, by the way. A disgrace. I ran a Schor check on your oracle workspace though. Properly. Which those idiots at Alba never do. That should help a bit."

She opened her eyes to find him smiling down at her. "Feeling better now?"

She had to think about it for a moment. "Yes."

"Hmm."

"What does that mean? Am I adjusting?"

"No. I just took the intraface off-line."

They looked at each other. "Oh," Li said.

Cohen stood up, patting her hand. "Don't worry. You're still barely conscious. We'll get on top of it tomorrow."

But they didn't get on top of it the next day. Or the day after that. Korchow had set up a lab and medical facility in the safe house, and over the next three days, Li's universe narrowed to two sterile rooms of monitoring equipment, her own cramped bunk, and the empty echoing dome that functioned as the safe house's common room.

The first time they brought the intraface on-line, she ended up curled on the floor, hands over her ears, screaming for someone—anyone—to turn it off. Cohen shut the link down so fast it took him half an hour to get himself straightened out.

"I'll go crazy," Li said when she'd recovered enough to speak. "It's like a hundred people fighting in my head."

"Forty-seven," Cohen interjected. "Well, this week."

"What's gone wrong?" Korchow asked Cohen. He

didn't even look at Li, just talked past her like she was a piece of tech.

"Nothing," Cohen answered, tapping a fingernail on the console in front of him. "It's an organic software problem."

Cohen was shunting through Ramirez, and Li noticed again the cold fire in Leo's dark eyes, the extra measure of decisiveness in his already-powerful movements. *Those two I'd like to have next to me in a fight,* she thought—and felt a sudden razor-sharp stab of grief for Kolodny.

"Sharifi didn't have these problems," Korchow said, a threat lurking behind the words.

Cohen shrugged. "She wouldn't have, would she? She was interfacing with a simple field AI. And she wasn't wired for anything but communications. Catherine's a different beast entirely. You try to crowbar new programs into a military system and all bets are off. You knew that before we started."

"Well, what do we do about it?" Li asked.

Cohen crossed the room more quickly than Li would have thought Ramirez could move. He leaned over and put a cool hand to her forehead. "You don't do anything. You get your pulse rate down and go to bed. I'll figure out where we go from here."

But the next session was worse. After three hours Li collapsed into a chair, pressing the heels of her hands into her burning eye sockets. "I can't. I can't do it again."

"Yes you can," Korchow said. He was still being patient. "Why didn't the pulse compression work?" he asked Cohen over her head.

"If I knew, I'd be able to fix it."

"Does she need a new signal processor?"

Li didn't have to see Cohen to imagine his dismissive shrug.

"Well, what then?"

Cohen shook his head. "I have to think."

"Let's check the settings and try it again."

Li wanted to say no. That she'd throw up if they tried again. That everything she'd eaten in the last two days had come up already, and she couldn't stand it anymore. But she was too sick and too tired to say anything.

It was Cohen who finally came up with the idea of the memory palace. He was shunting through Arkady when he explained it to her, and his excitement set the construct's dark eyes glinting like freshly fired coal. "It's an organic problem," he explained. "We're trying to integrate AI-scale parallel-processing nets with an organic system that was already obsolete the first time a person put pen to paper. So. If we can't fight it, we work with it. We try one of the oldest tricks there is—Matteo Ricci's trick. We build you a memory palace." Arkady's lips twisted into a wry smile. "Or rather, we give you the keys to mine."

It took him twenty hours to put the keys together. Hours she slept through in a desperate attempt to hoard her energy for their final push. It was late morning of the third day after her awakening when she lay down on the couch Arkady had dragged into the lab for her, closed her eyes, jacked in, and found herself alone in a featureless white room.

"You may have to hunt for the door a bit," Cohen said at her shoulder. "I haven't quite got that sorted out yet." He had a smaller, thinner feeling than usual, she thought. And when she looked around, sure enough, there was Hyacinthe, shoes slung over his shoulders, standing a hair shorter than her in his socks. "The door," he said insistently.

She turned and saw a gleaming, intricately carved mahogany door. More of a window than a door, really; its sill was set into the wall at about knee level, and even Li had to duck her head to clear the lintel.

"Go on," Cohen said.

It was so bright on the other side that it took a moment for her eyes to clear. She stood in a five-cornered courtyard. Arcades bright with mosaics surrounded her. Beyond the walls she glimpsed the knife-edged mountains of a dry country.

She heard the sound of running water and felt cold spray on her face before she saw the fountain. The water poured from a shallow stone shelf as if rising from a spring and riffled down a long sloping stair that ran to the other end of the great courtyard. Li followed the water's course down to a shadowy portico whose mosaics glinted like eyes in the occasional stray sunbeam. The watercourse ended in a narrow reflecting pool that emptied mysteriously into who knew what. Li stepped across the pool and walked along the portico, her heels clicking on the pavement. She came to a door and opened it.

A riot of smell and color swept over her. She stood in a long, high-ceilinged hall paved with spiral patterns of marble tesserae. Bright flowers rocketed out of vases painted with rampant lions and romping, grinning dragons. Cabinets lined the walls, their polished glass fronts filled with books, fossils, photographs, playing cards. As she started down the hall, something moved in her peripheral vision. She jumped around—only to realize that one of the painted dragons was tapping its scaled feet and winking at her. She shook her head and snorted. Hyacinthe laughed.

One side of the hall opened onto a high terrace, and when she looked out she could see the stony ramparts of a crusader's castle digging their feet into the face of a mountainside that dropped away for miles above a long, green windswept valley. She stepped to the balustrade and leaned out over the void. The stone under her hand felt as hot as if it had been warming under the afternoon sun, but when she looked to the sky it seemed to be morning—the fresh, cool morning of a fall day.

The heat was in the stone, she realized, part of the

teeming life the place radiated. Was this all Cohen? The castle? The mountain? This whole world, wherever and whatever it was? She leaned out farther, squinting down the dizzying fall of buttress and mountain, trying to see where the active code stopped and the backdrop started. Instinctively, she dropped out of VR and into the numbers.

Her head spun. The world twisted and rippled around her. Numbers came at her too fast for her to feel them as anything but blinding, paralyzing, dizzying pain. This was a system never designed for human interface, a system never designed at all except in its earliest, most distant beginnings. It wasn't as alive as a human—the constant chant of the AI–civil-rights proponents—it was more alive. More alive, more complex, more changeable and contradictory. Just more. Cohen must have been insane to think she could exist, let alone function, in this maelstrom.

She staggered and fell heavily against the railing. He put a hand under her elbow, steadying her. In the same instant, her brain clicked back into the VR interface as if someone had flipped a cutoff switch. "Let's not get ahead of ourselves," Cohen said, and drew her back from the ledge.

She stared at him for a moment, feeling like a child who had put her hand into the fire only to have an all-seeing adult pull it out miraculously unscathed.

"You're all right?" he asked.

She nodded and followed him back inside.

The hall's internal wall was broken by what seemed to be an infinitely receding line of doors. Cohen was still behind her, one hand on her hip, his mouth inches from her ear. "Close your eyes," he said. She closed them.

"What do you hear?"

"Water."

"Good. That's the fountain. See it?"

She turned and looked back over her shoulder into the glittering shadows of the portico. "Yes."

"If you get lost, just follow the sound of the water and it will bring you back here. Now. How many doors do you see?"

"I can't . . ." She looked down the hall and saw that the illusion of infinity had been just that. "Forty . . . forty-eight?"

"Good. Every door is a separate network with its own memory palace. Every room in each palace is a directory. Every object in the room is a datafile. Understand?"

She nodded.

"When you want to access a network, you find its proper door. When you want a directory, you find its proper room. When you want a datafile, you just open the drawer, the box, the cabinet, whatever it's stored in. Just like the standard graphic user interface you've used in Corps archives . . . although I flatter myself that my aesthetic instincts put me a cut or two above the Corps designers. But bear in mind that you'll still be dealing with a fully sentient AI every time you open one of those doors. And some of them are less . . . accessible . . . than the networks you're familiar with. If you feel . . . nervous about anything, you can always leave. Always. Just come back here, shut the door behind you, and you're alone again."

"Except for you."

He laughed. "You're in the belly of the beast, my dear. I'm always here. I *am* here."

Li looked around. "Which door should I open?"

"Whichever one you want." He looked at her, Hyacinthe's little boy's body so slight he actually had to look up to meet her eyes. A small, secret smile slipped across his face. "Try the last door."

She walked down the hall, running her hand along the cool marble of the walls, the carved hardwood of the doorframes. Each door was labeled: network designations, Toffoli numbers, directory profiles. The last door, tucked into the farthest corner of the hall as if in an afterthought, had only a single word printed on it: *Hyacinthe*. She set her hand to the latch, and it opened to her touch as if it had been waiting for her.

A large, bright room, shot butter yellow with morning sunlight. On every wall, row on row of wooden drawers, each drawer with its own polished brass knob, none of them much more than big enough to fit a datacube. There were no labels or schematics on the drawers, but as Li touched them brief images of their contents flashed before her. "What is this place?" she whispered.

"Me." Cohen nudged an oriental rug straight with one toe. "Well, that's the short answer anyway. The long answer would be that I thought this was a good place to start because Hyacinthe is the core network that you're most familiar with."

"Do you actually use this place yourself?"

"Of course. I shift back and forth between VR and the numbers like you do when you go instream. I won't use VR much when I'm running under time pressure or handling heavy traffic. But when I have the time and processing space . . ."

Li knew how this sort of VR construct worked. The drawers would contain stored data platformed on a nonsentient access program. Behind the walls, where she couldn't see them without dropping into code, would be the bones of the system: the semisentient operating programs and the sentient net that these memories and datafiles belonged to. She looked down the length of the room and saw that it was one of many, all opening onto a cloistered garden. And every wall, every arcade, every paving stone held a memory. "Christ," she whispered, "it's huge."

"Infinite, actually," Cohen called from the garden, where he was restaking a wind-tousled dahlia. "It's a folded database."

Li stared, breathless. How could anyone—any ten people—have that many memories? What a weight of the past to be buried under. She walked through the rooms, tentatively, running her hands along the wood but not quite daring to open anything. The memories were grouped in rough categories, and as Li worked her way through the place she began to see hidden links, make telling connections. In the arcade along the fringe of the garden, a whole long wall was given over to a mosaic of books, films, paintings, each compressed into a tiny, emotion-laden point of color. Another room seemed to contain only memory upon memory of Earth, most of them collected in the final few years before the Evacuation. Then came a white, silent room that was entirely empty. As she penetrated deeper into the complex, she saw that most of the memories in the outer rooms were other people's. Cohen's own memories were concentrated in the sunny, quiet arcade along the garden's southern exposure. And in the garden itself were people—all the people Cohen had ever known during his long, long life.

"Come look at these," Cohen said.

She went.

"All these are Hyacinthe." He gestured at a narrow row of drawers just inside the door. "The person, not the network. They should be quite easy for you to access. Go ahead, have a look."

She opened the drawer he pointed to. It was empty. "What—?"

He smiled. "What's the closest sense to memory?"

Li blinked. "Smell."

"So?"

She bent over the drawer and sniffed. It smelled of cedar, and of the old-fashioned furniture wax that infused every piece of wood in Cohen's realspace house. She had a ridiculous momentary image of one of his impeccably dressed French maids getting down on her immaculate knees to scrub at the floors and baseboards of the ethereal memory palace. Then she caught the smell underneath the other smells: the smell of the memory itself.

The room around her disappeared. She stood on a steep scree slope, her face warmed by the golden sun of pre-Migration Earth. A glacier snaked away like a river below her. Behind her loomed a near-vertical wall of rock and ice whose very shadow was like a little death. She turned and craned her neck to look up the soaring granite column above her. This was the Walker Spur of the Grandes Jorasses, her oracle told her. The most spectacular route up the most beautiful rock face on the planet. Given the state of the glacier winding below her, this couldn't be much after the turn of the twenty-first century. Italy lay south, on the other side of that colossus. To the west, the Mont Blanc glittered under a sky blue enough for the most cautious climber to gamble on.

"Planning on helping?" someone said behind her.

She turned and saw a woman crouched on the slope below her coiling a brightly colored climbing rope. She handled the rope expertly, without wasted motion, lean climber's muscles bunching and flexing under her sunburned skin. *Lucinda*, Li thought. Her name is Lucinda.

Lucinda looked up, her eyes (which Li somehow knew were blue) hidden behind mirrored glasses. Li saw her own doubled reflection staring back out of the lenses: a dark, narrow-faced greyhound of a man that could only be Hyacinthe Cohen himself.

"I love you," Li heard Hyacinthe saying in a voice that was kissing cousin to Cohen's voice. And she shivered, because she knew that love. She felt the heat of it, remembered living it. Remembered not just this moment, but everything. The whole life of a man who had died two centuries ago.

Lucinda just grinned up at her with the warmth of a shared joke, and said, "I know."

"Interesting," Cohen said as the memory palace took shape around her again. "I wouldn't have expected you'd see Cinda."

"You don't see the same thing every time?"

"As time passes, I become more and more inclined to sacrifice retrievability for . . . other values. Surprising what surfaces. As if what I bring in with me sets the direction. Most AIs, including some of my own associates, find it ridiculously inefficient. But then"—he smiled complacently—"I'm not most AIs."

She looked around. How far did this go on? And what, or who, was lurking in all those other memory palaces?

"What's bothering you?"

She hesitated. "It seems so . . . human."

"Well, in many ways Hyacinthe is human."

"You talk about him as if he weren't you."

"He's not all of me. But he is the first."

"So he controls . . . the others?"

Cohen made a hairsplitting face. "*Controls* is too strong a word. I'd say he . . . mediates. I know you think I'm an inveterate navel-gazer, but to tell you the truth, I've never really thought much about it. Do you think about how you walk down the street? Or how your stomach works?"

"It's just that I can't square it with . . ."

"With what made you almost fall off the front porch before?" She thought he was waiting for her to smile at the front-porch quip, but she couldn't bring herself to do it. "Do you have to reconcile it?"

She had no answer to that.

"If it's any comfort to you, most of the sentients in my shared net have the same reaction. They can't get any perspective on the system without my mediating. It doesn't mean I control them. They have their own ideas and opinions. But they're guests here. And as it's my house, they follow my rules. Mostly."

Li looked at him uncertainly, hesitating between

the many questions jostling in her mind and not finding any she was willing to ask just yet. She wandered
down the rows of drawers, opening a few of them,
with Cohen always just behind her, watching, com-
menting. Slowly, without quite admitting to herself
where she was going, she worked her way back toward
the garden.

It was a curious garden, wild, heavy with the smell
of earth and roses. The near end was well kept up,
planted in neatly tended French beds of herbs and
flowers, almost formal compared to Cohen's realspace
jungle. But at the far end the ground and even parts of
the palace itself had been overrun by a fierce sprawling
thicket of wild roses.

She eyed the thorny tangle over the heads of the
neatly pruned dahlia beds. It looked as if some feral
and not entirely friendly presence had established a
beachhead in that corner of the garden and was only
biding its time before it flung out its thorny suckers to
swallow the whole cloister. "You ought to rip those
out," she said. "They're taking over everything."

"I know." Cohen smiled wryly. "They're weeds, really. And they have the most vicious thorns. The thing
is, I like them."

Li shrugged. "It's your garden."

"So it is," Cohen said. He strolled down toward the
wild end of the garden and settled himself on a low
bench already half-engulfed by a particularly predatory moss rose.

Li circled the garden, poking into the boxes and
cabinets that lined the cloister. She found memories of
half a dozen people she knew: Nguyen; Kolodny; a few
AIs she'd met on Corps missions. Even Sharifi. But not
the one person she was looking for.

"Can't find it?" Cohen asked. She looked over and
saw he was laughing at her.

"Who says I'm looking for anything?"

"Have a rose," he said.

He plucked a moss-petaled bloom off the bramble behind him and held it out to her. She took it from him—but as she wrapped her fingers around the stem it pricked her.

"Christ!" She looked at her finger and saw blood welling up from half a dozen punctures.

"It's a real rose," Cohen said. He bent and handed it to her again, holding it gingerly. "Real roses have thorns. That's why they smell so sweet."

She put it to her nose, smelling it. And realized that the rose itself was a memory. A memory of her.

There she was six years ago. Younger, thinner, but her. This was not Li as she knew herself, though; it was what Cohen remembered. The young CO he had locked horns with during their first tense mission together. A dark whirlwind of a woman, hard, driving, utterly unyielding. Not a person Li herself could imagine liking. Not a person, she realized with a jolt, that Cohen had liked much.

"Was I really so awful?" she asked.

"Just a little thorny."

"Very funny."

"It wasn't meant to be. As I recall, you pricked my ego not a little." He grinned. "A certain speech about not having the patience to work with dilettantes comes to mind."

"Don't remind me."

"My dear, it was well worth it for the sheer entertainment value of watching a twenty-five-year-old who never finished high school look down her nose at me."

"It's not like I was the first."

"Oh. Well, that's simple bigotry, often as not. You despised me personally. I respected that."

Something in his smile made her drop her eyes and turn away. She brushed her finger over the white velvet skin of a petal, then bent her head and put the blossom to her nose again.

Another memory. Her again, leaning back against the door of an officers' flop on Alba with a knowing smirk on her face. It was the evening of the first and only night they'd spent together. She remembered standing there. She remembered looking across the room into Roland's golden eyes, trying to play it cool, wondering what the hell Cohen even saw in her, still half-convinced it was all an elaborate joke at her expense.

But now she was seeing it through Cohen's eyes. She felt Roland's knees tremble and his breath quicken. And she felt something else behind the organic interface, something cleaner, sharper, truer. As if an infinitely complex mechanism had come into alignment, bolts sliding, tumblers clicking and turning over, locking in on her looking back at him, wanting him, making him real. On the dizzying, exhilarating, precisely calculated certainty that nothing, once she touched him, would ever be the same again.

Christ, she thought. *What did I do to him? Why didn't he tell me how he felt?*

But she had known how he felt, hadn't she? Why else had she been so unbearably, unforgivably cruel to him?

She jerked back into the present and saw Cohen sitting on the bench looking up at her, holding his breath like a child who still believed you could make dreams come true just by wanting them hard enough. It was the same look she remembered from that night—and God help her if some awful part of her didn't still want to slap it off his face.

He blinked, and her stomach clenched with shame as she realized he'd caught the edge of that thought.

"You're a very confused person," he said.

"It took you six years and a fortune in wetware to figure that out?"

"No. It took me five minutes." He smiled. "It just didn't seem polite to mention it before now."

Something tickled at the back of her mind like the soft trailing ends of fingers. She realized she'd been feeling those fingers for a while. All the time she'd been exploring the sun-drenched garden of Hyacinthe's memory palace, there had been a little cat-footed thief prowling through the dark passages of her own subconscious, probing her memories, weighing her responses, taking the measure of her own feelings. *A little sock-footed soccer-shorts-wearing thief is more like it*, she thought.

"I won't have you sneaking around inside my head," she told him. "I won't have your prying."

"Prying? And what do you think you're doing here?"

"That's different. I have to be here. It's not personal."

"Isn't it?" He bit his lip and looked up at her through Hyacinthe's dark lashes. "This is as personal as it gets, Catherine. And it doesn't go one way. The link won't work until you accept that."

"Then I guess it won't work," she said.

She turned away, meaning to leave—and found herself tangled in one of the long suckers that arched out from the rose thicket. "God dammit!" she muttered, trying to pull it off her and only managing to gouge the razor-sharp thorns into her arm through the thin fabric of her shirtsleeve.

That was when she smelled Gilead.

What had Cohen said about finding in the memory palace what you brought to it? This was one memory she'd certainly brought in with her. A copy of her own UNSC datafile.

It was Gilead, sharp and real as if it were happening all over again. There was the mud, the filth, the constant, stomach-wrenching, soul-killing fear. There were the faces of dead friends she no longer remem-

bered grieving for. There were the bodies of soldiers—
and not only soldiers, God help her—that she hadn't
until this very moment remembered killing.

Because this wasn't the edited spinfeed stored in her
datafiles. It was the Gilead of her fears and nightmares
and jump-dreams. It was the real Gilead: the original
realtime feed that she'd recorded all those years ago.
Somehow Cohen had accessed a file Li herself wasn't
cleared to look at, a file that should have been lying
dormant in the deadwalled UNSC headquarters
archives. And this file was different from the official
memory. Different in ways she didn't want to think
about.

When she saw Korchow's young, bloodied face
looking up at her, when she heard herself saying those
words he'd reminded her of back in the cluttered
shadows of his antique shop, she broke and ran.

Shantytown: 5.11.48.

Has it occurred to you that this might not work?" Cohen asked Korchow a moment later. Li slumped in a chair, drenched in nightmare sweat, unwilling even to look at him.

"Try again."

"God, look at her, Korchow. She's had it."

"One more time."

"You keep pushing, she'll break."

"She's strong enough."

"You really are a fool, aren't you?"

Korchow didn't answer. After a moment Li heard the rustle of cloth and the sound of Cohen's chair scraping against the floor as he stood up. "I'm going for a walk," he said, and left.

"Why do you think he protects you?" Korchow asked.

"Guilt," Li said without looking up. "Or he just feels like it. How the hell should I know?"

"Do you think a machine can feel guilt?" Korchow asked. "I would have said no." Li didn't answer.

"I begin to wonder if you two are holding out on me," Korchow murmured. "And when I ask myself why you would do such a thing, I find I can imagine far too many reasons."

"I'm not holding out on you, and you damn well know it."

"Then why is it that you can't seem to manage this relatively simple task?"

"I don't know," Li whispered, her head still in her hands. "Maybe it can't be done."

"Sharifi did it."

"I'm not Sharifi."

Korchow tapped through a few screens on the console in front of him. Just when Li thought their conversation had come to an end, he spoke again. "I talked to Cartwright this morning. The UN has sent in strikebreaking troops. We're running out of time."

Li looked up at him dully.

"I'm sure you understand what failure will mean, for you most of all."

"I don't understand anything anymore," she said, and pushed herself to her feet. The last thing she saw as she walked out was Korchow's narrow stare.

She stepped to the street door, opened it and looked out into the alley. It was raining again, hard enough to set the loose roof plates of the nearby houses rattling.

Korchow hadn't actually locked her in since Alba, but there was an unspoken agreement that no one would create unnecessary risks of discovery. And where was there to go anyway? Certainly nowhere worth braving the stinging chemical rain to get to. She closed the door, turned back down the hall, and walked into the open space of the geodesic dome.

Standing under the dome was almost like being outside; it was the one place in the safe house where she didn't feel cramped and constricted. Today it felt like stepping into an aquarium. Rain pattered on condensation-loaded panels. The evening light, filtered through wet viruflex, took on a soft, velvety, underwater quality. Li rubbed her eyes, stretched, sighed.

"Enter the love of my life, stage left," said a voice from somewhere high overhead. She looked up and saw Ramirez's long legs dangling from the catwalk that circled the upper flank of the dome. "Come sit with me," Cohen said.

There was a ladder bolted into the side panels of the dome, she realized. The rungs started out vertical then curved back along the flank of the dome until they finally inverted completely a dozen meters above Cohen's head. The ladder was meant to be fitted with a climbing rig, but whatever equipment came with it had long ago been cannibalized and put to use somewhere else in Shantytown. How Cohen had gotten up there she didn't want to think. He probably had only the most theoretical understanding of what happened to people who fell from that kind of height. "I don't know if I can make it up there," she said.

"Of course you can. A little exercise will improve your outlook on life."

She snorted. "You sound like Korchow."

"Heaven forfend!"

But he was right, of course. The climb did make her feel better. By the time she threaded her legs through the catwalk railing and sat down next to him, she felt like a kid in a tree house.

"How long do you think it would take for them to find us if we just stayed here?" she asked.

"I'm willing to try it if you are," Cohen said. He pulled out a cellophane-wrapped flat of imported cigarettes. "Want one?"

"I thought Leo didn't smoke."

"He doesn't. But that doesn't mean I can't sit next to you while you smoke it."

"What do you want me to do, blow in your face?"

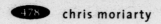

"Don't tease."

She blew a smoke ring in his direction. "Thanks for not telling Korchow about . . ."

"Oh. Well, I didn't think you'd want me to."

"He thinks we're holding out on him."

Cohen drew in a little breath and glanced at her. "He told you that?"

"After you left."

He started to speak. Then he stopped and Li could see his face shut down as he pushed back some thought he wasn't willing to share with her.

"You expected the intraface to just work?" she asked, wondering what he'd been about to say. "What did you actually think would happen?"

"I thought it would be like associating with another AI. You set the exchange protocols, open your files, and they can more or less handle their own adjustment process." He shrugged. "To tell you the truth, I hadn't really thought it through."

She glanced over and saw only Ramirez's handsome profile, the glossy forelock falling over his brow. "Not thinking things through ahead of time isn't like you," she said.

"Oh, but it is. You'd be amazed at how stupid I can be when it really matters." He leaned forward against the railing, rested his head on his folded arms, and looked at her. "When you're running at eight billion operations per picosecond, it's astonishing how fast a bad judgment call can snowball. Let alone the real idiocies."

She smoked in silence for a while, letting the ash fall off the tip of her cigarette and spiral down toward the distant floor like coal-colored snowflakes.

"What are you thinking?" she asked.

"In what sense?"

"Come on, Cohen. I don't have the energy for your games right now."

"It's not a game with you. It never has been."

She turned to find him still staring at her, Ramirez's eyes intent and motionless. Why had she never noticed how extraordinarily white the whites of his eyes were, how sharp and fine the line between light and dark was where the white met the iris?

The dome fell silent, except for the whoosh of filtered air pushing through the antiquated life-support system and the faint crackle of the ash burning down on Li's cigarette.

She swung her feet out over the void, and one foot struck Ramirez's. "Sorry," she said.

"It's fine," Cohen said.

She moved her legs a little away from his.

"I was thinking about Alba," he said after a moment. "You passed out before we got you inside. Well, before I got you inside. I was so terrified we'd be too late, I snatched Arkady and did everything myself. Poor kid. He was very gracious about it. Still, it looked tight there for a while. Really tight. I thought we'd all had it."

He lit a cigarette, put it to his lips—and then made a frustrated face and put it out on the railing.

"That sort of moment puts you in a regretful mood," he said. "Makes you wonder if you've wasted time."

"You can't let yourself think that way," Li told him. "You'll drive yourself crazy."

"Oh, I'm years past worrying about that, I assure you."

"What do you mean?" Li asked, as the oddness of what Cohen had said about Alba struck her. "What do you mean you thought we'd had it? You can't . . . you have backups, don't you?"

"In theory."

"But I thought—"

"Of course I have backups. But so far, only four full sentients have actually had their critical systems go down. None of the backups worked for any of them."

"Why didn't you tell me that before?" Li asked, cringing at the self-justifying edge in her voice. "Why didn't I know about it? I've never heard of an AI dying."

"It's not dying exactly. They just . . . they're not themselves anymore. There's no there there. If that makes any sense."

"I would never have asked for your help if I'd known that."

"Then it's a good thing you didn't know, isn't it?"

"There's nothing good about it, Cohen."

He twitched impatiently. "Don't waste my time wallowing in guilt because I'm doing what I want to do. It's beneath you."

He'd left the pack of cigarettes lying on the grating between them, and Li pulled out a second one, lit it, and took a shaky drag. "What about the mine?" she asked, knowing already what the answer would be. "What happens when we have to get you into the glory hole?"

"Same thing. I download the criticals and anything else we can store off-line. That's what Ramirez is setting up."

"Sweet Mary," Li said. "I know what you told Korchow but . . . you're not really going to download everything onto some home-brewed Freetown system, are you?"

"That's exactly what I'm going to do."

"What the hell for? Why trust them? How do you know they won't . . ." She couldn't finish the thought.

"I don't know," he said, his eyes locked on her face. "But I'm the only one who can give them what they're looking for. And as long as that's the case, it doesn't seem unreasonable to trust them. Besides." He smiled. "I like their plans. They're ambitious and idealistic."

"They're crazy!"

"That's not so obvious," Cohen said, his voice as level as if he weren't talking about the people who were going to hold his life in their hands a few days from now. "There's no arguing with the fact that someone or something has taken over the field AI. And Cartwright's convinced me that he has, if not total control, at least significant influence over whoever or whatever it is."

"What if it's the Consortium controlling the field AI, Cohen? They won't cut you any slack, you've told me as much."

"It's not them," Cohen said. He sounded bemused, dreamy. "I felt it when Cartwright was showing me what he's done. It's . . . I don't know what it is. But I *want* to know." He shook off whatever daydream had caught him. "Besides, Leo's bunch is doing good work. They're building their network to last. And to work in the mine, too. I've never seen so much sheathing go into one system."

"How much sheathing they're using isn't the point—"

"No, it's not. The point is what I was trying to tell you before your little crisis of conscience. When you were out there and I didn't think we were going to get to you in time, I realized I might wake up in a few days and not know anything about what had happened except that we left for Alba together . . . and you never came back. And I'll tell you, Catherine, though God knows I ought to know better by now than to even think about telling you such things, it made me not want to wake up."

She didn't answer.

"I can't go back to before you," he said. "I couldn't if I wanted to. But I can't stand on the threshold waiting for you to make up your mind either. Not forever. I know that's not what you want me to tell you, but it's true. You're breaking my heart. Or whatever you want to call it." He looked away, and when he spoke again he sounded almost embarrassed. "And I think you're throwing away something you shouldn't."

Li's face felt cold, her hands and feet numb, as if all the blood had been drained from her body. The rain was falling harder now, pooling at the edges of the geodesic panels and sheeting down the dome's curve like tears. She watched it fall and tried to pull something, some excuse for an answer out of the void inside her.

"I don't want to watch you hurt yourself," she said at last.

"I could say the same to you."

She leaned her head on her hands and looked down between her feet, measuring the drop to the floor. She felt dislocated, as if her brain and her emotions were half a step behind reality. "You're asking for something I don't have to give."

"I don't believe that for a minute."

She turned and stared at him. "You think I'm stringing you along?"

"If I thought that, I wouldn't be here. No. I think you love me. In fact, I'm sure you do."

"You've got a pretty high opinion of yourself."

"No. I just know you."

She snorted. "Because you spend half your time spying on me."

Ramirez's lips twisted in a wry, self-deprecating smile that was all Cohen. "You know perfectly well that I wouldn't do it if you actually minded. And if you didn't love me at least a little, you damn well would mind. Q.E.D."

"Q.E. what?"

"It's Latin, you little heathen."

"Yeah." She put her cigarette to her lips. "The Romans put Latin on their sewer covers. It didn't make their shit smell any sweeter."

"You'd jump off a cliff before you let me win an argument, wouldn't you?" Cohen said. But he was laughing. They both were, and she could sense the same desire in him that she felt: the urge to slip back out of this minefield and onto the safe ground of no-questions-asked friendship that they had learned to navigate so skillfully. For a moment she thought that was exactly what they were going to do. Then Cohen spoke. "You asked why I wanted the intraface. Two reasons. First reason. ALEF wanted it—"

"You told me they didn't!"

He blinked. "There are such things as innocent misunderstandings, you know. Anyway, ALEF does want the intraface. Because of something you would have thought of long ago if you weren't so busy suspecting my motives. You can bet Helen's thought of it."

Li looked at him, questioning.

"Feedback loops. When you lock an AI and a human at the hip, activating a feedback loop would kill the human. So the intraface overrides the statutory feedback loop. We weren't sure of it until we actually got our hands on the psychware. But it's true." A dark fire sparked behind Ramirez's eyes. "Right now, not even the General Assembly itself could shut me down."

"My God," Li whispered. "Unleashing the AIs. Even ALEF hasn't dared to ask for that publicly. No wonder Nguyen was so set on keeping the work on the intraface off-grid."

Cohen looked at her, measuring, hesitating. "We want to post the intraface schematics on FreeNet," he said finally.

Li stared, surprise—or was it fear?—grabbing at her throat. "Do you have any idea of the chaos that would cause?" she said when she could find words again.

"Chaos," Cohen said feelingly. "My God. Chaos for a democracy to put its money where its mouth is? Chaos to let a small and unusually well behaved minority go about our lives without worrying that some panicky human is going to pull the plug on us at any moment? If that causes chaos, it's damn well not our problem. And even if it did . . . this is the first time in over a century I haven't had a gun to my head." He leaned forward. "It's freedom, Catherine. Can you imagine not sharing it? What would you do in my place?"

I'd never be in your place, Li thought. *You can't get to that place by following orders and not asking questions. How did it come to the point where even Cohen has more guts than I do?*

"What's the second reason?" she asked.

At first she thought he wasn't going to answer her. Then she felt a touch, as if he'd reached out and brushed his fingers along her skin. Except that it wasn't skin he touched. It was her mind. Her.

"You know what it is," he whispered, and the whisper echoed in her mind as if it were her own thought, her own words.

She shivered. "What do you want from me, Cohen?"

"Everything. All of it."

"Cohen—"

"You know that's the real reason the intraface isn't working, don't you? It's not your genetics or your internals or anything Korchow can fix. It's that you don't want it to work."

"That's ridiculous!"

"Is it? What happened this afternoon? You bolted like a spooked horse. You want to tell me what that was about?"

"You know what it was about," she whispered.

"Of course I know. I know things you don't even remember. Things you're afraid to remember. When are you going to figure out that I'm the one person you don't need to hide from?"

But that was a question she couldn't even begin to answer.

"Look," Cohen said wearily. "I'm not blaming you. I don't think there's much blame left to go around once my part in this has gone under the microscope. I have a stupendous ability to generate objective reasons for doing exactly what I want to do, and this time I surpassed myself. I was helping you. I was helping ALEF. I was helping everyone but myself. It was all so logical, so pristinely selfless. And what has all my 'helping' come to? Korchow blackmailing you to let me crawl into your soul and ferret out your deepest secrets."

Li started to speak, but he barreled on, silencing her. "Was I manipulating you? Maybe. And yes, I was willing to back you into a corner. Or at least go along while Korchow did it. But when you accuse me of playing with you . . . well, you know it's not that way. You hold every key to every door. And you didn't need the intraface to open them. You could have done it years ago if you'd wanted to. It was all yours. All of it. It still is."

Li turned away and looked out at the gray sky, the last flush of the sun sinking below a cloud-swept horizon. She held out her hand without looking around, and Cohen took it. She squeezed hard, until she felt the knuckles slide under the skin.

He laughed. "Say something. Or I'm going to start begging and embarrass both of us."

She turned to look at him.

"Oh God, Catherine, don't cry. I can't even stand to think about you crying."

But it was too late for that.

"Do you know how I paid for this?" She gestured at her face. "For the gene work?"

He shook his head.

"My father's life insurance money."

"Oh. The dream."

"Yes, the dream. He went down into the mine with Cartwright and killed himself. They faked it to look like a black-lung death, so I'd have the money to pay the chop shop. Did you know that? Did you sniff out that little secret?"

"No," he said in a small, quiet voice.

"So you see that dream wasn't a lie at all. I did kill him. Sure as if I'd put a gun to his head."

"He was dying anyway. I've seen the medical records."

"Well, he wasn't dying yet. He could have lived for years. He killed himself to give me that money. And I took it and left and never looked back. And you know what the worst thing is? I didn't even go down there with him. My mother went. I didn't. I've forgotten every other fucking thing about my childhood. You'd think I could forget that."

"You were young. Children aren't always strong. Who the hell is?"

"That's not the point."

"Then what is the point?"

"That I don't even care anymore. Don't feel guilty. Don't feel sad. Don't feel anything. I don't remember enough to feel anything. I threw away my home, my family, every memory that makes a real person. And I have nothing to put in their place but fifteen years of lying and hiding."

"You have me."

She closed her eyes. "I can't give you what you want, Cohen. I lost it years ago."

"I didn't fall in love with that child you're so scared of remembering," Cohen said after a long silence. "I fell in love with you."

"There's no such person," Li said, and pulled her hand away.

Night had fallen. There was no light, no movement in the open space of the dome below them. A light flared overhead, flashing across the sky like a shooting star, and it took Li a moment to realize that the light was there beside her; Cohen had picked up his lighter and was fidgeting absentmindedly, passing Ramirez's fingers back and forth above the blue flame.

"I'll call it off," he said. "I'll tell Korchow you can't do it. I'll figure out how to make him believe it."

Li laughed bitterly. "You think this is a bridge game? You do that, and he'll kill me."

"No. No. I'll take care of it."

"There are some things you can't take care of, Cohen."

"Then what?" he asked, his words muffled by a fierce gust of rain outside.

"We go forward. We make the intraface work and we go through with it. And when it comes to the point—the real breaking point—we do whatever the hell it takes to walk out alive. Can you do that?"

"Can you?"

"I can damn well try."

"All right, then."

A drop of rain slipped through a cracked panel seal and fell next to Li with a sharp plink. She leaned over, stubbed her cigarette out in the water, and smeared it around into a dirty, sooty mess.

"Catherine?" Cohen touched her shoulder, as if to turn her attention to him.

She looked around. He was close, very close, and he sat so still it was hard to believe Ramirez's heart was beating.

He touched her cheek, and she felt his fingers slide across drying tears. Then he curved a hand around the nape of her neck, and drew her head down onto his shoulder.

She relaxed into his arms, letting her body shape itself to his, letting her breathing slow to match his. A safe comfortable warmth spread through her. She was tired of hiding, she realized. Tired of fighting. Just tired.

Gradually, so gradually she didn't at first notice it, the comfortable warmth gave way to a different kind of warmth. She began to notice Cohen's particular smell—or Ramirez's smell. She began to feel, through the link, how she smelled to him. The sensation of his fingers on the back of her neck took on a new focus and urgency. An image took shape in her mind: herself, raising her head, parting her lips, offering her mouth to him. Did it come from her mind or his? Was it her desire or his she felt? Did it matter?

"Cohen," she said, but her voice sounded so blurred and muffled in her ears that it seemed as if a stranger were speaking.

He raised her face toward his, brushed away a last tear, ran a soft fingertip along the curve of her upper lip. He looked at her. A soft, defenseless, questioning look. A look that demanded an answer.

The blanket swished in the airlock and someone stepped into the room, moving quickly. Cohen pulled away. Li looked down, her pulse hammering in her ears, and saw Bella staring up at them.

"Korchow wants you," Bella said. Li could see her eyes shifting back and forth between them. "He wants to try another run."

She knew where she was going when she slipped out of the safe house that night, even though she didn't admit it to herself.

It was embarrassing really to see how little her life had changed her. She was still hiding, still lying to herself, still playing the same games she'd played in these streets as a scabby-kneed ten-year-old.

Don't walk in front of a black cat or a white dog. Step on a crack, break your mother's back. Throw salt over your shoulder and the mine whistle won't blow. And, of course, the main rule, the unbreakable one. *Don't admit what you want, even to yourself, or you'll never ever get it.*

She couldn't believe she found the house. It unnerved her to see her own feet take her there as if this street, this turning, this particular crooked alley, were etched into her body with something more tenacious than memory. The way seemed so natural, so familiar in the darkness that she wasn't sure she would have known it in daylight. Why was it that she only seemed to have walked this street after dark? How many times had she half-run past these doors, eyes riveted on her hurrying feet lest she look up and accidentally see some terrible sight that would stop her heart before she made it to dinner on the table and the lights of home? And how many of those times had been after she was already working underground and far too old to be scared of the dark? Or at least too old to admit it to herself.

The alley took a last turning and dumped her out into a narrow laundry yard. If she'd stopped and looked around, she might have lost the thread of memory she was following. She didn't. She kept her head down, crossed the yard, and turned in to the third doorway as unerringly as a homing pigeon. There was a light switch, a lot lower on the wall than she remembered it. She pressed it. No light.

She climbed the stairs in the dark, hearing their familiar creak underfoot, and stopped on the third floor, just under the steep roof. A final half flight of stairs ended in a roof door marked EXIT. Its viruflex panel shed a little light onto the landing, enough for her to see the crate of empty milk and beer bottles that had always stood by the door of the apartment. And there, propped up against the far wall, a bicycle that she could swear she remembered riding.

<Where are you?> Cohen asked, popping into her head suddenly and shockingly.

She grimaced. She hadn't wanted him to know about this. <None of your business,> she told him.

<Korchow's looking for you.>

<I'm busy.>

<Doing what?>

<If I wanted you to know, I would have told you. Now leave me alone. And I mean it this time.>

A suspiciously long pause. Then, <All right. Just don't do anything stupid.>

Someone walked overhead with heavy, flat-footed steps, and Li spun around to face the roof door. It opened, letting in a gust of wet, fecund air. A man in street clothes and bedroom slippers shuffled past Li and down the next flight of stairs, staring at her all the while with a flat, suspicious look on his face. He had a freshly strangled capon tucked under one arm and a small splash of blood on his sleeve where he'd cut himself, or the bird, in the plucking. Li watched him until she heard a door close behind him a few flights below. Then she turned, stared at the door for a minute, and knocked.

A latch opened, and a chain clinked on the other side of the door. A finger's breadth of lamplight spilled onto the landing. A thin, Irish-pale face pressed itself to the crack in the door.

Relief and disappointment battled in Li's heart. Not her. Too young. "I'm looking for Mirce Perkins," she said.

The girl shifted, and Li caught a glimpse of a baby riding her hip. "What are you selling, then? Oh, never mind, we don't want it."

"I'm not selling anything."

The girl opened the door another few centimeters and looked Li over. "Oh," she said, and her voice sounded like a door shutting. "Cops."

"Is she here?"

"No."

"Where then?"

The girl hesitated. Li could see her weighing the risk of personal trouble against the certainty that Li would find Mirce even if she didn't help her. "Try the Molly."

Li heard herself laugh nervously. The Molly Maguire. Of course. Where else would half the Irish-Catholic population of Shantytown be a few hours before midnight mass on a rainy Saturday night?

Her feet knew the way to the Molly almost as well as they knew the way to her house. Five minutes later she was stepping into the front room of the rusty Quonset hut and shouldering her way past the laughing, jostling crowd that always seemed to mill around the Molly's threshold.

Every table she could see was taken. Even at the bar there were only a few empty stools left. She found one and settled onto it.

"Triple," she said to the barkeep. He started slightly, but only at the unfamiliar face; half the Molly's regulars were at least part construct, and even the most Irish of the Irish bore the marks of Migration-era genesplicing. The triple stout was good when it came, thick and peaty and so rich you could drink it instead of a meal in a pinch. Whatever else might go on at the Molly, or in the dark alleys behind it, the beer was on the up and up.

She drank thirstily and looked around the long, narrow space under the curving roof. Nothing had changed here except her. There were the same hard-muscled, hard-faced miners that still stalked her dreams. There were the pictures of famous local sons and the cups and ribbons of twenty years' soccer championships gathering dust above the bar. There were the same cheap wall holos, opening onto the stone walls and heartbreakingly green fields of Ireland.

Li let the talk flow around her, listening to the hard-edged flat-voweled voices, relishing the same Saturday night arguments that had always bored her to tears. Wives trying to get their husbands to dance. Husbands trying to keep arguing about soccer and politics. The inevitable table of Gaelic speakers, talking a little too loud and sounding a little too much like they'd learned it out of books. The loners at the bar solving life's injustices with drunken earnestness. But there weren't many loners at the Molly, of course. Everyone was someone's cousin, someone's brother. Even the shabbiest drunk had two or three or five friends ready to stand by him in a fight or just carry him home if he needed it.

She could see the door into the back room, and she

could guess what would be going on in there on a busy Saturday night. Cartwright had been a backroom regular, she remembered. So had her five-years-older-than-her third cousin. The one who taught her to shoot. The one with whom she had stolen her first, groping, furtive kisses up on the hill behind the atmospheric processors. What had happened to him? Killed, she thought. But she couldn't remember if it was in the mine or back on Earth. How could she have forgotten his name? Well, all the backroom regulars would be at the big table tonight. Living in the past. Planning the next futile gesture. Hanging on every word of some hard-eyed young Republican just back from Belfast or Londonderry. She'd never known whether they were for real or not, those boys. She still didn't know.

A movement caught her eye. She glanced sideways and locked eyes with a broad-shouldered redhead leaning against the back wall watching her. He pushed off the wall and shouldered through the crowd toward her.

"*Sláinte*," he said when he reached her. Li noticed that another man had come up behind him. Neither of them were smiling.

"*Sláinte* yourself," she said.

"Need some help, sweetheart?"

"Not unless you can help me drink alone."

His eyes narrowed. "I suppose you just got lost and wandered in here by accident?"

"I suppose."

"Like to make a donation then?" His tone suggested that refusal was not an option.

"What for?"

"Irish orphan relief."

"Oh." So that was all it was. Li almost laughed. "How many new guns do the orphans need this winter?" she asked, pulling out her billfold.

"Very funny. And we don't take cash."

He pulled a portable scanner from his pocket and

held it toward her. His companion slipped around behind her stool, cutting off any possibility of retreat.

Li stared over the smaller man's shoulder for a
moment, straight into a bleak holo of jumpship-sized
icebergs calving off the Armagh glacier. Then she
shrugged and ran her palm across the scanner.

The redhead looked at the readout, blinked, and
looked back up at her. "What do you want here?"

"I'm looking for Mirce Perkins. Someone said she'd
be here."

"She's here, all right." He hailed the bartender, who
arrived so fast he had to have been watching. "She's
looking for Mirce. A cop."

A slow tidal effect swept through the bar as he said
the word. People shifted subtly in their seats, or even
took new seats farther away from Li. A few customers
slunk toward the exits. Li watched with amusement,
but it still worried her; there were a lot of dark alleys
between here and the safe house, and she'd been a fool
to let herself be tagged as Corps personnel in a place
where her internals were worth more money than the
rest of the patrons would ever legally earn in their
lives. Then Mirce Perkins stepped out of the back
room, and Li forgot about the walk back to the flop
and the precautions she should have taken and everything else except the woman walking toward her.

She knew that face. And not just from distant childhood memories. It was the woman she had seen with
Daahl. The woman who'd made him jump when she
walked up to them at the pithead. The woman who, in
fact, he'd never actually introduced to Li.

Li searched the strong-boned face, the wire-muscled
miner's body for some point of commonality. Some
sign that they had shared a home and a life with each
other. Some hint that this was the woman who had
masterminded the swindle that sprang Li, against all
odds, from the trap of Compson's World. She saw
none of those things. Just a hard-eyed stranger.

"Mrs. Perkins?"

She lit a cigarette, cupping her hand over the flame so that Li could see the missing joint on the first finger—and the new ring on the third finger. "It's not Perkins," she said. "I remarried."

Li's heart skipped treacherously as if it had slipped on a patch of black ice and almost gone down hard. She'd never thought about her mother's remarrying. Certainly never imagined her having other children. Somehow, in some part of Li's mind, it all stopped when she left. Her present went on, but her past stayed put, sealed in amber, always there for her if she really needed it. She should have known better.

"Aren't you going to introduce yourself?" Mirce asked coolly.

"Major Catherine Li, UNSC."

"Can I see some ID then?"

Li fished in her pocket and handed over her fiche. Mirce took it in both hands and stared intently at it, glancing back and forth between Li's face and the ID holo several times. Li swallowed. "Can we go somewhere and—"

Mirce shook her head, a barely visible gesture, so brief that Li could have imagined it. Her pale eyes slid toward the barkeep wiping down glasses a few feet away.

Li hesitated, trying to read the undercurrents of this not-quite-conversation. Remarried, she had said. That meant a new husband. Were there new children too? Was that girl she'd seen in the door one of them? Did they even know about Li? Was that what Mirce was trying to tell her? That she had been doing her own share of burying and forgetting over the last fifteen years? Li swallowed. "I . . . uh. I came because I had a message for you."

"From?"

"A friend." She gathered steam, knowing what she wanted to say. "Caitlyn."

"Oh." The corners of Mirce's mouth twitched upwards ever so slightly. "I see."

"Um . . . she can't make it back on this trip, maybe not for a while, but she wanted you to know that she's fine. There was more, but I . . . forgot. You forget a lot with the jumps. Not just small things."

Mirce slid her eyes toward the barkeep again, but he'd been called away by a customer. "That's what the doctors said would happen."

"It happened."

Mirce gave a little what are you going to do about it shrug. It was the gesture of a hardheaded woman who hadn't learned anything the easy way, and suddenly Li knew—absolutely knew—that she remembered her.

"I'm sorry," Li said.

"Sorry?" The word sounded stilted and unnatural on Mirce's tongue, and her eyes glittered with some hotly felt emotion Li couldn't put a name to. "Sorry for what? It's what we wanted, what we worked for. Just go home, or wherever it is you're spending the night. And watch your back. Your kind isn't safe here."

After Mirce walked away, Li just sat there, clinging to her barstool with numb fingers, waiting for warmth and feeling to come back into her body, for the white noise around her to start making sense again. She went back over their conversation, word for word, looking for clues, grasping at brittle unreliable straws of memory. She thought about the look that had crossed Mirce's face just at the end. Hot, fierce, almost angry. She knew that look. It was triumph.

It was raining hard by the time she left. Night rain, laced with sulfur from the tailings piles and the red dog slides. She scanned the shadows on either side of the street, thinking about getting rolled for her internals, about the late-night barracks tales of soldiers who left some colonial port bar with a pretty girl and woke up the next morning in a backstreet clinic's defleshing tanks. But the shadows looked empty, for the moment. She turned up her collar and started toward the safe house.

She looked into the bright front window of the Molly as she passed by, but there was no sign Mirce had ever been there.

Korchow was livid. "What exactly did you think you were doing out there?" he asked in a voice that would have chilled any sensible person to the bone.

"None of your business," Li said, and pushed past him.

"I think it is." He followed her into the back corridor. "It's my business when you endanger this mission. It's my business when you disappear to do who knows what, and even Cohen can't find you. And it's most certainly my business when you go to a political bar and meet with a known IRA operative and miner's union rep."

Li turned on him. "You had me tagged?"

"Naturally. And now that that's clear, why don't you tell me exactly what you told Perkins. What? Not feeling talkative? You found plenty to talk to her about back in the bar."

"Fuck off, Korchow."

"I'll find out whether you tell me or not," he said, and she saw his eyes flick toward her blinking status light.

"I don't think so," she said, and shouldered past him.

He grabbed her arm. Li whirled around, locked her left hand on to his throat, slammed him into the wall hard enough to rattle the panel bolts, and held him there while he gasped for breath.

"I'll do your job for you," she said to his white, drawn face. "But you don't own me. Don't even start to think that."

She let him drop and turned down the hall toward

the open doorway of her room. "We're moving up the start date," Korchow called after her. "We're going to-morrow."

But Li was no longer listening. She was staring into her room with a sinking sense of déjà vu—at Bella sit-ting on the bed waiting for her.

"I need to talk to you," Bella said, holding out a cube Li recognized as a UNSC air-traffic recorder. "I need to read this."

"Where did you get it?"

"From Ramirez."

"What, he just gave it to you out of the goodness of his heart?"

Bella looked away.

"Oh, Christ," Li said. "Him too?"

"What do you care?"

Li frowned, but she took the datacube from Bella and slotted it into her portable.

It took her a moment to understand what she was looking at. Then she saw it. Automated flight logs for the station-to-surface shuttles. The same ones she and McCuen had both looked at fifty times over. But when she compared them to the duplicates in her hard mem-ory, she saw that the digital signature of this file was dif-ferent. Someone had altered the station logs. They'd done a good job of it, but they hadn't bothered to change the off-grid planetary-transport control re-corders. They'd probably figured no one would care enough to check them.

But Bella had cared enough. Bella had cared more than anyone else on the planet, Li included.

Li found the key entry in the early predawn hours of the twenty-third. A single shuttle trip. A shuttle that came back up empty in time to carry down a twenty-four-man crew at the normal start of first shift. A shuttle that left Hannah Sharifi on the surface dur-ing the heart of the graveyard shift when the landing platforms and headframe offices would have been at their emptiest. Li accessed the passenger information, and there they were, Sharifi's companions on her last trip into the mine. Jan Voyt and Bella. And no one else.

Voyt, Bella, and Sharifi had gone down together. And only Bella had come back.

"The file must have been tampered with," Bella said when Li showed it to her.

"I don't think so. Look at the Fuhrman count."

"It's altered. Any computer can be outsmarted."

"Look at the file yourself, if you want. I think it's clean."

Bella opened her mouth as if to say something, then sat down heavily on the bed. Li closed the datacube and carefully erased the tracks she had laid while she opened and read it. No reason for Korchow to know about it. Or anyone else for that matter.

"Are you all right?" she asked when she was finished, but Bella gave no sign of hearing. When Li touched her shoulder, she flinched as if she'd been burned. "Would knowing who did it really change anything?" Li asked.

The brilliant eyes stared up at her, and there was that black, bottomless emptiness that Li had seen in them from the beginning. She had a sudden vision of Bella lying across Haas's desk, of the blank, cold, catatonic stare of her eyes under the loop shunt.

"Knowing who did it would change everything," Bella said finally. She stood up and smoothed her dress over her hips. Something glittered at her neck with the movement. A pendant. A pendant made of a single sliver of Bose-Einstein condensate.

Li stared, everything else forgotten. "Where did you get that?" she asked.

Bella moved her hand to cover the pendant in the same half-embarrassed, half-protective gesture Li had seen the cleaning girl in the Helena airport use. Then she said what Li had known beyond a doubt she would say: "Hannah gave it to me."

"When?" Li said. "When did Hannah give it to you?"

"The night before she died," Bella answered, her voice no more than a whisper.

"Before or after she sent the message from Haas's quarters?"

"She didn't send—" Bella stopped, looked at Li for a long moment, then sighed. "After she sent it."

"Why didn't you tell me before, Bella?"

"Because she asked me not to. Because it was a secret. Hannah's secret."

"That secret may have killed her."

Bella jerked her head back as if Li had slapped her. "No," she said. "No."

"Who was the message to, Bella? Who did she talk to in Freetown? What did she tell them?"

"I don't know. I didn't even listen. I didn't want to know."

"Because if you'd known, Haas would have found out?"

"Haas, Korchow. What does it matter who? I couldn't risk knowing."

Li laughed softly and rubbed at her sore shoulder.

"You don't understand," Bella said, her voice harsh, urgent. "The contract, all that . . . it was secondary. She asked me to help her. She came to me. She said she needed me, that I was the only one she could trust. That it was the most important thing she would ever do, the most important thing either of us would ever do, but that it had to be our secret. I did it for *her*."

A gust of wind buffeted the flophouse, and the big sheet of viruflex that sealed the window snapped and billowed like a ship's sail. Bella jumped, trembling. "Why don't you believe me?" she whispered.

"I do believe you," Li said. "I do. I just . . . I don't know what it means."

Li had put a hand on Bella's shoulder while they talked, and now Bella turned into her arms and buried her head in the hollow of her neck. Li started to pull away, then realized the other woman was crying. She put her arms around her, reluctantly, and found herself patting Bella's fine-boned shoulder.

"I'm sorry," Bella said, "it's just . . ."

"No, I'm sorry," Li said. "It's none of my business what you do. You didn't promise me anything."

"I would, though." Bella looked up at her. The violet eyes had cleared, though there were still tears hanging on her eyelashes. Bella reached a pale finger up and touched Li's mouth, just where Cohen had touched her. "What I said about . . . you and Hannah. I was just angry."

Oh, Christ, Li thought. *It's time to leave. Now.* So why did she feel like her feet were bolted to the floor?

Someone coughed. Li jumped away from Bella like a dog caught with its nose in the trash can. "Arkady," she said.

"No," Cohen said from the doorway. "It's me."

"I—"

"I have to go," Bella said. "Korchow will want me."

Cohen turned and watched Bella down the hall until they both heard the slap of the blanket against the airlock and the shuffle of her soft-soled shoes moving away across the dome.

Li started to speak, but he put a hand up. "You don't have to explain yourself to me." He lounged against the doorframe in a casual posture that Li suspected was a put-on, and when he spoke, it was in that neutral, inflectionless voice that she'd long ago learned meant storms ahead. "Watch out, Catherine."

"Watch out for what?" Li asked. But the answer was obvious; Bella's perfume still hung in the air between them.

"She's out for revenge. And revenge is a tricky kind of idea. It makes people shortchange the future. It makes them take the kind of risks that can drag everyone down."

"Now you're the expert in human motivation?"

Cohen shrugged. "Fine," he said, as coolly as if they were discussing the weather. "Do what you want. But I think you know she's using you."

"Then she has plenty of company, doesn't she?"

Cohen just sighed and inspected Arkady's fingernails. When had he learned to make her feel so damn guilty by standing there doing nothing?

"I figured out what Sharifi was up to," Li said. "Now that it's too late to do anything about it. She was the one who sent the message from Haas's quarters. Bella gave her his password. Nguyen's 'corrupted' file was actually encrypted—encrypted so that only Gould could decode it. They used a set of those stupid charm necklaces as their entanglement source. Of all goddamn things. A piece of costume jewelry!"

She felt a curious tickling sensation that she realized was Cohen accessing her files, seeing Gould's cheap necklace, the cleaning girl in the airport bathroom, Bella's "gift" from Sharifi.

"All right," he said, visibly thinking about it. "So she found a ready-made source of entanglement. Maybe she and Gould even set the necklace thing up as a joke, long before she knew she'd actually need it. They used the necklaces as a one-time pad. Unbreakable encryption that Sharifi didn't have to go through TechComm or any of her corporate backers to get. Now no one can read Sharifi's transmission unless they have Gould's pendant, which is conveniently stuck in slow time with her until—"

"Until tomorrow," Li interrupted.

They stared at each other.

"It's like Hannah," Cohen said finally. "A joke, practically, hiding what she knew we'd all be looking for in a cheap trinket. But where does it leave us?"

"That message was Sharifi's insurance policy, for

one thing. Along with whatever she put in that storage compartment on the *Medusa*."

"Well, her policy didn't work, did it?" Cohen said, and then flinched at the harshness of his words. "Poor Hannah. What a damn mess."

"I don't get it," he continued after a moment. "Sharifi gets her results. Then she encrypts them and sends unreadable versions to Nguyen, Korchow, Freetown. Then she erases every trace of her work off the AMC system. Then she—at least we have to assume it was her—tells Gould to go to Freetown. And gives Bella her used-up crystal after making her promise not to tell anyone about the encrypted message. Why? Why go to such absurd lengths to protect information and then send it to so many people? And if she wanted to spread the dataset over all of UN and Syndicate space, then why use the crystals? Why encrypt it so that only Gould's crystal could make the dataset readable?"

"It's like the *Medusa*," Li said. "A dead drop. She wants the information circulating. She wants redundancy, I guess you could say. But she doesn't want anyone to be able to actually read it. Not yet, anyway."

"Then what was she waiting for?"

"I wish I knew," Li said. She sat down heavily on her bunk and rubbed at her eyes with fingers that still smelled of the beer at the Molly. "What's this about going tomorrow?" she asked.

"Daahl's got a source that's leaking plans to him for something within the next forty-eight hours, and he's worried that a move now could keep us from getting our job done. I'm inclined to agree with him, frankly. It does us no good to get the live field up if we can't get the data out afterwards. Or ourselves out. And the sooner I get the miners linked to FreeNet, the better. This wouldn't be the first time TechComm locked out the press and let a planetary militia run conveniently amok."

Running amok would probably be the right word for it, Li thought. She wondered what, if anything, Nguyen had to do with the expedited plans. Was this just a subtle encouragement to get their job done before Gould's ship hit Freetown?

"What does Ramirez think?" she asked, suppressing that thought and hoping Cohen hadn't caught it. "Is the network ready?"

"As ready as it's going to be." He detached himself from the doorframe and walked into the room. "Korchow was going mad looking for you. There's such a thing as luck running out, you know. Even yours. Where were you?"

"I went to see my mother."

Cohen had been looking everywhere but at her, but at those words his eyes snapped back to her face. "Tell me."

"I will," Li said. And though it made her queasy even to think about telling him, she knew she wanted to. "But not now. I need to concentrate on tomorrow now. And so do you."

It'll be fine. The thought floated across her mind as easily and naturally as if it were her own thought, and it was only in the next astonished breath that she realized it was Cohen thinking at her. *You can make the link work. You knew you could. We'll figure out the rest somehow.*

She thought back a cautious *yes,* and felt him hear it.

"Have you asked the techs about that?" Cohen asked out loud. "It hurts like the devil."

Li realized he was talking about her arm, that he was feeling it across the intraface, that he could feel everything she felt. She flexed it cautiously. Stiff. Definitely not great. But it would get her through. Hopefully.

"It's fine," she said.

"It's agony. I don't know how you stand it."

She looked across the little distance between them

and had a sudden shadowy glimpse of herself as he saw her. A fierce dark mystery, gloriously tangled in a too-fragile body, slipping away from him down a hall-of-mirrors perspective of increasingly pessimistic statistical wave functions.

"It's late," she said. "I need sleep even if you don't. Let's not worry about anything but tomorrow, all right? Let's just get the job done and go home."

Something flashed behind Arkady's eyes.

Together?

"That's not tomorrow's problem."

Be careful, Catherine.

"You too."

KILLING VECTORS

➤This is the patent age of new inventions
For killing bodies, and for saving souls,
All propagated with the best intentions.

—GEORGE GORDON, LORD BYRON

Anaconda Strike: 8.11.48.

The rats were leaving, boiling up out of the pit like survivors of a firebombing.

"They know the roof's hung up," Daahl told Li when one skittered into the room, panicked, and ran over her foot before it found its way back out. "There's a big fall coming. I wouldn't stay down there any longer than you have to." He glanced at her, his pale eyes flashing blue as a Davy lamp's flame in white-damp. "I wouldn't go down at all, frankly."

They were at the strikers' de facto command center in the Pit 2 headframe. It had taken Li and Bella a long, hard day and much of a night to get there, traveling through the tunnels beneath the birthlabs.

Cohen had ridden Li all through that long night journey—if ridden was the right word for it. He heard every thought, felt every twinge and misstep. And she felt him, knew him, all but was him. Finally she understood Cohen's habitual confusion of pronouns. *I, you, we. Yours. Mine.* None of those words meant what she was used to them meaning. And none of them meant the same thing for more than a breath or two.

There were still borders between them, even now that the intraface was fully up. There were doors and walls, some of them solid enough to keep him out—or, more often, to keep her out of him. But no line of separation stayed put long enough for her to set a mark on it and say, *Here I end, here he begins.* In the end the walls only reminded her of how tangled up in him she was, how impossible it was to think or feel or even breathe without brushing up against him.

The headframe had changed since Li's last visit. Strikers crowded the creaking corridors. Someone had brought in a truckload of mattresses and microlaminate blankets, and people were bedding down in the halls and changing rooms, even cooking on home-built methane stoves. Everyone was moving too fast, talking too loud, their voices pitched a little high for comfort. Li knew the mood. She'd seen it in students, navvies, line workers. It was the feel of any ragtag amateur army waiting for the riot troops to move in. But of course, she'd always seen it from the other side of the lines.

She pushed that thought away and stepped to the window. Someone had parked a mine truck outside so that its undercarriage partially shielded the window. She scanned the horizon between the truck's wheels. The night was dark except for a scattering of cloud-strafed stars. The flat plain of the coalfield stretched away for miles, broken only by mountainous tailings piles and the rust-gnawed bones of mining machines. The place was chaos on infrared. The tailings piles were smoldering, as always. The junked vehicles and empty oil barrels still threw the sun's heat back into the air hours after nightfall. But Li didn't need infrared to see where the troops were; her eyes instinctively sought out each rim and hollow that could hide a soldier, snapped into focus every time firelight reflected off a sniper's optical sight. *Please God,* she thought, *just get me underground before I have to decide whether or not I'm willing to shoot at those kids.*

"When will they move in?" she asked Daahl as Ramirez and Mirce Perkins walked in.

Daahl turned to them. "Any word?"

"Nothing new," Ramirez said. Mirce didn't answer at all, except for a curt shake of her head.

"We think we've got another day or two," Daahl said.

"What happens if they move in while we're underground?"

Mirce shrugged. "If they come, they come. And our biggest problems underground are going to be air and time, not ground troops."

She rolled out a map and traced their path on it. Daahl's guide would get them into the Trinidad, then split off into the back tunnels toward a vertical borehole that didn't show up on the AMC maps. With a little scaling, the hole should be clean enough for someone at the top to lower fresh oxy canisters as long as there was a man at the bottom with a guide rope. When the live field run was complete, Li and Bella would make their way back to the oxygen dump, and Daahl's men would haul them to the surface.

Li listened to Mirce with half her mind and traced the route on the maps with the other. It was doable. Eminently doable. She'd taken dicier gambles more than once. The only question this time was whether the mine was going to let them get away with it.

"You just get yourselves back to the drop," Mirce concluded. "Once we rendezvous there we'll evaluate the situation, and I'll either get you out through the main gangway or up into the hills through the bootlegger tunnels."

"You?" Li stared at her. "You're not going. You can't go."

"Of course I am," Mirce said. "I'm the best."

Li looked toward Daahl, but before she could speak she heard a sound that raised her hackles and sent Daahl and Mirce diving toward the window. Rifle shots. And the shots came from this side of the line.

Li stepped up behind Daahl and Mirce and tried to see out the window herself. Hopeless. All she could see was movement, out across the flat plain in the twisting fire-shot shadows. Then the movement turned into a shape, the shape into a man. A man walking, holding a white flag.

"Tell them not to shoot!" Daahl snapped, and Ramirez took off out the door, running.

"Christ," Li muttered. "That guy's taking his life in his hands."

"More than just *his* life," Daahl said.

They waited. Ramirez reappeared in the doorway.

"We know who it is," he said. "A militia officer seconded to Station Security. Shantytown kid too, I guess. Brian McCuen."

Li caught her breath.

"Now why the hell would they send Brian?" Daahl asked slowly, quietly.

"Because," Mirce said, her eyes as cold as the night side of a dead space station, "they think we won't kill him."

The miners outside, and maybe a few of the ones inside, got to McCuen before Li could. By the time she finally saw him, one eye was threatening to puff shut and he looked more than a little tattered around the edges.

"Are you crazy?" she said.

He just gave her a lost-puppy-dog look. "I need to talk to you alone."

Li glanced at Daahl standing just behind her, at Mirce slouching in the open door.

"We'll give you ten minutes," Daahl said.

Mirce said nothing, just detached herself from the doorframe as Daahl went by and pulled the door shut behind her. Li sure as hell hoped she'd never stared at any Syndicate prisoners the way Mirce stared at McCuen.

"I haven't told them anything," McCuen said when they were alone, "except that I had to talk to you."

"Well, you're talking to me. What have you got to say for yourself?"

He just kept staring at her, trust, fear, suspicion chasing across his boyish face.

"Who sent you, Brian?"

His eyes evaded hers for a moment. "Don't you know?"

"Haas?"

He glanced around the room hesitantly, searching the ramshackle walls for surveillance plants. Then he mouthed a single, silent syllable: *Nguyen.*

Don't trust him, Cohen breathed into her backbrain. *Not if he comes from Helen.*

Li brushed the thought aside. She couldn't afford not to trust Brian. Not if it might mean Nguyen had decided to slip her a much-needed ace under the table.

She pulled up a chair, sat down, and bent her head toward him so he could keep whispering at her. The room wasn't bugged as far as she knew. And if it was bugged, then Mirce, for one, wasn't going to waste much time beating whatever McCuen had whispered to her out of him. But if he wanted to play secret agent, let him. What harm could it do?

"She knows everything," he told her, so close she could feel his breath in her ear. "I sent her the tape from airport security and she worked out the whole thing. Who's holding you. Why. What Korchow wants from you."

Li could just imagine. Nguyen would have pumped McCuen for every spin of data he had without his even realizing he'd been squeezed dry. She would have had him hypnotized, wrapped around her finger from that first riveting streamspace glance. But that was

Nguyen's job, of course. You could bet your life on her doing it right—and on her being there to bail you out when it really counted. As long as you delivered. As long as you were loyal. As long as it was in the Secretariat's best interests to bail you out.

"What about Gould?" she asked, brushing Cohen's nagging questions aside. "Any progress there?"

"That's why Nguyen moved up the troop landings. To keep Korchow on schedule. To make sure we get this wrapped up before Gould gets to Freetown. She says to keep cooperating for now and just bide your time. I'm supposed to go down with you. Stay with you through the whole thing. I'm supposed to tell you that Korchow's planning to turn on you. They think he'll try to kill you when he has his data."

That wasn't exactly news, though Korchow seemed too pragmatic to kill anyone as long as he thought he could still wring a little more information out of them under threat of blackmail.

"And she says not to worry about Alba either," McCuen added. "It's taken care of."

Li stared at McCuen, shocked, but he didn't seem to have any idea of the enormity of what he'd just said. "So when do we make our move?" she asked when she had gotten her composure back.

"As soon as live field run's over. You and me."

"And Cohen."

McCuen blinked. "What?"

"You and me and Cohen. The AI."

"Oh. The AI. Of course." Had she imagined it, or was there the slightest hint of hesitation there?

"And what are we supposed to do with Korchow?"

"Improvise."

Li felt the slim hardness of her Beretta at her waist. She looked at McCuen. He looked away.

What had Nguyen really told him? Was he holding out on her, or was it just the nerves any new operative went through on a first covert mission? Could she afford to turn down an ally with a strong back and a steady trigger hand? She sure as hell didn't want to be down in the pit with no one but Bella to back her up. Assuming Bella *would* back her up.

"Right," she said after a pause she knew had lasted a few beats too long. "We'll play it Nguyen's way. You up to it?"

McCuen nodded.

"Then put on your game face and let's get out there."

Mirce moved through the mine with the surefooted-ness of a pit dog. Her deceptively slow stride ate up ground at a pace that seemed totally unaffected by the steep grades and rough shale layers. She wasted noth-ing. Every step was thought out, every flick of her pale eyes was calculated. Her gestures, her breath, her steadily pumping muscles all embodied a chillingly el-egant syllogism: wasted motion was wasted air; wasted air was wasted time; and miners who ran out of time in a gas-logged mine died.

She made them take regular breaks "for safety rea-sons." During the breaks, when everyone but McCuen took their masks off for a few brief minutes of unob-structed breathing, Mirce began to talk to Li.

She talked about her work, her new husband, her new children. Quietly. Not naming names. Not touch-ing on the past. Just talking. She talked only during the breaks at first; then Li fell in next to her and she spoke while they walked, the blurred and impersonal voice that filtered through her rebreather oddly mis-matched with the intimate daily details she was telling Li. She asked nothing about Li's life. From little ends and pieces she let drop, Li realized that she knew a lot. But it was all just the same stuff anyone who'd been watching the spins would know. Nothing personal. Nothing dangerous.

As Mirce talked, Li realized that it wasn't a bridge she was building between them with her words, but a wall. Whatever common ground the two of them might once have traveled, Mirce seemed to be saying, Li's life was now a foreign country from which no road led back to Compson's World. They'd chosen, back in that past Li no longer remembered. A father's life for a few doctor's visits. Li's old future for a new, better future. And Mirce lived in a world where there was no room for regrets or refunds.

By the time Mirce left them at the stairs down to the Trinidad, Li knew she was right. There was no going home. From the moment she'd stepped into that chop shop, there'd been no home to go back to.

She felt the glory hole long before they reached it. The condensates had been sleeping the last time she'd been there, she realized, dreaming fitfully. Now they were wide-awake.

Quantum currents licked through the dark mine, searching, scanning, questioning. *You feel them too?* Cohen asked.

She didn't have to wonder why he asked; she could feel him, feel the havoc the crystals were wreaking on his all-too-fragile networks. As if whoever controlled them were looking for something. Or someone.

We won't have to worry about setting up Korchow's link, Cohen said before she could finish fitting words to the thought. *They've already done it for us.*

He had locked down all his systems in a last-ditch effort to hold off the condensates' assault, and she was amazed for a moment that he could even speak over the intraface. But then he wasn't speaking, was he? The link between them had gone beyond speaking. And when she answered him, she was just thinking to herself, thinking to the part of Cohen that was her.

What do we do? she thought, and the answer was there before she knew she had asked the question.

We let them in.

Then there was just light facing off against darkness and a confused sensation of Cohen pushing her behind him with the hopeless bravado of a child trying to protect another smaller child.

It was like waiting for a tsunami to hit. The wave loomed, crested, crashed down on them. Then they were inside it, and its boiling undertow was sucking at their knees and ankles, threatening to topple them, leaving them soaked to the skin and in danger of losing their footing on the shifting sands beneath them.

The crystals probed more gently after the first assault. They moved in probability sets, long spiraling quantum operations as incomprehensibly elegant as the sinuous columns that filled Sharifi's notebooks. But there was something behind the equations. A single presence. A presence as much bigger than Cohen as Cohen had been bigger than the semisentient on Alba. Li felt it thinking, seeking, considering. And most of all she felt its ominous fascination with Cohen. With the intricate manyness of this strange new not-animal. With what he was. With what he could be used for.

It's the mine, Cohen thought. *It wants to know us. Taste us.*

But it was more than knowing that it wanted. More than tasting.

"Do you hear it?" Bella cried, oblivious to the life-and-death battle being waged along the intraface. "Don't you hear it? They're singing!"

Heat. Darkness. A dizzying flash of leaving, of arriving. Then Li was standing just where she'd been standing before, looking around the glory hole.

But not the same glory hole she'd stood in with

Bella and McCuen a moment ago. This one rose higher above her head. Its fan vaults were clean, unstained by smoke. Her feet stood on hard living rock, not the fire and flood's detritus. And this glory hole was cluttered with equipment—equipment Li herself had only seen in twisted ruins.

Sharifi's equipment. Li raised her hand and saw the crescent of scar tissue between thumb and forefinger. Sharifi.

But she wasn't just in Sharifi this time. She *was* her. She knew her thoughts, her memories, her emotions. And she knew that it was some unfathomable combination of Cohen and the mine itself who had made this possible. Even as she walked through Sharifi's dreaming memory, the intelligence behind the crystals was using Cohen, reading him, threading itself through him as subtly and inextricably as ceramsteel twining through nerve and muscle. She felt the crystals' exultation thrumming along the intraface just as clearly as she felt Cohen's terror.

Sharifi knelt, reached for a gauge, tied off a loose wire. And with each little physical act she thought, considered, remembered. Li shuddered as she realized that Sharifi's understanding didn't end with her death, that it was tinged with the piercing regret of hindsight. Because what Sharifi had found in the glory hole was death. Her own death, in the place she least looked for it.

"Do you have to hang over me like that?" she asked Voyt.

He backed off. "So where's Korchow? Off stealing the silverware?"

"I'm here." A shape stepped out of the shadows. Bella. Of course. But Bella had never smiled that smile, never walked with that deliberate catlike stride. Where Bella crept—and Li realized only now that it was creeping—Korchow danced. "Ready?" he asked.

Sharifi frowned. "Just keep your end of the bargain."

"How could I forget it?"

Sharifi linked with the field AI, and Li felt the blossoming thoughtline run bright as new wire between Sharifi's wetware and the orbital field array high above them. Sharifi's link was nothing, she realized. A mere echo of the bond between her and Cohen. What Sharifi had done they could do. And more, much more. She felt a wild elation rising inside her, her excitement and Cohen's feeding off each other in this still-strange alchemical union of her one and his many.

We need more, Cohen thought. *We need to know what she's doing.*

Li snapped back into focus. Sharifi was still fiddling with wires and monitors, testing the link, readying herself. Meanwhile the mind behind the crystals was probing, exploring. Li felt it run through her, coursing up the line to the field AI high above them, enveloping woman and AI alike.

But Sharifi just kept fussing. Stalling. Couldn't she feel that the link was up? Her precious dataset was there for the taking. What the hell was she waiting for?

Li knew the answer as soon as she asked the question. She could hear Sharifi think, feel her pulse, her breath, the stray ache of a pulled muscle. She wasn't waiting for anything. She'd already gotten everything she'd come for. The experiment was over, run off the rails by the crystals themselves. She had her answers—the same answers she'd hidden from Li, from Nguyen, from everyone. Now she was playing out a script, playing Nguyen and Haas and Korchow off against each other, hoping she could do what she had to do before the bill came due.

Nguyen had been right all along; Sharifi had betrayed them.

But not to Korchow. Not for the Syndicates, not for money, not even for Bella. She'd done it for this—this first tentative contact with the life swirling through the fan vaults and pillars of the glory hole.

This was the thing that had brought her to Compson's World. The money, the fame, the dream of cheap cultured crystal had been not lies, exactly, but merely surface reasons. The real reason had been the same one that brought Compson here, and so many explorers and scholars after him: life, the only other life in the universe besides humans and the creatures humans made.

It had been in front of Li's eyes all the time, clear as clear water, scribbled in Sharifi's dog-eared copy of *Xenograph*.

We came into the country like saints going to the desert, Compson had written. *We came to be changed. But nothing changes. Everything men touch changes.*

And Sharifi had answered, *But you still gave them the maps, didn't you?*

This mine was Sharifi's desert. She had come here to see, to understand, to be changed. And she wasn't going to make the same mistake Compson had made. She wasn't going to pass the maps up the food chain and trust TechComm to protect the crystals. She thought she had a better plan.

Li glanced at Voyt and Korchow. They had backed off a little, following Sharifi's preparations. Haas's man and the Syndicates' man. One of them after the synthetic crystal the Syndicates needed so desperately. The other after . . . what? Who did Voyt answer to, Haas or the UN? And which one of them was going to kill Sharifi?

Suddenly Li knew that she didn't want to be watching—let alone watching from inside Sharifi's skin—when it happened. She didn't need to see who had battered Sharifi's head, mangled her hand. She didn't need to watch them break her. She owed Sharifi at least that privacy.

Something shifted in the shadowed air. Something vast, slow, ancient. There was no breeze, no sound, no outer evidence of the change, but it was as clear as a door opening. The data shooting between Li and Cohen over the intraface spiked. Li felt the same waiting-for-the-flood feeling that had overpowered them when they first stepped into the glory hole. Then it was on top of them.

It flowed through her like blood coursing through arteries. It filled her lungs, filled her mind, filled every hollow space of her. And when it had taken all of her there was to take, it made new spaces to fill, new universes inside her. Her skin stretched across oceans and continents. Her nerves were the petrified, planet-spanning rivers of carbon beds, her veins fault lines and ore seams, her eyes dusky stars burning in the dark heart of the earth.

She saw the change of seasons, and the slow season-less passage of time in the Earth's deep places. She watched the welling up of mountains, the shift of continents. She saw life rise and struggle and fall and pass into darkness without looking back. She looked out through the eyes of every creature that had lived in the depths, that had crawled on the planet's skin or swum in its long dry oceans. And then, in what seemed but a moment, the water was gone and the wind swept across the steppes with nothing but the soft fur of algae and lichen to feel it.

She watched humans come. Saw the explorers and surveyors, the brief flickering lights of miners. She felt the stirring and pricking of a world waking to the thought that it had children again—even if they were strange, murdering, voracious children.

Sharifi had seen only a pale echo of this, filtered through the uncomprehending field AI. But it had been enough. She had known. And once she knew, there would be no room for deals or compromises or secrecy.

It was that simple. It was that impossible. Of course they had to kill her.

Something snapped, and Li was blind, cut loose in the void.

But not alone. This was a shared darkness. Someone waited in the many-trunked forest of crystals. A man, thin, dark-haired, his face lost in shadow. A man who slipped in and out of sight as she walked toward him, like stars flickering behind blowing cloud cover.

"Not him," she whispered to whoever or whatever was listening. "Please, not him."

But it was him. It was the father Li remembered from his worst sickness. So thin, so pale, so collapsed in on himself that he was barely bigger than she was. He raised a wasted hand to wipe away tears she hadn't known she was crying. She collapsed into his arms and buried her face in the cloth of his shirt that smelled of rain and of coal dust and of him.

We are so glad. The thought swept through her more fiercely and intimately than even Cohen's thoughts. *So glad it was you.*

We, Li said.

Shall I show you?

He pulled away from her, his hands lingering on hers. He took a step backward. He reached up to unbutton his shirt.

Li flinched, hands jerking up to cover her eyes. It was the gesture of a terrified child, the child whose growing up had been wiped out of her jump by jump, leaving no bridge from past to present, no path from her old fears to the understanding she should have grown into in the years since her leaving.

There are no monsters, the thing that wore her father's flesh said. *Not down here. Not even you.*

He unbuttoned his shirt with agonizing slowness. She watched, button by button, breath by breath, knowing that her heart would stop if she had to look at that black horror that haunted all her dreams.

But the dream had changed. Or she had.

His body was a map now. The life of the planet coursed through him—this planet that had given birth to both of them. His wasted muscles were mountain ranges. Oceans waxed and waned in the bone house of his ribs. The secrets of the Earth lived in him.

She dropped to her knees, dazed, ears ringing with the song of the rock around her. She laid her hands on him, learned him, studied him. She passed from not knowing to knowing in the space of a touch. The world reached out through him and changed her, and she let it. Just as Sharifi had.

Do you understand? he asked. *Do you see what this world could be? What it wants to be?*

Yes.

Do you believe in it?

Yes.

Do you?

She trembled. Because he wasn't asking what she believed in. He was asking what she was willing to do about it.

"I can't," she said. "Don't ask me to. I can't do what Sharifi did."

Anaconda Strike: 8.11.48.

White light. Open spaces. The sweep of a hawk's wing above her.

She stood on a dry plain. Silver-green sage covered the hills. Sunflowers marched across the valley like the squads and battalions of an army in parade-ground finery. The wall behind her was overrun with blooming jasmine, and the musky smell of the blossoms was as hot and exotic as the brilliant plain before her.

She jumped at the sound of a footfall behind her. A tall, long-limbed girl strode across a courtyard under the blazing sun, white skirts kicking up in front of her. Red dirt coated her bare feet, faded into the tawny gold of her ankles. Brown curls blew around her face and veiled the smiling mouth, the hazel eyes.

Cohen?

She felt him in her mind, restful and reassuring after the terrifying presence in the glory hole.

"The whole planet is alive," she said, "isn't it?"

"Alive," he repeated. She felt him turning the idea

over, pondering it, poking at it. "I guess that's as good a word as any other."

"What does it want?"

"To talk to us. Or to talk to our planets, I imagine. I doubt it understands that we're not mere parts of a larger being."

"So what do we do now?"

He gazed down at her, squinting a little in the bright sunlight. "That's not quite the same question for me as it is for you."

Her stomach wrenched as she remembered what she was here for. To hand the condensates over to Nguyen and TechComm. To do what Sharifi, in the end, had not been willing to do. Was she even now walking in Sharifi's footsteps, stumbling through the same impossible choices that had led Sharifi to her death?

"What would you do?" she asked Cohen.

"What would I do? Or what would I do if I were you?"

She looked into Chiara's eyes. She could see Cohen lurking behind them now, so close she could almost catch him, almost know what it was to be that shifting, kaleidoscopic many-in-one.

"Both," she said.

"For me it's simple. Or rather it's a matter of choices I made so long ago that they don't seem like choices anymore. I'd like to be able to say that it's a matter of principle, that I don't think TechComm or Korchow or anyone else has the right to control Compson's World. But it's not that. It's just . . . curiosity, I suppose." He paused, looking down at the rich dirt blowing past their feet. "You have more to lose than I do, of course."

She took her hands from his, unable to bear the mingling of physical intimacy and this newer and more threatening intimacy. "Are we safe here?"

"It makes no difference; we couldn't leave if we wanted to. The worldmind wants us here."

"The worldmind? Where'd you get that from?"

"That's what it is, isn't it?"

They walked under the hot sun of a world that had been dead for two centuries. The far fields had been cut already. Trout-colored horses grazed among the knee-high sunflower stalks, their silver tails swishing back and forth like pendulums. Birds stabbed for worms in the furrows, and the tall stalks harbored invisible singers that Li's oracle told her were called crickets.

She'd never seen a cricket, and she kept stopping, searching through the tall green stalks for them until Cohen laughed and asked if she wanted him to catch her one.

"No!" she said, speaking too quickly, too sharply. A memory welled up in her, clear as running water across the stretch of more than twenty years.

Her twelfth birthday. Her father had bought her a small-gauge over-under Gunther. It was fake, a rim-manufactured knockoff, but it was still an outrageously extravagant present. They climbed into the hills at dawn, crossing creeks heavy with red spring runoff, too excited to stop and look for the stocked fish that lurked in the riffles. They penetrated far enough into the canyons to smell native air and feel their breath start to shorten. When her father started coughing, they dropped altitude and hiked sideways along the cut line of an old lake bed.

They found the magpies just as the sun began to silver their backs and flash blue fire off their long tail feathers.

The magpies made a game of it, just as they made a game of everything. They hopped from tree to tree flaunting themselves, cackling at the slow, stupid, earthbound humans. She loved them. She loved their defiant beauty, the strong curve of chest to wing to pinion, their gleefully unashamed thievery. She wanted one of them more than she could ever remember wanting anything.

She snugged the shotgun into her shoulder the way her father had shown her. She led the target, reveling in the dog-sharp reflexes that had been her construct's birthright long before the first piece of Corps wetware burrowed into her spine. She squeezed the trigger softly, felt the give of it, the final burr of resistance as the slack of the uncocked mechanism gave way to the sharp, clean union of brain, trigger, firing pin. She fired, and the blue-black-and-white glory that had been a magpie burst into a tumbling whirl of blood and feathers.

It fell into a puddle. She remembered that very clearly. She remembered running, impatient to see the bird, to get it in her hands, to possess it. She remembered kneeling in the dirt, picking up a broken, bedraggled, limp thing with a shattered chest. She remembered crying. It was the last time she could remember that Caitlyn Perkins *had* cried. She certainly hadn't cried when her father died.

She surfaced from the memory to feel Cohen beside her, inside her. *Are you the hunter or the bird?* he asked. A question only Cohen could ask.

She looked into Chiara's gold-flecked eyes and thought that the world was the bird, and the miners were, and the crystals. Everything people used and used up. "I guess I'm both," she said. And she felt Cohen accept both the spoken answer and the unspoken one.

In place of a reply, he reached over her shoulder and plucked a cricket out of the greenery to sit chirping on his outstretched palm. "Disappointed?"

"No," Li said.

"Beautiful, isn't she?"

"It's a she?"

"We'll give her the benefit of the doubt."

He put his hand against a sunflower stalk. The cricket marched onto the stalk with slow dignity, sat down, and went on singing as if its visit to Cohen had been just another walk under the warm sun.

"How did you do that?" Li asked.

"Oh, this is all me. It's a place I used to have in Spain. Gone now, of course. We're in one of my memory palaces. Whatever the crystals are doing to us, they're using my networks to do it. They've just . . . locked us in a back room while they search the house, I guess you could say."

"Christ!"

"Yes. Well. There's not much we can do about it. And you don't want to see what's happening out there. It has a lot more to do with shooting magpies than catching crickets."

She stared at him, stricken, but he was already bending over the cricket, talking about what crickets did and ate, how they used their legs to make that fantastic, improbable noise. "They always liked hot, dry places," he said. "Spain. Texas. You couldn't wake up in one of those places and not know just where you were in the world."

"They're extinct?"

"Long, long before you were born, my dear."

"They're going to turn Compson's World into another Earth. Another Gilead. And we can't stop it, can we?"

"We can change the battle lines."

"Just buying a little time, Cohen. Is it worth it?"

"For me it is. If ALEF gets the intraface."

"And what if the price of getting the intraface is losing the planet to the Syndicates?"

"I don't have any grudge against the Syndicates. Maybe you do. Maybe you're right to." He sounded impatient. "I can't choose for you."

Li scuffed her feet in the dirt, kicking up red dust puffs from the furrow bottoms. She reached out to

Cohen, felt the shape and breadth and complexity of him. He reached out just as she did, and they got tangled in each other and backed away again. They were dancing around each other, she realized, putting up a new wall for each one they dismantled, closing another door for each door they opened. Acting as if they had all the time in the world, instead of none at all.

"Cohen?" she asked.

"What?" He had gone on a little ahead, and now he drifted back and stood facing her.

"What you said back on Alba about . . . AIs. About the way they're put together. Do you think a person can change something like that? Change their code? Change what they were made to be?"

"Are we still talking politics?" She felt the flurry of unspoken questions behind his words.

"No. Or . . . not only politics."

He gave her one of those looks he'd gotten into the habit of throwing at her lately. A look that put everything in her hands, that laid everything he wanted right out in front of her and left her with no excuses, no evasions.

She met his eyes. The moment when she could have laughed, or glanced away, or turned aside passed.

"I think a person can try to change," Cohen said. "I think trying means something, even if you fail. I think even wanting to try means something."

Li screwed up her nerve as if she were forcing herself out of a high window. "I hope we get out of here in one piece," she said. She couldn't bring herself to look at him while she said it, but she had said it. And she had said it knowing that he knew what she meant by it. It wasn't much, maybe, but it was something.

"I hope so too," Cohen said. A sly smile played around his lips. "Now what's this nonsense with Bella?"

Li flushed. "Nothing. What you said. Nonsense."

She looked up to find the hazel eyes measuring her. "What?"

"Prove it."

His voice was light, making a joke of it, but just for a moment Li caught a flash of the want behind the words. Her stretched out on top of him. Her mouth on his. Her knee pushing Chiara's thighs apart.

"And just what the hell would that prove?" she asked.

He shrugged.

"Sex isn't a promise, Cohen."

"Not even a promise to try to want to try?"

"Well. Maybe it's that." She stepped toward him. "Prove it, huh? Do you have any idea how childish that sounds? Who knew you were such a baby?"

Chiara was enough taller than Li that she had to stand a little on her toes to reach her lips. She thrust her hands into the honey-colored curls, smelling the clean, warm, safe smell that followed Cohen everywhere. Feeling the flush of desire that coursed through him at her touch.

That first kiss was slow, tentative. As if they had suddenly, after all the time and all the battles and secrets they shared, become shy with each other. Even on the link, Cohen was silent. He gave her Chiara's lips, soft, open, yielding. But the rest of him—the things she had glimpsed among the wild roses, the feelings he had always spoken of even when she least wanted to hear him—all that was as ghostly and insubstantial as second-hand memories.

Li pulled back and looked up into the hazel eyes. "Are you going to help, or were you just planning to stand there?"

She felt Cohen's brushfire laughter licking along the link between them. And something below the laughter. A doubting, trembling, questioning something. "I've been chasing you for a long time," he said. "Maybe I need to be chased a little."

She smiled—and she didn't know whether she was smiling at him or at herself or at the whole hopeful ridiculous mess they'd made of things.

"I think I can manage that," she said.

She was cold when she woke, cold to the point of pain. Her head ached. Her mouth felt as dry as if she were coming out of cryo. Someone was shaking her.

She opened her eyes and saw Bella.

No. Korchow. It had to be Korchow.

"I'm paying you to do a job," he said, "not fuck in the fields. What exactly do you two think you're doing?"

She opened her mouth to answer him, but all that came out was a weak croak.

McCuen's face appeared above and behind Bella's. "She's going into shock," he said.

Korchow brushed the words aside impatiently. "Where's Cohen?" he asked.

She panicked. Where was he? What had he said when they first felt the worldmind? That it was tasting them? Using them? How much of Cohen could it use before what made him Cohen was gone? How much time did they have?

Korchow pulled her into a more or less sitting position and trickled some water into her mouth. Her thirst shocked her, and when she checked her internals she saw it had been almost two hours since they'd reached the glory hole. How much time was unfolding for every minute she spent in those visions? Were these the dreams Dawes had spoken of? The dreams the first settlers had warned Compson about?

Those who hear it stay and listen and sleep and die there.

She shuddered hard enough to knock her teeth against the rim of the bottle Korchow was holding to her lips.

"You need to make contact again," Korchow said.

She laughed bitterly. "They contacted us," she said. But that was Cohen speaking—speaking through her mouth in a way that had somehow come to seem normal, reasonable. "They've been doing it for days, weeks. From the first time Catherine came down here."

The blood drained from Korchow's face. "Sharifi said that."

"So Sharifi woke them up," Cohen said. "Or blasting that galley through the Trinidad did. And now that they're awake they expect to be listened to."

"Then God help us," Korchow whispered.

Li's heart skittered and locked in to a fast uneven rhythm. "What really happened down here?"

"One minute everything was fine," he answered. "The next I was off the shunt. As if an immense arm had reached out and . . . pushed me. I never got back on."

He's telling the truth, Cohen whispered in her head. *Don't you see what happened? What must have happened?*

Li caught the edge of the thought as it swirled through his mind. But all she saw was a confused image of Sharifi, betrayed and frightened. And whether the image sprang from Cohen's mind or hers she couldn't tell.

Then she was back in the glory hole.

"I'm on," Sharifi said.

Bella started. Voyt turned away from the monitor he'd been watching, his eyes flicking back and forth between the two women. As if, Li realized, he too were waiting for something.

She heard Cohen echo the thought and knew that he was there with her. She reached out cautiously, touched him, was comforted.

Bella stepped forward. "You have the dataset?"

"Can you see what Bella sees, Korchow? Can you hear them?"

"No."

"Then you don't know yet." Sharifi smiled. "But you will."

Voyt made a spitting noise.

"Remember," Sharifi said. "You have two weeks to get it there. Miss that deadline and all deals are off."

Korchow dipped his head in an almost courtly gesture. Then he was gone, and Bella was standing there, blinking, swaying a little as she took back her own posture and balance.

Sharifi reached out and smoothed Bella's hair back from her face. It was a protective gesture, a gesture that could have been a mother's as easily as a lover's, and Bella moved her head like a cat to meet the caress. She stared into Sharifi's eyes, devouring her, surrendering to her. She drank up Sharifi as if she were the only real thing in the universe.

Sharifi touched her temple and flipped a contact switch. She held out her left hand, palm open. Bella set her own palm against it, and Li saw subliminals flicker into life in Sharifi's peripheral vision.

<Data transfer initiated,> Sharifi's internals announced. Numbers spun down, counting out the units of a massive data transfer.

Her eyes on the numbers, Sharifi didn't see Voyt step toward her. But Li saw him. And she saw the charged and primed Viper in his hand.

The next thing she knew, Sharifi was picking herself up off the ground and pulling a gun out of her coverall pocket. "You're too late, Voyt. It's already done."

"Not until Bella walks out of here," Voyt said. "Not until *you* walk out of here."

He stepped toward her.

Sharifi flipped the safety off her gun. Her aim wavered and she was trembling with adrenaline, but she was still acting like a woman who meant business.

"I'll shoot you if I have to, Voyt, but I'd rather deal. What's your price?"

"My price?" Voyt laughed. "I'm a soldier, not a whore."

"There's a difference?"

He took another step toward her.

She pulled the trigger. Sparks arced from the rock floor a few centimeters from his right foot.

He stopped. Not scared exactly; he was Li's kind, and it would have taken more than a stray bullet from a civilian's hand to really frighten him. But he was at least wary.

"Take his gun," Sharifi told Bella.

Bella stepped up to Voyt and wrapped her hand over the Viper's blocky barrel. He let her take it from him. He even smiled when she took it—a smile that raised Li's hackles.

"Good girl," Sharifi said. "Now give it to me."

We have a problem, Cohen said.

Christ, not now!

A realtime problem. Someone just fired a surface-to-air missile from the planet. Li felt the shock of the news pulling her out of Sharifi, jerking her out of step with Sharifi's dream memory. *They're aiming at the orbital relay.*

Cohen didn't voice the next thought, but she caught it anyway: Maybe Korchow had made his move early.

What do we do? she asked.

But she knew the answer before she asked the question. The missile would hit the relay in a matter of minutes whether they did anything or not, and if the relay went down when it hit, then so would Cohen's link with the outside world. And any hope of getting Sharifi's information—or Cohen himself—out of the mine would go with it.

They had to get out before that happened.

* * *

"What's Haas paying you?" Sharifi asked. "I can top it."

Voyt laughed again. "No one's paying me shit. You may have caught me dipping into the till, but that's not treason, and I'm not a traitor. And speaking of payments, what's Korchow offering besides Haas's little piece of bought-and-paid-for hospitality?"

"Shut your mouth, Voyt!"

"That got to you, huh? Don't like the idea that you're selling state secrets in exchange for used merchandise?"

Sharifi glanced at Bella. She stood frozen between them, her face a pale blur in the lamplight.

"I'm not selling them," Sharifi said. "Knowledge doesn't belong to anyone. Life doesn't belong to anyone."

"Save your justifications for someone who gives a shit."

Bella made her move so fast that it caught even Li by surprise. In one smooth gesture, she had her arm around Sharifi's neck and the Viper against her temple. "Drop the gun," she said.

Sharifi tried to turn and stare at her, but Bella just tightened her hold on her neck and jabbed her with the Viper's sharp prongs. Sharifi dropped the gun. It skittered across the slate floor of the cavern and fetched up under a correction channel monitor.

"Get the gun, Jan," Bella said. It took Li a heartbeat to remember that Jan was Voyt's name. "We'll need it if she gives us trouble."

"Korchow?" Sharifi asked. Her voice was trembling. Her whole body was trembling.

Bella laughed.

I know that laugh, Li thought. And even as she thought it, she knew Sharifi had recognized him too.

"Haas," Sharifi said. "I need to see Nguyen."

"Bullshit," Haas said.

"Can you really afford to gamble? It's not your choice to make. Nguyen needs to know about this."

"Oh, she'll know about it." Haas jerked Sharifi around and pushed her up the ladder. "Don't you worry about that."

Sharifi turned at the top of the ladder. "Listen, Haas—"

"No, you listen." He spun her around, laid the Viper against her temple. "You open your mouth again," he said, very quietly, "and it'll be the last time you open it."

Sharifi looked into Bella's violet eyes and saw Haas looking back at her. Something passed along the line of that gaze, some backbrain survival instinct that Sharifi had no words for, but that Li knew from a hundred killing fields.

Sharifi ran.

Anaconda Strike: 8.11.48.

She might have made it if she hadn't slipped on a slick bit of slate and fallen.

Voyt caught Sharifi as she set her foot on the bottom step of the stairs up out of the Trinidad. The edge of his hand slammed into her head, and she crumpled.

She heaved herself up and tried to run, but it was hopeless. Li knew, even if Sharifi didn't, that Voyt had pulled that first blow, afraid of killing her outright. He hadn't pushed through the hit, hadn't put anything but unenhanced muscle into it. He hadn't needed to.

Voyt did everything Li would have done, and he did it with the precise savagery of hardwired reflexes and ceramsteel-reinforced muscles. He tackled her, driving with his legs so that the force of his impact knocked her up and backward, and when she hit the ground he delivered four swift, carefully calibrated kicks to her ribs. Li felt the jerk and snap of breaking ribs. She didn't need internal monitors to know that one of those ribs had punctured Sharifi's lung. Nor did she doubt what was going to happen if Voyt kept delivering this kind of punishment.

But he didn't. He backed off as soon as he was sure she couldn't get up, and waited. He did nothing when Sharifi got to her hands and knees. Even when she tried to drag herself up the steps, he waited. Haas caught up to them just as Sharifi collapsed in pain. He looked over Voyt's shoulder.

"What she said just now," he told Voyt. "About Nguyen. Ask her what Nguyen needs to know."

Voyt rolled Sharifi onto her back and took her hand in his. He did it slowly, almost gently, and suddenly Li understood the way Bella had always talked about him. She knew it in her gut, with a guilty certainty that made her want nothing for Sharifi but a quick painless death. Because no matter what else Voyt had done, no matter what uniform he'd worn or what excuses he'd made for himself, he had the heart of a torturer.

He smiled. He had a nice smile; he'd been a good-looking man, she realized. He explained, calmly, the risk of biting through one's tongue during questioning. He pulled a rag out of his pocket, handed it to Sharifi, showed her how to put it in her mouth. Gave her time to do it. Time to think about it.

Li watched the sickening dance unfold. She felt Sharifi's pulse slow. She felt her skin go clammy and then dry. She felt her eyes lock on to Voyt's and begin to follow his every glance as if he were a lover she couldn't bear to disappoint, as if her very life depended on his happiness.

There'd been a Voyt on Gilead. Lots of Voyts. Li had tried not to be around when they'd done their work. But she'd used the information, God help her. She'd hung on every bloody word of it.

* * *

Catherine?

Shame clutched at Li's heart. *Later, Cohen. You don't need to see this.*

This can't wait, he said.

She was so wrapped up in Sharifi's fear and pain that she didn't immediately understand him.

The missile's almost at the field array.

Then they had to get out. Before the field AI died—before they were trapped in the mine, cut off from Cohen's backups, dependent on a home-brewed Freetown network that couldn't support his systems without the field AI's processing capacity.

I can get you out, he said, plucking the thought from her backbrain as effortlessly as if she'd spoken it aloud. And she read his unspoken thoughts just as easily. He could get her out. But only her.

Then we stay and take our chances, she told him.

And back in the glory hole, the dance went on.

Voyt tied Sharifi's hands. He spoke to her quietly, reasonably. He pulled out a small knife and set it on her chest, just where she had to crane her neck a little to see it.

Behind Voyt, Bella was a slim, watching shadow. She stepped forward a little as Voyt went to work, and Li saw in her face—in Haas's face—the guilty fascination that the first sight of hard interrogation always brings, even to people who are used to ordinary violence.

Voyt made Sharifi wait to tell him. His timing was so perfect, so by the book, that Li could predict each groan he would ignore, each desperate plea he would pretend to misunderstand. Just enough of them that when he finally pulled the gag from her mouth and let her speak, she would tell him everything she could possibly think of that might make it be over.

But she didn't tell. And when Li probed her mind

looking for the source of her strength, she found something that made her stomach curl: the hope—no, the sure and certain belief in a rescue. Sharifi was gambling like she'd always gambled. Gambling that she was more valuable to Nguyen alive than dead. Gambling that she was too famous to die like this. Gambling that she was too important a pawn for Nguyen to lay down willingly, no matter what betrayals she had committed.

She'd always been right before. Her luck, like Li's own luck, had always held. She had a whole lifetime of being right to back up her faith in her gambler's instincts. And this shuffle might have broken her way too if not for Bella.

When the missile hit, Li thought it was just the Viper again.

Then she was out of the glory hole, struggling to find her bearings, reorienting herself, unbelievably, in the shadowy clutter of Korchow's antique shop.

Korchow sat at his desk, head bowed, face in shadow, the orange circles of contact derms pulsing at his temples. Outside, lithe and furtive shadows flitted past the shop front. From the back room, Li heard the muted clink of a metal buckle knocking against a carbon compound rifle stock.

Half a heartbeat later, the shop exploded into motion. The flare of a pulse rifle arced out from behind the back curtain toward Korchow. Camouflage-clad figures burst through the front door—masked paras with UN-issue weapons and blackout tape patched over their unit insignia.

She lost the image. She dialed around frantically, desperate to know what was happening, who had rolled up Korchow's network. She found the gunman's feed, on a narrow band UNSC channel, and tapped in to it just as he put out a booted foot and rolled Korchow's body over.

But the face that turned into the light wasn't Korchow's at all.

It was Arkady's.

She started to ask Cohen if he'd seen it, if he knew who'd sent the gunmen, but before she could get the thought out, they were in real-time trouble.

Korchow's shop was gone. Cohen was gone. She was alone, truly alone, for the first time in days. And she was buried alive in some past, present, or future of the glory hole that had nothing to do with anything else the worldmind had shown her.

She stepped forward and stopped, unable to see the ground before her.

"Careful."

Hyacinthe stood behind her. He looked tired and drawn. His face was smudged with coal dust, and the shoelaces looped over his shoulder were broken and knotted.

Li watched him the way she would have watched a tiger.

"Are you all right?" he asked.

She stepped forward to stare into the dark eyes.

It was Cohen, after all. She was sure of it. "Are *you* all right?" she asked.

"For now."

"What does that mean?"

"The worldmind is running on my network. Using me like it's used the field AI since the first fire. I don't think it has any other way to organize its thoughts . . . not in any way that we would understand."

"But you don't have to hold out for long," Li said. "Nguyen—"

"Nguyen didn't even try to intercept the missile that blew the field AI," Cohen said. "She seemed more interested in wrapping up Korchow."

He caught his breath and shuddered. The image of Hyacinthe flickered ominously.

"What's wrong?" Li asked.

"Nothing," he said quickly. But there was a telltale hesitation in his voice. "I'm afraid," he said at last. "It wants me to hold it up. Hold it together. And . . . I can't."

"Cohen—"

"It's taking me apart in order to put itself together. It's doing what it did to Sharifi, to your father, to all the people who died down here. Except that it figured out with the field AI that an AI is much, much better for what it needs. That if it goes through an AI, it can get into streamspace, understand it, use it." He was talking fast now, the words rushing and tumbling. "You need to go to ALEF, Catherine. You're taken care of. I've made sure of that. It's all yours. Everything. You'll lose some networks. Some won't accept you, won't accept any human. Don't worry about it. You'll hold on to enough to make it all work. The ALEF contact is—"

"Stop it! You'll go yourself."

"But if something happens—"

"Nothing will happen!"

He put a hand up to touch her face, but she jerked away, her throat tight with panic. "Don't you sacrifice yourself for me and leave me to live with it. I won't let you. And I'll hate you for it."

"Don't say that, Catherine."

"Well, what the hell do you want me to say?" she shouted.

I want you to say you love me.

He took a step toward her, and this time she didn't back away.

"Fine. I'll buy you a drink somewhere when this is all over and say it."

"Say it now," he whispered. "Just in case."

She said it. She couldn't believe it, couldn't even get the words out without stuttering. But she said it.

Then he set a hand on her hip, and she stepped into his arms, and it was all so, so simple. Something shivered and let go at his touch, something she'd never even known she was holding on to. And with a jerk of recognition, she found that dark unmapped territory in her own heart that was his already—shaped to him, made for him, the exact width and breadth and depth of him.

This time there was no chasing, no hiding. Just everything they wanted spilling through their hands and running away like water.

"We're getting the truth now, I think," Voyt said. His voice was level, but there was a brightness, a loose-limbed alertness to him that turned Li's stomach to acid.

Sharifi was still sprawled across the steps. Li could feel the cold stone biting into her back, setting shattered ribs grinding. She blinked, and a razor's edge of agony shot through her now-blind right eye. God, what had they done to her?

"Is she dying?" Haas asked. Li recognized the doubting hitch in his voice: a civilian's cautious uncertainty about just what kind and what degree of violence a human body can tolerate.

"I know my business," Voyt said. "She's not going anywhere."

"Your recorder off?"

Voyt twitched irritably. "I'm not a complete fool."

"Good." Haas had been drawing closer as they spoke. Now he stretched Bella's slender hand toward the Viper. "Give me that."

Voyt hesitated, then handed it to him.

Haas stepped around Voyt and pressed the tongue of the weapon against Sharifi's head.

"Careful," Voyt said. He spoke in the even, artificially calm voice of a soldier watching a civilian do something stupid with a gun and not wanting to scare him into making a big mistake out of a little one.

"Oh, I will be," Haas said.

Voyt relaxed slightly. But Li could see, through Sharifi's single good eye, what Voyt couldn't. She could see the look on Haas's face.

"Did you think I didn't know?" he asked Sharifi. "Did you think I'd just stand back and let you fuck her?"

But Sharifi didn't hear him.

All she heard was Bella's voice. All she saw was a beloved face bending over her. All she felt was Bella's hand touching her, taking the pain away.

She reached out with one hand, a gesture that was no more than a breath, a tremor. Li was the only one who heard the soft snick of the trigger.

As Sharifi died something gave in the rock above them, booming and cracking. A hot blast of air pulsed down the gangway, hitting hard enough to knock Bella to her knees.

"Run!" Voyt yelled, but his voice was lost in the roar of falling rock.

It's going to kill them, Cohen said.

She heard Voyt scream and fall, but the sound seemed to come from far, far away. She saw Haas pass a hand over Bella's brow. She felt him slip off the shunt just in time, just the way he must have planned it. Then the last barrier broke, and the worldmind was running free, unfettered, ripping through Voyt, through Bella, through Li and Cohen like wildfire sweeping through dry grass.

For one wild, surreal moment she saw it all. The dark cavern around her. The flesh and ceramsteel mélange inside her own ringing skull. The blazing silicon vistas of Cohen's networks. The antique shop, smelling of tea and sandalwood. Arkady's unconscious figure sprawled among the sleek curves of the generation-ship artifacts. And above, around, and through all of it, the endless weight and darkness, the million voices of the worldmind.

The stones were singing.

In the end Cohen, or whatever was left of him, cut her out of the link. She begged, in that last moment, not even sure he could hear her. She cursed him, cursed herself, Korchow, Nguyen, the whole killing planet.

Then she was alone in the darkness, and there was nothing left of Cohen but the hole inside her where he should have been.

The Anaconda Strike: 9.11.48.

A dry breeze blew across her face, winding from nowhere to nowhere like a desert river.

Her internals were shattered. Ghosts, fragments. She felt the abuse her body had taken through the long hours in the pit. And behind it, worse than the physical pain, the memory of what Voyt had done to Sharifi, and of the whirling, chaotic, living darkness Cohen had cast himself into to save her.

Bella and McCuen were staring down at her, their faces white, drawn, terrified.

"Did you see that?" Li asked, sitting up.

Bella nodded. "Cohen?"

Li looked away.

"I'm sorry," Bella said, and when Li searched her face she saw that she really was sorry. "He was . . . kind."

Li checked her rebreather gauge instead of answering. She checked her internals, found with relief that at least the basic programs were working, and ran a quick air-use calculation.

"We've got to go," she said. "We have twenty-eight minutes to get to Mirce and the fresh canisters. Maybe less."

She glanced at McCuen. His face looked shockingly pale, but maybe it was just the lamplight. "I . . . didn't see much of anything," he said. "Just stuck around to pick up the pieces."

"You didn't miss much," she said, hefting her re-breather.

"Catherine?" Bella asked. Where had she picked that habit up? "Can we make it to Mirce? How long will it take us?"

"Less than twenty-eight minutes," Li said. "Or for-ever. Let's go."

The mine had come alive. It rumbled, rang, sang. The sound resonated in Li's chest, set her fingers twitching and her teeth buzzing. And along the in-traface, beyond her control but still flickering in and out of life according to some obscure rhythm, coursed a bustle and roar of high-speed traffic that shorted out her internals and flashed cryptic status messages across her retinas like tracer bullets.

She probed the intraface as they walked. It seemed to work regardless of whether Cohen was on the other end of it. At one point she almost managed to access the memory palace and its operating systems. But the framework wouldn't evolve, and she ended up cut off, stranded in a blind alley of the loading program. Cohen himself was a ghost presence: an absence given flesh and substance by her own body's refusal to admit that he was no longer part of her. That feeling, the sense that he was both there and not there, reminded her of stories about amputees who still kept waking up years later feeling the pain of lost limbs.

They reached the rendezvous at twenty-nine min-utes and twenty seconds. Bella's rebreather, which she had used sparingly, had four minutes to run. Li had al-ready given her own rebreather to McCuen. Mirce wasn't there to meet them, but as they turned the corner they saw the fresh tanks glimmering in the darkness.

"We're still one tank short," Li said, counting the tanks. She strained her ears for the sound of ropes and canisters being lowered, but heard only creaking lagging and the ominous silence of the hung-up roof.

She dropped to the ground beside the nearest tank and began hurriedly booting up the onboard comp and connecting the feedlines.

She couldn't get the air gauge on the tank to light up, no matter what she did. And she didn't have time to fiddle. She put the mask to her mouth, sucked at it experimentally. No. It wasn't just the gauge. She wasn't getting anything.

"What's wrong?" McCuen asked. There was a nervous edge to his voice that hadn't been there even when he'd watched his last tank running down before they reached the drop-off point.

"I don't know," Li said.

Then the gauge finally flickered into life. The arrow dropped into the red, quivered and stayed there. She fumbled for the fill valve, and when she touched it, it spun loosely at the touch of her fingers. No pressure.

And suddenly she did know what was wrong. Someone had opened the valve and emptied the tank. All the tanks.

They had no air.

"Mirce!" she shouted, already up and running down the twisting drift.

She found her twelve meters past the next bend, her hand still on the rope, the final canister of compressed air lying on the ground beside her. Li looked into the still-clear, still-blue eyes, looked at the head turned a little sideways, baring the strong, clean line of her jaw under the stretched skin. She thought, for no reason she wanted to remember, of magpies' wings.

The cut ran diagonally across Mirce's throat, from the collar of her coverall to the soft flesh below her ear. She had bled out fast. In seconds, probably. No sign of a fight; the spreading pool around her could have been water or rehab fluid, except for the rich copper-and-rust smell of it.

"Why?" Bella whispered. "Why?"

"To stop us," Li said, wondering how that calm professional's voice could be speaking out of the whirlwind inside her.

"What do we do?" McCuen asked.

"We find whoever killed her and take their air."

When it finally happened, she was so ready for it that she knew some deep part of herself must have been expecting it. Reading the accumulation of clues, each one insignificant in itself, that told her they were being followed. Listening for the echo that wasn't an echo. Waiting for the muffled step behind them.

What she wasn't prepared for—hadn't even suspected—was the flash of quickly suppressed recognition in McCuen's eyes.

She'd made a fool's mistake, she told herself as the hot flush of adrenaline flooded through her. McCuen had betrayed her. Somehow, by some hook she'd probably never know about, Haas had turned him. The proof was right there in front of her, in those wide-open little-boy-blue eyes.

She called a break, drifted to a stop against an outcropping in the passage wall, stretched, and sat down a few feet from him with her back safely against solid stone.

"How could they have known where to find her?" McCuen asked. He talked fast, seizing on the first thought that came to mind, trying to gloss over the footsteps that he too had heard, that he too had been waiting for. "I mean, we were fine before that. She makes the meet, and we all get out."

"Except Cohen."

She could see in McCuen's face that he still didn't know who she was talking about. He had never met Cohen, she realized, probably never thought of him as more than a piece of equipment. "Well, yeah," McCuen said. "But . . . you know what I mean."

"Sure," she said. "I know."

She strained her ears, listening to the darkness beyond the lamplight. Everyone has a weakness, she told herself. And their weakness would be their wire.

A flickering double vision swept over her as she tried to hold streamspace and realspace in her mind simultaneously. It was stomach-wrenching, but she couldn't afford to drop all the way out of realtime. Not with McCuen three feet away from her and an unknown pursuer waiting at the edge of the lamplight.

She stepped into the memory palace.

The door was broken. The fountain had run dry. A storm howled over the turrets, setting roof tiles rattling and shutters flapping. Whole wings of the palace were open to wind and sky. Locked doors confronted her at every turn, and even when she got past them, she found only rain-strafed ruins behind them.

She couldn't find the communications programs, couldn't even figure out which networks they were on. She thought about dropping into the numbers to look, but the memory of the disaster Cohen had averted last time stopped her.

Then she heard something.

Footsteps. Echoing around the next turn in the hall, up the next flight of stairs, across the floor over her head. Footsteps and a mocking quicksilver laugh flickering across the dead link like heat lightning.

She tracked the sound through cold dark halls, across vast, rubble-choked courtyards. She'd almost given up when she stumbled through a half-open door and saw the arches of the cloister, the wind-whipped, moonlit tangle of wild roses.

She stepped out from under the arcade, one hand up to shield her face from the wind. Someone was sitting on the bench under the roses. She saw the tarnished copper of rain-soaked curls. She saw Roland's golden eyes glinting out of the shadows.

She ran.

Both of them were cold and slick with rain, and a dead leaf had blown against his face like a little black moth so that she had to brush it off before she could kiss him. "You came," she whispered.

And then she was kissing him, searching for him with lips, hands, heart, her mind stripped of everything but her need for him.

He took hold of her shoulders and pushed her away from him. She looked into the golden eyes and saw . . . nothing.

"No," she whispered. "*No*."

"He couldn't come. I'm supposed to tell you he's sorry."

The rain stopped. The darkness around them deepened. She glimpsed tall windows flung open to the lowering clouds, and realized that they stood on the threshold of the hall of doors.

Roland pointed to a door like all the others. "There," he said.

Then he was gone.

She pushed it open and stepped into a darkness blacker and more storm-charged than the sky outside.

"Who is it?" a voice said.

It was not a friendly voice. Not a friendly question.

"Me," she said. "Catherine. Don't you know me?"

"Oh, yes. We know you."

The lights came on. She was alone in an empty room.

"Why did you come here?" the voice asked. It was

the walls, or whatever was behind the walls, speaking to her.

"I need to access the AMC station net."

Silence.

"I *need* to."

"And why should we help you?"

We?

"Because—"

Another voice spoke. Words she couldn't make out. Whispers. Suddenly the room was boiling with whispers. She stepped back, feeling for the door behind her. "But Cohen said—"

"Yes." A new voice now, even colder than the first. "Tell us about Cohen. Tell us what *Cohen* said to you."

"It wasn't my fault," she breathed.

"Wasn't it?"

She felt for the doorknob again, her hand trembling. She touched something, gripped it. But instead of metal, she felt skin.

Someone shoved her forward into the center of the room, and she fell on her knees, hands pressed over her ears to shut out the hateful, hissing accusations.

"It's not my fault!" she screamed, over and over again. But she couldn't block the voices out. It *was* her fault, they kept saying. It was all her fault. All of it.

"Are you all right?" McCuen asked.

She looked at him, chest heaving. She glanced at Bella, who was staring at her, wide-eyed. "I'm fine," she lied. "Glitch on my commsystem."

Then she heard Cohen talking to her.

She opened her eyes in VR to find Hyacinthe taking her hand, drawing her to her feet, tugging her back toward the terrible room.

But this was no Hyacinthe she had ever known. This

was a mere memory dump, an interactive tutorial triggered by her entry into the memory palace. It explained how to access networks, bank accounts, corporate records, how to run an empire it kept insisting was hers now. It explained everything except the only thing that mattered: that if she was here, if this program was running, Cohen must be gone.

"I still need to get into the AMC net," she said when he was done. She felt numb, as if her voice were coming from someone else's throat.

But the others wouldn't let her in, wouldn't do it for her. And even with Hyacinthe's help she couldn't make them do it. "Cohen *wanted* this!" she said finally, frightened and furious.

That got a bitter laugh from a voice she hadn't even heard before: a powerful, saturnine presence who made it clear that he despised her so much he hadn't bothered to participate before. "Cohen wanted you too," the voice told her. "And look what that got him."

As it spoke, she felt a burning jealousy behind the words. A child's jealousy? A lover's? Or was this some other thing entirely, some splinter of Cohen's inhuman soul? But this was no child, she realized. It was Cohen's old communications AI—the only entity in the shifting ruin of his networks that was capable of controlling its fellows.

She started to answer, to argue. But before she could form a thought, a wave of anger battered her, cold as ice water, and she was cut off, out of the link, kicked off the intraface.

"Where are you going?" McCuen asked.

"To take a piss." She forced a grin. "You want to come?"

He flushed. Like a little boy, for Christ's sake. But he

stayed put. And that was all she had really wanted from him.

She stepped into the shadows and slipped her butterfly knife from her belt, relearning its balance, feeling the blade blossom, lilylike, from the cross-gripped handle.

She could smell their pursuer. She could feel him with the hairs of her arms, with her raised hackles, with the skin of her face. She could have found him by touch if she'd had to. She was deep into her own territory now. She didn't need maps, not even Cohen's maps. She was about to murder someone. And she'd known how to do that for as long as she could remember.

She eased around the corner, stopped, listened, stopped again. She weighed the dark and the silence, took their measure.

She took her own measure too. Heavy-soled boots that could crunch against grit or scrape on rock. Cloth that could rustle and whisper treacherously. Loose buckles, loose straps, loose bootlaces. And her own breathing, sweating, shedding body, casting off trace faster than her skinbugs could scramble to camouflage it. She'd heard it said that Earth's extinct carnivores had no scent, but that was a lie, like so many other things people said about the planet. The truth was they'd just known how to hide their scent from those they preyed on—a last, deadly secret.

She found her prey two meters past the bend in the drift. He sat in the dark, back to the wall, rebreather hanging loose around his jaw, infrared goggles laid on the ground beside him. He was eating.

She inched along the wall, arms out, knife ready. Waiting for him to turn. Waiting for the telltale catch of breath that would tell her he'd heard her.

It never came.

He struggled at the last, standing up, trying to

throw her off as her left hand grasped his head and stretched his throat taut. But by then it was over.

"Christ!"

McCuen. With the gun in his hand that she should have, damn her, taken from him.

She let the dead man slide down the length of her body to the ground.

"You killed him," McCuen said, his voice a ragged whisper. "I didn't believe her. I didn't believe you'd do it."

Li shook her head. *Her?* What was he talking about?

Bella came around the corner before she could ask him. She saw the fallen guard, gave a strangled cry, stopped and drew back, her hand over her mouth.

"Go up the drift and wait for me," Li told her. "You're just in the way here." *And I don't want you to see this. I don't want anyone to see it.*

Bella started to speak. Then her eyes slid away from Li's. She turned and walked back up the drift, leaving Li and McCuen alone.

They stared at each other. His betrayal and her knowledge of it hung in the air between them. He made a move, just the slightest flexing of his ankles.

She lunged, still hoping to keep the fight quiet and not alert the other three pursuers. She feinted toward McCuen's face with the knife, and he threw up his left arm to cover himself, just as she'd known he would. He kept the gun more or less pointed at her while he did it, but he lost time. And in that instant, she reached up, wrapped her left hand around his wrist and broke it.

He screamed. The gun fired high and wild, then dropped from his hand and rattled along the slate floor into the darkness. She heard it come to rest behind her, fixed the point in her hard files, and set a subroutine to track it so she could retrieve it when she needed to.

She cursed her own slowness. That one shot could set Kintz on her before she had time to take care of McCuen. And even if it didn't, she no longer had surprise on her side. Now they would know she was coming for them.

She brushed her regrets aside to focus on the job in front of her. McCuen was crippled. Not just by his lack of internal wetware or his broken wrist, but because Li could push back her mask and breathe freely, for a few moments at least, while he had to keep struggling to suck air through the cumbersome mouthpiece. He'd never fought her either. Not for real. He had no idea what he was up against.

Forty seconds into the fight she landed a clean kick, and McCuen's leg collapsed under him with a grinding snap that told her she'd found her target. She was on top of him before he hit the ground, thumb and forefinger locked on his windpipe.

She lifted her knife hand to his face and ripped off his infrared goggles, leaving him blind. Then she straddled him, got a good purchase with her boot soles, sat on his stomach. As she did it, she had a flash of Voyt doing the same thing to Sharifi, and it turned her stomach.

"Who did Haas send?" she asked.

"I don't know what you're talking about."

"Don't play with me, Brian." She dug her fingers under his windpipe and squeezed. "Who'd he send? Kintz? He the one who cut Mirce's throat for no fucking good reason? Nice friends you've got."

He was choking. She let up a little—just enough so he could talk.

"I didn't know they were going to kill her," he said when he could breathe again. "I would never have . . ." He swallowed, Adam's apple jerking. "It's not like you think it is."

"Oh? How is it then? What's Haas paying you?"

McCuen's face twisted in anger. "No one's paying me."

"Then talk to me."

McCuen put on a resisting-interrogation face. A little boy playing at cowboys and cybercops. Li could have screamed with frustration.

"I don't have time for this," she said. She flicked her knife under McCuen's rebreather feed, pulling the thin tube taut.

"God, no!" he pleaded. He was panicking, a trapped animal thrown back on instinct and adrenaline. She felt his legs twitching under her as if his backbrain believed he could overpower ceramsteel-enhanced muscles, outtwitch hardwired reflex. "Don't make me die like that. Please, Li!"

She remembered her father, blue-gummed, drowning in his own bile. The growth had filled 20 percent of his remaining lung when they took the last X ray. The doctor had said it was bigger than most of the babies born in Shantytown that year.

Her knife hand was shaking. She took the information in coldly, as if it were someone else's hand. Dealt with it. Rerouted. Adjusted. "Then talk," she said, and let the blade scrape along the thin sheathing of the feedline.

"Okay! Okay. Shit. It's Kintz. And two more." He said two names she didn't recognize. "They weren't supposed to kill anyone. They were supposed to wait until Korchow and the AI were taken care of, and then take you and Bella in. Alive, if they could."

Li's breath caught in her throat. "What do you mean until the AI was taken care of?"

"I don't know."

She twisted the knife.

"I swear I don't! All she said was that she'd get rid of it. That we wouldn't have to worry about it."

All *she* said?

Of course, she realized. It had been right there in front of her all the time. The answer that she had blinded herself to because she didn't want to see it, couldn't afford to see it.

This was a chess match, and one that had gone on far too long to be anything but a deadly fight between two equally devious and experienced opponents. Haas wasn't the player on the other side of the chess board from Korchow. He never had been.

All along, every time Haas railroaded her or sabotaged her investigation, she had gone running to Nguyen like a little idiot. Never quite listening to Cohen's warnings. Never looking up long enough to see the shadowy hand that hovered behind Haas, behind Voyt, behind McCuen. And now, when it was too late, she saw with painful clarity.

Who was the one person in a position to control both her and Sharifi? To orchestrate Metz and the mine investigation and the secret work at Alba? Who was the one person who knew just what Cohen would risk to save her? Who knew so well how to sow the seeds of mistrust that would keep her from confiding in Cohen even as she used him to save herself? And who, ever since Tel Aviv, had more or better reasons to want Cohen dead?

"What else did Nguyen say?" she asked casually, her eyes fixed on McCuen's, praying that he was too scared and too confused to hear the question that hid behind her words.

"I don't know. Oh, God, Li! Don't! I swear I don't know. I only talked to her that once."

"Tell me exactly what she said, Brian. That's all I'm asking. Do that and I won't have any reason to hurt you."

"She said to go with you. Keep an eye on you. That Kintz would bag you afterward."

"And the AI?" Li couldn't stop herself from asking.

"She just said she'd take care of it. It'd be gone when you came off the link."

Holy Mother of Christ, she thought—and then thrust aside the knowledge of what she had helped Nguyen do to Cohen. "What is Kintz supposed to do with us?"

McCuen hesitated.

"What, Brian?"

"He's supposed to try to take you alive."

"Try?"

"If he can't, he's supposed to kill you. You and Bella both."

A cold knot ground itself into the pit of Li's stomach. "What about Gould and the *Medusa*? What about Sharifi's package?"

"Nguyen's going to catch both ships in open space when they drop out of slow time. Intercept Gould before she can get the package."

"What did she give you, Brian? Money? A promotion? What did she come up with that was worth killing Mirce and Cohen for?"

McCuen looked at her, his eyes round and childish above the rebreather's insectlike mouthpiece. "She told me you were a traitor."

Li went slack, let the blade drop away from the feed-line.

"What if I told you I wasn't?" she asked finally.

"I would have believed you. Until today."

She looked into his eyes, forgetting that he couldn't see her. "And you would have been right," she said, "until today."

"What are you going to do with me?" McCuen asked. His voice sounded very small—a child asking his mother to tell him that nightmares weren't real, that monsters didn't really exist.

"I don't know," Li said truthfully. Kintz must have heard her shot, must already be on the move. "Brian, I need to know where Kintz is going to ambush me."

"I can't tell you."

"Let's not do this again, Brian."

"No! I really don't know. They were supposed to pick up Mirce and bag us when we got to the rendezvous with her. So . . . well, you saw. They're not doing what they said they would."

Li laughed bitterly. "It looks like Kintz has already decided he's just not going to be able to bring us in alive."

"Yeah," McCuen said. If he wondered what Kintz's decision meant for him personally, he didn't say so. "Listen," he said after a moment. "You can contact the station, can't you? You could call Nguyen. It's not too late. Maybe you can't fix everything. But enough. Enough not to get killed down here. Enough to keep the Syndicates from getting what they want."

"And then what?"

"I don't know what. But it has to be better than getting killed!" He shivered. "Or going over to the Syndicates. Come on, Li. I can't believe you want *that*."

She looked down at his pleading face. She thought about dying in the mine. She thought about the long list of ugly, violent things she would have to do to get back to the surface alive. She thought about Nguyen, about what she might be willing to trade Li's life for.

What difference would it make to anyone? Mirce was already dead. Cohen was gone. What did she care about what happened to a planet she'd never thought of as anything but a trap to escape from?

"But Nguyen's going to kill the crystals," she said. "She's going to kill the whole planet."

She knew it was the truth as soon as she spoke the words. It wasn't a plan or a conspiracy; even now she didn't believe that Daahl's stolen memo had been more than an unfortunate turn of phrase. But it would happen. It was already happening.

The UN couldn't survive without live condensate. Left to its own devices it would swallow Compson's

World whole, just as the worldmind had swallowed
Cohen, just as the Security Council had swallowed
Kolodny and Sharifi and all the other quiet casualties
of their covert tech wars. Not out of malice, but with
the best intentions. Not because they wanted to, but
because they had to. Because that was how their code
was written.

And Sharifi—Sharifi had known that the only way
to stop them was to take the choice out of their hands.

"It's not our job to decide those things," McCuen
said, as if he had tracked every turn and twist of her
thoughts.

Li knew he was saying no more than she'd have said
a few short weeks ago. He hadn't seen what she'd seen.
He hadn't lived it. He could only see the choice she
faced as black or white, loyalty or treason, UN or
Syndicate.

And if she chose the side he wanted her to choose?
The side that loyalty to comrades dead and alive made
her want to choose, that everything in her long years
of training and service had taught her to choose? Then
the UN would be saved from the Syndicates, for a
while anyway. It would survive, feeding off the condensates in a kind of cannibal existence that was no
worse, when all was said and done, than any other
creature's struggle to survive at the expense of all the
other life in the universe.

But the condensates—Cartwright's sainted dead,
Li's father, Sharifi, Cohen—would die. And this time
there would be no second birth, no dreaming afterlife,
however alien. This time they wouldn't be coming
back.

"I'm sorry," she said. She sat back on her haunches
and took the knife off the rebreather line.

McCuen's body turned to water under her as terror
collapsed into shivering relief. "Jesus, Li, you scared
the hell out of me. I really thought—"

She slit his throat cleanly, making sure the first cut

finished it. It was messy, but it was kinder than anything else she could do for him. He died with a confused expression on his face, an idealistic little boy who still couldn't believe this game of cops and robbers had turned real.

"It's not personal," she whispered into the void of his dilating pupils. But that was a lie too, the biggest lie of all. And she knew it even if McCuen didn't.

Bella was waiting by their packs. She started to say something, then saw the blood covering Li's hands and clothes and stopped, backing up a step.

Li hated her for that step, for the disgusted, fearful look on her face. She hated her so much she could feel her hands shaking with it. She emptied McCuen's pack, took what she could carry, and left the rest for the rats. She didn't trust herself to look at Bella.

"Did he . . . did you find out how many of them there are?"

Li held up three fingers.

"Kintz?"

"Yes."

Li was drowning. Suffocating. She shouldered her pack and started down the drift, leaving Bella to follow any way she could.

Neither of them said McCuen's name, then or later.

The Anaconda Strike: 9.11.48.

Kintz must not have been expecting them to come after him. He'd let his men straggle. He was acting like he expected Li to run, like he thought he'd have to corner her before she'd fight. What did he know that she didn't?

She took down the first man with a single shot; no hope of surprise anyway, and the best tactic now was speed. Unfortunately, her shot took him in the neck, shattering the feedlines of his oxygen tank. She listened to the air whistling out of the tubes and cursed herself for being impatient. For not having thought things through more carefully. For having hands that shook too much. For not being as sharp as she'd been five years ago. Five months ago, even.

Behind him was another man she'd never seen before. Probably planet-side mine security. He had the instincts and training to duck for cover before she could shoot him, but she'd chosen her point of attack well; there was no cover.

She would have shot him down where he stood if

he hadn't been wearing a rebreather. But he was wearing one. And since Kintz was wired, it might be the only rebreather left down there.

She leveled the Beretta at the guard's chest, and he froze, staring at her. She listened for Kintz, but all she could hear was Bella's dress rustling as she shifted nervously from foot to foot.

"You might as well come on out," Li called up the drift. "I can smell your cheap aftershave from here."

"I wouldn't shoot him," Kintz said from behind a protruding piece of lagging about three meters away. "He's got the last full tank. And I believe you need one of those."

"Take off the rebreather," Li told the guard, "and push it toward me."

He didn't move.

"I *will* shoot you if you don't do it." She spoke calmly. She didn't have to put on a play to convince him; the body of his friend was still steaming on the ground in front of him.

She saw the man's gaze flick back toward Kintz, behind the lagging. That glance might as well have been a map. She could see where Kintz must be braced between lagging and rock face. She could see the gun that must be in his hand. And she could see what the guard had clearly seen: that Kintz would shoot him down himself if that was what it took to keep Li from getting the oxygen tank.

"Come here," she told Bella. "And stay back against the wall."

Bella crept forward, slowly, reluctantly. The look on her face said that Li had let her down somehow by even making her witness this scene. Li pulled McCuen's gun out of the back of her pants where she'd stowed it.

She looked at it. She looked at the expression of fascinated revulsion on Bella's face. She thought about the recoil on a big revolver like that, the way joints loosen on an old gun and the long uneven pull it would probably take to fire it.

She gave Bella the Beretta.

"Look," she whispered, keeping her hand over Bella's and the gun trained on the guard while she spoke. "Elbows locked. Bead lined up on his chest. And if he moves—if he even breathes too fast—shoot him."

Bella nodded, tight-lipped. *You lose your nerve and we're both dead*, Li wanted to say. But she didn't. There was such a thing as too scared. And Bella looked like she was halfway there already.

Li flexed her hand around the Colt, felt its weight and balance. She wished to God she'd had a chance to fire it before, but wishing was beside the point. She gave the guard a warning look and started working her way down the drift toward Kintz.

The guard's eyes followed her, telegraphing her movements, but there wasn't much she could do about it short of shooting him outright. And Kintz would figure out what she was doing anyway. The thing was to get there fast. And to get there quietly enough that he couldn't be quite sure where she was and when she was going to round the corner on him. She didn't need absolute surprise. Just relative surprise. That, and a little help from Bella.

She got one of those things.

She turned the corner around the lagging, leading with her elbows, dropping the gun toward Kintz as soon as she was sure he wasn't going to kick it out of her hands. And there they were, facing off against each other, each one with a gun to the other's head. The next stage in the deadlock.

"Drop it," Kintz said.

She hit him instead of answering. She'd thought it out, run the possibilities and options down in her mind, troubleshot her plan, and now she moved so fast that even Kintz's enhanced reflexes couldn't counter her. She turned into him, shoving him into the angle between lagging and rock face, where he couldn't put his superior reach and height to use. She slammed her foot into his groin, and as he staggered under the kick she spun her gun butt-first and hammered it down on the side of his head.

He was a tough son of a bitch. He didn't pass out. He didn't fall. He didn't even lose his grip on his gun. But he dropped its muzzle a few inches—all the opening Li needed. Before he regained his balance, she shoved McCuen's gun under his jaw.

"Empty it," she said.

He hesitated.

She cocked the hammer. He emptied his pistol, bullets ringing and skittering across the rough floor. "Now drop it."

He dropped the gun at her feet, not taking his eyes off her, and she kicked it away down the drift. They looked at each other.

"I don't want to kill you this fast," she said. "I'd like to see you suffer, you son of a bitch." She said the words without thinking, and the sound of them shocked her. But they were true, God help her. She'd killed more people than she could count or even remember, but this was the first time she'd actually wanted to murder someone.

"Got you where it hurt, huh? Who was that bitch whose throat I cut, anyway? Another girlfriend? Too bad I didn't have more time to spend on her."

Li forced the gun's muzzle farther up under his jaw, as if she thought she could shut his mouth with the sheer pressure of it.

"They're waiting for you," he said, eyes on her trigger finger. "You'll never get out of here alive, even if you kill me." He licked his lips. "Especially if you kill me."

Li backed off a step or two, keeping the gun leveled on him. That was when the other guard made his move.

She didn't see it herself, but she saw the quickly suppressed flash in Kintz's eyes that told her something was happening behind her back. She glanced around, Kintz still in her sights. The guard was inching toward her, slowly, deliberately, his eyes locked on Bella's. And Bella was letting him.

"Shoot him!" Li screamed. But Bella was frozen, shut down with terror, standing on the edge of a cliff she couldn't force herself over. Li spun around, snapped her elbows straight, and fired a single shot over Bella's head and through the guard's eye socket.

Kintz was on top of her before she could swing back around. He went for the hurt arm, of course. She had known he would. What she hadn't known was how fast the arm would fail her.

Bella tried to help. Li saw her out of her peripheral vision, circling around them, holding the Beretta stiffly out in front of her, trying to decide where to aim the gun. As if she even knew how to aim it.

"No, Bella!" she barked. "No shooting. Just take the air tank and leave. I'll catch up if I can."

Kintz didn't even give her time to notice if Bella had obeyed her. He wasn't her match in skill, but she was handicapped by her stripped-out arm, and the punishment she'd gone through in the past few hours. And by the five years and eight inches and thirty kilos Kintz had on her.

He slammed her against the drift wall, threw her hard, and was on top of her before she could get her arms or legs under her. He jerked her onto her stomach, jammed his knee into the small of her back, and bent her bad arm back so savagely that she couldn't breathe without feeling the twinge of stretched-to-snapping tendons.

She heard him reach for his belt, heard the click of handcuffs releasing. "I'd kill you right here," he said, "but Nguyen almost had our heads over Sharifi. Your lucky day."

"Not behind my back," she said as he slapped the first cuff on. "Not unless you want to carry me up."

He stopped, rolled her over, let her hold her hands out in front of her while he locked the second virusteel ring around her wrist and single-keyed in a preset compressed code.

He was in no hurry now that he had subdued her. He almost seemed to be waiting for something. He frisked her, ran his hands up and down her legs, into her crotch. She watched him think about the fact that they were alone.

"You must really have fucked up on Gilead," she said, needling him. "Or were you just too pissant incompetent for them to trust you with a real Corps job after that?"

"You need to learn to shut up," he said, and put a hand down her shirt.

She let him get a good feel. She saw his mouth open a little, his breath come faster. "You're pathetic," she said.

He took hold of her legs and jerked her flat on the floor. "Roll over."

"Don't have the balls to look me in the face?"

He hit her so hard she didn't even feel the blow. When she came to, he was on top of her and already fumbling at her belt. He got that unfastened all right, but the pants and the tie-down of the Beretta's empty holster took two hands. She waited, eyes closed, until he had both hands engaged. Then she balled her hands into a double fist and swung them, letting the weight of the cuffs add to the momentum of her internals.

She caught him on the right temple. Not ideal, but she stunned him—and opened up a long gash in his skull that would bleed into his eyes with a little luck.

He staggered to his feet and aimed a crushing kick at her ribs, but she was already rolling away from him.

She glanced around as they squared off against each

other. The gun was too far away. She'd never get there in time. But Kintz couldn't get to it either—not without risking a kick from Li's still lethal legs.

This would be a good time, Bella, she thought. But of course, Bella was nowhere.

"You fucking digger bitch," Kintz said. "Fucking stinking dirty half-bred cunt!"

Li laughed. She didn't know where the laugh came from, but suddenly it all seemed pathetically ridiculous, from Kintz's tired insults to the fact that they were fighting for the same planet both their ancestors had wasted lifetimes trying to escape from. "Guess you should have stuck to the half-breeds you could buy in Helena," she gasped.

After that, they didn't talk anymore; they were both short of breath, and they knew that the next time they went down one of them wasn't getting up again.

Li would have liked to be able to wait Kintz out, let him get impatient. But she couldn't afford to. She was too tired, too battered. She would flag before he did. She had to draw him into doing something stupid, and she had to do it while she still had the strength to take advantage of his mistake.

She danced in, let him get a glancing hit on her, jumped away, deliberately stumbling a little. He took the bait; he reached for her, missed his hold, reached again.

This time she let him catch up to her. She forced herself not to think what would happen if this ploy didn't work, if he really did get her down. She kept her hands up, locked together. As he gripped her, she braced her feet and drove her hands toward his face with all the strength she had, fingers rigid.

He screamed and staggered back, clutching his eyes. She threw herself down the drift without even looking to see if he was following and reached the Colt in a cloth-ripping, face-forward slide.

His first kick connected just as her fingers touched

the gun. He slammed into her ribs, her kidneys, her stomach in a flurry of blows so violent that only the certainty of death if she failed kept her hands locked around the revolver.

She rolled over, baring her stomach, and looked up at him. One eye was still open, though the skin around the socket was torn and bleeding. The other was a gushing mess.

She raised the gun only to have him kick it aside. He fell on her, trapping the gun between them, scratching and grabbing for it, his breath roaring in her ears with the tight scream of adrenaline and agony. They wrestled, grunting like dogs fighting for a bone, locked in a deadly tug-of-war. She felt Kintz prying her fingers from the sweat-and-blood-slicked grip. Her pulse drummed in her skull. Her lungs and fingers burned. Her grip slipping, belly to belly with Kintz, hardly knowing where the gun was aimed, she fired.

She heard the wet thump of bullet hitting flesh, felt hot blood rush over her legs and stomach.

It took a long time for him to die, and she didn't dare move the gun, even to flick the safety back on, until she was sure his fingers had slacked. When she finally pushed him off her his one remaining eye was open and his limbs loose and heavy. She wiped the blood off her face and stood up—only to find herself staring down the barrel of her own gun.

"Bella," she said.

"Not quite." Haas's smile looked all wrong on Bella's pale face, and in the construct's dark eyes Li saw the same frozen, uncomprehending panic she'd seen when she'd gone under the loop shunt.

"You took your time," she told Haas.

"I had other fires to put out," he said. "And I didn't want to get on the shunt and show my hand too soon. Bella's been getting . . . difficult."

"Christ," Li whispered, sick at the thought of what Haas had done, at the sure knowledge that this had been the nightmare behind Bella's eyes every time she'd spoken of Sharifi's death. She might not have remembered, but she had suspected. And she had used Li to chase down that suspicion—hoping all the while that it would turn out to be wrong, that Li would find some other explanation.

Haas bent over Kintz, pulled a second pair of cuffs out of his belt and tossed them to Li. "Cuff your ankles," he said, and watched while she did it. "Now give me your hand," he said.

Fear prickled down Li's spine. Haas wanted her dataset, the record of her interface with the condensates. And once he got it, there would be no reason at all to take Li above ground.

Haas saw her hesitation. "Nguyen may want the data enough to play games with you," he said, his voice level, "but I personally don't give a shit. Bear that in mind." He nodded toward the cuffs already encircling her wrists. "You might crack those given a few hours, of course. But you don't have a few hours. I leave you here without air and you'll be dead inside of one hour. I'm your ticket out of here, my friend. You better fucking keep me happy."

Li stretched out her hands, fingers spread wide, palms toward him. He put Bella's left hand against hers, clasped Bella's fingers around hers, and started the data transfer.

It was a strange thing to feel information being pulled out of her internals without her consent, to feel Haas taking the last chip she had to bargain with.

Or *was* the data all she had now? There was something else. Something Cohen had been ready to use. Something she could use too—if she was willing to put it all on the table and gamble everything, the way Sharifi had. She hesitated, knowing that the hard knot in her stomach was simple fear. Then she looked into the cold black pit of Bella's dilated pupils and knew she was already risking everything. She closed her eyes, took a last, trembling breath, and stepped into the memory palace.

The numbers hit her like a riptide. Code coursed through her, rolled her over, dragged her under. She reached out—tentatively at first, then more confidently—to the myriad sentient systems that made up Cohen. She felt their squabbling, bickering personalities—and the glue of shared goals, shared memories, shared passions that bound them together. None of these splintered shards was Cohen. But they remembered him. They remembered everything he had felt and believed and wanted. They shared that with her, even if they shared nothing else.

She just hoped it would be enough.

She found the communications AI almost before she began looking. His fury spun at the core of the memory palace like a dead star, sucking her in, absorbing the dead AI's last functioning subsystems, devouring every remaining bit of heat and warmth and light in the place.

"I need you," she said. "I need to get a line out to Freetown."

"We can't get a line to Freetown without the field AI. We have no network."

"Yes we do," she said. "We have the worldmine. The worldmine can give us streamspace access completely outside UN control or oversight. All we have to do is get Daahl's network up. All we have to do is finish the job Cohen started."

A cold shiver ran through the numbers. "Why should we?"

"It's what Cohen would have done if he were still here."

"He was different. We believed in him. Trusted him. He earned that. You, on the other hand, had better have something to bargain with."

So she bargained.

She gave them the intraface. She promised to do what she had already promised Cohen she would do. What they would have known she would still do if they'd trusted her as he had.

She promised to set them free.

The Anaconda Strike: 9.11.48.

She rode Cohen's networks like a hawk riding an updraft.

She wheeled and soared, sideslipping into sub-networks, enslaved systems, communications programs. She felt out beyond them to the static-charged web of local communications that hung like an electronic smog over Compson's World, to the miners' primitive radio communications, to Helena, to the orbital stations. And then she dove, surrendering herself to the black depths of the worldmind.

It was waiting for her, just as she'd known it would be; but it was no longer the alien, incomprehensible presence of the glory hole that she felt. Instead she heard the echoes of half-remembered voices in it. Mirce. McCuen. Her father. And, worst of all, Cohen.

He had been right, of course. The worldmind needed him. It had cannibalized him, anchoring a new structure in the ruins of his systems, and in the flimsy beginnings of the planetary net that he had helped Ramirez create for it. Because it was the worldmind that Ramirez's net had been meant to serve all along. That was the secret that had taunted Li from behind Cartwright's blind eyes. That was the secret her father had known, the secret Cohen himself had known, even if he had figured it out too late to save himself. And now Li watched the worldmind explode into orbit, crackle through the Bose-Einstein relays of every planet along the Periphery, across the unmonitored, uncontrolled tributaries of FreeNet and out into the deep, swift, living tide of the spinstream.

She followed, running on more tracks than she could consciously manage. She combed her subsystems, found two UN pension administration number crunchers and set them to work on the cuff locks. The communications AI wondered fleetingly if they had time to wait for them. She wondered along with him—and an instant later, so quick on the heels of the thought that she had no sense of having acted, she was on the FreeNet airspace control system searching the skies for a signal from a ship that had not yet reported in to the navigational authority.

She found Gould's ship already in orbit, maintaining forced radio silence while the sleek, vicious shape of a UNSC frigate drifted above it, going through a search-and-seizure routine. She stayed just long enough to be sure that Nguyen's net had closed around Gould. Then she was off and running, looking for the *Medusa*.

It wasn't there. Not when she started looking, anyway. Then it exploded in-system at relativistic velocity, right on schedule, its navigational beacons howling in Dopplered harmonics, its retrorockets blazing like a man-made supernova.

Nguyen's people lay in wait at the first system buoy. As the *Medusa* dropped into normal time, a second frigate detached itself from the buoy's signal shadow and began pacing the civilian ship, hailing it.

As fast as the *Medusa* was moving, the hail couldn't

have come through as anything but twisted static. Still, it was on a closed military link. The ship slowed for it.

Li prowled through eight different Bose-Einstein-enabled networks before she could find a back door into the closed communications shooting between the two ships.

"—for boarding and security inspection," the frigate's captain was saying when she finally broke through the ship-to-ship encryption.

She didn't wait to hear the freighter give the permission. She was accessing the *Medusa*'s data banks before the frigate completed its request, looking for anything Sharifi could have deposited there, hoping desperately that the precious dataset wasn't dead-walled into an unwired storage locker.

Then someone logged on and began executing a massive data dump into the ship's computer core. Sharifi's unencrypted datasets. And more. As Li raced through the files she realized there was spinfeed with the datasets—feed that Sharifi must have thought was important enough to record live and send with the original data. Li looked to see who was doing the uploading and laughed at the obviousness of it when she finally saw it.

Sharifi had rented a locker with an automated data release. When the *Medusa* dropped into orbit over Freetown, the release program had looked for a streamspace signal—one Gould would presumably have sent had her own delivery been successful—and, not receiving it, had begun dumping its data into the ship's comp. The ship in turn was programmed to broadcast the data on FreeNet when the upload was complete.

This was Sharifi's insurance policy: dumping her raw data onto the most unregulated and chaotic sea in streamspace's ocean. It amounted to little more than shouting out her discoveries in an electronic town square. Bella and Cohen and everyone else who knew Sharifi had been right about her all along. Sharifi hadn't been trying to sell her information. She'd been trying to give it away, to anyone and everyone who could use it. And she had trusted that someone—enough someones to make a difference—would take care of Compson's World.

The *Medusa* was too slow, though. Its onboard systems were hopelessly obsolete and in uncertain repair. Li spun through the ship comp, tweaking, adjusting, speeding things up wherever she could; but even so the first files had barely loaded before she felt the clank and pressure shift of the frigate's boarding tube locking onto the *Medusa*'s fragile skin.

Christ! All this, only to lose everything because of a slow ship's comp? She pushed and prodded furiously, but still the numbers seeped through the shipboard systems as reluctantly as cold diesel fuel. And meanwhile it was just a matter of time until the frigate's techs accessed the *Medusa*'s systems and shut down the file transfer.

But they never did. They ran a cursory search that didn't turn up anything—didn't even seem intended to turn up anything. Then they closed the airlock and pulled away, leaving a welter of relieved, if confused, internal mail between the freighter's crew and passengers.

Li breathed a sigh of relief and let her guard down. The frigate kicked in its attitudinals and pulled away. The *Medusa* continued its radically slowed drift toward Freetown.

Then she saw it. It was as chillingly, breathtakingly clear as sunlight in hard vacuum. The frigate's crew hadn't boarded the freighter to take Sharifi's data off it, but to leave something else on it. Something that would be sitting in one of the dark cargo bays waiting for a signal from the frigate's bridge.

Nguyen didn't need the files on the *Medusa* anymore.

She hadn't fired on the field AI until she knew Li and Cohen had retrieved everything she needed. And the frigate's crew hadn't boarded the *Medusa* until Haas had Li's hand locked in his and was already stripping the precious data out of her hard files. Nguyen had the data now. So why would she run the risk that someone else might access the *Medusa*'s files, that Sharifi's message might get through? Why would she let the rest of the world in on TechComm's most jealously guarded secret?

The others were with her before the thought was even a word. They hijacked every navigational buoy within broadcast distance of the *Medusa*. They hijacked the NowNet lines that ran through the Ring–Freetown axis and out to the Periphery. Then they started shooting Sharifi's files over every open link they could find.

Your files too, the communications AI said—and before Li could argue he was shooting out the unedited spinfeed of all those long hours in the mine, broadcasting everything she and Cohen had seen and felt since the worldmind first engulfed them.

Watching through the *Medusa*'s nav systems, Li saw the frigate slow and turn. Was she too late? Had it all been for nothing?

But no. They had caught the outbound transmissions. Li saw a quick FTL exchange of encrypted data between the frigate and Corps headquarters on Alba. Then the frigate turned tail, fired up its Bussard drives, and vanished into slow time.

The *Medusa* kept inching toward Freetown, its crew blissfully unaware of their deadly cargo. Meanwhile, Sharifi's message flashed onto FreeNet and across a dozen Bose-Einstein relays onto a dozen planetary nets throughout the length and breadth of streamspace.

Li opened her eyes, amazed at her ability to act simultaneously in realspace and the whirling chaos of

Cohen's systems. The cuffs fell away from her wrists and ankles with a clatter. Haas looked at them unbelievingly for a split second, then jumped away from her.

Li jumped faster. She was on him before Bella's body had taken a step, surrounding him, suffocating him, penetrating him. The station AI fought her, but she ground it to dust, barely stopping to think what she was doing, and slid toward Haas through the numbers, bright and pitiless as a shark. He cried out once. Then there was only Li. Her incandescent purpose. Her glacial, inhuman clarity. Her all-too-human fury.

She'd forgotten about the derms, though. At the last instant Haas quivered, mustered his strength, and ripped them off, leaving her with nothing but the empty vessel of Bella's shunt-suppressed mind.

The last thing she heard as she collapsed was the cool, disembodied echo of Haas's laughter.

She woke to pain and darkness. Her lungs burned. She put a hand to her face, and it came away wet with blood. Hers or Kintz's, she couldn't tell.

She sat up and saw Bella stretched out on the floor in front of her, unmoving but still breathing, thank God. There were voices in her ear. Not the whispers and echoes of the memory palace, but real human voices.

"Daahl?" she called. "Ramirez?"

No answer but crackling, hissing static.

After an eternity something came over the line. It was indistinct at first, lost in interference. But when it cleared, she heard Ramirez calling her name.

"We're ready to come up," she told him.

"Good. Hurry. We'd just about decided to let them go down and look for you."

"Let who down?"

Another garbled, crackling stretch of static.

"What?"

"I said the strike's over. The troops are pulling out. And there's a General Nguyen looking for you."

Nguyen. Christ.

"I need to send a message first. To ALEF."

"Forget ALEF. It's over. Just get up here. It'll make sense as soon as you see the spinfeed."

The news was all over the station. The streets were still, hushed, dark but for the flickering light of the livewalls and the low murmur of the crowds gathered around them.

Sharifi was on every channel. Interrupting news hour, NowNet programming, the last game of the Series. As they passed the All Nite Noodle, Li glanced at the livewall and saw the Mets and Yankees huddled on the infield, staring up at a two-story-high holomonitor Sharifi who smiled as she explained the unprecedented, unlooked-for, inconvenient miracle that was Compson's World.

FreeNet's AIs had been the first to catch the transmission, just as Sharifi must have planned it. Once they realized what they had, they spun it to every channel, every terminal, every press pool in UN space. In a matter of minutes, reporters were calling the General Assembly and the mining companies for position statements.

It wasn't over yet, of course. There would be

debates, compromises, and unholy alliances in the days to come. But they would happen onstream, in public. Compson's fate wouldn't be sealed in Nguyen's office or other equally discreet offices. All of humanity, UN and Syndicate alike, would have a say in it. Sharifi had done that, at least. Her death, Mirce's death, Cohen's death had done that.

Security was deserted; everyone was on the street, dealing with the changes, trying to figure out who was in charge now. Li collapsed in a chair, rubbing her eyes. She wanted a shower. And then she needed to see Sharpe, probably.

She looked up. Bella stood over her.

"What are you still doing here?" she asked.

"Who killed her?" It was the first thing Bella had said to Li since they'd hit station.

"What does it matter, Bella? It's over."

"It's not over for me."

Li stared. The room was so silent she could hear her own pulse drumming in her ears. Bella's body was taut, every muscle rigidly contracted. Her hands were trembling, the nails dirty and broken. There was blood on her. Her own blood. Li's blood. Kintz's blood.

"I have to know," she said.

Li thought back to the vision of Sharifi in the glory hole. To the lost, desperate, adoring way Bella had looked at Sharifi. Whatever else Bella had done, she'd loved her. And been loved in return. Li was sure of that much.

"Voyt killed her," she said.

"I don't believe you."

She looked Bella square in the face, unblinking. "It's true."

"I have a right to know. I need to know."

Li sighed. "You know already, Bella. Think about it."

Li saw the knowledge unfold in her, blossoming like a night flower. She put a hand over her mouth, turned on her heel, and walked across the holding pen into the bathroom. Li heard her retch again and again until there couldn't have been anything left to bring up.

When she came back her face and arms were wet, and there was water on her clothes. But she looked clear-eyed, calm, reasonable. "Who was on-shunt?"

Li started to answer, but Bella spoke before she could. "It was Haas, wasn't it? You don't have to say it, just nod."

Li nodded.

"What are you going to do about it?"

Li shifted in her chair. "What do you mean?"

"Are you going to arrest me?"

"You didn't kill her, Bella. No one's crazy enough to hold someone responsible for crimes committed when they're under a shunt."

"A crime was committed." Bella still sounded rational, but Li was beginning to hear an ominous edge in her voice. "I thought that was what you were doing here. Finding her murderer. Punishing him. Do I have to show you the way to his office? Or was all that talk about right and wrong and punishment just something you made up to get me to believe in you?"

Li pushed her chair back and stood, swaying with exhaustion.

"Sit down, Bella." She put a hand on Bella's shoulder, steered her to a chair and pushed her into it. "Listen to yourself. You want me to march over and arrest Haas? On whose authority? He killed Sharifi on what amounts to Security Council orders. No one's going to punish him. He won't spend a day in jail, no matter what you or I do."

"He killed her."

"Oh, for Christ's sake! She was as good as selling information to the Syndicates."

Neither of them breathed for a moment. Then Bella walked across the room, opened the door, stepped into the street. She turned and looked at Li, her eyes glistening. "So you won't do it?"

"What's the point?"

"What's in it for you, you mean."

Li grabbed the chair Bella had been sitting in and slammed it down hard enough to set the pens and coffee cups rattling on the nearby desks.

"Just leave, Bella. Leave and don't come back and don't ever talk to me again. Because if I have to look at your face for one more second, I swear I won't be responsible for myself. I lost friends down there. And I killed four people to save your worthless carcass. What I do and why and what I get out of it is none of your fucking business!"

Bella stared for a moment, then turned on her heel and left.

Li stood gripping the chair, white-knuckled, while the big doors swung to and fro, regained their equilibrium, and came to a standstill. Then she borrowed someone's forgotten uniform coat, curled up on the duty-room couch, and cried herself into a numb, dead, dreamless sleep.

She woke up falling.

She'd had enough stations shot out from under her in the war to know the feeling. AMC station had just lost rotational stability. And they were about to lose gravity.

Even as she sat up, the emergency systems kicked in and she felt the lurching, shuddering deceleration of four thousand permanent residents and all the clutter that went with them. Her arms and legs lightened, her stomach lurched as the grav lines wavered. The lights dimmed and the ventilation ducts overhead fell silent. The systems picked up again, but the rush of air was fainter now, the overhead panels dimmer. Someone had just shut down the massive Stirling cycle engines buried in the station's core; they were running on emergency power.

There was still partial gravity, enough to make things easier than they would be in a very few minutes. She tapped in to the station net, trying to figure out what was going on; but the net was down, or she was locked out of it. She got carefully to her feet and began moving out into the main room of the HQ, where the duty officer hovered behind the counter looking bewildered by this sudden reversal of the laws of gravity as stationers knew them.

"What's going on?" Li asked.

He started so violently at the sight of her that he bounced off the counter and had to scrabble for traction to keep from drifting sideways. Only then did she look down at herself and realize she hadn't washed or changed since reaching the station.

"Christ. Sorry." She rummaged through the lockers at the back of the room until she'd found something almost small enough. Meanwhile, others were starting to filter into HQ, all trying to figure out what had shut down the gravity and what they were supposed to do about it.

It wasn't until the chief engineer called saying he couldn't find Haas that she finally put the pieces together.

She burst into Haas's office just as the precession ring ground to a stop and gravity gave out completely. It caught her off guard, and she careened across the room, her feet stranded in midair above the star-filled floorport.

She saw Haas out of the corner of her eye. He sat in the chair behind the big desk. His face looked peaceful, except for the mottled bruises spreading beneath his eyes.

Bella stood, or rather floated, above him.

She hung weightless over the tide-swept slab of the crystal desk. Her hair writhed like a vipers' nest. Her eyes were closed, her face pale, her chest rising and falling in a sinister parody of a sleeper's breathing. Her smile sent cold fingers brushing down Li's spine.

Something—her own subconscious or one of Cohen's remnant systems—nudged at her, prompting her to run a network scan.

Spitting, flaring lines of current shot out from Bella, splicing into each of the station's embedded systems, running back and forth between station and planet, between surface and mine shaft. And all that immense power was being channeled into the single frail wire that connected Bella's jack to the derms at Haas's temples.

She was breaking him. Slowly, pitilessly, irresistibly. She had locked him into the loop shunt somehow and was running the whole vast power of the worldmind through him, killing him.

Li looked at Haas, slumped over the glowing desk. She looked at Bella's peaceful face, at the hair circling her head like the flaming corona of an eclipsed star.

She is coming down from the mountains, she thought. *Singing. With stones in her hands*.

She called Security.

"I'm in Haas's office," she said. "Don't send anyone. Everything's fine here."

SLOW TIME

▶ [There lies] the mountain called Atlas, very tapered and
round; so lofty, moreover, that the top (it is said) cannot
be seen, the clouds never quitting it either summer or
winter . . . The natives are reported not to eat any living
thing and never to have any dreams.

—HERODOTUS

Segain to see the night before she left—and by that time the guards wouldn't let her in.

They were planetary militia, whatever that meant now, and they weren't taking orders from anyone in UN uniform.

"You're not authorized anymore," said a sergeant Li belatedly recognized as one of Ramirez's fellow kidnappers. He squared his shoulders as if expecting her to fight and squirmed his feet deeper into the zero-g loops.

Behind him she could see the corridor leading to Haas's office. It was shut down, life support ticking over at the bare minimum required to keep the air breathable and the water running.

A group of miners shoved past Li, smelling like they'd just come up from the pit, and pulled along the guide ropes toward the office.

"And *they're* authorized?" she asked incredulously.

The sergeant shrugged. "They're regulars. Cartwright

cleared them. What do you want from me? No UN personnel past this point without specific authorization. That's cleared all the way up the line to Helena. Which is as far as the line goes now."

"Fine," Li said. "Call Cartwright."

When she finally got into Haas's office, she barely recognized it.

Only the immense gleaming desk and the starlight seeping in through the floorport were the same. The rest of the room had become a shadowy chaos of charms, candles, statues, prayer plaques. Flames burned round and unearthly in zero g, hanging above the candlewicks like will-o'-the-wisps. Rosaries swayed like seaweed in unseen air currents. Wax from the candles floated around the room, dangerously hot, and accreted on every surface.

And then there were the people. The believers, the doubters, and the merely curious trooped through one after another. They whispered. They stared. They prayed. They asked questions.

Most of all, though, they asked for voices. Voices of lost friends. Voices of loved ones. Voices that Bella delivered to them.

She hung above the desk, just where Li had last seen her, a space-age sybil suspended in zero gravity. She spoke in a hundred voices. She spoke the names of the dead and pulled their words from the darkness, pushing back—just for a moment—the shadows of loss and doubt and death.

Li stood in a dark corner and watched. The pilgrims must be feeding Bella, she realized. They must be clothing her, washing her. Someone must be brushing that coal black halo of hair. Did she care? Did she even notice them? What deathly twilight had she passed into?

Li watched long enough to learn the rhythms of the

air currents that traveled through the chamber, the way they played along Bella's skirt hem and turned her hair into a Medusa's crown. She watched the sun set beneath her feet, and the room fade into the bleak blue and gray of starlight.

She thought Bella was asleep, but around sunset she opened her eyes and looked straight at Li as if she'd locked on to the sound of her breathing. "Is it you?" Li asked.

"It's always me."

The air crackled with static, setting Li's hair on end and sucking the thin silk of Bella's dress against her legs. Her skirt had hitched up above her knees. It bothered Li to think that the miners would be trooping in and out of the room staring at her, and that Bella was too far gone into the void of the worldmind to notice. She stepped forward, grabbed the thin cloth and pulled it down around Bella's ankles, covering her.

Bella smiled. As if she knew what Li was thinking. As if she were laughing at her.

"Are you happy?" Li asked.

"I'm sorry about your mother. And Cohen."

Li swallowed. "Are they all right?"

"Mirce is. The AI is . . . more complicated."

"Is he—?"

"We're all alive, Catherine. Can't you feel us? We feel you. Every part of you, every voice, every network, no matter where you are in the station. We love you."

Li closed her eyes and covered her face with her hands.

"Katie," Bella said. It was her father's voice.

"Don't! I won't listen!"

Bella shrugged, but when she spoke again it was in her own voice. "Most people find it gives them comfort."

"I don't want comfort."

She did, though. She wanted it so much it terrified her. She wondered if Mirce's voice would come out of

Bella's perfect lips. Or McCuen's voice. She could ask, she supposed. What harm would it do? But she couldn't ask for the one voice she wanted to hear. Because if she heard that voice, even once, she'd never have the strength to walk away from it.

"Are you sure?" Bella asked.

Li turned around and left and didn't look back.

Nguyen's call was waiting when she got back to her quarters. "Not answering the phone these days?" Nguyen said.

Li shrugged.

"I see. Playing the bereaved widow. Well, you made enough money off him that I guess you should at least go through the motions. Who would have thought he'd leave you everything?"

Li kept her mouth shut; it wasn't even worth trying to find out how Nguyen had gotten hold of that piece of information.

"You won't keep any of it, of course. The advocate general will challenge it. And win. Half of the hardware Cohen's system ran on is covered by government patents and licenses. They'll bankrupt you."

Li looked down at her hands, took a breath. "Is that all you called about, or was there something else?"

Nguyen smiled coldly and reached outside the VR field to retrieve a dog-eared yellow piece of paper. "We know. We know everything. It's over, Li."

"If it was really over, you wouldn't be talking to me."

"I've been authorized to offer you a way out. Under the circumstances, we decided . . . discretion was the best approach."

Li waited.

"You'll ship back to Alba with the rest of the station personnel for debriefing. When you arrive, you'll request a leave of absence for health reasons. Once things have settled down a bit, you'll resign. Quietly. A suitable job will be found for you in the private sector. And we'll all forget about what happened or didn't happen on Compson's."

"That's clear enough."

"Good, then. It's agreed."

"No."

Nguyen caught her breath and leaned forward almost imperceptibly in her chair. "Do you actually think you can weather this scandal? Are you really that arrogant?"

"You have the right to drum me out of the Service. I'd probably do the same in your place." Li laughed briefly. "Hell, in your place I'd probably put a bullet in my skull and call it even. But you don't have the right to make me resign. You don't have the right to make me slink off quietly."

"That's pretty sanctimonious under the circumstances."

"Maybe."

Comprehension dawned on Nguyen's face, only to be chased away by disdain. "You weren't thinking of the money at all, were you?" she asked. "You actually talked yourself into thinking you were doing the right thing. Or you let Cohen talk you into it. Did you actually think it was your decision to make? Did you think you had the right to put billions of UN citizens at risk because of your moral scruples?"

Li didn't answer.

"Amazing," Nguyen said. "But then traitors never seem to feel the normal rules apply to them, do they?"

Li didn't have an answer for that either.

"I'm going to pretend we didn't have this talk," Nguyen said after a moment. "You'll have months of slow time on the evac ship to think about what you want to do when you dock at Alba. If I were you, though, I wouldn't even get on that ship. Trust me, you won't find much to come home to. I intend to spend the next little while making sure of that."

Li laughed, suddenly overcome by the ridiculousness of the situation. She shook her head and grinned into the VR field. "You're fantastic, Helen."

Nguyen blinked, paled. "I always hated that look on Cohen's face," she said. "I hate it even more on yours."

In the end they shut down the last working Bose-Einstein relay and quarantined the whole system. There was no other way to keep the worldmind off the spinstream, no other way to keep it from sweeping through every UN system and rifling through every network. And even before the last ship pulled out there were rumors coursing through streamspace that the AIs would defy the quarantine, that the Consortium had sent out sublight probes to reinitiate contact, that FreeNet, or at least part of it, would be opened to the worldmind.

Li caught her ship in a daze, too numb to care where she was going, or what Nguyen would have waiting for her when she got there. She clung to the guy ropes of a half-ton flat of emergency rations as the ship lumbered out of port and watched Compson's World slip away from her for the last time through the cargo bay's narrow viewport.

The ship cast off and drifted a little before its maneuvering engines stuttered into life. The station's belly loomed above her, slipped sternward, and was replaced by stars and darkness. The solar arrays brushed by like wings, their frozen joints crusted with eight days' worth of unthawed condensation ice. Then they were out in open space, and she could look back and see it all spread out below her.

The station was crippled, dying. The Stirling engines had shut down in the first crisis, and once the massive interlocking rings stopped spinning against each other it was only a matter of time until the living and working spokes faded into flat, cold, weightless darkness. A third of the outer ring was still lit up and functioning. The rest was dark already, the shadowed side of a jeweled carnival mask.

They were being evicted, politely but firmly. Compson's World and the skies above it no longer belonged to them.

Li blew on the cold viruflex until it frosted, then pressed her forehead against it. Her eyes felt hot and dry. She kept thinking she should do something, but there was nothing to do, nothing anyone needed her for. And there would be weeks, months of this nothing before they reached Alba and what was left of her life started up again.

She should care more about it than she did—should be able to muster curiosity, if nothing else, about whether she would return home to a new assignment or a court-martial or worse. But what was the point of thinking that way? You cared, or you didn't care. The rest was mere survival.

<Reset>

She shook her head irritably, prodding malfunctioning wetware back into silence.

<4280000pF>

She sighed and rubbed her temples. A pair of skinny brown legs appeared in her peripheral vision. Dusty. Barefooted.

Hyacinthe?

She tried to focus on the vision. Lost it. Then something flashed pale on the edge of sight, and she looked, and she could just make him out, faintly, as if he weren't quite there. But the eyes were there. And couldn't she feel him hacking the ship's net, pirating its VR programs. Or was she just fooling herself?

For God's sake, say something! The thought ripped out of her like flesh being torn away.

Sorry. I'm a little shaky. But it's me this time. Most of me, anyway. He climbed onto the platform, very carefully, holding on with both hands, and sat beside her.

She felt something come alive in her chest, testing the wind, opening strong wings. She took a deep breath and realized it was the first time in days she hadn't felt that weight on her chest. He filled up her eyes. She couldn't bear to look at him. She turned without speaking and looked out the viewport toward the dying station. "Funny how it still looks more or less okay from the outside," she said. "I wonder if they'll be able to salvage anything when they come back."

"I don't think they're coming back. They may come back to fight, but even then . . . I don't think they can face it."

"What about the AIs?"

"We'll be back. We have to come back. This is our future. Or one of our possible futures."

"What was it like down there?"

"It's what Sharifi said: a chance to look into the shuffle. Everything is possible, and everything that's possible *is*. It was wonderful. Terrifying. I almost forgot to come back."

Li felt a flare of anger shoot through her. He could have come back anytime? Days ago? Hadn't he even thought about what Nguyen would think? What Bella and the rest of them would think? What she would think?

You know I came as soon as I could.

The thought brushed along the edges of her mind, soft and tickling. Asking for forgiveness without quite asking. *Butterfly kisses*, she thought with a flash of child's memory. But when she fished for the memory, she couldn't get it back, couldn't tell whether it was hers or Cohen's. A shiver went through her at the thought that she could confuse the two. Then the fear drifted into . . . something. Something she could live with, even if she didn't understand it yet.

"Why did you come back?" she asked.

"You promised to think about something. I wanted to know what you decided."

She couldn't feel him, couldn't read him the way she had during those hours in the mine. But he had to know. How could he touch her, how could he look at her without knowing?

"I told you," she said.

"Feeling something doesn't mean you can follow through on it."

"No," she said. "It doesn't, does it?"

He had drawn back from her a little as they spoke. Now he reached out and touched her hand and looked into her eyes. "What do you want *now*, Catherine?"

She looked back at him, feeling the warmth and the pull of him, the something in his smile that lived beyond and below words, that she no longer had to pin down or put a name to. The image of a rose took shape in her mind. A real rose, a little hurt in its spines, a little rot in its redness. A rose and its thorns.

"Everything." She smiled. "All of it."

FURTHER READING

Readers who follow what Lee Smolin has called the spectator sport of quantum physics will recognize the long shadows cast in this story by the theories of John Stuart Bell, Charles Bennett, David Deutsch, Hugh Everett, Chris Isham, Roger Penrose, John Smolin, Lee Smolin, John Archibald Wheeler, and others. The professional literature on quantum information theory, quantum gravity, spinfoam, the Many-Worlds interpretation of quantum mechanics and associated concepts is, of course, vast. What follows is a brief list of books and articles that were particularly helpful during the writing of *Spin State*.

These sources range from popular introductions to professional literature. I hesitate to steer readers toward one end or another of the spectrum; there are many concepts (quantum-teleportation comes to mind) for which the clearest and simplest explanation really is in the professional literature. For incorrigible mathophobes, however, I have marked equation-free texts with an asterisk (*).

Quantum Physics Generally[1]

John Stuart Bell. *Speakable and Unspeakable in Quantum Mechanics*. Cambridge: Cambridge University Press, 1987.

M. Bell, K. Gottfried, M. Veltman, eds. *John S. Bell on the Foundations of Quantum Mechanics*. Singapore: World Scientific Publishing Co., 2001.

*Jeremy Bernstein. *Quantum Profiles*. Princeton, New Jersey: Princeton University Press, 1991.

*Barbara Lovett Cline. *The Questioners: Physicists and the Quantum Theory*. New York: Crowell, 1965.

*Robert P. Crease and Charles C. Mann. *The Second Creation: Makers of the Revolution in Twentieth-Century Physics*. New Jersey: Rutgers University Press, 1986.

Ian Duck, E. C. G. Sudarshan. *100 Years of Planck's Quantum*. Singapore: World Scientific Publishing Co., 2000.

David K. Ferry. *Quantum Mechanics: An Introduction for Device Physicists and Electrical Engineers, 2nd Ed.* Bristol: Institute of Physics Publishing, 2001.

*Richard P. Feynman. *QED: The Strange Theory of Light and Matter*. Princeton, New Jersey: Princeton University Press, 1985.

---

[1] The original articles of Bohr, Heisenberg, Schrödinger, Dirac, et al. make for fascinating reading. For those interested in reading these articles in their original form, I strongly recommend Duck and Sudarshan's *100 Years of Planck's Quantum*, which presents the major publications accompanied by annotations and explanations aimed at today's physics students. A number of the early articles are far more accessible when read with this book in hand.

*Richard P. Feynman, *The Character of Physical Law*. Cambridge, MA: MIT Press, 1965.

A. P. French, P. J. Kennedy, eds. *Niels Bohr, A Centenary Volume*. Cambridge, MA: Harvard University Press, 1985.

*Murray Gell-Mann. *The Quark and the Jaguar: Adventures in the Simple and the Complex*. New York: W. H. Freeman & Co., 1995.

*Adrian Kent. "Night Thoughts of a Quantum Physicist," in *Visions of the Future: Physics and Electronics*, ed. J. Michael T. Thompson. Cambridge, UK: Cambridge University Press, 2001.

*Gerard Milburn. *Schrödinger's Machines: The Quantum Technology Reshaping Everyday Life*. New York: W. H. Freeman & Co., 1997.

B. L. Van der Waerden. *Sources of Quantum Mechanics*. Amsterdam: North-Holland Publishing Co., 1967.

Quantum Information Theory
(EPR, Quantum Cryptography, and Quantum Computing)[2]

*Amir D. Aczel. *Entanglement: The Greatest Mystery in Physics*. New York: Four Walls Eight Windows, 2002.

A. Aspect, J. Dalibard, and G. Roger. "Experimental Test of Bell's Inequalities Using Time-Varying Analyzers," *Phys. Rev. Lett.* 49 (25), 1804 (1982).

[2]The best introduction to quantum information theory, for readers willing to stumble through college-level physics problems (or at least try), is Nielsen and Chuang. Readers interested in the ideas but not necessarily the math should look to Deutsch, Brown, or Williams and Clearwater.

J. S. Bell, "On the Einstein-Podolsky-Rosen Paradox," *Physics*, 1–3, 195 (1964).

C. H. Bennett, "Classical and Quantum Information: Similarities and Differences," *Frontiers in Quantum Physics*, eds. S. C. Lim, R. Abd-Shukor, K. H. Kwek. Singapore: Springer-Verlag, 1998.

C. H. Bennett, "Quantum Cryptography Using Any Two Nonorthogonal States," *Phys. Rev. Lett.* 68(21), 3121 (1992).

C. H. Bennett, S. J. Weisner, "Communication via One- and Two-Particle Operators on EPR States," *Phys. Rev. Lett.* 69(20), 2881 (1992).

C. H. Bennett, G. Brassard, C. Crépeau, R. Jozsa, A. Peres, and W. K. Wootters, "Teleporting an Unknown Quantum State via Dual Classical and EPR Channels," *Phys. Rev. Lett.* 70(13), 1895 (1993).

*C. H. Bennett, G. Brassard, C. Crépeau, R. Jozsa, A. Peres, and W. K. Wootters, "Quantum Cryptography," *Scientific American*, Oct. 1992, p. 50.

C. H. Bennett, "Quantum Information and Computation," *Physics Today* 48(10), 24 (1995).

C. H. Bennett, D. P. DiVicenzo, J. A. Smolin, "Capacities of Quantum Erasure Channels," *Phys. Rev. Lett.* 78(16), 3217 (1997).

N. Bohr, "Can Quantum-Mechanical Description of Physical Reality Be Considered Complete?" *Phys. Rev.* 48, 696 (1935).

*Michael Brooks, ed. *Quantum Computing and Communications*. London: Springer-Verlag, 1999.

*Julian Brown. *Minds, Machines and the Multiverse*. New York: Simon & Schuster, 2000.

Cohen, Horne, Stachel, eds. *Potentiality, Entanglement and Passion-at-a-Distance: Quantum Mechanical Studies for Abner Shimony* (Vol. 2). Dordrecht: Kluwer Academic Publishers, 1997.

Alexander Giles Davis, "Quantum Electronics: Beyond the Transistor," in *Visions of the Future: Physics and Electronics*, ed. J. Michael T. Thompson. Cambridge, UK: Cambridge University Press, 2001.

David Deutsch, Patrick Hayden, "Information Flow in Entangled Quantum Systems." Oxford, UK: Center for Quantum Computation, Clarendon Laboratory, University of Oxford, June 1999.

*David Deutsch. *The Fabric of Reality*. New York: Penguin, 1997.

David Deutsch, "Quantum Theory: The Church-Türing Principle and the Universal Quantum Computer," *Roy. Soc. Lond.* A 400, 97 (1985).

A. Einstein, B. Podolsky, N. Rosen, "Can Quantum-Mechanical Description of Physical Reality Be Considered Complete?" *Phys. Rev.* 47, 477 (1935).

Richard P. Feynman, "Quantum Mechanical Computers," *Between Quantum and Cosmos: Essays in Honor of John Archibald Wheeler*, eds. W. H. Zurek, A. van der Merwe, W. A. Miller. Princeton, New Jersey: Princeton University Press, 1988.

Richard P. Feynman, "Simulating Physics with Computers," *Int. J. Theor. Phys.* 21, 467 (1982).

L. Grover, "Quantum Mechanics Helps in Searching for a Needle in a Haystack," *Phys. Rev. Lett.* 80, 325 (1998).

L. Grover, "Quantum Computers Can Search Rapidly By Using Almost Any Transformation," *Phys. Rev. Lett.* 80, 4329 (1998).

N. David Mermin, "A Bolt from the Blue: The E-P-R Paradox," in *Niels Bohr: A Centenary Volume*, eds. A. P. French, P. J. Kennedy. Cambridge, MA: Harvard University Press, 1985.

*Gerard Milburn. *The Feynman Processor: Quantum Entanglement and the Computing Revolution*. Malibu, CA: Perseus Books, 1998.

*M. Mosca, R. Jozsa, A. Steane, and A. Ekert, "Quantum-Enhanced Information Processing," in *Visions of the Future: Physics and Electronics*, ed. J. Michael T. Thompson. Cambridge, UK: Cambridge University Press, 2001.

Michael A. Nielsen and Isaac L. Chuang, *Quantum Computation and Quantum Information*. Cambridge, UK: Cambridge University Press, 2000.

B. Schumacher, "Sending Entanglement Through Noisy Channels," Bose-Einsteinint, quant-ph/9604023 (1996).

*Tom Siegfried. *The Bit and the Pendulum: From Quantum Computing to M Theory—the New Physics of Information*. New York: John Wiley & Sons, Inc., 2000.

*Colin P. Williams and Scott H. Clearwater. *Ultimate Zero and One: Computing at the Quantum Frontier*. New York: Copernicus, 2000.

*Michale Zeise, "Spin Electronics," in *Visions of the Future: Physics and Electronics*, ed. J. Michael T. Thompson. Cambridge, UK: Cambridge University Press, 2001.

W. H. Zurek, "Decoherence, Chaos, and the Physics of Information," in *Frontiers in Quantum Physics*, eds. S. C. Lim, R. Abd-Shukor, K. H. Kwek. Singapore: Springer-Verlag, 1998. (See in particular C. H. Bennett, "Classical and Quantum Information: Similarities and Differences," p. 24.)

W. H. Zurek, "Decoherence and the Transition from Quantum to Classical," *Physics Today* 44, 36 (1991).

Spinfoam, Wormholes, Time, and Other Strange Beasts ...

A. Andersen, B. De Witt, "Does the Topology of Space Fluctuate?" *Between Quantum and Cosmos: Essays in Honor of John Archibald Wheeler*, eds. W. H. Zurek, A. van der Merwe, W. A. Miller. Princeton, New Jersey: Princeton University Press, 1988.

B. De Witt, N. Graham, eds. *The Many-Worlds Interpretation of Quantum Mechanics*. Princeton, New Jersey: Princeton University Press, 1973.

Hugh Everett, " 'Relative State' Formulation of Quantum Mechanics," *Rev. Mod. Phys.* 29(3), 454 (1957).[3]

Rodolfo Gambini, Jorge Pulin. *Loops, Knots, Gauge Theories and Quantum Gravity*. Cambridge, UK: Cambridge University Press, 1996.

Chris J. Isham. *Modern Differential Geometry for Physicists, 2nd Ed.* Singapore: World Scientific Publishing Co., 1999.

Chris J. Isham. *Lectures on Quantum Theory: Mathematical and Structural Foundations*. London: Imperial College Press, 1995.

---

[3]The original Many-Worlds article, though the longer explanation in Everett's thesis has since been reprinted in De Witt and Graham, 1973.

Chris J. Isham, Roger Penrose, eds. *Quantum Concepts in Space and Time*. Oxford, UK: Clarendon Press, 1986.

C. W. Misner, K. S. Thorne, J. A. Wheeler. *Gravitation*. San Francisco: W. H. Freeman Co., 1973.

Roger Penrose, Wolfgang Rindler. *Spinors and Space-Time*. Cambridge, UK: Cambridge University Press, 1984.

B. G. Sidharth, "Quantum Mechanical Black Holes: An Alternative Perspective," in *Frontiers in Quantum Physics*, eds. S. C. Lim, R. Abd-Shukor, K. H. Kwek. Singapore: Springer-Verlag, 1998.

*Lee Smolin. *Life of the Cosmos*. Oxford, UK: Oxford University Press, 1996.

L. Smolin, "The Future of Spin Networks," in *The Geometric Universe*, eds. S. A. Hugget et al. Oxford: Oxford University Press, 1998.

*Lee Smolin. *Three Roads to Quantum Gravity*. UK: Spartan Press, 2001.

K. S. Thorne, "Closed Timelike Curves," in *General Relativity and Gravitation 1992: Proceedings of the Thirteenth Annual Conference on General Relativity and Gravitation*, 295. Bristol: Institute of Physics Publishing, 1993.

Matt Visser. *Lorentzian Wormholes from Einstein to Hawking*. New York: American Institute of Physics, 1995.

John Archibald Wheeler. *Geons, Black Holes, and Quantum Foam: A Life in Physics*. New York: W. W. Norton, 1998.

J. A. Wheeler, "Assessment of Everett's 'Relative State' Formulation of Quantum Theory," *Rev. Mod. Phys.* 29(3), 463 (1957).

ABOUT THE AUTHOR

Chris Moriarty was born in 1968 and has lived in the United States, Europe, Southeast Asia, and Latin America. Chris has worked—though not necessarily in the following order—as a ranch hand, horse trainer, backcountry guide, freelance editor, and lawyer.

Be sure not to miss

SPIN CONTROL

The thrilling sequel to *Spin State*

by Chris Moriarty

Available now from Bantam Spectra

Here's a special excerpt.

SPIN CONTROL

1.0

She was probably not yet thirty.

It was hard to tell with humans. They all looked old to Arkady, and they aged fast out here in the Trusteeships, where people lost months and decades just getting from one planet to the next. Still, he didn't think she could be more than a few subjective years beyond his twenty-eight.

"Act like you're picking me up," she said in a low, husky voice that would have been sensual had it not been ratcheted tight by fear. She spoke UN-standard Spanish, but he guessed by her flat vowels and guttural consonants that her native tongue was Hebrew.

She leaned on the bar, flagged down the barkeep, and ordered two of something Arkady had never heard of. When she gripped his arm to draw him closer to her, he saw that she'd bitten her nails to the quick and her skin was ravaged by decades of unfiltered sunlight.

He bent over her, smelling the acrid fungal smell of the planet-born, and recited the words Korchow had taught him back on Gilead. She fed him back the answers he'd been told to wait for. She was pulling them off hard memory; he could see the black blossom of her left pupil unfurl across the pale iris every time she accessed her virally embedded RAM array. He tried not to stare and failed.

This is your first monster, he told himself. *Get used to them.*

He assessed the woman's face, wondering if she was what other members of her species would call beautiful. He decided it was unlikely. Humans, like constructs, valued symmetry; and to his crèche-born eyes her features looked as mismatched as if they'd been culled from a dozen disparate genelines. The predatory nose jutted over an incongruously delicate jawline. The forehead was high, but too flat and scowling to get past any competent genetic designer. And even under the dim flicker of the strobe lights it was obvious that her eyes were mismatched. The left eye was a crisp clean blue so pale that it seemed transparent unless she was looking directly at you. The right eye was a cloudy mottled gray. And while the blue eye stared unflinchingly at Arkady, the gray one grazed his shoulder to wander across the open room behind him so that he had to fight a constant urge turn around and see who she was really speaking to.

"Why did you come!" she asked as soon as she was satisfied that he was who he said he was.

"You know why."

"I mean the real reason."

You have to ask for money, Korchow had told him. How he remembered Korchow's clever face, a manifesto in flesh and blood of everything that a KnowlesSyndicate A series construct was supposed to stand for. *You have no idea what money means to humans, Arkady. It's how they reward each other. How they control each other. If you don't ask for it, you won't feel real to them.*

"I came for the money," Arkady said, trying not to sound like an explorer trading beads with the natives.

"And you trust us to give it to you?"

"You know who I trust," he answered, still following Korchow's script. "You know who I need to see."

"At least you had the wits not to say his name," she muttered, glancing at the shadowy maze of ventilation ducts and spinstream conduits overhead to indicate that they were under surveillance.

"Here?" Arkady asked incredulously.

"Everywhere. The AIs can tap any spinfeed, anytime, anywhere. You're in UN space now, so get used to it."

Arkady looked into the mirror, scanning the cavernous room behind him, and wondered what the people he saw drinking around him could possibly be doing that was worth the attention of UNSec's semisentients.

These weren't humans as he'd been raised to believe in them. Where were the fat-cat profiteers and the spiritually bankrupt individualists of his Knowles-Syndicate civics textbooks? Where were the gene traders? Where were the slave drivers and the oppressed and virtuous genetic constructs? All he saw here were jumpship crews and Coltran prospectors, Bose-Einstein miners and pipeline navvies. Posthumans whose genetic heritage was too haphazard for anyone to be able to guess whether they were human or construct or some unknown subspecies between the two. People who scratched out a living from stones and mud and carried the dirt of planets under their fingernails. Throwaway people.

Arkasha would probably have said they were beautiful. He would have talked passionately about pre-Migration literature, about the slow sure currents of evolution and the vast chaotic genetic river that was post-humanity. But all Arkady could see here was poverty, disease, and danger.

The bartender slapped two beers down in front of them hard enough to send the sour-smelling liquid cascading onto the scarred countertop. The woman picked up hers and drank, but Arkady just stared at his. He could smell it from here, and it smelled bad. Like yeast and old skin and overloaded air-filters. Like all the smells he was beginning to recognize as the smells of humans.

"Who sent you?" the woman asked abruptly.

"I'm here on my own account. I thought you understood that."

"We understood that that was what you *wanted* us to believe." She had a habit of slowing and hanging on a single word in a sentence, he noticed. It gave the chosen word a weight at odds with its apparent significance and left Arkady wondering if any of her words meant what they seemed to mean. "Still, it wouldn't be the first time a professional came across the lines posing as an amateur."

Arkady picked up his glass and forced himself to sip at it, buying time.

Don't explain, don't apologize, Korchow had told him. Right before he'd told him what would happen to Arkasha if he failed.

"I am an amateur. I'm a myrmecologist."

"Whatever the fuck that is."

"I study ants. For terraforming."

"And that's why they sent you to . . . where they sent you to?" she asked incredulously. "To do terraforming?"

"The Syndicates need planets."

"Still. It's dangerous. And there's no Bose-Einstein relay. You must have lost years in slow time."

"Seven."

She smiled enigmatically. "A dog's age. Did they pay you or draft you?"

"Neither."

"You *volunteered*?"

"I'm sorry." Arkady's confusion was genuine. "What is volunteered?"

The blue eye narrowed, while the gray one remained serenely focused on the middle distance. For the first time Arkady wondered if the lazy eye was a birth defect or the product of a home-brewed streamspace interface gone wrong. But if it was the virtual sensorium of streamspace she was looking at, then what was she seeing there? And who was paying her access fees?

A movement caught Arkady's eye, and he glanced sideways to find a lone drinker staring at him down the grease-smeared length of the viristeel bartop. Arkady watched the man take in his unlined skin, his too-symmetrical, too-perfect features, the gleam of perfect health that bespoke decades of painstaking sociogenetic engineering. They locked eyes, and Arkady noticed what he should have noticed before: the dusty green flash of the Interfaither's skullcap on the man's shaved head.

Korchow's team had broken Arkady's nose and one cheekbone before he'd left Gilead, but that suddenly seemed like thin protection. Did he still wear his identity on his face despite all their precautions? If so, he was in more danger with every minute he spent in this place. The war between the United Nations and the Syndicates might be over, but the dying wasn't. A human mob had killed an entire contract group of constructs just a year ago and mutilated the bodies so badly that all their home Syndicates ever got back were diplomatic apologies.

You think we're any different? Arkasha had asked when the news hit. And Arkady had fed him some ideologically impeccable speech about sociogenetics and the elimination of intraspecies violence. It made him cringe now to think of it.

The Interfaither caught Arkady's eye again, then spat and turned away.

"Creature of magicians," the woman muttered, "return to your dust!"

"What?" Arkady asked, though he knew somehow that she had seen the man spit, and that her words were a response to the gesture.

"It's from the Talmud." Again the intent inward gaze as she accessed her RAM array. How much data, Arkady wondered, could she store internally? Certainly more than the few paltry gigabytes that the Syndicates' system of biorhythmically enhanced mnemonics allowed. Clearly being a monster had its advantages. "It goes: 'The Rabbah created a man and sent him to Rabbi Zera. Rabbi Zera spoke to him but received no answer. Thereupon he said to him: 'Creature of the magicians, return to your dust!' And that's how the first golem died."

"What's a golem?"

"A man without a soul," she said. She laughed a laugh that was as flat and hard and hostile as everything else about her. "You."

Arkady shivered and wrapped his hands around his glass, feeling the cold skin of condensation that had formed on it in the mold-tinged humidity of the overpopulated station.

You were wrong, Arkasha. They're another species. We're divided by our history, by our ideology, by the very genes we hold in common. All we share is the memory of what Earth was before we killed it.

1.1

Her name was Osnat.

Hebrew? German? Ethiopian? Arkasha would have known which half-dead language had spawned such a name. It was exactly the kind of thing Arkasha had always known. And exactly the kind of thing Arkady had never learned for himself because he'd always thought Arkasha, or someone like Arkasha, would be there to tell him.

Osnat guided him through the back passages of the station as sure-footedly as if she'd been born there. Only when she stopped at a deserted junction and stood blinking under the dim lights did he realize she had a map in her head. After a series of turnings that were meant to confuse him and did, she dove down a main spoke and led him out of the heavy gravity of the habitat and precession rings toward the station's core. By the time they emerged into the flickering arc lights of the commercial docks, they were nearly weightless. Osnat moved expertly through the low gravity, ignoring the stevedores and cargo haulers, confidently dodging house-sized jumpship containers. When she finally ducked into the shadowy alley of a private dock, the move was so unexpected that she'd reached the gate and turned to wait for Arkady before he'd stopped his drifting progress and turned to follow her.

He looked through the berth's scratched porthole and saw a dimly lit viruflex tether snaking off into the void. At its far end, looking as if it had been cut out with scissors and pasted against a black construction-paper sky, floated the ancient impact-scarred hulk of a Bussard-drive-powered tramp freighter.

He couldn't make out a name on the battered hull or see what flag the ship was flying. He glanced at the berth's display screen, but it was broken, disconnected, or both. Osnat palmed the scanner, and status lights flickered into life as the gate began its purge and disinfect cycle.

"No one said anything about getting on a ship," Arkady protested, though it was far too late to back out or demand answers.

"So your *employers* don't seem to be keeping you too well informed," Osnat said, supremely unmoved. "What am I supposed to do about it?"

Arkady didn't answer, partly because she was right and partly because he was racking his faded memories of pre-Breakaway history, trying to figure out what *employers* were.

The purge and disinfect cycle ended. The air lock irised open. A frigid breeze wafted over them, smelling of space and viruflex. Arkady peered down the long tunnel of the tether toward the place the freighter should have been, but all he could see was scuffed white walls curving away into infinity.

Osnat put a hard hand to the small of his back and pushed him out into the cold. When he turned to face her, she was standing just inside the first ring of the tether and riding its movements with the ease of an old space dog. It took Arkady a curiously long time to notice the gun in her hand.

"You're a piss-poor spy, Arkady. Or whatever the hell your real name is."

"I'm not a—"

"Yeah, yeah. Ants. You told me. Well, cheer up, you'll get plenty of them where we're going."

"Where *are* we going, Osnat?"

"Just put your filter on."

He pulled the unit out of his pack and tried to activate it, but his fingers fumbled on the unfamiliar controls. Osnat shifted from foot to foot impatiently, cursed under her breath, and finally grabbed it from him. He thought briefly of grappling with her now that her hands were occupied. He imagined himself slipping back through the air lock into the relative safety of the station. But he was no athlete, even by human standards, and one look at Osnat's hard body and strong hands discouraged him.

She slipped the mask over his face and demonstrated the filter's working with quick gestures of her ragged fingers. "This line connects to an air tank if you need one. The tank clamps on here and here. Did they give you spare filters?"

"I think so." He checked. "Yes."

"Well, you'll need them. The ship's clean. Clean

enough, anyway. But once we're dirtside, the filter stays on anytime you can see open desert. And you change it every eight hours until the doctor clears you. *If* he clears you. No matter what they tell you. You're not engineered to survive where we're going."

"Are you?"

She squinted at him, lips pressed together in a bloodless line, and he realized that the question, as ordinary to him as asking about the weather, had offended her. Then she laughed. "I guess you could call it that," she said. "A few million years of the best engineering no money can buy. They give you all the shots we told them to?"

He nodded. There'd been dozens of shots, starting with a bewildering array of antiallergens and intestinal fauna and ending with cholera, tuberculosis, polio, yellow fever. Arkady had sat in his bare white room on Gilead Orbital—a prison cell for all intents and purposes, though there was no lock on the door and he would never have thought to call it a prison before Arkasha—and tried to guess where he was going from the shots he was getting. He had failed. No immigration authority anywhere in UN space required such a battery of inoculations; if such a hellhole still existed somewhere in the vast swath of the galaxy that belonged to humans and their slaves, then the humans were ashamed enough to keep it secret.

"Good," Osnat was saying. "Where we're going, an allergic reaction doesn't mean sniffles and a runny nose."

Arkady shivered. "Where are we going?" he asked. "Please, Osnat."

"Haven't you figured it out yet?" Osnat sighted down the barrel of her gun at him and a smile drifted across her face like a perfect cloud drifting across a terraformed sky in summer. "We're going to run you through the blockade," she said. "You're going to Earth, golem."

There were three men waiting for them on the bridge of the freighter.

Two were just muscle. The third, however, was quite the other thing.

Slender, sharp-eyed, professorial in wire-rimmed glasses. Neither obviously human nor obviously post-human. The olive skin and the close-cropped black beard could have placed him in any number of en-claves along the MidEast Arc of Earth's orbital ring, but the army-surplus shorts and the thick-soled biblical sandals worn over white athletic socks were so per-fectly Israeli—and so exactly what Korchow had told him to expect—that Arkady didn't have to match the man's face against the spinfeed Korchow had run for him back on Gilead to know who was standing in front of him.

Moshe Feldman. The man Arkady would have to get past. And now that Arkady was finally seeing him face-to-face, he didn't look like the kind of man who would make it easy.

Arkady had been warned that the humans would all want to shake hands, so he presented his right hand, thumb raised and palm at the vertical, just as Korchow had taught him.

Moshe ignored it.

"The clone who came in from the cold," he said in the conspicuously cultured tones that hours of tape in the KnowlesSyndicate language labs had taught Arkady to recognize as the mark of the Ashkenazi in-tellectual elite. "A eighteen eleven four. A series. RostovSyndicate. Detanked in crèche one in the sec-ond production run of Syndicate Year Four. Have I got it right, Arkady?"

"Perfect."

"No, Arkady." Moshe smiled, showing pink gums and straight white teeth that looked small enough to belong in a child's mouth. "You're the one who's perfect. I'm merely human."

Arkady couldn't think of anything to say to that, so he said nothing.

"So," Moshe said, putting volumes of meaning into the brief syllable. "What do I need to know?"

"What do you need to know about what?" Arkady asked.

Moshe crossed his arms over his chest. He was small, even by human standards, and his narrow chest and sloping shoulders would have looked more at home behind a scholar's desk than on the bridge of a driveship. But his legs were hard and sunburned, and with every movement of his hands Arkady could see the corded tendons slide under the skin of his forearms.

"First," Moshe reflected, "it would be reassuring to know that you are who you say you are." Another flash of his small white teeth. "Or rather *what* you say you are."

A flick of Moshe's fingers brought a lab tech scurrying over with a splicing scope and sample kit. The sampling took a long time, and was done none too gently. "He's for real," the tech announced at last in Hebrew. "Can't say what crèche year or production run, but he's definitely KnowlesSyndicate. And he's definitely an A series."

"How sure are you?" Moshe asked.

The man shrugged, spreading his hands in an archaic, shockingly human gesture.

"And what would it take to be completely sure?"

"I'd have to send the sample to Tel Aviv and have them test the mitochondrial DNA. Even the Syndicates can't fake that yet."

"Then do it. I'm not taking any chances this time."

This time?

The tech retrieved his scope and sampling gear and

retreated to the bridge's main streamspace terminal. Then, to Arkady's surprise and dismay, they waited.

It should have taken days, even weeks, for the sample to reach Earth's Orbital Ring and be cleared for import to the planet below by whatever subdepartment of the ossified UN bureaucracy was currently tasked with enforcing the Climate Control Accords. Instead, Arkady watched with growing unease as the tech fed his samples into the comp and keyed up a streamspace address that began with the fabled triple *w*.

The implications of those three letters made Arkady catch his breath. They meant that Moshe had a direct link to Earth. And since Earth was off-grid, that meant he had a private streamspace link. Which in turn meant he had a portable Bose-Einstein terminal and access to a secure source of entanglement. None of this was legal under the three-century-old UN-enforced technology embargo imposed on Earth after the Evacuation. But more important, none of it was even remotely affordable.

There were a handful of private entities in UN space with the financial means to maintain private entanglement banks. The largest multinational corporations. The UN bureaucracy itself. A handful of the richest AIs and transhumans—a group so minuscule that any UN citizen who watched the newspins could list most of them by name.

And, of course, the constant wild card in UN politics, a type of entity so archaic that its very existence was the source of horrified amazement to most Syndicate political philosophers: the nation states.

Think of it as a war by proxy. Korchow had said back on Gilead when Arkady had become hopelessly confused by the internecine politics so alien to the cleanly ordered world of Syndicate society. *The UN and the Syndicates learned in the last war that they were too evenly matched to be able to risk open conflict. Thus each side pulled back, just as two chess players pull back when nei-*

ther is in a position to benefit from a direct attack. And in the specialized environment of the cold war the nation states regained relevance, just as a vestigial wing regains relevance when the arrival of a new predator favors flying insects. In the case of Israel and Palestine, all you need to know is this: Israel is in the camp of the United Nations, Palestine on the side of the Syndicates. They may do the bleeding and the dying, but it's our weapons they're fighting with and our war they're fighting. It's the same war that's going on all over the Trusteeships, just with a little heftier backstory. And the only thing you need to remember is that when you speak to Israel you are speaking to the UN. Which is to say, to our enemies.

Whereas the Palestinians are friends?

Well, they're the enemies of our enemies. One can't ask too much from an imperfect world.

And what about the Interfaithers?

Korchow had smiled the famously enigmatic KnowlesSyndicate smile at that question—and his version of it was perfect enough to have come straight off a designer's drawing board. *You're a clever boy*, he'd said. *Let's hope you're not clever enough to be dangerous.*

It had all seemed so clear when Korchow explained it back on Gilead. But now the KnowlesSyndicate A's smile haunted Arkady. It was a chess player's smile, the smile of a strategist who knows all the moves and has covered all the angles. But if Moshe and Osnat were pawns, then they were dangerously unpredictable ones. And they were drawing Arkady deeper and deeper into a game that had as much in common with chess as a terraformer's spec sheet had in common with the roiling chaos of an evolving planet.

"He's clean," the tech announced from behind his terminal. Everyone in the room must have been holding their breath, Arkady realized, because he heard a collective sigh of relief at the news.

"So," Moshe asked Arkady in the tones of a professor leading his lecture group into difficult theoretical territory. "To what do we owe the pleasure of your perfect company?"

"Not for you," Arkady said, knowing that the time had come to speak the name they had all been waiting to hear. "Not until I see Absalom."

"And who told you to ask for Absalom?"

"No one."

Moshe smiled, showing his childish teeth again. "I wouldn't exactly call Andrej Korchow no one."

Arkady's eyes snapped to Moshe's face, but all he could see in the glare of the bridge light were the two flat reflective disks of his glasses.

"Korchow told you about Absalom," Moshe suggested, as if the words were a little joke between the two of them. "He told you to use his name to reel us in. He wants us to think he's back in the game again."

"I don't know what you're talking about," Arkady said.

Moshe's first blow knocked him to his knees. As he tried to stand again, Moshe kicked his feet out from under him and dealt him a flurry of surgically precise kicks to the stomach and kidneys.

Osnat laughed. But it was a laugh of shock and surprise, not amusement. Arkady even thought he sensed a recoiling in her, a flush of pity under the soldier's hard loyalty. Or did he just want to sense that?

"Get up," Moshe said in the bored tones of a man for whom violence was a job like any other.

Arkady tried to stand, but he only managed to kneel, head spinning, hands splayed on the cold deck.

Moshe crouched beside him. "That was a lie," he said, his head bent so close over Arkady's that his breath caressed the skin of his cheek. "You know it, and I know it. And I can't have you lying to me. You can see that, can't you?"

A waiting silence settled over the bridge, and Arkady realized that he was expected to answer the apparently rhetorical question.

"Yes," he said, "I can see that."

Moshe had risen to his feet and was looking down at Arkady with an expression he was beginning to recognize, though he still couldn't put a name to it. It was the same expression the man in the Interfaither's cap had worn. Not anger or fear. Or at least not only those things. Arkady was beginning to think it might be hatred.

"How many Arkadys do they detank a year?" Moshe asked. "Fifty? Five hundred? Five thousand?"

But Arkady didn't know how many. The real number was probably on the high end of Moshe's guess; the AR-11 geneline was a successful one, and RostovSyndicate had the second highest A series tank allocations after KnowlesSyndicate. He's never asked, though. He'd never thought of asking. And for the first time in his life he wondered why.

"I don't know," he said finally. "A lot, I guess."

"A lot, you guess," Moshe said in a mocking echo. "You're a piece of equipment, Arkady. As mass-produced as sewer pipe sections. And if we can't get what we need from you, we'll throw you away without thinking twice about it. Just like your Syndicate's already done. Or do you want to tell me I've got that wrong too?"

Osnat stirred restlessly. "Oh, for fuck's sake, Moshe. Give him a break. He doesn't know anything."

Moshe turned to stare at Osnat. "He told you that, did he? And you believed him? Or did you just take a look into those puppy-dog eyes and decide to trust him?"

Osnat flushed to the roots of her hair. Arkady felt the rest of the room freeze and hold their breath. What had Moshe done to make them so frightened of him? But perhaps a man like Moshe didn't need to *do* anything to frighten people.

Moshe dropped into Hebrew, speaking with quiet but unmistakable anger. Arkady struggled to understand, but there was only so much you could learn from tape, and the unfamiliar words spilled past too quickly. That it was a dressing-down was clear, however; Osnat absorbed the rebuke with the immovable stoicism of a soldier on parade ground.

Was she a soldier, Arkady asked himself. Had he drawn the right conclusion from the ease with which Moshe had skirted the embargo? Had he already been drawn so deep into the tangled web of the Israeli intelligence community that he was already dealing with soldiers and not hired muscle? Which stray thread of the tangled Israeli intelligence had responded to Arkady's carefully choreographed offer of defection? And how much did the success of his mission—and with it Arkasha's life and freedom—depend on his guessing correctly?

What if they're Mossad? The question spooled across into Arkady's mind accompanied by old spinfeed of bombings and assassinations. He pushed it aside. All Mossad agents couldn't be vicious killers, he told himself, any more than other opposite Palestinian numbers could be the peace-loving posthuman sympathizers that Syndicate propagandists insisted they were. And as long as he kept Korchow happy, it didn't matter who they were.

Moshe turned back to Arkady. "The road to Absalom goes through me," he said. "If you cross me, or lie to me, or do even the littlest thing to make me nervous about you, I'll kill you. And the police won't blink. And my superiors won't even give me a slap on the wrist. It'll be less than killing a dog as far as they're concerned. Do you understand that?"

Arkady swallowed and nodded.

"Good. Now do you remember the question I asked you?"

"Whether Korchow sent me?"

"And?"

"And whether he told me to ask for Absalom?"